EXPLOSIVE

BETH KERY

BERKLEY SENSATION, NEW YORK

THE BERKLEY PUBLISHING GROUP
Published by the Penguin Group
Penguin Group (USA) LLC
375 Hudson Street, New York, New York 10014

USA • Canada • UK • Ireland • Australia • New Zealand • India • South Africa • China

penguin.com

A Penguin Random House Company

EXPLOSIVE

A Berkley Sensation Book / published by arrangement with the author

Berkley Sensation Books are published by The Berkley Publishing Group.
BERKLEY SENSATION® is a registered trademark of Penguin Group (USA) LLC.
The "B" design is a trademark of Penguin Group (USA) LLC.

For information, address: The Berkley Publishing Group,
a division of Penguin Group (USA) LLC,
375 Hudson Street, New York, New York 10014.

ISBN: 978-0-425-26683-0

PUBLISHING HISTORY
Heat trade paperback edition / December 2010
Berkley Sensation mass-market edition / February 2014

PRINTED IN THE UNITED STATES OF AMERICA

10 9 8 7 6 5 4 3 2 1

Cover photo by Jasmin Awad / gettyimages.
Cover design by Jason Gill.
Interior text design by Tiffany Estreicher.

ACKNOWLEDGMENTS

Many thanks are due to several people for this book. I'm so grateful to have a husband who knows the world of business as well as he knows technology, tax law, and how to fix a sink. His information is always invaluable to me when it comes down to the details. I'd like to thank Lea, Sabra, Mary, and Robin for beta reading *Explosive* and providing feedback. I'd be lost without you, ladies. Thanks to Sabra and her husband for giving me valuable information on the EOD. And Fi—you're a saint for helping me brainstorm and putting up with me when I worried incessantly. I would also like to extend my gratitude to the members of my Yahoo reader group, Total Exposure, for cheering me on and offering me support. Your kind words of encouragement keep me going at times.

CHAPTER **ONE**

She was so caught up in the lazy mood of the first evening on her summer holiday that at first she couldn't compute the fact that Thomas Nicasio was standing on her dock. He stared fixedly at the rippling lake, the golden sunlight bringing out the burnished highlights in his uncharacteristically mussed brown hair. If it weren't for that singular profile she would never have recognized him in these surroundings.

Thomas was an inhabitant of her work world, after all, a denizen of the city and the high-rise where they both worked. For Sophie, he only lived within the confines of 209 South LaSalle, wearing his perfectly tailored Armani suits, always moving with a brisk sense of purpose through the corridors or paging through his BlackBerry distractedly while he waited for his brother in the waiting room of the medical practice where Sophie worked.

They'd shared nothing more until that moment but heated glances, a few flirtatious conversations. On several occasions, she'd noticed Thomas sitting in the waiting room, studying her covertly while she interacted with her patients as she escorted them to the reception desk. It was clear to Sophie that Thomas was attracted to her, but he'd always seemed to make a point of keeping his distance.

The single exception to their sterile acquaintance had been the charged, brief exchange they'd shared in the waiting room of her office just last evening. Thomas certainly hadn't seemed contained or aloof on *that* occasion.

Still, until that moment he'd always hovered on the periphery of her life, never fully entering it, but never totally absent from it, either. She thought of Thomas Nicasio a lot, usually in a sympathetic manner following her consultations with her psychologist friend, Andy Lancaster.

More recently, she had good reason to consider Thomas with compassion while watching the ten o'clock news.

He might occasionally creep up into her thoughts whenever she saw another tall man out of the corner of her eye while she was grocery shopping or jogging by Lake Michigan. Certainly the faces of her fantasy lovers often morphed into Thomas the closer she got to climax, but surely that was no surprise. Sophie suspected the same was true of a majority of the women who caught sight of him.

Still . . . she wondered at times if his sober, watchful gaze had the same effect on most females that it did on her.

Usually Thomas existed for Sophie only within the confines of her office lobby or the eight-by-eight confines of a crowded elevator, his head easy to see over the other early-morning elevator riders, his eyes unfailingly meeting hers, his gruff, quiet, "Good morning, Doctor," tickling her ear before the elevator doors opened and Sophie stepped off on the twenty-third floor.

The overlap of their lives was so minimal that it made her wonder if she was hallucinating—conjuring her dreams into reality—when she saw him standing on her dock wearing a pair of jeans and a black T-shirt.

Her brain just couldn't seem to get a handle on the image.

And there was something about his stance that caused a muted alarm to start ringing in her head. She considered calling Andy Lancaster, who had been treating Thomas's brother, Rick. Thomas had been asking to see Andy just last night.

But what could Andy do, even if she got a hold of him? He was in Chicago, after all, over one hundred fifty miles upstate.

And *Thomas* had never been his patient.

Sophie knew that multiple tragedies had befallen Thomas Nicasio's family recently. His brother and nephew were dead. Thomas's adoptive father, Joseph Carlisle, was being investigated for several federal crimes. The FBI was in the midst of building an indictment against the wealthy businessman.

Did those things relate to the fact that Thomas was standing on her dock, looking dazed and shell-shocked? And if so, what was he doing *here*? There was no way he could understand that *she*, of all people, knew details about the dark labyrinth of his family life.

She placed the paintbrush she'd been gripping into a coffee can filled with water and headed toward the side door. She glanced down at herself, hesitating. A few swipes of dried lavender tempera paint decorated her bare ribs and abdomen. She wore a bikini with a pair of jean shorts pulled over the bottoms and white canvas tennis shoes that were so ancient the cloth was separating from the soles in spots.

She should go and change—throw on a shirt at the very least.

But then she recalled the way his head hung at a queer angle as he stared at the sunset-infused lake and she descended the steps.

The closer she got to his rigid figure, the more anxious she became. Before her feet hit the dock, she saw the way that his rib cage moved in and out. It struck her as strange— eerie, even—how he stood so still and yet appeared to be panting, as though from some invisible exertion.

She gasped when he spun around as her foot hit the wooden dock, looking like a ready, lethal warrior anticipating attack. A sensation like flowing, hot liquid sank through her lower belly.

For a few seconds, they just stood frozen in each other's

sights, his stare unnerving her. His jaw was covered with whiskers that were two shades darker than the hair on his head. He typically combed his long bangs back in a conservative style that suited his polished work image. Currently, they hung loose, bracketing his dark brows and eyes that had always reminded Sophie of a deep forest wood with shards of sunlight breaking through the topmost branches.

Sophie heard a speedboat motor hum in the distance through the increasingly loud throb of the heartbeat in her ears.

After a moment she summoned her voice, trying to grasp on to a fleeing sense of reality.

"Thomas? What a surprise. It's me—Dr. Gable? Sophie? From Dr. Lancaster's office?" She waved lamely at the glistening waters and laughed. "I hadn't realized we shared space at Haven Lake as well."

Despite her growing uncertainty, she'd forced her voice into the level, reassuring tone she took with someone who was agitated or panicked. She'd had her share of crisis training to become a physician, but even before she'd gone to medical school she'd worked for a year as a clinical social worker with abused children. She'd long ago learned to soothe instinctively . . . without thought.

She was so caught up in the bizarre, electric moment that it never occurred to her to question why she would treat a six foot four male in his prime, a man who typically moved through the minutes of his life with the easy grace of a prince, like an agitated child. Especially since Thomas Nicasio hardly seemed childlike to her at that moment. If anything, he reminded her of a wild, cornered animal.

A wild, *dangerous* animal?

The worn black T-shirt he wore carried the inexplicable caption *Mighty are those that flirt with fate, EOD.* The material skimmed across his long, lean torso, making it easy for her to see his rapid breathing. She'd never seen him in anything but a suit before, but she had to admit his broad shoulders, narrow hips, strong thighs, and long legs were perfectly suited to jeans. Her gaze skittered across his crotch. She glanced guiltily back up to his rigid face in time to see a spark ignite in his eyes.

Her heartbeat amplified in her ears.

A strong sexual current had often leapt between them in the past, but at the moment, Sophie felt burned by the heat of his stare. She tensed when he took a step toward her.

"Tom. Call me Tom."

Her mouth fell open at the sound of his deep, hoarse voice. Why did he sound like he hadn't spoken in days? Her expert eye took in the pinched look of his bold, masculine features, the whiteness at the corners of his mouth, the look of exhaustion that seemed to reside behind the maniclike intensity of his gaze.

She turned her shoulder to him in a nonthreatening stance and beckoned with her hand.

"Why don't you come inside, Tom. You must be thirsty."

For a few seconds she had no idea what he would do, this man who was both familiar to her and yet a stranger, a man who had never said much more than a few dozen words to her at a time if he spoke at all. He might have laughed. He might have flown at her in a rage. Anything and everything seemed possible in that gravid moment. Considering her readiness for catastrophe, what he did next should have seemed mild.

Instead, it jolted her to the core of her being.

He walked toward her with a long-legged stride that ate up the space between them in a second. She tensed and a tingling sensation ran beneath her skin when his gaze traveled over her naked torso.

He halted less than a foot away from her.

Close.

Closer than casual human contact.

"I came looking for you."

She felt his warm breath tickle her upturned face. He reached for her. His hand felt hot and dry encircling her own, as if he had a furnace working overtime inside him. She just stared up at him, speechless.

"I came looking for you, Sophie," he repeated.

"Why?"

He just nodded soberly toward her house. She was still stunned when he gently urged her to accompany him, his stare never leaving her face.

The wraparound porch was a landscape of golden light and shadow when they approached the side entrance to the house. The door squeaked open, and she led him onto the screened-in portion of the porch. Their hands were still locked, so she felt it when he paused. She turned back to see him staring at her work in progress. He glanced from the painting to the lake, and back at the canvas again, his expression unreadable.

"It's not very good. I just do it for fun," she said, wondering why she whispered. Maybe it was because the atmosphere suddenly seemed electrically charged, expectant . . . like the air before a storm. Her breath stilled when he suddenly transferred his gaze to her naked abdomen.

"I was wondering why you had purple paint on you."

She gave a small laugh when she saw how his well-shaped lips quirked—very slightly—in amusement.

"I used to tell Rick you were like the little girl in the neighborhood who was always so clean; the kind that Mama wouldn't let play rough with the other kids . . . the kind that was never allowed to get dirty." His palpable gaze flickered over her breasts and neck before he met her stare.

Her mirth faded.

"Rick said that was just my lame excuse not to ask you out," he finished.

Sophie swallowed thickly. This situation just kept getting more and more bizarre. She knew from her friend Andy how close Thomas had been to his brother, Rick Carlisle. Not that she wouldn't have already guessed it the few times she'd witnessed the two men's easy camaraderie when she'd glimpsed them together in her office or in the building.

"You must be upset, Tom," she whispered. "Is that why you're here? Are you hurting . . . after your brother's and nephew's deaths?"

His eyes glittered with emotion in an otherwise masklike countenance.

"Come inside." She tightened her hold on his hand and guided him down the dim hallway to the kitchen. The windows there faced east, depriving them of the sunset light. She flipped a switch, chasing away the dark shadows.

If she'd thought that electric lights and her cheery, homey kitchen would bring a sense of normalcy to this surreal situation, she'd thought wrong. One glance at Thomas's tall, whipcord lean body and rigid features and she existed in the *Twilight Zone* all over again. Perhaps it was the thick, nearly tangible cloud of tension that surrounded him that contributed to her sense of floundering for familiar territory.

She released his hand and headed toward the refrigerator, trying to shake off her sense of unease.

"I made fresh lemonade earlier today. Would you care for some?"

"Do you have anything harder?" he rasped.

She glanced back over her shoulder. "I have some wine in the pantry."

"Never mind. Lemonade is fine."

She studied him anxiously. Under the bright fluorescent lights, she could more easily see that a fine sheen of sweat covered his face.

Fever, she thought.

"Why don't you sit down at the bar," she suggested before she headed toward the refrigerator. She filled two glasses with ice and lemonade and handed him one. He hadn't taken her advice to sit down and still stood in the precise spot where she'd left him. He took the glass and drained the contents in two seconds. When he'd finished, she took the empty glass and gave him the other one. While he drank, she encircled the wrist of his free hand with her own.

He swallowed the second glass of lemonade almost as quickly as the first. When he'd finished, she sensed him watching her from above, his head lowered while she concentrated and counted the beats of his rapid, strong pulse while watching the seconds pass on her kitchen clock.

The silence seemed to press on them like a thick cloak.

"Would you like some more?" she asked after she'd finished and dropped his wrist.

"No. I've had enough."

"Tom, you're ill," she said, looking up at him.

He blinked. He glanced around her kitchen with a slight scowl on his features. His confusion seemed to fade when he looked at her face again.

"You might be right. I'm not sure how I got here."

She took the glass he held from his stiff grip and set it along with the other one on the kitchen island.

"Do you mean you don't remember?"

For a few seconds he seemed uncertain. "I remember driving here. I had to get away."

"Had to get away from what?" she asked slowly.

He just stared at her with those brooding green eyes flecked with gold. Sophie supposed that given everything that had happened to Thomas Nicasio lately, he had plenty of reasons for needing an escape.

He remained immobile when she reached up to touch his forehead and cheek. His skin felt clammy. She mentally cursed when she recalled she didn't have a thermometer in the lake house. Still, she'd guess that if he ran a fever, it wasn't an alarming one.

Her fingers delved through thick, surprisingly soft hair, searching for wounds on his scalp. A shiver coursed through him when her hand reached the base of his skull. She caught his scent. Despite his obvious illness and uncharacteristically disheveled state, Thomas Nicasio smelled *good*.

Cautiously, she met his stare.

For a few seconds, neither of them moved. Sophie suspected neither of them breathed.

"Did you hit your head, Tom?" she asked eventually, her fingers resuming their careful search.

"I don't think so."

"Have you been drinking?" she asked, even though she'd inhaled his breath and already suspected that he wasn't drunk. He shook his head.

"Drugs?"

Again, he shook his head. She pushed back his hair. Her gaze shot to his when she saw the discoloration near his hairline on his left temple.

"You *have* been hit." She reached for the wrist of his right arm, holding his stare all the while. Her mind churned when she glanced down and saw the abrasions and flecks of dried blood on his knuckle.

"You've been in a fight," she stated tersely. Did a shadow of defiance cross his features, or was that her imagination? Well, perhaps she had sounded accusatory. It wasn't her place to judge him, after all. "Are you in any pain?"

"No."

"Sick to your stomach?"

He shrugged negligently.

"How is it that you're *here*, Tom?" she asked, despite the memory of what he'd said earlier.

I came looking for you, Sophie.

He wasn't entirely lucid, after all.

"Do you know someone who lives near here?" she prompted when he didn't speak.

"No. I only know you."

"Well . . . why did you come looking for *me*?" she couldn't resist asking in an anxious rush. "Did you find yourself getting ill on the road and need a doctor? Did you remember me telling you I was vacationing here, at Haven Lake?"

A spasm went through him and he cupped his right brow with his palm, squeezing his eyes shut.

"I'm taking you to the emergency room in Effingham," she declared, alarmed by the sight of what must have been a jolt of intense pain going through him.

"I'm not going anywhere."

"But you've *got* to, you're not well and—"

"I'm *not* going to the hospital," he grated out between clenched teeth.

She went completely still at his harsh tone. She considered calling the police, but then he opened his eyes.

"All right."

The two words leaving her own lips surprised her a little,

but she felt as if she didn't have a choice once she'd looked into those twin pools of turmoil and anguish. "You might have a concussion, but you're feverish, as well. I'll get you some Tylenol and then you need to rest. Will you at least promise me to do that for now?"

"I'm not sleepy," he said hoarsely. His gaze lowered. Heat flooded her cheeks. He stared at her breasts covered in the thin bikini top. Her body responded to his blatantly sexual gaze against her will. Her nipples stiffened beneath the flimsy fabric.

He stepped toward her.

Sophie stepped back.

"You're ill. You need to rest. Is there someone you want me to call? Will someone be missing you in Chicago? Never mind. Come on," she said when he just stared at her. She waved her hand and led him down the dim hallway to the guest bedroom. She turned on the light and inspected the state of the room. She hadn't been in it since early June, just after Andy and his wife, Sheila, had visited for a weekend.

Her mind sifted through his symptoms, trying to make sense of his bizarre presentation as she bustled around in the guest bath, laying out clean towels and getting Tylenol out of the medicine cabinet. His feverish state implied that something physical was going on, but the pain she'd seen in his eyes just moments ago argued for something psychological. The bruise on his temple wasn't massive, but she knew the brain could sustain considerable injury from a blow without any obvious external trauma.

Of course there was no reason why his condition couldn't be *both* physical and psychological, considering the amount of stress Thomas must have been under recently.

Who had he been fighting with, and why? Oddly, it didn't surprise her to consider Thomas engaging in a brawl, despite the fact that she was used to seeing only his polished work image. She'd always sensed a rebel existed beneath the smooth exterior of his perfectly tailored suits. Maybe it was the tilt of his jaw that made her think it, or the gold flecks that flashed and burned in the deep green of his eyes; or a smile that was sweet, but just a tad cocky . . . slow in coming and breathtaking upon arrival.

Or maybe it was just because Sophie knew he'd spent the first years of his life in a working-class Southside neighborhood far from the perfectly manicured, sweeping green lawns and multimillion-dollar homes of Lake Forest, where Thomas had gone to live with the family that adopted him, the Carlisles. A kid growing up in Morgan Park would have known how to use his fists. Besides, he'd only worked in the private sector for the past few years. Before he'd taken up the reins of his own business, he'd been in the military, but Sophie couldn't recall at the moment if Andy had ever mentioned in what branch he'd served or what his duties had involved.

She grimaced as she filled a glass with water from the tap. She felt guilty for not taking him to the hospital, even though the chances were that the emergency room physician would recommend nothing more than close observation of Thomas's symptoms for the next forty-eight hours.

And either way, Thomas had flatly refused to go, so what choice did she have?

Her level of anxiety upon entering the bedroom was unprecedented since her first year of medical school.

She carried the Tylenol in one hand and the glass of water in the other. He still stood just inside the threshold of the door. She was relieved when he took the Tylenol without argument. He stood behind her while she turned down the bed, making her highly self-conscious of her bent-over position.

She added his blatant sexual stare into her formulary of symptoms, even though Thomas Nicasio's hot eyes hardly left her feeling analytical. Was he in a manic state, perhaps? That would explain his hypersexuality, the sudden need to impulsively escape . . .

. . . but not the bruise, fever, or dazed confusion.

Was she *safe* with him there in the house with her? She glanced back at him and their gazes held. She exhaled slowly.

"Why don't you get into bed?" she asked, glad to hear

that her voice didn't audibly tremble. He stepped toward her and Sophie glanced down, avoiding that laserlike stare. She knew she should have backed away, but she didn't.

Not even when he spread one hand along her naked hip.

She held her breath and clamped her eyes shut when she felt his thumb gently rub across a dried smear of paint. Her lungs burned by the time he bent his long legs at the knees, and he wrapped her in his arms.

He encompassed her. In that full, fertile moment, she felt Thomas Nicasio in every cell of her being.

He nudged her hair back with his nose and pressed his entire face to the side of her neck. His hardness pressed against her softness, stark and potent.

"Sophie."

Her heart throbbed erratically in her chest at the sensation of his hot mouth moving next to her sensitive skin.

"Sleep with me, Sophie. I need your cleanness so much right now."

CHAPTER **TWO**

Her eyes burned when she heard those roughly uttered words. His hand moved. He palmed her left breast, his thumb efficiently flicking aside the thin fabric. Her nipple tightened almost painfully as he stimulated it with deft fingertips. Molten fire flashed through her pussy, making her whimper. His other hand opened along her spine. He leaned over her, forcing her back to bow. His mouth, voracious and gentle at once, awakened her nerve endings, creating a prickling trail of pleasure as he moved along her neck, cheek, and jaw. He seemed so hungry . . . so starved for her. His raw need caused something sweet to unfold in her chest like a blooming flower, a feeling of tenderness twined with raw lust, a potent sensation unlike anything she'd ever known.

Her lips parted as if of their own volition, forming a target for his kiss, but then his unnatural heat penetrated her bewitched state.

He was ill. Fevered.

"No," she mumbled shakily in the second before his mouth closed on hers.

He didn't try to stop her from staggering out of his arms,

but she could tell by the slant of his mouth that he wasn't pleased. Her lungs froze at his abrupt absence, as if she'd suddenly plunged into icy water. She saw the glint of his eyes in the shadows cast by his lowered brow and mussed bangs.

"You're ill. You need to sleep." Her voice sounded tiny and muffled in the still room, as though someone else spoke from a distance.

She shut the door behind her and rushed to the kitchen. She poured herself a glass of lemonade and gulped it down nearly as rapidly as Thomas had earlier, trying to quench a burning thirst. Eyes clamped shut, she tried to ignore the hot, thick sensation that pooled in her lower belly and plagued her sex, but the ache was too sharp . . . too imperative. She placed a hand between her thighs and pressed as though trying to staunch a wound. The resulting stab of sharp pleasure made her wince.

For a full minute, she stood gripping the empty glass and staring down the dark hallway, panting softly. The magnitude of her arousal was something she associated with wild animals or teenage boys with potent hormones racing through their blood. It flabbergasted her, this unprecedented reaction to a man's touch. Rest would not come easy tonight.

Would *he* sleep?

Would he stay put?

She didn't know if she was glad, worried, surprised, or disappointed when she didn't hear a single sound emanate from the guest bedroom. After several minutes, she opened the back screen door.

The sun had nearly set as Sophie walked through the yard. The tall trees that lined the long, graveled road leading to the lake house were cast in a muted, golden-pink glow.

He'd turned off the engine in his dark green Lexus sedan, but he'd left the driver's-side door wide open. She leaned into the vehicle, catching the pleasant scent of leather mixing with the lingering fragrance of Thomas's spicy cologne.

Some of the contents of the glove box were spilled onto the passenger seat. She removed the keys from the ignition and shoved them into the pocket of her shorts before she walked around the car to the passenger door. She replaced the miniature flashlight, a map folded so that Haven Lake was easily seen, and a phone battery in the glove box. She bent to retrieve a newly opened bottle of Tylenol from the floor of the car.

He'd been trying to stop the pain, she realized sadly.

The bottle was small, the kind you bought at a gas station or convenience store. She quickly counted the remaining pills, wanting to make sure he hadn't taken several before she'd given him even more just minutes ago. Only two were missing; not enough to harm him even if he'd taken the two tablets just seconds before he'd staggered onto her dock.

She snapped the cap on, placed the bottle in the glove box, and secured Thomas's car.

The rest of the evening was spent trying to reach Andy Lancaster—which she never did successfully—cleaning up her makeshift studio on the screen porch, and then watching the end of a comedy on the television in her bedroom. When she finally shut out the light to sleep, there was nothing left to distract her from recalling Thomas Nicasio's presence in her house . . . or from his unexpected embrace.

She tried to make sense of her potent reaction to his touch. She'd long known that she was attracted to Thomas Nicasio. But the extremity of her current arousal confused her. Did it somehow relate to her knowledge of his life . . . to the fact that though she'd never been invited by Thomas, she'd peered into the secret realms of his private world?

She was a voyeur, of sorts. Not the sexual kind, but perhaps Thomas would think her knowledge was even more disturbing?

She thought of their brief, charged meeting just last night, trying to understand Thomas's sudden appearance at Haven Lake.

Every time she started to fasten her briefcase, she thought of another item she'd need while she was on vacation. Sophie scowled at the stack of journals on her desk and then irritably shoved the whole pile in her bag. She was sure to need the precise one she'd left behind. Why not take them all?

She wanted out of this damn office. She craved Haven Lake.

The only other physician besides Sophie who worked late on Wednesday evenings was Alex Fitzsimmons, their OB/GYN. Andy Lancaster, their psychologist, used to work late on Wednesday evenings, but he was notably absent at the moment.

Andy wasn't there tonight, of course, because Rick Carlisle wasn't there. Sophie thought of how she'd occasionally hear Rick and Andy as they passed her office on the way to Andy's, Rick bemoaning the Cubs latest loss or teasing Andy about his awful haircut.

Sophie would never see Rick Carlisle again; nor would she see his adoptive brother, Thomas Nicasio, waiting in the lobby for Rick to finish his psychotherapy appointment. A pang of loss went through her and she chided herself for the selfish thought. Rick Carlisle hadn't existed for the purpose of throwing Thomas Nicasio in Sophie's path.

She had run into Thomas frequently under those circumstances, though. Not *every* Wednesday evening, by any means, but often enough for her to take note of it.

Maybe it was her imagination—or plain old wishful thinking?—but it did seem to her that her chance meetings with Thomas were increasing greatly in the past few months. Never enough for her to depend on. Never enough for her to make *sure* she was in the office toward the end of Rick Carlisle's regular Wednesday appointment.

But enough to make Sophie suspect she might not be the only one who was nudging the odds to increase the likelihood of crossing paths with Thomas.

She thought wistfully of the excitement of those chance encounters with Thomas as she hauled her briefcase onto her shoulder and left her office, casting a sad glance in the direction of Andy's closed door.

The flap on her briefcase gave and a sheaf of paper and

several journals spilled onto the lobby carpet. A pair of tanned, masculine . . . very capable-looking hands beat her to the task of retrieving the spilled contents.

She glanced up from her kneeling position. His face was less than a foot away from her own.

"Thomas," she exclaimed, surprised. She tensed, knowing from experience that Thomas's smiles, while slow in coming, were every bit as disarming as his eyes. At this close of a range, one of those smiles might be explosive on impact.

But his smile never came, of course.

This Wednesday night was different from every other one that had come before it.

"What . . . what are you doing here?" she asked breathlessly.

Thomas just stared at her for a second, his face rigid.

"I was looking for Dr. Lancaster," he said before he returned to gathering her papers.

"He's not here. He didn't have any other appointments on Wednesday evening, aside from . . ." She faded off, but rallied when Thomas glanced up at her soberly. " . . . your brother. Do you want me to call Andy?" she asked. It would be understandable if Thomas requested a consultation with a psychologist.

"No, that's all right. I'll try to catch him another time."

"I was so sorry to hear about your brother and your nephew."

The words spilled out of her throat in a rush of compassion. She hoped she hadn't offended him when he merely resumed picking up her papers and journals. Sophie knew it was best to follow a grieving person's lead in these situations, so she busied herself with helping him retrieve the fallen items. She shouldn't have spoken to him in such a familiar fashion.

"Sorry about all this," she said, nodding to the papers. "I'm flustered . . . trying to get out of this place and wondering if it's even possible."

She reached to take the papers and journals that he held, but Thomas didn't release them.

She glanced up at him to see that he studied her. If there was one thing about Nicasio, he really made a woman feel like he wasn't just looking, but saw. That's how he always had managed to make *her* feel, anyway.

"Your mind isn't the only thing that has ten million things stuffed in it." He nodded at her briefcase. "You're busting at the seams, Dr. Gable."

Dr. Gable. Several months ago, the *Doctor* had become *Dr. Gable*. Since she'd never formally introduced herself, Sophie found herself wondering how he'd discovered her name. She liked to think he'd asked someone, even though it was more likely he'd seen her name on the front door of the medical offices and figured out which doctor she was by a process of elimination. She was the only female in the group practice.

She gave a shrug, her flickering gaze taking in his slightly amused expression. It struck her suddenly how intimate their postures were, kneeling on the floor there together, her face only inches apart from a casual acquaintance who she felt an almost overwhelming need to embrace . . . to comfort.

She relinquished the papers into his hold and rose to her feet. For a few seconds, he remained kneeling, his face near her thighs. She stepped back and brushed the wrinkles out of her skirt, trying to smooth not only the fabric, but her ruffled nerves.

"I'm about to go on vacation at Haven Lake, downstate. It's a pain, tying up so many loose ends," she explained with a smile, trying to lighten the tension-filled moment.

His eyebrows rose on his forehead. He stood slowly, uncoiling his long body. He'd removed his jacket and tie and wore dark blue pants that rode low on his narrow hips. A navy and white striped dress shirt set off his golden brown tan. Sophie'd often speculated how he'd acquired that tan. Did he spend his weekends playing tennis at a club? Boating? Swimming?

Something in the long, lean lines of his torso and powerful shoulders and chest seemed to argue for the latter. Somehow, she could perfectly imagine Thomas Nicasio knifing through the water, mastering that domain just like he appeared to so effortlessly master the rest of his world.

"Surely that's not a good explanation for the state of your briefcase. You're supposed to leave work behind when you go on a vacation, aren't you? Not that I'd know that from personal experience or anything." The twitch of his lips struck her as a little sad, as though he wanted to grin but some unseen weight prevented it.

"I'm fortunate enough to be able to take off a month every summer, but there's a price to pay. It's when I do all my writing." She hitched her stuffed briefcase for emphasis. "I plan to write three, maybe four medical articles while I'm relaxing."

This time, the smile did find expression on his lips, but Sophie noticed it never reached his eyes. He cast an anxious glance toward the corridor—in the direction of Andy's office.

"That's what you plan," he murmured when his gaze returned to her face. "But will you actually get around to work once the vacation atmosphere sets in?"

Sophie froze for a moment when he stepped closer.

"Well, I'm a bit of a procrastinator. But I'll get to it. Eventually, anyway, when I see the end of my vacation start to loom on the calendar."

Her reply sounded a bit breathless as she watched him slide the journal and loose papers into her briefcase, careful not to crinkle anything. He glanced down at her face with a hooded stare. The look in his eyes had made the breath freeze in her lungs. For a few seconds, Sophie thought the moment had come.

Thomas Nicasio was finally going to cross the invisible boundary that kept them existing in separate worlds.

But then he looked away and briskly pulled the zipper, closing her briefcase.

"Life's short, Dr. Gable," he said gruffly. "I'm finding that out firsthand. You never know when fate might step in and make it even shorter. I hate to think of you wasting your vacation hunched over a computer screen. It just doesn't seem right, somehow. Not for you."

She held her breath in her lungs when he gently smoothed back a strand of hair that had fallen on her cheek.

He stepped away.

As Sophie lay there a little over twenty-four hours later while Thomas Nicasio slept a few dozen feet away from her, the memory made her heart squeeze tight in her chest.

For the hundredth time, she replayed his embrace in her mind, recalled in graphic detail the sensation of his hard, hot body pressed so intimately next to her own, the way he'd fit against her so well. Her nipples tightened against her T-shirt.

Sleep with me, Sophie. I need your cleanness so much right now.

She groaned softly and turned onto her side, curling into a fetal position in an attempt to alleviate the ache at her core that would not dissipate, no matter how much she tried to distract herself. She prayed for sleep, for the oblivion of unconsciousness that would stifle the fire in her flesh, but her prayers went unanswered. Thoughts of Thomas swelled in her awareness until her body heat escalated to a low boil.

One hour passed—two, then three. Every nerve in her body seemed to be buzzing with electricity, making sleep seem a ludicrous proposition. Her entire awareness stretched down the hallway to the room where Thomas slept.

She lay on her side, her face turned toward her shut bedroom door, her body throbbing with heat.

She heard the muted sound of a door latch clicking open down the hallway. Her heart swelled in her chest and began beating erratically. She wasn't really surprised. It struck her suddenly that she'd been *waiting* there in her bed . . . anticipating this moment.

And not just for the past several hours . . . for a long, long time.

She held her breath when her bedroom door opened quietly. He stood in the opening for several seconds, as if unsure. A dim light from the living room reflected behind him, allowing her to see he'd taken off his shirt and wore only his jeans.

The moment felt heavy, tense . . . pregnant with possibilities she couldn't fully comprehend.

"Sophie?"

She swallowed thickly. "Do you feel better?"

He nodded, his gaze glued to her face.

"Let me feel your forehead," she whispered.

He came toward her. Her gaze was filled with the vision of taut muscle . . . strained virility. She remained unmoving, spellbound. He knelt next to the bed, his posture striking her as a silent plea. She placed her fingertips on his cool forehead, but hers was a lover's touch more than a clinician's.

He needn't plead.

She put her hands on his shoulders and felt dense muscle gloved in smooth, warm skin. He came at her urging, his big male body a welcome weight pressing her down into the mattress, his demanding, urgent kiss a dark, thrilling promise of what was to come.

The next morning, he was gone.

Sophie jogged out the back door wearing a hastily donned cotton robe over her nakedness, already knowing from the leaden sensation in her gut that the dark green sedan would be absent from her driveway.

She went back inside the house and for a few minutes, just stared blankly at her sunny kitchen, feeling every bit as dazed as Thomas had appeared last night.

A decision struck her brain like a gong of clarity.

She showered, packed, and made a quick stop at her elderly neighbors, the Dolans, in order to ask them to pick up her mail—she wasn't sure how many days she'd be gone. While she was at the Dolans', Daisy Dolan asked her if it'd been all right that she'd told that nice man who was asking for directions to her house last night where Sophie lived.

"He seemed so anxious to see you. I thought perhaps he was ill," Daisy said, her forehead crinkled in concern. "I hope I did the right thing. I tried to call you afterwards, but you must have been out in the yard."

Sophie kissed her friend on the cheek in reassurance. "I was painting. It's okay, Daisy. I'm glad you gave Thomas directions to my place."

She was on the interstate headed toward Chicago within an hour of discovering Thomas Nicasio had fled her life just as dramatically as he'd entered it.

CHAPTER **THREE**

Sophie bit at a fingernail nervously before she realized what she was doing. She hadn't bitten her nails since she was fourteen years old.

She plopped down at her desk, her mind replaying all the while what had occurred this afternoon, when Thomas Nicasio had walked onto the elevator at 209 South LaSalle today with two soberly dressed men whom Sophie strongly suspected from their manner were federal agents.

Whoever the two men were, Sophie knew one thing from Thomas's furious scowl and the formal manner in which the two men flanked him like they would a prisoner: These men were no friends to Thomas Nicasio.

Something had told her not to speak when she saw him; not to acknowledge their acquaintance in front of the two men. Part of her was glad to see Thomas's ambivalence about ignoring her. Apparently, he hadn't been left completely unaffected by what she'd considered a soul-wrenching night of lovemaking, even if he had gotten up the next morning and driven away.

She couldn't judge him too harshly for his erratic behavior. He wasn't well, after all.

She'd returned to the city to have a serious talk with her friend Andy Lancaster and then to find Thomas . . . to assure herself that he was all right. Andy was off on Fridays, so she'd met with him earlier that afternoon in the tiny, messy den in his Lakeview condo. Andy's new wife, Sheila, had gone through his bachelor-pad condo in a whirlwind of redecorating soon after they'd married, but she'd agreed not to touch Andy's den with so much as a paintbrush.

Andy had listened with intense focus while Sophie explained about Nicasio's appearance at Haven Lake last night. He'd asked her a series of pointed diagnostic questions and then leaned back in his leather chair, his high forehead wrinkled and his kind face shadowed with worry.

"We have to do something, Andy," Sophie stated unequivocally.

"*What*, exactly?" Andy countered. "It sounds like Nicasio was in a brawl and suffering from a head trauma. We can't force a grown man to go to the hospital, Soph. I've never even been formally introduced him."

"But those diagnostic questions you were asking just now . . . It sounded like you think he's suffering from a psychological trauma, as well. What if . . . ?" Sophie glanced around nervously, as though she thought someone sinister was lurking in the dusty corners of Andy's den. "What if Thomas knows something about what Rick Carlisle told you during his sessions? What if he's discovered something more? What if he's in danger?"

Andy's expression froze. "Sophie . . . I never *told* you that the person who I was doing a case consultation with you about was Rick Carlisle."

Sophie made a sound of disgust and stood. She found herself staring at an Escher print that hung on Andy's wall, feeling every bit as trapped and confused as the creatures in the optical illusion drawing.

"Andy, we've been good friends now for thirteen years. Have a little respect for my intelligence, will you? Do you think I don't notice the comings and goings in our office? Do you really believe I didn't know perfectly well that the patient you were so concerned about, and who you've been consulting with me about for over a year on an anonymous basis, was Rick Carlisle, Nicasio's adoptive brother?"

"Sophie—"

"I know you're bound by an oath of confidentiality," she exclaimed as she spun to face him, "but a man may be in danger. There are limits to your oath."

Andy stood slowly and pushed his wire-rimmed glasses back on his nose. "Sophie, Thomas Nicasio *isn't* my patient."

"But Rick Carlisle was, and look what happened to him! He's *dead*."

She instantly regretted her impulsive words when she saw Andy's face drain of all color. She knew how attached Andy was to all of his patients. Rick's death had been a heavy blow for him.

"Even if you *were* right about the identity of my patient, the officials called what happened to Rick Carlisle an accident. An *accident*. Besides, you can't really believe that Rick's father would murder his own son and grandson in cold blood, can you? Isn't that what you're implying, Sophie?"

Her cheeks warmed. It did sound a little melodramatic, but—

"Joseph Carlisle is being investigated by the FBI for organized crime activities. And you know what Rick had discovered in his own research into the Outfit for his book. His journalistic source fingered Joseph Carlisle as the main boss of the Chicago Outfit," Sophie hissed. "How do I know what men like that would do and not do to keep their secrets? Do *you* really know, Andy?"

Andy sighed wearily when Sophie stared at him imploringly.

"This is *outside* my realm of control," he insisted. "If I were in possession of specific evidence that suggested a murder of two innocent people had occurred, that'd be one thing. But I *don't* have any concrete evidence. Even Ri—*the patient*—wasn't fully convinced about the allegations this man—Bernard Cokey—made in regard to his father being the head of Chicago organized crime. Please understand,

Sophie. The ethics of my profession clearly state that I'm powerless to act given these circumstances."

Sophie inhaled slowly, gathering her fragmenting thoughts. Andy had to be one of the most thoughtful, compassionate men she'd ever met, and here she was, practically accusing him of negligence. Andy would have done everything in his professional power to keep Rick safe if he possessed solid evidence his patient was in danger.

"I understand. I do. But *I'm* not operating under any such constraints, Andy. Thomas Nicasio is in trouble. I just know it."

After her meeting with Andy, she'd gone to the office, planning on looking for Thomas. That's when she'd unexpectedly come face-to-face with him as he was being escorted onto the elevator by the two men. She'd altered her plans and gotten off on the twenty-third floor, highly conscious of Thomas's stare on her back as she did so. She'd gone to her office, checked her voice mail, returned a few phone calls . . . brooded while she waited for Thomas to be alone in his office.

She repeated the details of her conversation with Andy earlier in her mind, trying to decide what her course of action should be.

Or even if there *should* be a course of action.

It was true that Andy was hamstrung by his oath of confidentiality. But what about *her* obligations? Although Rick Carlisle had unburdened himself to Andy during his psychotherapy sessions, Rick himself hadn't entirely believed in the incriminating allegations his source had made.

Unlike New York, where several crime families vied for control, the Chicago Outfit had long held sole control and monopoly on organized crime in the Midwest. The Outfit still remained draped in mystery and shadow. Despite the FBI's increased efforts to infiltrate and break the legs out from under the powerful, widespread criminal organization, so many things still remained secret, including the identity of the top man.

Rick Carlisle had been part of the force that was chipping away at the power of the Outfit. His award-winning investigative reports for the *Chicago Tribune* had given the FBI important fuel for the arrests of fourteen key members of Chicago organized crime. During the trial, federal prosecutors were able to strike a serious blow against the criminal syndicate, sending multiple Outfit members to prison. However, corruption among federal officials remained problematic, and the ability to identify and prosecute the top boss and completely cripple the crime syndicate remained out of the FBI's and other federal investigators' reach.

But the FBI was gaining ground. They'd recently stated that they'd soon be announcing an indictment against Joseph Carlisle for tax evasion and money laundering; although rumor had it he was guilty of much, much more. Word on the street had it that Joseph Carlisle was the top man of the Outfit. There was little doubt that the mob felt the law watching their every move, waiting for a slipup.

It was under this tension-filled environment that Rick Carlisle had recently procured a journalistic source, an individual who had been a small-time criminal in the Chicago crime syndicate for decades, a man that went by the name of Bernard Cokey. A high-ranking soldier in the Outfit had owned a restaurant where Cokey had worked as a cook. Cokey's position was such that other mobsters came to think of him as part of the woodwork; they didn't trust Cokey so much as consider him insignificant.

In this environment, Cokey had collected quite a cache of valuable insider information. He was now retired, and somewhat bitter at the way his higher-ups had always treated him like a harmless mascot.

Rick had written a number of award-winning articles on organized crime under his journalistic pseudonym, Joshua Malenic. When he decided to write his latest book, he'd chosen to focus on the most famous crime syndicate in his hometown of Chicago. Cokey had agreed to provide Rick with anonymous information.

A dazed and disoriented Rick Carlisle had told Andy during a psychotherapy session several weeks ago that Cokey had given him the elusive name of the Outfit's boss.

Much to Rick's disbelief, Cokey had indicated that his own father and Thomas's adoptive father—Joseph Carlisle—was the top man.

Rick hadn't been convinced of his source's honesty. He'd certainly never indicated to Andy Lancaster that he believed he was in danger.

And there was always the possibility that Rick had good reason to feel safe, Sophie thought. Joseph Carlisle might be innocent. It might be just as the police said: Rick Carlisle's and his son's death might have just been a tragic, freak accident.

Sophie found herself chewing on her nails again and made a disgusted sound. She stood and began pacing next to her desk. The fact of the matter was the circumstances had left her in the singular, uncomfortable position of having slept with a man she knew a hell of a lot about, unbeknownst to him. And she had a feeling Thomas Nicasio was not only ill in some fashion, but in a lot of trouble because of those circumstances.

She glanced at her watch. It was 7:45 P.M. The authorities must have finished talking to Thomas by now. She stood from her desk, intending to take the elevator to the forty-sixth floor . . . to walk into Thomas Nicasio's offices for the first time in her life.

Someone knocked on her door instead.

"Come in," she called, thinking it was probably the cleaning staff. It was late on a Friday and the office was empty, save for Sophie.

The door swung open and Thomas walked in.

Sophie froze, shocked by the unexpected sight of him. He kept his eyes trained on her as he shut the door behind him. She'd always thought her private office large enough, but the walls shrunk with Thomas Nicasio in the room.

"Thomas. Are you all right?"

"No."

She saw him push the lock on the door handle. He stepped toward her. She recognized that hot look in his eyes. Recognized it all too well. She'd seen it countless times last night.

"I'm not going to be all right until I bury myself in you."
He stalked across the room and reached for her.

"Tom—"

He cut off her soft whimper of mixed need and uncertainty when he seized her mouth with his own. He proceeded to consume her.

Thomas felt fevered, but not by illness. By lust. He'd never experienced anything like it in his life.

When he'd walked into the lobby this afternoon and come face-to-face with two badge-waving federal agents he'd been frothing with a different emotion: *fury.* Wasn't it bad enough that his brother and nephew were dead? His family had been floored by Rick's and Abel's deaths, but the FBI continued to nose around relentlessly, investigating his father, accosting him—Thomas—in the lobby of his building and treating him like he was a suspect in some crime, as well.

In the midst of his angry ruminations, he'd suddenly glanced up and seen Sophie Gable standing in the elevator, looking as fresh, golden, and lush as a newly plucked peach.

He'd frozen on the threshold. The sight of her had struck him like a stinging slap.

A wave of intense lust flooded his body, shocking him, given the situation. You would have thought she'd stood there stark naked instead of wearing one of her many conservative skirts and low-heeled pumps, her shoulder-length, wavy blonde hair pulled up onto her head in a no-nonsense, effortlessly elegant style.

He saw her dark brown eyes widen when she saw his strange reaction to seeing her. Pink lips that were naked of all artifice parted in surprise.

How *the hell* had he ever managed to rein himself in when it came to Sophie Gable before?

Agent Fisk noticed his odd reaction and gave Sophie a sharp, speculative glance. Thomas got a hold of himself and turned his back to her. Still, he was hyperaware of Sophie behind him, her presence pulling at him like a magnet.

When he glanced back at her, he saw something on her face that he couldn't quite interpret.

Had it been alarm?

She probably *was* alarmed, given the strange way he was acting. Those dreams he'd been having about her—dreams that redefined the meaning of sexual need and pleasure—*those* were responsible for his bizarre reaction to Dr. Sophie Gable.

Thomas noticed Agent Fisk's second glance at Sophie and turned away from her again. He didn't want these assholes noticing her.

What was wrong with him? It had shocked him, to feel something so inappropriate—so powerful—in the midst of such a volatile moment. His brother and nephew were dead and federal agents were investigating his father for federal crimes. And all he could think about was stripping off Sophie Gable's clothes and fucking her until all of his anguish and fury exploded into a cataclysm of nirvanic forgetfulness.

He was losing control of his chaotic emotions.

Losing control, period.

His family was suffering from unspeakable grief; his mother shrouded in a thick veil of sadness that Thomas couldn't penetrate, no matter how hard he tried; his sister-in-law shell-shocked and only beginning to recognize the black abyss of her loss; his father's charisma and heartiness suddenly diminished so that he looked like a husk of the vibrant man he used to be.

Now the FBI had barged into their private family grief, stirring up an already frothing cauldron of anguish by never missing a beat in their investigation of Joseph Carlisle, by alleging his adoptive father had perpetrated crimes so widespread, Thomas couldn't even consider them without alternating between feeling hollow, numb shock and sheer outrage at the offensive insinuations the FBI was making in their investigations.

Truth be told, as irritated as he'd been when the agents approached him in the lobby, he'd been glad to have a target for the anger, helplessness, and grief that had been building in him since his mother had called last week and told him Rick and Abel were dead.

He'd been on a Diversey Harbor dock at the time he'd gotten that call, waiting for his brother and ten-year-old nephew to come and collect him in the boat—the same boat that had exploded.

Once he was behind the closed doors of his office with the two agents, he hadn't made a secret of his contempt. Fisk had stayed silent, watching him like a bird of prey as Larue began questioning him. Thomas, who'd had years of experience both as an enlisted man and later as an officer in Somalia and Iraq, immediately understood that Fisk possessed the brains and savvy between the two agents, despite his younger age.

It surprised Thomas when Larue started asking questions about his background and Nicasio Investments instead of his father.

"Nice place," Larue commented as he glanced around Thomas's large, luxurious office and out the floor-to-ceiling glass windows that faced Lake Michigan. The golden summer evening outside stood in stark contrast to Thomas's stormy mood. The headache that had been plaguing him nonstop made things even worse. Every time he tried to concentrate on something, to focus on his thoughts, it became so severe it felt like his head was splitting open.

He frowned as he sat down behind his desk, staring at the two interlopers coldly, refusing to make this easy for them.

"Where did you get the money to start up your firm three years ago, Mr. Nicasio?" Larue had asked as he opened up a small notebook and began taking notes.

"The Navy provided well for me since I was a teenager, and I never had need for most of my salary. I compiled quite a savings, which I was able to add to the trust fund my father reserved for us," Thomas answered, restrained anger making his voice sound stiff.

"You served in the EOD unit, isn't that correct?" Larue asked, never glancing up as he scribbled in his notebook.

"That's right," Thomas replied, tight-lipped. Larue referred to Explosive Ordnance Disposal, the elite unit of the Navy responsible for safely disarming bombs or other types of ordnance, including chemical, biological, and nuclear. As an eighteen-year-old, Thomas had risked his adoptive father's disapproval by enlisting in the Navy instead of going to college right after high school.

It had been one of only a few, but notable, moments when Thomas's stubborn nature superseded one of Joseph Carlisle's authoritarian decrees. Joseph had wanted him to attend an Ivy League university right out of high school. But even in this clear-cut instance of filial rebellion, Joseph had ended up respecting Thomas's decision, saying that a man had to find his own path and test his own legs. The fact that Thomas had gone on to earn his college degree in business administration and become a decorated officer in the EOD unit only seemed to reinforce Joseph's respect for Thomas's proclivity for independence. Deep down, Thomas knew that Joseph respected his ability to make a mark on the world without patronage.

It was an approval Joseph had never bestowed on Rick, his eldest son, even though Rick had been even more deserving of it than Thomas.

"And when you say that your father set up a trust fund for you, you really mean your adopted father, isn't that correct?" Larue persisted.

"I was adopted, yes, but Joseph Carlisle *is* my father," Thomas bit out irritably. He felt Agent Fisk's stare on him and returned the look with a frown. *What's your problem, asshole?* He wondered if Fisk understood his volatile thought when the young agent dropped his gaze to his lap, his brows knitted in consternation.

"Your real parents were killed during a burglary, I understand?" Larue continued.

"That's right. It happened when I was ten years old. Is that what you two came here to discuss? The fact that my parents' murderer was never found? Wonderful." He leaned back in his leather chair and gave a fake sigh of relief. "I'm glad to know the investigation is still underway. And here

I'd been suspecting that you two were just here to waste my time."

Larue looked up sharply, his pen frozen on the paper. Fisk wiped his hand across his jaw and mouth, but not quick enough for Thomas to miss his slight smile.

"Your parents' murder investigation isn't under the auspices of the FBI," Larue explained.

Thomas's pointed, annoyed glance told the agent loud and clear he'd been being facetious. Larue must have understood, because he cleared his throat and turned his attention back to his notebook.

"So it's safe to say that Joseph Carlisle supplied you with the majority of the capital to start Nicasio Investments?" Larue asked.

Thomas made an irritated, slashing motion with his hand. "No, I'm not saying that at all. I started Nicasio Investments mostly with my own savings. But let's cut the bullshit. I have no doubt you guys have all the banking numbers. It's not illegal for a father to set up a trust fund for his children. Why don't you get to the point? You two are here to ask me questions about my dad. If you think I'm going to tell you something that will bolster your investigation, you're dead wrong. What you're digging around for—what you're alleging about Joseph Carlisle is ridiculous. My father is a hardworking man who would do anything for his family. My brother's death is ripping him apart. Haven't you guys got anything better to do than to kick a man when he's down?"

Fisk met his stare and shifted in his chair uneasily, but his blistering question bounced off Larue like raindrops on rubber.

"It's my understanding that Joseph and Rick Carlisle had been on the outs with each other for years," Larue commented.

"Yeah? Where'd you hear something like that, Larue? Listening to gossip in the girls' john?"

"Actually, I heard it from your brother's wife, Mr. Nicasio. Are you insinuating Kelly Carlisle is a gossip?"

Thomas leveled a malevolent stare, refusing to respond.

He loved Kelly like a sister; he hated the fact that Joseph had disapproved of not only Rick's career as an investigative journalist, but his choice of wife. Thomas'd worked tirelessly to try to bridge the gap between father and son. The peace-making role was one he'd become familiar with since he was thirteen years old. He doubted his father would ever fully recover from the fact that he and Rick hadn't been talking at the time of Rick's death.

But he'd be damned if he was going to talk out loud about such painful, private family matters to a sanctimonious FBI agent. Larue waved at his right hand.

"What happened to your knuckles?"

Thomas glanced at his knuckles in mixed surprise and irritation. What the hell was Larue talking about?

"You know a man named Douglas Mannero?" Larue persisted. Thomas could tell by his tone the agent thought he was being stubborn by not answering his former question for a stretched moment, but in truth, a wave of nausea had rolled through him when he'd seen the abrasions on his knuckles. He became uncomfortably aware that he was sweating. He struggled to focus on Larue's latest unexpected question. Douglas Mannero was one of the clients in his investment firm.

"What's *that* got to do with anything?"

"We know he's one of Nicasio Investments' clients. You've been handling his money for two years now." Larue flipped back a few pages in his notebook. "Mannero runs a large, lucrative West Side vending machine business—manufactures, repairs, and distributes vending machines all over the city, downstate, Ohio, Wisconsin, and northern Indiana."

"So?" Thomas prompted, bewildered by the turn of the questioning.

"Who referred Mannero to Nicasio Investments?" Larue asked.

Thomas narrowed his gaze on Larue.

"What are you digging at?"

This time, Larue didn't respond, just fixed him with that

stony, cocky G-man stare. Thomas's fury escalated in the tense silence that followed, making his chest burn.

Agent Fisk suddenly leaned forward in his chair, speaking for the first time since the meeting had begun.

"Douglas Mannero was arrested earlier today as part of our ongoing investigation into organized crime in Chicago, Mr. Nicasio. Thanks to the cooperation of the IRS, we have good reason to believe that the vending machine company was being used to launder money that the Outfit made from illegal gambling operations."

"Should I call my lawyer?" Thomas seethed. "Are you accusing me of being involved?"

"No. We have no evidence that would indicate you understood that the money was dirty when Mannero asked you to invest it," Fisk said.

Larue gave his partner a surprised, irritated glance, which Fisk ignored. Fisk held Thomas's stare. "We didn't come here today to accuse you of anything, Mr. Nicasio. But as part of our investigation, we would like the name of the person who referred Mannero to Nicasio Investments."

"I don't recall," Thomas replied.

Fisk nodded his head and studied Thomas narrowly. "We won't take up any more of your time, then."

Larue looked up at him, his widened eyes saying loud and clear that he was stunned by Fisk's actions.

"You're mistaken about Mannero," Thomas said coldly. "I've seen the company's books. I made a study of them, in fact. They're clean. You're even more wrong about your allegations against my father."

"We have information from a very reliable inside informant that tells us otherwise," Fisk said with a level stare before he hitched his chin at Larue, indicating to his partner that it was time to go.

Thomas curled his lip in disgust. "You guys are fucking hypocrites. You say you want justice, but you're willing to take the word of some slimy little two-bit criminal over a respected businessman like my father?"

Fisk stopped dead in his tracks and spun around. "What slimy two-bit criminal are you referring to, Mr. Nicasio?"

Thomas rose slowly from his chair, glaring at Fisk. "The one you must be talking to who is feeding you all these lies about my father."

For a few seconds, Fisk didn't move.

"Our informant isn't a criminal, Mr. Nicasio. Not in the slightest. Have a good evening, sir."

Thomas had just stood there, watching the two agents march out of his office, boiling in a vat of bewilderment and rage. Even in the midst of his emotional turmoil, the image of Sophie Gable standing in the elevator leapt into his mind's eye. It only added to his volatility that he couldn't stop thinking about her, even under these circumstances. He didn't want to think about *a woman* now, not when the FBI was hounding Joseph Carlisle, making preposterous claims about him being involved in organized crime, badgering Thomas about a client his father had referred to him a couple years back.

Despite his mental prohibitions on lusting after Sophie, he detailed the vision of her once again in his mind's eye, fantasized about peeling off that crisp white blouse she wore and baring her succulent flesh for his hungry mouth.

His blood sizzled in his veins; his cock twitched.

What the hell was wrong with him?

After several minutes he rifled around in a desk drawer to retrieve some keys and called his administrative assistant, Erin, telling her she was free to go home. He'd go over to Doug Mannero's office/warehouse and have a look at the books himself. He'd gone over them carefully when he took on Doug as a client. He'd recognize if there'd been any changes made . . . any cover-up. Thomas had a good head for numbers.

But when he got on the elevator, instead of hitting the button for the lobby, he hit the one for the twenty-third floor instead.

He knew he should stay away from Dr. Sophie Gable. She didn't deserve to be the unsuspecting target of the cyclone of emotion that whipped and whirled around in his head.

But he couldn't seem to stop himself from seeking her out. It puzzled the hell out of him, this sudden fixation he had on the doctor. Sure, he'd been strongly attracted to her ever since the first time he'd laid eyes on her. And he wasn't a fool. Thomas liked women, and they typically liked him. He was experienced enough to know that Sophie Gable was very aware of him, as well; knew instinctively she returned his interest.

But he'd always shied away from her, wary of her clean scent, girl-next-door glow . . . an appeal like body-warmed, sex-mussed sheets on a sunny bed. He was too complicated for Sophie Gable. Too dark. He'd get her dirty; mess her up. It amazed him to know he'd actually avoided her to protect her as much as himself.

Despite his self-imposed prohibition against Sophie Gable, something about her called out to him; always had from the moment he'd first set eyes on her.

And God help her, in the midst of his turmoil and grief, he suddenly found he didn't want to spare her any longer. No longer *could* spare himself. He would quench his fires in Sophie Gable tonight. His cock craved her, but his mind did as well.

After the storm was spent, Thomas knew—somehow—that peace would come, even if it was temporary.

The door to her office was unlocked. The lights were still on in the empty lobby. He headed down the hallway, a sense of sharp anticipation building in him. He knocked on her door and opened it when he heard her low voice bidding him to enter.

She stood by her desk, looking like a graceful gazelle caught in headlights. His gaze trailed down over her elegant throat and the front of the simple, white cotton blouse she wore. Sophie could try to disguise her assets by putting on a professional appearance all she wanted, but Thomas was a connoisseur who instinctively recognized quality when he saw it. He didn't care if she wore a nun's habit, nothing was going to hide the fact that Sophie Gable was built like a brick house.

Nothing could hide it from him, anyway.

"Thomas," she whispered. "Are you all right?"

"No," he replied, mesmerized by the movement of her lips. His fingers itched to delve through her soft, wavy hair, to ruin the knot that restrained it at the back of her head. He pushed the lock on her door, examining her reaction to his boldness.

Would it frighten her?

When he saw her furtive gaze drop down over his abdomen and crotch, and then the convulsion of her elegant throat, he got his answer. Whatever the magic—whatever the insanity—that was brewing between them was affecting her as much as him.

The realization made his cock stiffen and throb next to his left thigh. He stepped toward her.

"I'm not going to be all right until I bury myself in you," he said truthfully.

"Tom—"

He bent down and covered the lush confection of her lips with his mouth. The sensation of her firm flesh amplified his hunger exponentially. He ate up her sexy, tiny whimpers and parted her lips with his tongue.

He groaned as her taste registered in his brain.

Christ, this was gonna be good.

He lost himself in her, welcoming pure sensation, intoxicated by the feeling of her hips curving into his palms, made drunk by her sweet mouth and her fresh, floral woman-scent filling his nose. She slid her tongue against his eagerly, turning her head and pressing closer, the evidence of her returned ardor making lust roar like a torrential current through his veins. Sophie didn't kiss like the innocent girl next door. No, she tangled her tongue with his wildly, shaped his mouth and created a suction his cock responded to wholeheartedly.

His hands opened over her round ass. He pushed her against his erection and rubbed her softness against his hardness, uncaring about the lewdness of his actions . . . just feeling. Every nerve in his body screamed with need, just like they had as he dreamed last night. Kissing Sophie was like dipping his tongue into sex-sweet honey.

He lifted his head after a moment, molding her lips with his own, nipping at her hungrily.

"I have to have you. Now."

"Yes," she whispered. The feeling of her hands moving anxiously over his back and around to the front of him, stroking his ribs, drove him crazy. He hissed when she drove her fingers through an opening in his shirt and touched him, skin to skin.

He stared into her wide, liquid brown eyes as he began to unbutton her blouse. As he brushed his knuckles against the fullness of her breasts his cock lurched with longing. She might have felt it, because she murmured his name shakily and craned up to kiss him again.

"No. Let me look at you," he ordered tensely.

She remained unmoving as he finished unbuttoning her blouse and parted the fabric, making his fantasy reality. Her skin had been sun-kissed light gold with just a hint of apricots. The simple, modest white bra she wore turned him on more than the raciest, skimpiest lingerie he'd ever seen. She shivered when he slid his hands along the satiny skin at the sides of her torso and reached for the clasp.

"Oh, Sophie," he mumbled in awe when he'd bared her pale, full breasts. Her nipples were delicate, pink and tight. Lust lanced through him when he held her firm, warm flesh in his hands and lightly ran his thumbs over the succulent tips, making them bead and stiffen even more. He glanced up at her.

"You're beautiful."

"Thomas," she whispered. She placed her hand on the back of his head and brought him down to her. He nuzzled the silky curve of a breast, inhaling her scent, before he slipped a nipple into his mouth, laving it with his tongue. His eyes burned with emotion that he couldn't comprehend as he suckled her first softly and then, as his desire built to almost unbearable levels, ravenously.

The pain of her gripping his hair as she held him down to her brought him back to himself—that and the sharp ache of his near-to-bursting cock. He raised his head, searching for a trace of sanity in Sophie's eyes.

Instead, he saw the glaze of a fevered lust shining in their depths and knew she suffered as much as he did. He would have hurried things for himself, but what he saw in the depths of Sophie's eyes made him frantic.

Or at least that's what he told himself later when he was trying to justify his actions.

He held her gaze as he placed his hands on her skirt and began to slide the fabric up her hips. They both panted into the thick silence. When his palms ran over the tops of smooth stockings and onto the warm silk of her upper thighs, a low growl vibrated in his throat.

An explosion seemed to detonate in his brain. He turned her in his arms and pressed his cock against her ass. She didn't balk when he pushed her upper body down, forcing her to bend at the waist. Her hands went out to brace their weight on the desk.

"I'll go slow next time, Sophie. Right now, I'm going to go crazy if I can't get inside you."

She didn't speak, but she turned and met his gaze as he lowered her panties. The sight of her damp parted lips and wide, glazed eyes caused his cock to jerk viciously in his boxer briefs. His face pinched in an agony of lust when he glanced down at her bared ass.

God, he should stop this. It *was* madness. The things he wanted to do to her . . . lovely, kind Dr. Gable with the face of an angel and a smile that could warm a man on the coldest, bitterest days of his life.

He wanted to fuck her like an animal.

"Spread your thighs some, Sophie."

She followed his gruff order, her panties stretched tight where he'd lowered them to just above her knees. He unbuckled his belt rapidly, his eyes glued to the erotic image of Sophie bent at the waist, her skirt bunched around her hips, her white ass and the tantalizing glimpse of her pink sex between her spread thighs. He'd fantasized about how she looked under those prim, nondescript skirts, salivated at the visions his mind conjured.

His fantasies paled. Nothing compared to the rich, carnal feast spread before him.

He'd never wanted to put on a condom less, but he was careful to do so, mindful of her cleanness, of not wanting to dirty her with his bitterness and rage. His loneliness.

And yet . . . he experienced a simultaneous need to take her like a savage, to desecrate her with his essence and scent . . . to mark her.

His strange, mixed feelings created an unbearable friction in him; one that would only diminish once he'd exploded in her depths. He glanced up. She'd been watching him roll the condom onto his painfully sensitive erection. When he took his cock into his hand, her tongue slicked her lower lip anxiously.

He palmed a round ass cheek, lifting her flesh, parting her slit. They both gasped when he pressed the tip of his cock into her.

He groaned, deep and savage, when he slid several inches into her tight, sultry heat. He pumped his hips, trying to be as gentle as his fevered, pounding blood would allow, silently praying for admittance to heaven. She was gratifyingly wet. He heard himself moving in her juices as he moved his cock into her snug channel.

His blood boiled in his veins. He *required* release. "Let me in, Sophie. Let me in."

He slapped her bottom.

She gasped. Heat rushed around his cock. He slid into her to the hilt, grunting in sublime pleasure. Her pussy clutched at him like a hot, silken fist. He grabbed her hips and began to pump without pause, starved to feel every nuance of her tight embrace. His shirt kept getting in the way, causing him to curse. He spread a hand on Sophie's buttock, his cock fully submerged, and ripped at the buttons of his shirt. When he'd shoved aside the cloth, baring his chest and abdomen, he noticed Sophie had once again turned her chin.

Her hungry eyes made the skin on his torso prickle.

He stroked her buttock softly while his cock throbbed deep

inside her. Their gazes held while he began to fuck her, his strokes long, thorough, and forceful. Her mouth dropped open and her face tightened every time his pelvis smacked against her ass and thighs.

After a moment, a low keen exuded from her throat and she dropped her forehead to the desk. He used his hands to lift her hips slightly, allowing him to take her at a downward angle that made him growl in feral satisfaction.

The final shreds of his restraint evaporated. He took her in a fluid, frenzied fuck. Her desk rattled and scooted a few inches on the floor. Maybe he could have stopped himself if she protested his forceful possession.

Maybe. Thomas didn't know what the hell to expect from this frenzied, wild stranger that had taken over his body.

But he needn't have worried about her compliance. Sophie whimpered and moaned in pleasure. She bucked her hips eagerly. Despite the fact that he liked her display of eagerness, he swatted her ass. His cock leapt in her tight sheath at the smacking sound of his palm against firm flesh.

"Keep still. Please," he grated out. "I'm about to lose control as it is."

He began fucking her again with long strokes, his face clenched tight in an agony of bliss. Still, he wanted more of her, was wild to find some secret in her darkest depths.

He pressed her chest and belly flat to the desk and lifted his knee, rising up partially over her. He placed his knee on the desk and fucked her with deep, short, frantic strokes, his eyes rolling back into his head at the delicious friction the new angle provided him.

Sophie mewled in stunned pleasure.

"You're so damned hot. So tight. I'm not going to last," he muttered as he thrust madly. He slid his hand to the front of her, his finger burrowing between her labia, seeking out her most sensitive flesh, needing her to share some measure of the burning inferno about to consume him.

His curse was an acknowledgment of a blessing. She was wetter than a man could imagine in his most illicit fantasies.

When she cried out and he felt her begin to convulse in

orgasm around his pistoning cock, a red haze of lust clouded his vision, the mindless nirvana he'd sought so desperately.

He placed his foot back on the floor and grabbed her hips. He thrust again and again, jerking her hips toward him, his arm muscles straining as he served Sophie's sweet flesh to his raging cock.

He bit his lip to stop himself from shouting when he came. He shook as he poured himself into the condom.

"Sophie, Sophie," he muttered between clenched teeth as wave after wave of blistering pleasure flooded his senses and all thought was blessedly erased from his brain.

CHAPTER **FOUR**

He fell down over her, gasping for air, feeling raw and exposed, like a fish tossed up on the beach. She'd turned her head, resting her right cheek on the desk. She panted, but nowhere near as hard as he did. He was in good shape, but Christ . . . fucking Sophie had been like racing toward heaven with the devil fast on his heels.

He pressed his forehead to her temple, wanting the small contact with her while his body recovered from the raging storm. He wanted to hold her, but his heart and lungs demanded their due, paralyzing him for a moment.

By slow degrees, he returned to himself. She shifted and murmured softly, lifting her chin and brushing her lips across his cheek. He realized he was pressing her soft body down onto the hard desk. His eyes sprang open when her vagina contracted around him. Need swelled inside him once again, fierce and raw.

Grief had transformed him into a fucking animal.

"Thomas?" she whispered when he abruptly stood. He clenched his teeth at the sensation of his cock leaving the warm, slick clasp of her body. It pained him for some reason, to see her bent over the desk like that, her white cotton underwear callously shoved down to her knees. He placed his hands on her lower legs and gently pulled up her panties, lingering to let his fingers slide across the curve of her naked hips.

He winced as he removed the condom from his restiffening penis.

He didn't respond to her one-word query while he jerked up his underwear and pants, then knotted the condom, wrapped it in some Kleenex from her desk, and disposed of it in the wastepaper basket.

She straightened as he came back toward her, pushing her skirt back down over her legs. Her cheeks were flushed pink from her arousal. Her glance held traces of confusion and concern, causing regret to lance through him once again.

He took her in his arms and brushed back tendrils of hair from her cheeks. This close, he could see the gold strands seemed to hold onto the muted light, making them incandesce and shimmer. He pressed his lips to her temple. For a full minute, neither of them spoke.

"What can I say?" he eventually asked next to her skin. "I don't know where that came from. 'Sorry' doesn't really seem adequate, seeing as how I just barged in your office and made love to you with all the finesse of a locomotive going at full steam."

She leaned back and studied him. He closed his eyelids when he felt her fingers burrowing through his hair. Her massaging fingertips caused a wave of heaviness and exhaustion to sweep through him. He dropped his forehead to hers. His world was spinning out of control, but Sophie's touch steadied him. Maybe that's why he'd entered her office earlier with such a single-minded purpose.

"I am, though," he mumbled. "Sorry I mean. I don't know what's wrong with me."

"You don't have to apologize. You're in pain. I wanted you just as much." She glanced down between their bodies. "What's happening between us has been a long time in coming. Thomas?"

He lifted his head slowly, surprised by her words. *What's happening between us has been a long time in coming.*

She started to say something, and then seemed to edit herself at the last moment. "Are you all right?"

He nodded.

"I've been worried about you," she whispered. "Those men on the elevator—were they cops or federal agents?"

Irritation pierced his feeling of languorous comfort. He should have known it felt too good to last long.

"Yeah. FBI."

"What . . . what did they want?" she asked shakily.

He inhaled through his nostrils, trying to calm his anger, which was never far from the surface these days. "You've probably heard on the news? About the FBI investigating my father . . . the allegations that . . ." He swallowed in order to get the bitter words out of his throat. " . . . he's involved in organized crime?"

She nodded.

"They were here asking me questions about a Nicasio Investment client."

He felt her go still next to him.

"Were they accusing you of being involved in organized crime as well, Thomas?"

"No. But they *were* trying to link my father to a huge gambling operation, and using one of my clients to do it. They've already arrested my client for supposedly using his vending machine plant and distribution business to launder mob money. They were trying to use me to get a link between my client—Doug Mannero—and my father." He glanced away from Sophie's luminous face and inhaled slowly. "Tax evasion and money laundering are the least of the crimes the FBI would love to pin on my dad. Agent Fisk claimed they have someone on the inside providing them with information, but the only thing they're being fed by that slimebag is lies," he finished grimly.

"You believe entirely in your father's innocence?"

He turned abruptly, causing pain to slice through his head.

"Thomas?"

He shook his head briefly, trying to bring her into focus as well as shake off a momentary vertigo. He peered at her closely. Why was he telling her this stuff—a virtual stranger?

"Of course I believe he's innocent. The FBI must be getting desperate these days. They were trying to get me to say my dad had referred Doug Mannero to me, but I refused to give them any fuel. I went over Mannero's accounts myself when I first took him on. They were clean."

She swallowed convulsively and spread her hand on the side of his head. "What are you planning to do?"

He glanced around her private office dazedly, feeling like he was just seeing it for the first time—which maybe he was, as consumed as he'd been by a fever to fuck earlier. Her office was about a sixth of the size of his, but the cinnamon-colored walls, tasteful paintings, and candles on the end tables next to the ivory couch gave the room a warm intimacy that his workspace had never known.

"I should go over to Mannero, Inc., and look at the books. I was actually on my way over there when I came here . . ." He faded off, once again focusing on her somber face. Regret lanced through him. "I can't imagine what you must be thinking of me."

Her brow crinkled. "I think you're not yourself, Thomas. You loved your brother and nephew. You're drowning in grief. The FBI's investigation of your father must feel like another blow when you were already spinning. I can only imagine what it's doing to your family."

He watched himself as he ran his fingertip over the soft shell of her ear. She was so delicate . . . so exquisite.

He felt like swine when his cock tightened.

"Abel was my godson, you know," he murmured distractedly as he stroked her. "He was ten years old. I was teaching him how to water-ski. Rick and he were going to be picking me up at Diversey Harbor on that day. They never came."

She didn't reply but she placed her hand over his heart. Her simple gesture made something dangerous swell in his chest.

"I should go," he said roughly.

"Where?"

The sharpness of her query made him blink. She probably thought he was abandoning her after he'd just fucked her like a madman.

"Can I see you . . . later tonight?" he asked.

"Come with me *now,* Thomas."

A trickle of unease went through him. She'd sounded soft, but the thread of steel in her tone confused him.

"Listen . . . I know how strange the way I'm acting must seem to you," he tried to explain. "You must be thinking I'm a real asshole for busting in here and making love to you so . . . forcefully for the first time while you were bent over a desk."

She paled and her mouth dropped open. She looked stunned, but he rushed ahead, needing to tell her this. Jesus. Here stood a woman who likely had an IQ that would put him to shame, forget about the body of a Venus, and look how he was treating her? He rushed ahead anxiously, trying to explain, even when he himself couldn't understand what the hell he was doing.

"I'm not trying to get away from you, Sophie. I'm just . . . something . . . *something's* happened."

Her expressive, dark eyes made him want to relent, to stay there with her, to forget all the horror and chaos that was his life.

"But I need to go and have a look at those books at Mannero, Inc. I need to know what I'm dealing with as far as this FBI investigation," he finished regretfully.

For a split second, he saw panic flicker across her flushed face. "Thomas, don't go there. Please. You . . . you need to rest. You're not well."

He brushed his thumb across her cheek and attempted a smile. "Is that your professional opinion?"

"*Yes.* I don't think you should go. Come with me now. I'll make you dinner at my condominium. We'll talk . . . or . . . or not, if you don't want to."

He leaned down and kissed her opened lips, lingering

when he caught her taste on his searching tongue. He felt guilty. She sounded so worried . . .

After a moment, he lifted his head reluctantly. He'd be a liar if he said he wasn't fantasizing about having her yet again . . . taking her in another fevered frenzy. He'd heard death could heighten the sexual instinct. People needed to feel alive in the midst of their anguish . . . to celebrate the fullness of existence when death hovered and beckoned into the void.

Thomas now knew firsthand how true it was.

"Tell me your address," he muttered as he nudged her middle with his once again stiff cock before he backed away, depriving himself. At least for a while. His body was far from being done celebrating Sophie Gable's vibrant existence. Next time, he'd take it slow. Now that he'd consumed her, next time he'd savor her.

If he could get a handle on himself, anyway.

He nodded when she said her Gold Coast address. He'd remember, even if his concentration hadn't been that great for the past several days . . . even if the past few days had been a strange collage of too-bright, vivid images and darkness. Thomas didn't forget numbers.

"I'll meet you at your place in a few hours. I *promise*. No one and nothing is going to keep me away from a second time, Sophie."

A shadow flickered across her beautiful face, but Thomas determinedly levered his body away from hers.

He hadn't remembered.

The thought kept replaying like a skipped record over and over again in her brain as she locked up her office after Thomas left. He hadn't remembered last night . . . hadn't remembered making love to her.

He thought he'd just made love to her for the first time.

Her brain couldn't quite seem to wrap around the reality of it. She'd known he'd been traumatized . . . unwell, but she hadn't guessed he wouldn't remember, that he'd become amnesic to those hours in her bed, to their raw, volatile lovemaking. Another thought made her freeze while her key was in the door.

What else didn't he remember?

The thought sent her brain into another riot of uncertainty. She'd been stunned when he'd mentioned that he'd just made love to her for the first time in her office just now. At first, she'd thought it must be a joke, but then she'd taken in Thomas's rigid muscles and tortured glance and known in a rush of dread that it wasn't.

She'd stopped herself from spilling the truth. He was like a walking time bomb. Who knew what would happen if she suddenly forced him to recall what he'd forgotten?

She shouldn't have let him leave, she thought as she pulled her key out of the door and swiftly turned. She slung her purse over her shoulder and headed toward the elevator, but came up short when a man called her name.

She recognized the young, sharp-eyed FBI agent who had been on the elevator earlier with Thomas. He leaned casually against the hallway wall.

"Dr. Sophie Gable?" the man repeated. She nodded. He reached into his pocket. Sophie's gaze lowered over the official-looking badge he held up. "My name is Fisk. I'm with the Federal Bureau of Investigation. I was wondering if I might have a word?"

"About what?" Sophie asked.

"Thomas Nicasio."

Sophie just stared at the agent while her pulse began to throb in her neck. It struck her that Agent Fisk wasn't that much older than she was, but his clean-cut, dark good looks, serious expression, and sharp eyes gave the impression of talking to an older man. Despite her wariness of him, Sophie had to admit that Fisk had the type of face you trusted. And maybe she would have trusted him . . . under different circumstances anyway.

"Where's your partner?" Sophie queried briskly after she'd glanced around his shoulder and ascertained that she was indeed alone in the deserted hallway with Fisk.

"Working on something else."

"So you work alone at times?"

"Yeah. I do, Dr. Gable," the agent replied after a pause. "I saw Nicasio leave your office." His perceptive eyes flickered over her body. Sophie glanced down, following the trail of his brief assessment of her appearance. She held the agent's stare, her chin tilted upward as she rapidly shoved the side of her shirt into her skirt. It'd remained partially untucked, a telltale sign of her heated lovemaking with Thomas.

"Have you known Nicasio long?"

"No," Sophie admitted brusquely. "What is it that I can help you with, Mr. Fisk?"

He smiled at her small show of defiance. "I'm not your enemy, Dr. Gable. I'm not Thomas Nicasio's enemy either."

"Thomas seems to feel differently."

"Does he?" Fisk asked, his air of slight puzzlement ratcheting up her own confusion. "You were just with him. As a physician, I'm wondering if you noticed anything . . . unusual about him?"

"What do you mean?" Sophie asked slowly.

"He seems extremely upset . . . overwhelmed."

"Is it a wonder?" she snapped, hoping the observant agent didn't notice her pulse throbbing at her throat. "Thomas has been through hell in the past week, Mr. Fisk."

"And by all the evidence, hasn't made the return trip yet," Fisk muttered.

He knew, Sophie thought. He knew Thomas wasn't right. But when she noticed Fisk's searching expression, Sophie wondered. He seemed to be looking for answers as much as Sophie was.

"Why do you keep staring at me like that?" she demanded suddenly.

Fisk shrugged, unaffected by her outburst. "I was trying to figure you out, that's all, Doctor, wondering if you're really what you seem. Your professional history is pristine; a complaint has never been made to the American Medical Association in regard to your practice. You pay your taxes on time. As far as I can tell, you've never even gotten a speeding ticket."

Her eyes widened. "You did a background check? On *me?*"

"It seemed prudent, given the circumstances."

Sophie shook her head and smiled sarcastically. "If you were interested in speaking with me, you're not choosing a very wise way to get my cooperation, Mr. Fisk. If you'll excuse me, I need to be going."

She turned and started down the hallway.

"Thomas Nicasio is in grave danger," Fisk called out behind her.

Sophie's feet came to an abrupt halt. She slowly turned around and faced him.

"You care about him. Even if you two did just recently become . . . acquainted." His eyes flickered once again over her waist where she'd just tucked in her blouse. It hadn't been a question, but a statement, Sophie realized. When she didn't respond, Fisk just nodded as though she had. Sophie had to admit she'd never been very good at hiding the truth.

"And you're worried about him, aren't you, Doctor?"

"Yes," Sophie replied hoarsely. She swayed slightly in her heels, unable to decide if she should go or stay. "What . . . what made you think that Thomas isn't well?" she asked warily.

"He's either not well or he's a hell of an actor," Fisk mumbled. He grimaced slightly when he saw her concerned expression. "Look . . . I'm not at liberty to give you any details of the investigation."

"I'm not interested in details of your investigation," she bit out. "I'm interested in Thomas's well-being."

"I'm interested in that, too."

"You certainly weren't acting like a concerned friend when you came here with your partner to badger him today."

She straightened when he didn't respond. "If you're so worried about Thomas Nicasio, what are you doing *here*? Shouldn't you be looking out for Thomas's safety?"

"I have someone looking out for him," Fisk replied levelly.

She raised her eyebrows in query, but once again, he didn't respond.

"Is there anything specific you can tell me about why you're hovering around in my hallway? Because I haven't got time for your warnings about Thomas's safety if that's all you've got to say. Your dire predictions aren't helpful to me."

"Let's just hope my predictions aren't accurate as well, Dr. Gable."

CHAPTER **FIVE**

Thomas turned his head, squinting when a car's head-lights shone directly in his face as he pulled into the Mannero, Inc., parking lot. Darkness shrouded him as he stepped out of his car. The factory was located on Laflin Street on the West Side, far enough away from the Loop that the city lights didn't have much more effect than a string of Christmas tree lights would in illuminating a football stadium.

Whoever had just left had been working late. The parking lot was completely empty with the exception of his vehicle. He was glad he wasn't going to run into any question-asking employees. He glanced at the illuminated dial on his watch as he walked toward the entrance, grimacing when he saw that it was a little after nine.

He'd kept telling himself to call his mother, to check in on her, but he'd never gotten around to it. He recalled something she'd said to him at Rick and Abel's funeral as they both stared across the room at Joseph Carlisle.

"Make sure you try to talk to him, would you, Thomas? You always seem to cheer him up when no one else can," his mother had said.

Her statement had made a familiar, paradoxical feeling

of pride and guilt stab through Thomas. Any evidence of Joseph Carlisle's affection had always filled him with a sense of self-worth. It bolstered his confidence to know that Joseph considered him a true son, that his father didn't regret taking in a vulnerable, confused, and angry ten-year-old orphan.

But his pride twined with guilt, because Thomas knew the special relationship he shared with his father should have been reserved for Rick.

For his *real* son.

He'd hated the fact that two of the most important people in his life had been on the outs. He'd done whatever he could over the years to improve Joseph and Rick's relationship.

Now it was too late . . . too late for so much.

Another car pulled into the dark, vacant lot. He stopped dead in his tracks when the vehicle headed straight toward him, holding his hand up to shield the bright headlights from his eyes.

"Shit," he muttered disbelievingly through stiff lips. Every muscle in his body tensed in preparation to dive when the car showed no sign of stopping.

The wheels skidded in the gravel as the car came to an abrupt halt just feet away from where he stood. Someone—a woman—clambered out of the still-running vehicle. He blinked in amazement when he recognized Sophie Gable's face.

"What the hell—"

"I'm sorry, Thomas. I . . . I had to come," she said breathlessly. Her upswept hair had become partially unfastened. Had he done that during their heated lovemaking earlier? Her face looked entirely washed of color in the bright headlights.

"Why? What's wrong?" he asked slowly, still recovering from the unexpected sight of her. What the hell was she doing *here*? Had she followed him? he wondered with rising suspicion.

"Thomas . . . I . . . I was thinking that . . ."

"Yes?" he prompted when she licked her lips nervously and glanced around the empty parking lot. Her white throat convulsed.

"I think it'd be a good idea for you to come with me. To Haven Lake?"

"What? *Now*?"

He just stared at her in rising disbelief when she nodded her head soberly, as though his question had been entirely serious.

An incredulous bark of laughter popped out of his throat. Before it'd cleared his lips entirely a flash of light caught his attention out of the corner of his eye. Both he and Sophie turned toward the warehouse. He saw a flickering, swelling, enormous gold and orange ball of fire through one of the windows. He cursed and reached for Sophie.

A boom tore through the still summer night as he fell to the gravel, Sophie beneath him. He ducked his head, covering her and clenching his eyes as fragments of shattered glass fell around them. Sophie cried out. She wiggled beneath him, but he held her immobile. Thomas knew explosions like most people knew what to expect when their alarms went off in the morning.

He knew explosions . . . and bombs.

Sure enough, a second boom vibrated the air around them. A smoking, sizzling piece of metal girding clanked heavily just feet away from their heads.

Thomas hissed and rose on his hands and knees. They needed to find cover. Flames surged out of the warehouse's broken windows, licking hungrily at the rich oxygen source the outdoor air provided. A wave of heat struck his face like a slap.

"Tuck your head into my chest," he ordered as he lifted Sophie. Thankfully, she didn't argue with him or choose that moment to ask questions. He crouched down over her, giving her the meager protection of his back, as he raced toward his car. The roar of leaping flames entered his ears. He whipped open the passenger door and set Sophie on her feet, placing his spread hand over her head in a protective gesture. It took him a moment to realize she was resisting him as he tried to push her into the seat.

"No, Thomas. Let me go to my car. You have to follow me!"

He yanked his gaze from the flaming building.

"Forget about your damn car—" His sharp rebuke was cut short when he looked down the empty, darkened street. A block and a half away he saw movement. With the help of the dim streetlights he made out the outline of a man rushing toward them. The light was sufficient for him to catch a brief image of Agent Fisk's face. Several car lengths away, another man was running toward them.

"Hey!" Fisk called out, his voice cutting through the distance that separated them and the roar of the flames.

"Thomas! Get in your car and follow me. *Now*."

He blinked and stared down at her. The moment couldn't have lasted much longer than a second, but it stretched surreally long. The authority in Sophie's voice had amazed him. She'd sounded a little bit like Colonel Harvost at that moment—his former commanding officer. Her face was cast in flickering shadow and bloodred light from the fire. Fisk's feet tapping on the pavement sounded abnormally loud despite the agent's distance.

He didn't think Fisk could have made out their identities. They were still far enough from the fire to be shrouded almost completely in darkness.

Had Fisk just arrived or had the FBI been staking out the Mannero warehouse?

He'd be nuts to flee the scene of a crime, but the last thing he wanted to do at that moment was confront Fisk or Larue . . . or face what the exploding warehouse really meant to him and his family.

And . . . Jesus. He was an expert on bombs, given his military experience. He could assemble one just as easily as disarm it. What if the feds tried to pin the torching of the warehouse *on him*?

Maybe it wasn't such a bad idea to try to escape without detection.

He glanced from Sophie's rigid features to the burning building. The explosions seemed to have ceased, but the warehouse had become a flaming torch.

"Yeah. Okay. Cover your head on the way to your car and take the rear exit," he commanded tersely as she moved fleetly away from him.

He got in his car and gunned the engine, watching as Sophie slid into the driver's seat of her own vehicle. She put the car into drive, her wheels scattering gravel in a three-foot arc as she whipped around and shot toward the back entry of the parking lot like she thought her life depended on it.

Maybe it did?

He followed just as rapidly, leaving his headlights off, not wanting to illuminate Sophie's license plates or the make and color of her car for the eyes of the rushing Agent Fisk. He heard Fisk's distant shout as he turned into the narrow alley that ran the length of the block. The sound of his squealing tires prevented him from making out what it was that he actually yelled.

Thomas's concern that Fisk had made out their faces or their license plates in the darkness faded the farther he and Sophie traveled down I-57 South. They'd passed two state troopers on the three-hour trip, but no flashing lights and wailing sirens had followed them.

They reached Haven Lake at around 12:30 A.M. after stopping only once at a gas station an hour outside of Chicago. Their conversation there had been brief and charged. Thomas had immediately recognized the signs of shock on Sophie's face when she'd exited her car. He'd become far too familiar with the signs—the rigid facial features, the glassy appearance of the eyes, the flattened mouth. He'd seen it in combat. He'd witnessed it on his mother's, father's, and sister-in-law's faces far too often lately not to recognize it in an instant.

He'd seen it a time or two when he looked in his own reflection, as well. Maybe that's why he'd been avoiding mirrors ever since he'd learned of Rick's death.

When he'd seen Sophie's shock he'd suggested they stop somewhere for longer—a restaurant or even a hotel—not liking the idea of her driving in that condition. But she'd just shaken her head, her solemn expression and big eyes causing a squeezing sensation in his chest cavity.

Another two hours alone in the car had caused him to reevaluate his strange, strong feelings for Sophie Gable, however. It slowly dawned on him as he stared at the back of Sophie's BMW sedan that her behavior tonight had been odd. *More* than odd.

Suspect, even?

Why had she showed up in that parking lot, intent on preventing him from entering the building? It'd almost been like she'd known Mannero, Inc., was about to explode into flames. And Fisk had been there, as well. Thomas couldn't help but draw the lines between the unexpected bystanders at the crime scene.

Was *Sophie* somehow connected to the FBI investigation of his father?

The thought unsettled him for several reasons, some of which he could put into words, and some which were unformed, but caused an uneasy feeling in his gut.

The main reason he didn't want to be suspicious of Sophie was selfish. He wanted her more than he ever recalled wanting a woman. The realization didn't diminish his slightly queasy feeling.

He noticed a storm brewing as they pulled off the interstate. Gold light flickered in the western sky, briefly illuminating the outline of ominous-looking thunderheads.

Thirty minutes later, Thomas followed Sophie down a pitch-black, tree-lined lane. He admitted to himself that there could hardly be a better place than the secluded Haven Lake to get his footing after everything that had happened lately—Rick's and Abel's deaths, the soul-scarring funeral, the FBI's investigation of his father. . . the exploding warehouse.

Besides, it wouldn't hurt to feel out the lovely Sophie even further, to spend an uninterrupted weekend with her . . . to plumb the depths of her secrets and her soft, inviting body as well.

Fortunately, the sharp lust he felt for her would only help him in getting closer. If the elusive Dr. Gable was keeping something from him, Thomas vowed she wouldn't keep her secrets for long.

Sophie felt as if the entire scenario from the previous evening—*had it really just been a little over twenty-four hours ago that Thomas had wandered, shell-shocked and dazed into her life?*—had been reversed after they'd entered the lake house kitchen. The long drive to Haven Lake had kept her from dwelling on the explosion, but nothing prevented it now.

She stood next to the sink, glancing up when she felt the glasses she'd been holding slide out of her gripping hands. Thomas touched her upper arm, capturing her attention. It took her a few seconds to realize she'd been standing at the sink, holding onto two empty glasses, staring at the faucet and all the while seeing that silent, expanding bright orange ball of flame and then hearing that boom rip through the night.

She said nothing, just watched him numbly as he set down the glasses and opened a few cabinets.

"There's wine in the pantry," she said, sensing he was searching for something stronger than the water she'd been about to get them.

His purposeful, confident stride across the kitchen struck her as being the polar opposite of his appearance last night. He came out of her small pantry holding a bottle of Cabernet Sauvignon. She recognized the label and suspected Thomas knew his wine. That particular bottle was the most full-bodied, potent spirit she had here at the lake house. She'd been saving it for visitors and steaks on the grill.

He didn't fumble through the cabinets this time, but walked directly to the drawer that held her wine opener. He uncorked the wine with a brisk efficiency of movement that she admired, even in her muddled state.

"Drink," he said firmly when she accepted the filled glass he handed her.

She tipped the red wine between her lips, her gaze never leaving Thomas's stare as he did the same.

"Sophie, what were you doing there . . . at Mannero, Inc.?"

She shivered at the impact of his low, hoarse voice. She experienced a nearly overwhelming desire to ask him to hold her. But she needed to accept, here and now, that their potent physical attraction to one another didn't give her the right to run for reassurance into Thomas's arms.

Especially when he didn't even recall some of that volatile lovemaking; especially when *he* was the one who suffered so greatly.

"I don't know, Thomas. I just . . . I had a feeling you were in danger. I didn't want you to go to that place. Not after what you'd told me earlier."

She shifted uncomfortably beneath his hard stare and took another sip of the rich wine.

"You expect me to believe that? That you had a 'feeling' that warehouse was going to be torched?"

"No!" she corrected abruptly. "I never said I thought that place would explode. How could I know something that bizarre would happen? I said I thought . . . *felt* as if you were in danger."

"Who or what would I be in danger from?" he demanded, taking a step closer to her.

"I don't know, exactly. It was just a hunch."

"A hunch," he repeated flatly. His gaze narrowed. "I thought doctors were scientists. The other physicians in your practice must be surprised when you have these precognitive moments."

She threw him an irritated glance and set the glass down on the counter. She stepped a few paces away from his burning stare, needing the space his dominant presence refused to grant.

"You have to admit it's strange, Sophie."

"I could say the same about you. You've been acting strangely around me, as well." When he didn't speak, she inhaled slowly, steeling herself before she faced him. "Is it any wonder I was worried about you? You've been behaving very erratically."

She waited, her breath stifled in her lungs, for him to reply. What, exactly, would cause a memory to trip in his brain?

Light flashed outside the window and thunder rent the night, startling her. Thomas never stirred. From the fierceness of his stare, she was convinced for a few seconds that he was about to close the distance between them and shake the truth out of her.

Instead, his jaw stiffened and he took another swig of the wine. His put-together business look had started to come apart at the seams given the events of the past several hours, reminding Sophie of the tense, desperate, slightly disreputable appearance he'd had last night when he appeared on her dock. His long hair had fallen forward, bracketing his cheekbones and shadowing his eyes. Whiskers darkened his lean jaw. Her gaze flickered down over his neck and broad shoulders.

She muttered under her breath and headed toward the hallway.

"Sophie?"

She turned at the sound of his harsh query.

"Where are you going?"

"Your neck is cut, Thomas. From the glass," she replied softly.

He touched the skin above his bloodied collar.

"Just give me a moment to get some things to clean it up. Why don't you sit down in one of those chairs," she suggested, nodding at the breakfast bar that took up one side of the kitchen. Her gaze skimmed over the long length of him. "I'll be able to reach you better from there."

For a second she thought he'd accuse her of purposefully changing the subject, but then his face settled into an impassive mask.

In her bathroom, she wrapped some cotton balls, tweezers, a bottle of hydrogen peroxide, adhesive bandages, and some antibacterial ointment into a clean towel.

She paused when she walked out of the hallway, carrying her supplies.

Thomas stood by one of the chairs she'd indicated earlier, unfastening the last button on his dress shirt. Her gaze stuck on the tantalizing strip of bronzed skin and ridged muscle between the stark, white fabric. The memory of him shoving apart the placket of that very same shirt impatiently while his cock was buried deep inside her flashed into her brain in graphic detail. She noticed that he'd frozen just like her, his stare on her unwavering. Outside, lightning flashed and thunder answered.

She swallowed thickly when she saw the flicker of his eyelids. Had he guessed what she'd been thinking?

His long fingers worked the button through the last hole. He whipped the shirt over his shoulders and draped it across the back of the chair.

"I thought you'd want me to take off my shirt. So you can tend to my wounds. Doctor."

Sophie ripped her gaze off the glorious expanse of lean, prime male flesh. The sight of his sexy lips shaped into a small smile was nearly as unsettling as his naked torso.

"Thanks. It'll help," she said, infusing a brisk sense of purpose into her voice. He must be used to having females temporarily short circuit at the sight of his body, after all. No reason to swell his male ego even further.

She scowled at her automatic thought as she set down the items on the counter and tore two paper towels off the roll. She was honest enough with herself to recognize her own defensiveness. Thomas never acted like a strutting rooster, despite his rugged male beauty, so it was unfair to cast him in that light. Just because she had a father whose conceit exceeded his considerable good looks didn't mean that every man who was handsome was equally invested in his appearance.

He sat compliantly in the chair when she approached, saying nothing while she inspected the cuts on his neck.

She extracted most of the slivers easily, but one large piece was more deeply lodged than the others. He didn't flinch when she finally removed the shard using the tweezers, but she saw how his shoulder muscles tensed, absorbing the pain.

"Sorry," she murmured as she placed the glass and tweezers on the paper towel. "It looks like that's all of it."

"How'd you ever find this house?" Thomas asked a moment later, interrupting the silence between thunder bursts.

She paused in the action of cleaning his neck with cotton balls soaked in hydrogen peroxide. She'd been doing her damndest to attend to her task and ignore the compelling odor of combined male musk and spicy cologne that lingered so richly at his nape.

"My parents left it to me." She noticed he was staring at some photos on the wall—black and white, highly stylized images of a beautiful couple walking and posing on the beach. "That's them—there in the photos."

He twisted his chin around to see her. "Have they passed away?"

"No. They're just sort of absent. Psychologically speaking, anyway," she said matter-of-factly. She looked up from unscrewing the antiseptic and noticed that his dark brows were furrowed in puzzlement.

"My parents are completely, utterly involved with two things: each other and their careers. They moved me to Hollywood when I was eleven years old. My father was chasing after a dream to become a famous actor, and my mother wanted to be in the thick of things, as well. She modeled when she was young, and started writing screenplays after she had me." She glanced around the comfortable lake house with the mismatched furnishings, embroidered pillows, the old stereo with her parents' extensive—and probably valuable, at this point—record collection stored in painted wooden crates. She loved the homey appeal of the house—perhaps because it represented what she'd never really had.

"We used to come here when I was little," she explained in a low voice. "I usually got to bring a friend. It was a childhood dream come true: swimming until nightfall, running around the woods like savages, roasting marshmallows over a bonfire at night. My parents became a little less obsessive while they were here . . . a little happier."

Thomas didn't speak as she rubbed the antiseptic cream into his skin, but she sensed he waited expectantly. "Once my parents moved to California, they never came back to Haven Lake. The house stood empty until I returned when I came to Chicago for college."

Thomas peered at her over his shoulder.

"You said you came here for a month every summer?"

"That's right."

"And they've never come back? Never met you here?" he asked as she rubbed cream into the final cut. Fat raindrops began to spatter on the window panes. She tried to ignore how intimate the scenario was—their quiet conversation about family, the cheerily lit kitchen, the storm outside.

Her fingertips on Thomas's skin.

"No. I have to go to California to see my parents." She nodded distractedly toward one of the photos on the wall as she peeled the paper off a Band-Aid. "That's their house there, in the background of that picture. It sits right on the beach; it's modern, fashionable . . . very *clean*."

She paused in the act of affixing the bandage to his neck when he twisted his chin around farther and forced her to meet his stare. Even though she'd kept her tone level, he'd sensed her irony anyway. She read something in the depths of his eyes. A memory from yesterday evening came back to her in graphic detail.

I used to tell Rick you were like the little girl in the neighborhood who was always so clean; the kind that Mama wouldn't let play rough with the other kids . . . the kind that was never allowed to get dirty.

She held her breath when he suddenly grabbed the wrist of her outstretched hand and turned himself on the swivel stool. He widened his long legs, bracketing her hips between his knees.

"So what you're telling me," he began, his low, gruff murmur causing goose bumps to rise on her neck. "Is that it wasn't your parents who made you all prim and proper? You did that on your own, didn't you, Sophie? They were too busy with each other . . . fulfilling their own dreams to make you into a good little girl."

"They weren't negligent, if that's what you mean. I had everything I needed."

His dark eyebrows went up on his forehead in a wry expression. "So you didn't starve and you had clothes on your back."

She smiled. "My upbringing would be considered 'privileged' by most," she said as she began to clean up the items on the counter. "I'm far from being the only person on earth who had self-involved parents. I was lucky to have my mother and father in the household at all."

Her smile faded when she saw his mouth flatten. She didn't tell herself to move, but suddenly she'd stepped deeper into the harbor between his spread knees. She cupped his jaw with her palm.

"I'm sorry," she whispered.

"Why?"

Awkwardness crashed through her at his taut inquiry.

"I . . . I had heard that your parents were killed."

His hand covered hers. "That was a long time ago. I was lucky enough to be blessed with two sets of parents. Iris and Joseph Carlisle have loved me like their own son."

She glanced down. "I must sound ungrateful to you. Complaining about my parents."

He lifted her chin. "I didn't hear you complaining. We were having a conversation. You were just telling it like it is."

For a full few seconds, their gazes clung. Sophie was distantly aware that the storm had swelled to its full fury. Rain lashed at the windows and thunder rumbled all around them. She blinked when she realized she'd been staring fixedly at Thomas's mouth. His hands settled on her waist and his head came nearer.

"I should put another bandage on your neck," she warned.

"Later," he muttered before his mouth brushed hers in a questing kiss. His lips felt warm and firm. She opened her mouth, sandwiching his lower lip between her own, caressing him and biting softly.

He groaned and pulled her tighter against his body.

"What am I doing here, Sophie?" he asked in a gruff whisper, his mouth hovering a fraction of an inch above hers. His fingers delved with a gentle possessiveness into the flesh of her hip.

"You need time, Thomas. To heal."

He lifted his head, looking a little stunned, perhaps at the sound of her authoritative tone. He abruptly slid to the edge of the chair and pressed her into his body.

"And you think you can heal me, Sophie?" he rasped, a sardonic smile tilting his lips. His hands opened over her buttocks. She whimpered at the feeling of his cock hardening against her belly. Her hands rose to his waist where her fingers relished the feeling of thick, smooth skin. She found she couldn't get enough of the sensation. She'd learned last night that Thomas possessed a proclivity for restraining her during sex. The moments when he'd allowed her to touch him, to get her full fill of him, had been too few and far between.

"I . . . don't know," she responded, distracted by the feeling of his body beneath her fingertips. "Time is what you need. But . . . I want to be here. With you," she added, holding his stare.

She felt the tension rise in his muscles. He shook his head slowly. "I feel like someone else has come and taken over my body. You have no idea the things I want to do to you. If you knew, you'd run. Take your chance now, Sophie. Tell me to go."

She felt her pulse throbbing madly at her throat when she saw the feral gleam in dark green eyes.

Maybe she should heed his advice? She *knew* that it would be the smart thing to stay away from him. But for some reason, Sophie didn't want to be careful and rational. Not in the case of Thomas Nicasio.

"You're not going anywhere," she whispered.

His mouth slanted into a snarl before he seized her mouth

with his own and flexed his long fingers into her ass. Sophie moaned into his hot, consuming mouth as desire swelled in her breast and lust tore through her veins. She would have thought such a ravenous kiss would bank their fires but by the time he raised his head both of them panted with need. One look into Thomas's blazing eyes and she knew what was coming.

"I should shower first," she said, thinking of their former heated lovemaking, of lying on the gravel beneath Thomas while glass and singed fragments flew through the air, and then the long car ride that followed.

He stood from the chair, sliding his body against her. His height and presence—the sheer impact of him—struck her as if for the first time.

"You'll shower later. Much later," he mumbled. "Personally, I want my scent all over you, Sophie."

Her mouth hung open as she stared at his retreating back. He paused and looked back at her, his manner perplexed and a little impatient. He grabbed her hand.

Wild anticipation swelled in her as he led her down the hallway.

CHAPTER **SIX**

When they got back to her dark bedroom, Thomas flipped on the lights.

"I want to see you naked. Take off your clothes, Sophie."

Her heartbeat escalated in her rib cage when she heard his gruff request. Request? More accurate to call it a command, Sophie admitted as she swallowed heavily. It occurred to her that he likely could see her pulse throbbing frantically at her throat.

She wished he'd left the lights off. She wished he'd resume his consuming kiss, making her forget everything else but the need to quench her desire for him. Instead, his stare made her skin prickle in anxious excitement.

A sense of self-consciousness came over her, an awkwardness she couldn't recall feeling so acutely since she was a teenager with breasts and hips that were suddenly bursting out of her school uniform. When it came to appearances, Sophie had been much more comfortable being an awkward pre-adolescent than a teenager. She'd hated having to think about herself as a sexual being that attracted other people's gazes. She'd rather meld into the background while her beautiful parents dazzled the eyes of onlookers.

Her father had teased her mercilessly about her blooming body, sending hot spikes of shame through her, making her wish she could just fade into the sleek Corian and chrome kitchen counters of their Los Angeles home. She could still hear him teasing her while her mother looked on, a typical distant, vaguely amused expression on her breathtaking face.

"You're going to be built like your mom—not a straight line on you except for those teeth we're paying a fortune for. Meg—we should take her down to audition for that new teenager show. You know which one I mean? It's being directed by that snot-nose kid that turned me down for that sitcom last year. We'd have him begging if he had one look at our Sophie."

Her mother had rolled her eyes. "Sophie's thirteen years old, Bastian."

"If we'd started that young, who knows where we'd be?"

Sophie could still hear the trace of resentment in her father's tone. If they'd started young . . . if they hadn't unexpectedly been burdened by an infant girl . . .

"Sophie?"

She started at the sound of Thomas's voice and began unbuttoning her blouse. It wasn't like she hadn't slept with plenty of men between the time she was eighteen and thirty-three. She'd had her share and become accustomed to taking her clothes off in front of men.

But there was something about Thomas's incising stare here in the lit room that made her feel vulnerable for some reason, more *naked* than usual. It had little to do with whether her clothes were on her or not.

When she'd removed her blouse and let it drop to the carpet, she started to unfasten her bra.

"No. Take off the skirt next," Thomas muttered. Sophie paused with her hands behind her back. He sat on the edge of the bed, his manner intent, his attention entirely focused on her. She swallowed thickly and unfastened her skirt. When it fell down her legs and bunched around her feet, she stepped out of it. She picked up both garments and neatly folded them across the back of an upholstered chair.

When she turned around, she saw amusement had joined the heat in his forest green eyes.

"Are you always so neat?"

She shivered at the impact of his gruff query.

"I'm only asking, because I tend to have a dirty mouth when it comes to fooling around," he added wryly. He placed his hands behind him and leaned back on the bed, regarding her soberly. Sophie's gaze flickered down over the expanse of his naked chest, fixing on his groin. Tingling heat swept through her pussy, making her clit tingle deliciously when she saw the shape of his cock outlined against the fabric of his trousers. "Do you think that's going to bother you, Sophie?"

She glanced into his face. His voice had changed into a low purr, and she knew he'd noticed where she'd been staring. She shook her head.

"Good. Now take off your panties."

Her mouth went dry as she stepped out of her white underwear. Her discomfort at undressing in front of him mixed with a rising sense of excitement at following his instructions. She couldn't say for sure what turned her on more: doing what Thomas asked or seeing the growing tension in his muscles when she did.

"Give them to me," he said when she turned and started to lay her underwear on the pile of clothing. She twisted around in surprise, pausing when she saw his stare glued to her ass. He put out his hand. She licked her lower lip anxiously.

The crotch of the panties were actually quite wet—a remnant of their heated lovemaking earlier in addition to touching and kissing Thomas just minutes ago. His outstretched hand didn't waver, though, and neither did his demanding stare.

She stepped toward him and placed the panties in his hand.

He smiled, slow and potent, when he saw what must have been wariness on her face. His eyelids lowered. He lifted the panties to his nose. Sophie pressed her thighs and whimpered, shocked by the sharp pang of arousal that stabbed at her genitals.

"Hmmm, white cotton and sex," he growled. His hand went to his crotch and he rearranged his erection, pausing to tug lightly at the thick head. She saw him grimace and wondered dazedly if he'd experienced the same surge of lust that shot through her body. He inhaled once more before his eyelids opened slowly. He stared at the juncture of her thighs and her body answered in kind. Her vagina tightened as another pang of desire went through her.

He tossed aside her panties. His gaze trailed up her belly and ribs.

"Now take off your bra," he ordered thickly.

Sophie removed it fleetly, the majority of her self-consciousness gone now. All she could think of was stilling the mounting tension in her pussy. She let her bra fall to the floor, heedless of where it went, and stood before Thomas wearing only her thigh-highs and the low-heeled pumps she favored for work. Her nipples prickled and tautened under his hot stare. He reached out and put his hands on her hips.

Sophie held her breath as he opened his long legs and pulled her between them. He leaned down and placed his hot, open mouth on her abdomen. Her chest tightened with emotion and she exhaled raggedly.

"Thomas," she hissed as her fingers delved into his thick hair.

He turned his face, his lips caressing her skin. She saw his ribs expand as he inhaled.

"I can smell you, Sophie, and you're sweet." His voice sounded hushed in the still room. "Do you need to come, beautiful?"

Her response was unintelligible, but Thomas must have recognized it as a wholehearted assent. He glanced up at her, his chin still pressed against her stomach.

"Hold up your breasts for me."

Sophie swept her palms beneath her breasts, all too eager to comply. His eyelids narrowed as he studied her for a few breathless seconds. His nostrils flared. "So lovely." He met her stare. "When I tell you to hold up your breasts, I want you to hold them from below just like you are, but I also want you to pinch the flesh about an inch below the nipples. Not hard," he murmured as he watched her try to follow his instructions, "I just want you to present your nipples to me. That's right," he added in approval.

Sophie looked down at him, her entire body in the clench of desire, as he sighed and leaned forward, slipping a nipple into his warm mouth. She cried out at the sharp, delicious jolt of pleasure that shot through her flesh. He treated the nipple to a gentle form of torture, laving it sensually with his tongue, drawing on it until Sophie cried out again plaintively.

He worshipped; he coaxed.

He demanded.

When he switched to the other nipple, he became more stringent in his ministrations. His cheeks hollowed out as he suckled her firmly. She resisted an almost overwhelming need to press her hand to her clit. Her fingers tangled in his hair as she pressed him to her breast. She closed her eyes and chanted his name mindlessly.

When the word *please* fell past her lips, he put his hand to her pussy. She moaned in wild gratitude. The ridge of a long finger pressed between her creamy labia. He vibrated her burning clit while he continued to suck on her nipple.

This time, her cry sounded surprised. Orgasm shuddered through her, harsh and sweet at once.

"That's right," she heard him say as if from a distance. "Come for me, Sophie."

She choked on her desire when he thrust a finger into her slit while she was still in the midst of climaxing. He opened his hand over her outer sex while he pressed a long finger deep, moving his hand in an erotic, tight circular motion that caused a shout to erupt from her throat. Her hands dropped to his shoulders. She held on for dear life. He continued to stimulate her while she came, drawing out her pleasure to lengths she'd never before experienced.

Distantly, she was aware of him speaking to her, his low, raspy voice adding spice to an already potent release.

I can feel you coming. Give me more, Sophie. Give me more of that sweet honey.

She fell forward, bracing herself on his shoulders, gasping for air. He corkscrewed his finger in her and grunted in satisfaction as he withdrew.

"You're pulling on me," he murmured as he transferred both hands to her hips. He rubbed her softly. Sophie leaned back, panting. He smiled when he saw her look at him. "You were pulling on me like you wanted me back inside you. Is that what you want?"

"Yes," she whispered as she brushed her hand over his jaw. The fingers of her other hand dropped over his chest, exploring the feeling of thick skin stretched over dense muscle and bone. Her fingertips trailed down his abdomen, seeking out his heat. He stopped her when she began to unfasten his belt. He held her wrist captive.

"That's what you want inside you?" he asked, never interrupting his exploration of the curve leading from her waist to her right hip.

She gave him a wry glance and noticed his small smile. "What do you think?"

"I think I'd like to hear you say it, Sophie." The grin on his lips faded when she just stared at him. "Go on. Say it. What do you want?"

Her mouth opened, but the words wouldn't come. She wasn't accustomed to putting her desires into words.

His brow wrinkled as he studied her intently. "It's okay. You'll say it when you're ready," he said after a moment. He stood, making Sophie shiver as his body ran against her naked skin. The feeling of his cock pressing against his pants and her lower belly made her desire burn on her tongue. She strained up to meet his descending mouth. She suspected his kiss was meant to reassure her, but instead, Sophie found herself melting beneath his firm mouth. He seemed to be asking her a question with that kiss. Her mind might not have known the answer, but her body did.

"Lie back on the bed, Sophie," he whispered next to her lips a moment later.

She climbed onto the bed, eager for the sensation of his naked skin sliding against her own, hungry to feel his weight on top of her. He stood next to the bed, watching her as she settled back onto the pillows.

"Now spread your legs."

She parted her thighs, her breath starting to come quicker. He crawled onto the bed. Sophie was disappointed that he didn't remove his pants, but she was too mesmerized by the expression on his handsome face as he stared at her pussy to complain. Her clit twanged with renewed arousal, as though he'd touched her instead of looked.

It felt too intense when he lowered over her. She started to close her thighs, overwhelmed by his palpable stare. But he placed his hands on her, blocking the motion . . . keeping her open to him. He leaned down until his mouth was just an inch away from her outer sex.

"Shhhh," he soothed. A shudder went through her at the sensation of his breath on her sensitive lips. Her muscles grew tight with anticipation.

"Thomas," she groaned. She watched as his head lowered. She cried out when he swiped his tongue between her labia, parting the folds firmly, seeking out her secret flesh. He teased her clit with the tip, making her squirm in pleasure. He laughed softly and spread a big hand over her hip, pressing her down onto the mattress, immobilizing her.

Then he parted her with two fingers and began to eat her in earnest. A low, incredulous keen vibrated her throat. It felt decadent . . . delicious to lie there while he made love to her in such a concentrated, precise manner. His tongue was a sleek, firm master, pressing against her clit, vibrating it, agitating the helpless flesh until a scream erupted out of her lungs. She tingled. She burned.

She hurt, but God, was it a sweet pain.

When the pleasure became too intense, she tried to get away from him. But he put both hands on her hips now, keeping her captive for his torturing tongue and agile lips. He lifted her hips slightly, altering the angle of his mouth on her. He turned his head and suckled her gently, his tongue demanding its due all the while.

Orgasm crashed into her with the force of a tsunami. She

clenched her eyelids and teeth. Her fingers formed claws as she gripped the bedspread, needing to hold on to something as pure bliss blazed through her body.

A moment later, she gasped for air as her eyelids blinked open. Her eyes went wide. Thomas leaned over her on his hands and knees. He looked magnificent with his hair bracketing his gleaming eyes and his defined muscles tight with desire as he held himself off her.

"Tell me what you want, Sophie. I'm going to give it to you anyway, but I'd love to hear it coming out of those sweet lips. Tell me," he coaxed raggedly.

Sophie swallowed as her gaze traveled down his body. "I want your cock. Inside me."

"That's right," he whispered. He reached in his back pocket, taking out his wallet, searching for a condom. He tossed the leather wallet aside carelessly.

He tore at the fastenings of his pants and lowered his white boxer briefs to his thighs. His cock sprung free of the material. It looked a little intimidating, aroused as he was— tumescent and flushed with blood. He rolled the condom over the tapered, succulent cock head, his movements hurried but efficient.

She watched, mesmerized. His motions at that moment called powerfully to mind last night, when he'd done very much the same thing the first time they'd had sex. He paused when he glanced up at her.

"Sophie?" he asked uncertainly.

Her breath froze in her lungs, when she saw the sudden confusion on his face. Two tense seconds seemed to stretch into an eternal moment.

"*Tom*?" she whispered incredulously . . . hopefully. Had that been recognition she'd seen flicker in his eyes? Had he remembered? But then the moment passed . . .

"You're not afraid of me, are you, Sophie?"

She rolled her head on the pillow and mouthed *no*.

He finished putting on the condom. He lowered over her, his cock held in one hand. She moaned when he pressed his mouth to her neck at the same time that he nudged her slit with his cock.

"Good. Because it isn't like we haven't done this before," he muttered as he braced himself on one elbow and thrust. Sophie inhaled sharply as he slid into her vagina several inches.

"I know that. I know," she mumbled. He flexed his hips and pressed into her deeper. He groaned gutturally.

Both of them gasped when he slid into her to the hilt.

"God, you feel so damn good," he said.

Their bellies lay flush, expanding and contracting against the other's as they panted for air. Sophie gritted her teeth in agonized pleasure as her body stretched to accommodate him. He was so big. It felt as if he filled up every empty space in her.

"I want to make it last," he said. "But you do something to me, Sophie . . ."

"Take me fast, then. Just *take me*, Thomas." The words popped out of her throat in a pressurized hiss.

He grunted and began to move. *The man knew how to fuck,* Sophie thought dazedly as she watched him and the nerves in her sex fired madly beneath his stroking cock. She'd never thought about a man's skill in moving inside a woman: for her, intercourse always shared the same basic mechanics.

But Thomas turned it into an art form. His lean hips and muscular ass and thighs orchestrated the movements of his cock into an intense sexual symphony. He didn't just piston his cock in and out of her, he shifted his hips ever so slightly, massaging her with the most intimate strokes, firing this piece of nerve-packed flesh just so, kissing her deep with the thick rim below his cock head.

Sophie just stared up at him, her mouth hanging open . . . made speechless as he rocked her in a cradle of pleasure. He paused with his cock fully submerged in her and leaned down to suckle the tip of her left breast. She whimpered and tightened around him. His cock lurched at her instinctive caress.

He lifted his head, and Sophie saw his anguished expression. Or was it anger she saw etched on his face?

"I want to savor you, but I can't. I *can't*." Sophie inhaled sharply when he pumped his hips, fucking her with short, shallow, forceful strokes. He pinned her with his stare as their bodies smacked together and the flames he'd been carefully building in their flesh surged into a flash fire. He pushed at her thighs, rolling her hips until her ass came off the bed. He spread her legs until they splayed wide in the air. When he thrust, he grimaced at the new angle.

"Aww, yeah," he grated out.

Sophie cried out as her pleasure swelled. He closed his eyes and fucked her until the bed rattled beneath them and the headboard smacked rhythmically against the wall. Her world quaked around her, yet all she could consider was the need for release from this glorious tension. Her entire focus narrowed to the beautiful, primal male who possessed her so thoroughly.

She moaned in wild arousal and anguished need. His eyelids cracked open at the sound. His face, chest, and abdomen were slicked with sweat from the exertion of his hard ride.

"I'm going to come in your sweet pussy," he muttered thickly.

"*Yes*," she agreed, straining for her own orgasm, meeting his forceful thrusts with her own pumping hips, matching him stroke for stroke.

He opened his hand over her buttock and greedily molded the flesh to his palm, using his hold to increase the friction of his driving cock. "I want you to come with me."

I want that, too, Sophie thought wildly as she reached for it, strained for her release.

He lifted his hand and slapped her ass once, then twice. "*Come*," he ordered tautly.

Sophie opened her eyes in shock as her body instinctively followed his order. Orgasm crashed into her. She had a flashing vision of Thomas's face—tight, wild, and determined—before he drove deep. She felt him swell and jerk inside of her, the sensation causing a fresh wave of climax to surge through her. He gave a sharp yell and grimaced in pleasure. She felt his cock twitch as he came and his shout segued to a low, primal growl as he flexed his hips and fucked her while he exploded into the condom. Sophie grabbed onto his shoulders while they weathered the storm.

Slowly, she felt the tension leave the rock-hard muscles she clutched in her hands. His pumping hips stilled. He held himself off her with his arms, his chin falling forward to touch his chest.

Their heavy, ragged breath twined in the still room. Sophie became aware by degrees that a soft rain pattered on the windowpane. Without thinking about what she was doing, she placed her palm on Thomas's chest, wanting to feel his heartbeat, wondering if it raced just as madly as hers did.

He looked up slowly, his bangs casting his eyes in shadow. His nostrils flared slightly when he glanced down at her breasts.

"I feel like there's a bomb ticking inside me."

She reached and pushed his hair off his damp brow.

"Maybe it would help if you talked about it. You need to try to put it into words, Thomas," she whispered.

She sucked air into her lungs when he suddenly withdrew. His grimace told her the abrupt separation hadn't been pleasant for him, either. He came down next to her on the bed.

"Talking isn't going to bring Rick and Abel back. No amount of 'processing' can bring a person back to life," he stated starkly when his head hit the pillow. "I warned you to stay clear of me, Sophie."

His voice had gone so quiet, she barely heard the last.

"Do you *want* to leave, Thomas?"

He lifted his head and looked at her before he sagged back on the pillow. "I don't. I want to be here for some reason. At least for a few days . . . or for however long you can put up with me."

"I asked you to come here for some peace and quiet while you try to come to terms with things, Thomas. I haven't changed my mind."

Neither of them spoke for a moment as they listened to

the rain falling. Thomas stared up at the ceiling. Sophie wondered if he thought of what had occurred that evening: the FBI agents calling upon Thomas, their heated lovemaking in her office . . . the frightening explosion at the warehouse.

How was he making sense of it all?

"Sophie?" he asked gruffly after a moment.

"Yes?"

"Are you sure you don't know anything about that explosion?"

"I know I'm still freaked out about it." He turned his head and gave her a searching look. "I know as much as you know about that explosion, Thomas."

"How did you know to warn me? From going inside Mannero's warehouse?"

"I told you, I didn't know what was going to happen. I was just worried about you. Your behavior has alarmed me."

"And you genuinely believe that asking me to Haven Lake," he paused and she felt his stare all the way down to her navel, "is going to *help*?"

Sophie inhaled slowly. She, more than most, knew the power of placebo. She met his gaze unflinchingly.

"*Yes.*"

CHAPTER **SEVEN**

The ringing phone didn't disturb his wife's sleep. It didn't surprise him. He'd seen her take the sleeping pill her doctor had prescribed her last week and had already learned of the medication's profound effect on her.

He, on the other hand, had barely slept in days. On one or two occasions, he'd been tempted to take one of his wife's pills, but there'd been too much at stake to be caught unaware, befuddled and vulnerable from chemically induced sleep.

Plenty of time to sleep when you were dead.

He didn't answer the phone until he'd walked into the large den that was down the hall from the master bedroom suite and shut the door. It was a residential phone, one that was regularly checked for surveillance.

"What took you so long in getting back?" he growled into the receiver without a greeting.

"I'm sorry. Things got a little hectic."

"Don't *tell* me you didn't pull it off."

"No . . . no, the deal went off just fine. From what I've heard, it was quite a fireworks display."

He paused, his jaw clenching tight as realization hit him. "Jesus. By 'a little hectic' don't tell me you lost him? *Again*?

After he fell right into your pocket today by showing up at his condo and then his office?"

"It wasn't my fault. Listen, we tailed him from his office building, but then he went to the one place in the city where you specifically said you didn't want us anywhere near tonight."

"He went to the *warehouse*? Is he alive?"

"Yeah. I thought at first he might have caught the heat there himself, but I told Flavio to cruise down the street while things were still hot. He doesn't have a record," Garnier said rapidly, obviously sensing he was about to be reprimanded for the news. "There's nothing on Flavio, nothing the feds could trace back to us even if they did have the area under surveillance."

"And?" he asked tautly.

"Nicasio's car wasn't in the parking lot," Garnier admitted.

A pain went through his chest at the news. His goddamn acid reflux had been biting at him from the inside out for weeks now. "Do you mean to say you have no fucking idea where he is?"

"Don't worry," Garnier said grimly. "We have his condo and his office staked out, his club, favorite restaurant, Kelly's house, plus the residences of most of his friends. He hasn't been seeing anyone regularly for the past few months, but I put a couple guys on the residences of two of his former girlfriends. Figured it couldn't hurt."

"He's seeing that redhead. The interior designer."

"Not according to the redhead," Garnier said flatly. "He hasn't called her in weeks. But like I said, we're watching her place, just in case."

He inhaled slowly, tamping down his temper with effort.

"We need that tape. Are you sure you've checked everywhere that you can?"

Garnier grunted. "He's got it with him. He has to. Try not to worry too much. All it takes is one phone call from his cell phone and our contact at the phone company will be able to give us his location within fifty yards."

"All it will *take* is one phone call from him, you asshole!"

A silence ensued following his outburst. He clutched at his chest, knowing his employee had been caught off guard by his uncustomary show of fury.

"If he uses his cell phone to contact one person—*just one*—we'll have him. How much damage could he actually do in a few hours?" asked Garnier.

"Think *apocalyptic*, you stupid son of a bitch. You'd better rattle around those rocks in your head, Garnier, and figure out exactly where he is. If you think I'm going to wait around for him to make the phone call that'll ruin me in order to find him, you're even more of an idiot than I thought you were."

When Garnier was chastised into silence, he cursed under his breath and sagged into his leather desk chair.

"He's just like his father," he mumbled after a pause.

"Leave it to me, and he'll end up *exactly* like his father," Garnier promised.

He hung up the phone a few seconds later, willing the stabbing pain in his chest to ease. After a moment, he stood and shuffled down the hallway toward his sleeping wife, weariness weighting every muscle in his body.

A lifetime of effort, and for what? he thought bitterly.

He could withstand many things, and fate had forced him to do so. But if there was one thing he couldn't tolerate, it was disloyalty.

Disloyalty had to be stamped out at all costs.

Thomas listened to the shower running in Sophie's private bathroom. She'd insisted upon showering after they'd made love, and he'd been too tired to protest her absence in his arms.

The thought of her warm and naked in the shower made his cock stir. Again. He told himself to get up and join her in the shower. He even prepared to do so by fully removing all his clothes. Once he'd stripped, however, a wave of exhaustion struck him.

He hadn't been sleeping well since Rick's death.

No, that wasn't right. His sleep had been fractured and irregular for a week before Rick died. Ever since his brother had come to him, distraught and agitated about what he'd discovered in his investigative report about the Chicago mob.

He shut his eyelids and pressed his chest into the mattress, as though he were applying pressure to a gaping wound. He turned his face into the pillow and inhaled Sophie's scent—floral, female . . . clean.

She'd implied he was ill . . . sick at heart, that a few days of relaxing at Haven Lake would serve him well. Thomas didn't know if he believed her or not, but the thought of staying in the peaceful house . . . the prospect of spending time with Sophie appealed to him, feeling like a balm on the bloodied edges of his ragged spirit. He'd call his parents tomorrow; tell them he'd decided to get away for the weekend.

A pang of guilt and unease went through him when he thought of how his father would react to the Mannero warehouse explosion. He'd call Joseph Carlisle first thing in the morning, he promised himself. Thomas should be the one to tell his father instead of having him hear it from Fisk and Larue, who would be eager to somehow implicate his father in the arson.

For the destruction of those records Thomas had gone to examine.

He clamped his eyelids shut, willing his mind to clear. While he'd been making love to Sophie, he hadn't even noticed his pervasive headache, but it throbbed to life now, the pain dull and muted, but still clouding his thoughts.

He knew the real world would interfere at some point with his avoidance of it. Chances were Fisk hadn't identified them at Mannero's warehouse. Even so, the FBI would want to question Thomas in regard to the explosion. They'd be asking for him. It was only a matter of time before he'd have to return to Chicago to be with his parents during this trying time.

But didn't he deserve a temporary escape?

He buried his nose farther in the pillowcase and breathed Sophie's scent, letting it soothe his agitation. The clean, white cotton reminded him of her underwear. It'd been incredibly exciting watching her undress, seeing her reveal all her firm curves and skin that reminded him of apricots and cream. He would never have guessed he'd find a modest, low-heeled pair of pumps, an old-fashioned padded brassiere, and white cotton panties sexy, but on Sophie, it was an image that defined erotic.

For him, anyway.

He'd insisted upon inhaling the scent from her panties while she'd watched. The memory of how wet the panel had been; the image of her wide eyes when he'd inhaled her delicate, delicious fragrance made his cock stiffen next to the cool sheets.

He'd wanted to shock her a little. He hated himself for always wanting to dirty her, but that didn't stop the beast in him from craving to do just that: to desecrate the shrine of sex and innocence that was Sophie. When he thought about how he'd fucked her so savagely in her office . . . how he'd ridden her so hard just minutes ago, he twisted in discomfort on the bed.

But his damn cock swelled to full readiness yet again.

He knew it wasn't right for him to take out all his unrest, his grief, his fury on her . . . but his regret wasn't sufficient to make him walk away from her potent allure.

And it wasn't as if she didn't seem interested. Her large, dark eyes may hold a hint of trepidation at times, but she couldn't hide her arousal. He'd never known a woman to get so wet. *All that warm, sweet cream,* Thomas thought as he wrapped his hand around his erection and stroked himself. Eating her had been like drowning in sex-honey. And when he'd spanked her, the flush of liquid heat around his cock had sent her right over the edge.

Sophie may look like the image of wholesome beauty, but she'd been turned on by being spanked.

He groaned when he realized he was pumping his cock . . . recognized he was conjuring all sorts of fantasies about Sophie in his mind. *Stupid* fantasies. Like he was a horny seventeen-year-old all over again.

He pictured himself getting up and entering the humid

bathroom, joining Sophie in the shower . . . bending her over and driving his cock into her tight, warm heat. The fantasy was so realistic that his hand moved desperately.

Why didn't he get up? Why didn't he walk into that bathroom and just *do* it?

But he knew why he didn't, Thomas realized as he graphically imagined his cock hammering into her soft, giving body while he gently smacked her firm, damp ass. He'd already fucked her like a maniac twice tonight. Held her down on her desk and slaked his monumental thirst; spread her wide here in bed and drilled her until she'd screamed in release.

Sophie'd had enough. Even if he hadn't.

He winced as he came, careful to keep the erupting semen from soiling her sheets. When he heard the shower shut off, he reached for some tissues from the bedside table and cleaned himself off. He'd thrown away the tissues and gotten back in bed by the time she came out of the bathroom.

She believed he was sleeping, he realized, as he watched her pad quietly toward the bureau. She carefully opened the top drawer. He said nothing, enjoying the chance to observe her while she was unaware. She dropped the towel that she'd wrapped around her. His eyebrows went up in interest when she bent to lace her feet through some clean panties. She silently opened another drawer and started to withdraw a T-shirt.

"Uh-uh. Come to bed, Sophie."

She started and looked over her shoulder. She set the shirt on the dresser and walked toward him. He watched, appreciating the erotic contrast between her round hips and narrow waist . . . the slight sway of her breasts as she moved.

It was a good thing he *had* masturbated, he thought wryly as she slid beneath the sheet. She switched off the lamp and he pulled her into his arms, appreciating the shower-warmed softness of her skin in the air-conditioned room. The odor of some kind of fruity soap or lotion and Sophie just beneath it filled his nose. He settled her back against his chest and kissed the top of her head. Her soft sigh brushed across his forearm, making his skin prickle.

It didn't matter that he'd just come. He wanted her again. Some powerful combination of grief, anxiety, and Sophie Gable had transformed him into something insatiable.

He determinedly closed his eyes and let the exhaustion that was never too far from the periphery of his consciousness claim him.

He dreamt of the summer following his parents' murders—the summer he'd gone to live with the Carlisle family. In his dream, Rick and he were kids again in the outfield at Briar Park on a muggy summer day. Joseph—their Little League coach—was in the dugout, a powerful presence always at the periphery of Thomas's awareness.

Thomas's depression and grief over the sudden, inexplicable loss of his entire world had taken the form of surliness and anger. At ten years old, Thomas more resembled a teenage rebel than the vulnerable child that he was. Joseph had recruited him onto Rick's baseball team in order to give him something to focus on other than the empty hole that had opened up in the center of his chest.

The only person in the Carlisle household he didn't cop an attitude toward was Joseph. In the beginning, Iris Carlisle, Joseph's wife, seemed at a loss for how to reach him. He'd wanted nothing to do with her maternal warmth and kindness. She wasn't *his* mother, and Thomas resented her for reminding him of his mom with her concerned eyes and soft touches.

Joseph, on the other hand, had been a good decade and a half older than both Iris and his own parents. His thick mane of iron-gray hair, broad grin, and sparkling blue eyes made Thomas associate him more with a grandfather or uncle than the father figure he would have likely rejected out of grief from missing his own dad.

His adoptive father took pride in his working-class roots

despite having risen through the ranks of the business world to be the owner of a large, prosperous trucking company. Joseph Carlisle was a man's man, and it didn't take a young Thomas long to discover that Joseph was impatient at Ricky's lack of interest in sports and other stereotypical boyish activities. Ricky had no talent for sports, and that simple fact acted like a splinter under Joseph Carlisle's skin.

Rick had been a year older than his adoptive brother, but Thomas was bigger, even when they first met. Not in weight—Rick actually still carried his baby fat, which he never lost until adolescence—but Thomas was the taller of the two. Thomas possessed a whole different set of genes than Ricky, genes that had made him enjoy and excel at the things Joseph Carlisle found worthwhile like sports. Ricky, on the other hand, would have been happy to be left alone, reading his novels of high adventure or dreaming up his own stories, which he recorded in a black notebook he kept carefully hidden beneath his bed.

Joseph Carlisle's square jaw would have clamped tight and his eyes blazed with anger if he'd ever discovered that notebook full of his son's dreams.

You need to get out of the house, get some fresh air . . . run around like a normal *boy,* Joseph used to growl in frustration. In his first few months at the Carlisle house, Thomas had smirked every time he'd heard Joseph admonish Ricky. He'd been so confused and bitter by the abrupt absence of the two pillars that had previously held up his entire world that he'd taken a kind of sick satisfaction from seeing the pinched, pained expression on Ricky's face when he heard his father's familiar litany.

In Thomas's dream, he stood on the pitcher's mound and followed a fly ball headed toward right field. Ricky staggered around on his chubby legs, trying to follow the ball as he squinted into the bright sunlight. Thomas'd once heard Joseph tell one of the assistant coaches that since Ricky was their weak spot, they'd put him in right field to diminish their losses.

Ricky looked sweaty and slightly panicked as the ball arced downward out of the sky. The back of Thomas's neck prickled with the awareness of Joseph Carlisle's observance from the dugout.

In the dream, he was able to sense his adoptive father's thoughts. Joseph knew his son was going to drop the ball. Thomas knew it, too.

A deep, nameless dread filled him.

"You can do it, Ricky! Concentrate," he shouted at the dark-haired boy. In the dream, time stretched. Ricky glanced over at him. He seemed to gain confidence at something he saw. A smile tilted his lips.

He looked up and caught the dropping ball. Thomas whooped loudly.

"I'll practice hitting with you later on," he shouted when Ricky joined him at a jog, still clutching the ball victoriously. Love for his brother felt like it'd burst from his chest.

"You will? *Really,* Tom?" Ricky asked, surprised by his unexpected generosity. A flash of guilt stabbed through him. He'd been so rude and sarcastic to Ricky since he'd arrived at the Carlisle house, feeling like an unwelcome guest, an ugly, pulsating blemish on the smooth, lovely façade of the Carlisle family.

"Sure," he assured Ricky as they ran toward the dugout and a watchful Joseph Carlisle. Thinking about Joseph's reaction to Ricky catching the fly ball made him beam with happiness. "We'll practice out back after dinner. I don't care how many nights it takes. You're gonna hit the ball wherever you want."

Thomas started into wakefulness, the image of Ricky's dawning smile fresh in his mind and spirit. He stared blankly out the curtained window, seeing the gray light of dawn. It took him a moment to recall where he was, but then he inhaled Sophie's scent combined with that of the clean cotton sheets.

He just lay there for a few seconds, letting his pounding heart slow, allowing Sophie's fragrance and the sensation of her warm, even breath falling on the skin of his chest soothe him.

What had occurred in the dream had never happened in

real life, and that was what pained Thomas in that moment more than anything. In reality, he'd been rude and sullen to a hopeful, eager Ricky for over a year before he ever came out of his shell and befriended him. Thomas'd watched for nearly two whole summers while Ricky suffered during baseball season under the eye of his irritated, disappointed father.

Why had the ancient, nearly forgotten childhood regret risen so powerfully tonight?

After a moment, he swiped at his damp cheeks and rose from the bed, careful not to wake Sophie.

Sophie's heart seemed to leap up into her throat when she awoke the next morning and discovered she was alone in the bed.

Dear God, she thought, as she flung back the sheets. *Not again.* She grabbed a yellow sundress out of her closet and hurried into it, tying the straps at her shoulders in a haphazard fashion and rushing out of the room.

"Thomas?" she called out anxiously. Something about the flatness of her query in the silent house warned her she was alone. She held her breath as she raced to the back door. Warm, cheerful sunlight bathed her face, chest, and arms as she stepped out onto the back stoop. The storm had passed. They'd been gifted with a dewy, golden day sent straight from heaven.

She exhaled the breath that had been burning in her lungs when she saw Thomas's car directly behind hers in the drive.

She hurried around the house, hearing the buzz of bees and flies over the field of prairie grass and wildflowers next to the cut grass of her lawn. A decent-sized town had never sprung up around Haven Lake over the years, and Sophie was thankful for that. Without restaurants, movie theatres, and strip malls, the sleepy lakeside community had never really caught on as a vacation getaway. Haven Lake today was nearly as populated as it had been twenty-five years ago, when she came here as a child.

There were a number of houses rimming the lake, but she could only make out two secluded residences on the far shore through the dense oaks, maples, and locust trees. They were permanent residences; she was one of the few vacationers on Haven Lake.

The closest house was about a quarter of a mile down Lake Road. It belonged to the Dolans—a friendly couple who had retired relatively young. They occasionally stopped by to chat when Sophie was in residence, oversaw her lawn maintenance, and collected her mail for her when she wasn't there. She couldn't make out their home due to the thick foliage, but she could see their white dock running out into the still waters.

The lake and surrounding woods showed a different face to her every day, it seemed. Today the lake was a dark blue, reminding her of a sparkling sapphire set in a bowl of lush viridian.

The scenery usually captured her focus utterly, but today another natural wonder vied for her attention.

He wore a pair of blue swim trunks and nothing else. His torso gleamed with sweat as he pulled himself up until his chin was above a six-inch thick oak branch.

Sophie walked toward Thomas slowly.

His abdominal muscles must be working nearly as hard as his bulging arms and shoulders because they were tight as a ridged drum as he completed pull-up after pull-up. His gaze remained fixed on some distant point in the sky as his muscles flexed and then stretched with his falling weight, and flexed again. He grunted each time his body contracted before he uncoiled his lean, glorious length. Something about his hard, constricting muscles, the savage jerk of his sinews, and his soft grunts made her think of sex.

Then again, it was impossible to look at Thomas adorned only with trunks and golden brown skin that gleamed with sweat and think of anything *but* sex. She thought of last night—how he'd eaten her up with the single-minded intensity of a wolf at its supper. Her pussy tingled at the memory.

After another minute of heart-pumping activity—both

for him and increasingly for Sophie—he dropped to the ground, limber and sinuous as a panther. She'd thought he hadn't noticed her presence, as rigid and unwavering as his expression and gaze had been, but she realized he'd known she was there all along. He spoke without looking at her as he picked up a discarded T-shirt.

"I'll bet you're wondering where I got the clothes?" he asked as he wiped the sweat off his neck and then his brow with the shirt.

Sophie's mouth fell open. She hadn't been wondering about that at all. She'd been too busy salivating at the sight of all that flexing, pumping male muscle.

"Where *did* you get them?" she asked, suddenly curious now that he'd brought it to her attention.

"I was up early, so I drove into Effingham and found a store open," he murmured. Now that he was looking at her, he seemed distracted by the sight. His gaze dragged over her face, neck, shoulders, and chest slowly. Sophie forced her attention back to the conversation even if her body was far more aware of the undercurrents sizzling between her and Thomas.

She smiled at what he'd said. The only store where he could have bought clothing at 6:00 A.M. was a Wal-Mart.

"What are you grinning at?" he asked softly. Sophie unglued her eyes from the mesmerizing vision of him running his hand slowly over his sweat-glistening abdomen.

"The thought of you shopping at Wal-Mart for clothing. I'm used to seeing you in expensive suits."

"I'm used to seeing you all buttoned up as well."

She glanced down at herself self-consciously. She couldn't be any less put-together than she was at the moment. She hadn't combed her hair and the straps of her dress were haphazardly tied. Once again, a sense of awkwardness seeped into her awareness, an acute consciousness of the unusualness of the situation with Thomas. He was practically a stranger to her, despite the fact that she knew so many secrets of his private life . . . despite the fact that she'd let him repeatedly consume her with his raw passion.

She cleared her throat and glanced at him uneasily. "Did you eat while you were in town? Would you like some coffee, or maybe some—"

She blinked in amazement when he dropped the crumpled T-shirt on the grass and stepped toward her. He cradled her head in his hands. His thumbs beneath her jaw urged her to look up into his face.

"I don't think I've ever seen a grown woman blush as much as you do, Sophie," he murmured distractedly.

The heat in her cheeks amplified at his words. *Damn it*. She hated the telltale sign of what was happening in her inner world and had done battle with blushing since she was a child, although it'd been most acute in adolescence. It took something pretty major to get to her nowadays. Still, it happened more often than she'd prefer. She was an experienced, professional woman and it infuriated her, this proclivity to turn red when she least wanted to show her vulnerability.

She twisted her chin, breaking his intense study of her. If he'd laughed at her or insisted on talking about her sudden discomfort, she probably would have withdrawn even further. But instead—in what she was learning to be typical Thomas fashion—he acted as though her blush was not only beautiful, but a sign of much more than embarrassment.

Which it was, Sophie realized when he slipped a long finger beneath the strap of her sundress and leaned down to gently kiss the heat in her cheeks.

"You look like sunshine in this yellow dress with those pink cheeks," he murmured next to her skin. Sophie couldn't help but smile then, even if her blush didn't dissipate. She turned toward him, liking the sensation of the warm, fragrant puffs of his breath on her upturned lips, shivering as he stroked her shoulder with a magical touch. He peered at her upturned face intently and returned her smile. "I wonder . . ."

"Wonder what?" Sophie murmured. She went up on her tiptoes to try to brush her lips against his, but he was too tall and he didn't lean down toward her.

"Why every time I look at you, I want to fuck you until my ears ring."

If her cheeks had been warm before, they burned now. She felt liquid seep from her pussy. Maybe Thomas noted the arousal that surged through her veins because he slowly brushed the pad of his thumb across her cheek, as though tracing her heat. She murmured his name when he pressed his fingertip into her lower lip, his gaze turning hot and wanting. He lowered one arm and opened his hand over her hip.

"Are you naked under this dress?" Even though his tone was like a low purr, she heard something just beneath it . . . something that reminded her of a motionless panther about to pounce.

She nodded, spellbound by the sensation of him rubbing her hip and ass cheek through the thin dress. His gaze lowered, as though he were gauging her reaction to his bold caress. Sophie knew she should suggest they go inside the lake house—his palm was now boldly cupping and massaging her ass—but her pussy had gone molten, making her forget purposeful speech. She panted softly, her gaze fixed on Thomas's mouth.

He moved suddenly, pulling her with him. He pushed her back against the trunk of the oak and stood in front of her, his body ghosting hers within an inch . . . just out of contact, almost as though he was worried about touching her with his sweat. Sophie was preoccupied by the opposite. She experienced an overwhelming need to press against his hard length. His heat and scent pervaded her awareness. That was when she knew the real reason she'd blushed. Her own thoughts about what she wanted to do with this man both shocked and thrilled her.

Despite his perspiration-gilded muscles, he smelled wonderful—salty and spicy, like prime male flesh. Her mouth watered for him. She leaned forward and licked a tiny, puckered nipple, covering her tongue in his sweat. He hissed and plunged his fingers into her loose hair roughly. Still, he held himself off her, restraining himself.

She pressed her lips against his hard chest and moved her head slightly, coating her lips in his essence, too, before she licked again, intoxicated by his taste. He growled, deep and rough and cupped her jaw in his hand. Sophie glanced up at him, her parted lips slick with his sweat. His mouth slanted into a snarl when she glided her tongue along her lower lip, tasting salt and musk. His nostrils flared.

"You're going to have to pay for that, Sophie," he warned as he pressed his thumb to her damp lip, forcing her mouth open slightly more.

She went with him willingly when he grabbed her hand and led her across the expanse of the yard. He took her behind the boathouse, where it was shaded and cool. Her breath was coming in short, ragged gasps by the time he pressed her back against the boathouse wall. Her heart began to throb with excitement against her breastbone when he leaned down and ran the tip of his tongue over her lower lip, mingling their flavors.

"Such a sweet mouth," he muttered against her lips before he leaned down and pillaged what he'd admired with his lips and tongue. Sophie groaned in rising excitement. Her palm slid across his sweat-dampened ribs while her other hand found his cock unerringly. He groaned into her mouth when she cupped his erection through the swim trunks and stroked the long, thick column of his penis.

Her hunger swelled.

She panted when he lifted his head and stared fixedly at her mouth. A ray of sunlight filtered through the trees, bringing out the golden glints in his dark eyes.

"Down on your knees, Sophie."

She sunk before him, using her hold on his waist to stabilize herself. She reached for the waistband of his trunks, all the while wondering why she wasn't even remotely offended by his demand. The memory of how full and firm his cock had felt in her hand gave her the answer. She wasn't offended by his command to give him head because his wish matched hers perfectly at that moment. She couldn't wait to touch him, to fill her mouth with his teeming flesh.

He placed his palms on her hands, stilling her attempts to lower his trunks.

"Put your hands behind your back," he murmured. Her

eyes went wide as she glanced up at him. Just inches from her face his penis lurched against the fabric of his trunks. Doubt suffused her. His cock was too large for her to successfully bring him off with her mouth alone. She'd need her hand to attend to the flesh she couldn't get to with her lips.

"I'm all sweaty. I don't want to mess you up, but," his deep voice broke slightly, "God, I need to do this, Sophie."

When she heard the apology twined with his desire, her doubt evaporated. Slowly, keeping her eyes locked with his, she moved her hands behind her back.

"I'm going to fuck that beautiful mouth of yours." Sophie's vagina contracted almost painfully at him whispering something so illicit while she knelt before him here at the edge of the silent woods with the sun-dappled lake sparkling out of the corner of her eye. His words had landed on her ears like a dark angel's blessing. "And it's going to feel so good, Sophie. All right?"

Her gaze dropped down his magnificently naked, glistening torso to his crotch. She merely nodded her head, too overwhelmed by a sexual hunger that was more powerful than she'd ever known to speak. She watched, mesmerized, as he lowered the trunks and let them fall around his ankles. When he stepped out of them, he was completely naked. He stood before her, his muscles still hard and delineated from his workout, his golden brown skin shiny with perspiration. His cock hung thick and heavy between his strong, hair-dusted thighs, the color of it golden like the rest of his skin, but flushed with a ruddy hue. She could see several veins at the surface, feeding his arousal. The sight of the fleshy, delineated cap made her salivate. She longed to feel his weight in her palm, thirsted for the sensation of the fat, tapered crown sliding between her lips.

He cupped his hand at her nape and caught her forward movement when she leaned down instinctively to slip the cock head into her mouth. She caught his male scent and liquid heat surged from her vagina.

"Stay still," he rumbled above her, his voice rough with arousal. He kept one hand lightly encircling her neck while he lifted his cock with the other. Sophie stared, entranced, as he brought the smooth head within an inch of her parted lips and began to stroke himself. He lightly caressed her nape, making her shiver uncontrollably, as his fist ran up and down the crown and top half of his penis. When she parted her lips farther and craned toward him, his hold on the back of her neck tightened, restraining her.

She glanced up at him, feeling irritable at his deprivation but also nearly at the boiling point of excitement.

"Let me suck it," she whispered.

He smiled, slow and brilliant. He took a small step toward her, positioning himself.

"Open your mouth, but keep your eyes on my face, Sophie," he rasped.

She did what he asked. It stunned her to realize it, but she literally shook in anticipation. He cupped her skull and pushed his cock head between her lips slowly, his girth causing her mouth to part wider. Overwhelmed by the sensation, she shut her eyes so that she could completely focus on the feeling of his cock stretching her lips, the softness of his skin sliding next to her tissues . . . the salty, musky taste that filled her mouth.

He paused when her lips encircled the thick, delicious rim beneath the cock head.

"I told you to keep your eyes open, Sophie. Look at me."

She pried her eyelids apart and stared up at the glorious length of him. His face looked set and rigid as he looked down at her; his eyes glittering in the shadows caused by his falling bangs bracketing his cheekbones.

"God . . . your eyes, Sophie," he muttered gruffly. "Maybe I'd be better off having you close them. But don't . . . just . . . stay still. Do you understand?"

She nodded, making his cock bob in the air.

He flexed his hips and firmed his hold on the back of her head. His cock slid along her tongue. She stared up at him as he slowly filled her mouth with his throbbing flesh. When her eyes went wide in alarm as he neared her throat, he eased out slowly, grunting in pleasure. He held her immobile while he repeated the process, thrusting shallowly into her again and again, fucking her mouth more rapidly now, pushing a millimeter or two more of his long cock between the ring of her lips with each lusty stroke.

The only control she had in the situation was how firmly she clasped his cock and the magnitude of her suck. She took full advantage of what control she possessed, making her lips a tight clamp and creating such a fervid suction that her cheeks hollowed out and their inner lining touched his thrusting penis.

He watched himself penetrating her mouth for several taut moments before he met her gaze. "That's right," he said thickly, still pumping between her lips. "Give in to it. Let me use you . . . just for a little bit, Sophie."

She moaned at his volatile words, vibrating into his flesh. What he'd said had paradoxically shamed and aroused her. Perhaps her shame came from enjoying this so much, relishing in seeing his pleasure. It was a little like watching him masturbate, but different because she knew his excitement came from what he did to her.

A dove crooned in the woods, the noise calm and soothing, strangely at odds with Thomas's rigid muscles and grunts and growls of mounting arousal as he thrust into her mouth. Sophie's lips and jaw grew sore from her tight hold on him and her efforts to maintain a healthy suck, but she didn't let up. She loved observing her effect on Thomas.

She could smell his arousal with every inhale now, and tasted it as well, as his cock left an occasional stream of pre-cum on her tongue. She longed to put her hands on him, to feel the tight flex of his hard buttocks as he thrust in and out of her mouth, but he'd indicated she should keep her hands behind her back. Her sex had grown warm, wet, and achy. She felt her juices lubricating her inner thighs, but her own arousal didn't detract from her pleasure at observing Thomas in the midst of sexual excitement . . . in fact, just the opposite. She wanted to take him deeper, to throw him into a frenzy of need.

As if he'd read her mind, he paused with several inches

of turgid flesh filling her mouth. He studied her as he ran his fingers over her neck and stroked the base of her skull. His tender caresses on the new, fine hairs at her nape caused her to tremble.

"Do you want more?" he asked in a hushed tone.

She nodded eagerly and sucked hard on his cock, making him grimace. She flinched when the tip of his cock brushed the back of her throat, but he withdrew almost immediately. When she resumed her lusty suck and looked into his face entreatingly, he flexed his hips and slowly penetrated her again. This time, she controlled her body's defensive reaction when he touched her throat and continued to breathe evenly through her nose.

"Aww, Sophie. Your eyes are going to be the death of me," he grated out between a clenched jaw. He slid out of her throat, the spasm in his cheek making it clear to her how difficult the withdrawal had been before he tested her once again.

Sophie's sexual arousal was so great, her concentration on bringing Thomas pleasure so immense, that the sound of the car approaching never even penetrated her awareness. A woman's shout coming from the direction of the lake house made her pause, however, with Thomas's cock filling her mouth, the tip lodged in her throat.

"Sophie!" Daisy Dolan called cheerfully. "I've got your mail."

CHAPTER **EIGHT**

Thomas's entire attention was focused down to the narrow channel of immense pleasure Sophie granted him. He could have forgotten anything with Sophie's lips wrapped so tightly around his cock and her huge, velvety eyes staring up at him as he had his way with her. He knew he was behaving like a barbarian, but he couldn't seem to stop himself from relishing what she offered so freely. Besides, knowing he was desecrating Sophie just a little added an intoxicating spice to his arousal.

He wanted to be tender with her . . . but he wanted to dirty her just as much.

He never heard the woman's first call, too preoccupied with Sophie's delicious mouth, too busy drowning in the liquid sex of her eyes . . . too wrapped up in the building pressure of the explosive orgasm building in his testicles. Thomas only knew something was wrong by the sight of Sophie's eyes suddenly going wide and panicked while half his cock was buried between her lips. At first he'd thought he'd pushed too hard or far into her throat, but then the woman's call pierced the roar of lust echoing in his ears.

"Soo-phee," a woman crooned. Thomas guessed the

intruder on their carnal interlude stood at the back corner of Sophie's lake house. When she called again, it was clear she was walking down the length of the yard toward the lake.

Toward them.

Sophie started in shock, but Thomas's fingers were already rubbing her scalp, soothing her. "Shhhh," he whispered softly. "She won't come back here."

For a few taut, electrical seconds, they remained immobile, staring into each other's eyes, both of them still and alert for sounds of the visitor . . . Thomas's throbbing cock lodged in Sophie's wet, warm mouth. He heard the woman's footsteps on the dock and knew Sophie had heard them, too, when her eyelids flickered anxiously. Whether on purpose or not, she tugged gently on his cock.

Sweat trickled down his abdomen. Damn, it was the purest kind of torture to stay still under these circumstances. He grimaced as he slid his swollen cock out an inch and then back into Sophie's mouth, the small stroke sending tingles of excitement up his spine.

"I'm sorry," he told her silently as he continued to fuck her mouth with tiny, electrical thrusts. His cock looked enormous now, stretching her lips wide. He was about to come and he couldn't stop himself. Perhaps he could have ceased if Sophie had jerked away from him, but instead her dark eyes glazed with lust as she stared up at him and she pulled on his cock hard enough to make sweat pour off his brow. There was something else that he saw in her gaze that made him lose all vestiges of control.

Permission.

One hand fell to the back of the boathouse, bracing himself, as he gave himself wholly to the experience. When he felt Sophie's throat muscles tighten around the tip of his cock, squeezing him, he knew he'd reached his limit. At the moment of his crisis, guilt stabbed through him for the way he'd been using Sophie so selfishly for his pleasure. He wanted like hell to explode in her mouth, but hadn't he been forceful enough with her as it was? His entire body went tight as a coiled spring, his jaw clenched to prevent a shout of bliss from ripping out of his throat. He winced in unbearable pleasure, but the second before he came, he jerked his cock out of Sophie's mouth.

The resulting deprivation was too powerful to prevent a low growl of mixed pleasure and pain from leaving his throat. He turned his hip to Sophie and desperately pumped his fist over his spasming cock, his semen shooting in an arc into the grass. As his convulsions waned, he distantly became aware of the footsteps on the dock slowing and then increasing in speed as the visitor walked off the dock.

If that damn, interfering woman is stupid enough to walk back here, she better not have the nerve to look shocked when she sees what's going on, Thomas thought wildly as another convulsion of pleasure wracked him and he barely contained a rough groan as more come spurted from his cock.

His eyes sprang wide when suddenly Sophie was there, her hands turning his hips demandingly. She sunk his cock into her mouth and bobbed her head over him several times, taking him deep. He grunted in helpless pleasure when he felt her flickering, hungry tongue licking at his slit. All was forgotten as another wave of climax tore through him, nearly as powerful as that first nirvanic jolt, and Sophie sucked at him while he gasped and gave her everything he had to give.

Sweat ran into his eyes when he blinked his eyelids open a pleasure-infused moment later. Sophie's eyelids were closed now, but she still suckled gently on his softening cock. He shivered as echoes of his previous ecstasy rippled through his flesh. He raised his hand and ran his fingers through her silky hair before he palmed her scalp.

Slowly, almost regretfully, she slid her lips off his cock. She didn't move from her kneeling position. The vague memory of the female intruder struck his dazed brain and he glanced around in confusion.

"It was Daisy Dolan, bringing my mail. I heard her car pull out of the drive a few seconds ago."

His hand went to her elegant throat. He stroked it, wanting to soothe the rasp he'd heard in her voice, feeling guilty for being the one to cause it by thrusting his cock so deep into the heaven of her.

"I'm sorry," he said. He meant it on so many levels. Daisy Dolan had undoubtedly heard his muffled grunts and groans. His pleasure had been too immense to contain.

Sophie gave him a little smile. She looked as lovely to him at that moment as she ever had, with her blonde hair mussed from his hands, her lips reddened and swollen from his thrusting cock . . . her cheeks not just pink, but crimson from her arousal.

When he recognized that a fever still raged in her, when his had been quenched so well . . . so thoroughly, he bent down and pulled her to her feet. Saying nothing, he pushed her back against the boathouse. Holding her gaze, he lifted the hem of her dress.

He'd been feeling so guilty for glorying in what she offered him so generously that it stunned him—gratified him deeply— to see how much it had aroused her to do it. When he dipped a forefinger into the warm, abundant cream between her labia, he closed his eyes, humbled by the sweetness of her.

"Aw, Sophie," he murmured close to her upturned face as he slicked his finger over her swollen clit and she vibrated in pleasure. He opened his eyes into slits and witnessed her cheeks flushing even deeper in color. "Why are you so wet, beautiful?"

He made a flicking motion with his forefinger and she gasped.

"Did you like it?" he whispered as he caressed her intimately and his lips brushed against hers. "Did you like having me fuck that sweet mouth?"

She groaned softly as he vibrated her clit. He wanted her response, found himself hungering for it, despite his recent powerful climax—but he could be patient. When Sophie finally gave him what he wanted—when she was ready, her admission would be all that much sweeter for both of them.

"Spread your thighs," he muttered thickly.

When she followed his instructions, he paused in his

ministrations. He carefully untied the strips of fabric that held up her sundress and lowered the clingy fabric below her full breasts.

He smiled when he looked at her face and saw she'd been watching his actions with huge eyes.

"Isn't that a pretty sight?" he murmured as he fixed his gaze on her full, flushed bare breasts and lifted the hem of her dress once again. He longed to slip the fat, pink nipples into his mouth, but he enjoyed looking at her almost as much. He slid a finger into her slit and ground the ridge of his palm lightly against her clit. He groaned at the same time she did. Her pussy drenched his palm.

Her head thumped back against the siding of the boat-house as he slowly drew his finger in and out of her slick, clinging vagina.

"Thomas," she moaned in anguished arousal as her head twisted against the wall, and he understood why she begged. He wasn't giving her quite enough pressure to send her over the edge. When he continued to coast her just below the crest of climax, she groaned in frustration and began to make tiny undulations with her hips against his hand.

"Go ahead, Sophie," he encouraged as he dropped a quick, hot kiss on her parted lips, savoring her taste . . . savoring everything about her. "Use me for your pleasure like I used you."

Her back teeth gritted together and her eyelids opened. Her usually soft, doelike eyes looked determined as she began to grind her pussy into his hand more insistently. It drove him a little crazy to see her so insistent, so desperate. He snarled as he plunged another finger into her tight, wet pussy, wishing it were his cock.

He licked at her lower lip and she nipped at him. He laughed softly, delighted with her open display of greedy pleasure.

"Tell me you liked it, Sophie. Tell me you liked my cock desecrating that sweet mouth."

Her facial muscles pulled tight. "I loved it. Loved it . . . *Thomas*?" She gasped.

He moved his hand, massaging her clit more briskly, and leaned down to suck a succulent nipple. She cried out as orgasm crashed into her. Her shudders of climax vibrated into him. His touch on her turned gentle as he nursed her through her storm.

Once again, he couldn't understand why he wanted to cherish her when he clearly must want to violate her just as much. He clenched his eyes shut tightly and moved his hands until they encircled her waist. Her breasts were a delicious pressure against his chest when he drew her against him, his pleasure at doing so overriding his regret at pressing her against his unshowered, overheated body.

He buried his face in her perspiration-damp neck, wondering at the fact that even her sweat smelled clean and delicious. He became absorbed in the sound and sensation of her ragged, rapid breath, mesmerized at the profound vibrancy of her being. A tenderness unfurled inside him, feeling like a living thing awakening inside his body, as he recognized her stark vulnerability at that moment. She felt so intensely alive, so *real*, in his arms.

To be alive is to be vulnerable.

He blinked, banishing the thought. A moment later, the low-grade anxiety that had plagued him for weeks seeped into his consciousness.

But he couldn't completely forget those wondrous seconds as he held a trembling, gasping Sophie Gable in his arms. He couldn't stop himself from wanting to experience it all over again.

CHAPTER **NINE**

Sophie turned her head when Thomas nuzzled her jaw. She met his mouth and they shared a questing, delicious kiss. Strange, how he could be so demanding at times . . . volatile in his manner; and yet so tender and prizing at others.

She heard a soft, furtive sound in the woods behind them and opened her eyelids heavily. The combination of her post-climactic state, the contrast of the warm summer day and the cool, comfortable shade, and Thomas's languorous, exploratory kiss had a similar effect on her as a good glass of wine or two. When she heard the scraping of brush and tree limbs again, she started slightly in Thomas's hold. He sealed their kiss.

"Look," she whispered.

She noticed the wariness that crept into his expression and tightened his muscles. His sudden tension eased when he turned and saw what crept up on them. The little red fox remained suspicious, however, as it stared at them from where it stood at the very edge of the woods with glassy, beady eyes.

"Be careful," Thomas said when she made to leave his arms and head toward the fox.

"It's okay. I leave food out for him sometimes. He knows me," Sophie assured as she briskly pulled up her dress and retied the straps. She rubbed Thomas's forearm in an "it's okay" gesture, but he still seemed doubtful about releasing her from the circle of his arms.

"He's just a little guy," Sophie told him with a smile and upraised brows.

"Little guys have been known to have big teeth . . . and become rabid."

She shook her head and stepped slowly toward the fox. Thomas watched her with a scowl on his face as he scooped up his swimming trunks from the grass.

"Guy isn't rabid. His brothers and sisters and mother were all killed by some kind of predator last summer while I was here, probably a coyote," Sophie murmured as she approached the fox, which appeared to be wavering between staying put and running. "I used to see the lot of them occasionally in the yard, or in the woods, while I was walking. Then suddenly there was just little Guy here, all alone. I got into the habit of setting food out for him here behind the boathouse. I call him Guy . . . hey, Guy," she crooned as she neared him. She started to reach for him. The fox flinched before baring white, sharp teeth.

"Sophie, step back," Thomas growled.

"It's okay," she soothed both males with whom she shared the clearing.

She crouched slowly, assuming a less threatening posture with the wary animal. From her new angle, she was able to see how the fox didn't put any weight on its left front foot. "Aww, here's the problem," she sighed regretfully. "Your paw has been injured, huh, little Guy?"

She rose cautiously and began to back away.

"Sophie?" Thomas asked sharply when she started toward the house.

She spun around and faced him in a distracted fashion. He'd put the swim trunks back on and stood watching her with a bewildered expression on his handsome face.

"Oh . . . I'm sorry, Thomas. I need to go to get him some

food and something to drink. See how skinny he is? He can't hunt with his paw injured like that. I'll feed him first, and then try to figure out a way to get him to let me take a look at his paw. Some jerk set a trap in the woods, I'm guessing. It's illegal, but people *will* be idiots."

"You make a habit of this sort of thing, I guess?"

She shrugged and gave him an apologetic grin when she noticed his expression of amazement had morphed into humor.

"I was about to take you up to bed, you know."

"Oh . . . you were?" She fumbled, caught off guard by his forthrightness, not to mention the appeal of his proposition. "This won't take me long, I promise," she said as she started to turn. "Oh, and Thomas?"

"Yeah?" He was now exchanging suspicious glances with Guy.

"You probably should give Guy some space. Male territory and all that. This patch of grass is where he always fed last summer."

Thomas's eyebrows shot up. He gave a sharp bark of male laughter that made Guy inch back toward the woods.

"*Thomas*—" she hissed

"All right, all right. I'll go and take a swim," he assured her, laughter still shaping his mouth. He took several backward steps toward the lake and the fox came to a halt in its departure. "First time I've ever been beat out for a woman by a guy with four legs, though."

"Three and a half, actually," Sophie muttered, giving him a reproachful glance even though she was glad to see his smile.

CHAPTER **TEN**

She saw him swimming when she came out the side door a minute later with a dish of hamburger and a bowl of milk. He was past the Dolan's dock, still moving in a direction away from her at a brisk pace. He stayed in a straight line forty or so feet from the shoreline, safely within the buoys where boats were required to proceed with caution due to swimmers.

"I was right about him being a swimmer, wasn't I, Guy?" she murmured to the small fox once she'd placed the dish and bowl several feet away from where he still hovered anxiously at the edge of the woods. When she backed away, granting him ample room, he limped toward the food. *Poor thing*, Sophie thought when he left the cover of the woods and she saw how thin he really was. He finished the hamburger and milk in seconds, and then glanced up at her a little reproachfully, as if to say, *Is that all?* She laughed.

"That's it for now. You come back in a few hours for more. You'll get sick if you eat too much so quickly, starved as you were."

She started coffee and showered quickly when she returned to the house, then put on her standard lake clothing—a bikini and shorts. Thomas had just risen out of the water when she walked out onto the dock carrying a towel and a tray ten minutes later.

"Thanks," he murmured when she handed him the towel. He idly dried off his wet hair and face as he watched her set down the tray and sit cross-legged on the dock. Her skin prickled with awareness when his gaze trailed down over her bikini-clad torso. She was having difficulty not eating up the sight of him, as well, as he sat there with his long, well-formed legs hanging over the dock, his taut abdomen moving in and out slightly from the exertion of his exercise.

"Coffee?" she asked breathlessly, pulling her gaze off the vision of his succulent shoulder and upper arm muscles beaded with water. He nodded and she poured him a cup from the small carafe.

"Time for you to feed me now, huh?" he teased warmly as he accepted the coffee.

She arched an eyebrow. "I would imagine you've worked up a good appetite."

His smile widened rakishly before he helped himself to a slice of buttered toast. "Tastes good," he said appreciatively a moment later before he grabbed another slice.

"You sound surprised."

"I haven't had much of an appetite lately."

"And haven't been sleeping well, either, I'm willing to bet," Sophie added evenly before she took a sip of coffee. She immediately regretted her words when a shadow fell across his features. She'd been facing his profile, so when he turned and glanced out at the calm lake, munching his toast more slowly now, she couldn't observe his expression.

"Thomas—"

"I don't want to talk about my brother right now," he said quietly, but she heard the warning in his tone. He turned and gave her a brooding glance.

Maybe he'd read her mind. She *had* been planning to subtly encourage him to put his grief into words. The trauma of Rick's and Abel's deaths was festering inside of him, making him suffer. And Sophie suspected that was only part of what he grieved. If only he'd release some of the poison, the chances were his memories from that dark period of time would slowly start to come back to him. Trauma amnesias—both physical and psychological—were much more common than people realized, and they usually resolved given a supportive environment where the mind had a chance to heal.

But Sophie also knew he had to process his grief at his own pace. If she pushed him too hard, she'd pay for the error. He'd flee . . . or do something rash, given his volatile state.

"All right," she said evenly.

He looked a little sheepish and relieved at once at her agreement. He leaned back on one arm and lifted his coffee, his large hand encircling the entire cup versus utilizing the handle.

"So . . . what do you like to do while you're here, Dr. Gable?" he asked gruffly.

Sophie swallowed some toast. "Oh . . . a lot of this," she glanced between them and out toward the lake.

"So you haven't been working frenziedly on your research articles?"

"No, I told you I'd procrastinate. Once I get used to swimming any time of the day I want, taking long walks, reading until the wee hours of the morning, and creating awful paintings, I'll get around to the articles."

He smiled. "How long have you painted?"

"I just started a couple years ago. I was getting really stressed with my job, and I have a friend—a psychologist—who insisted I start doing something to unwind. I signed up for a couple classes at a community college—tai chi, sailing, painting, ceramics. Only the painting took. It relaxes me."

"The psychologist who's your friend—is he the one who works in your office?"

She examined him closely as she nodded her head, but she couldn't decipher his expression.

"Andy Lancaster. We met during undergrad at the University of Chicago. We'd both volunteered to take part in a psych experiment for extra credit. It was about conformity and obedience, and we were supposed to shock a puppy when it did anything but sit still. Both Andy and I refused point blank, but Andy was so stressed out by the whole thing, he practically had a breakdown, even when they told him the puppy really wasn't being harmed, that the subjects just needed to think it was for the purpose of the experiment. Andy doesn't have a mean bone in his body, though, and it really shook him up. I took him for a beer afterwards to unwind and we've been friends ever since."

Thomas's smile dawned slowly, snagging her gaze. She realized she was grinning back at him. "Picking up strays even as a girl," he murmured. "It's easy to see why you became a doctor. You practice internal medicine, right?"

Sophie nodded.

"I've watched you with your patients a couple times while I was in the waiting room. They trust you. I can tell. They really believe you care."

He said it with such genuine warmth that Sophie blushed in mixed embarrassment and pleasure. "Thanks. What about you?" she asked, longing to turn the topic away from herself. "Does it make sense that you became an investment advisor?"

"No sense whatsoever," he replied before he tossed the last of his toast in his mouth and washed it down with some coffee.

"Why'd you do it then?"

He shook his head while he chewed, a grin still shaping his mouth. "I had to do something once I left Mama's arms."

"Mama?"

"The military," he chuckled, seeing her stunned expression.

"Hardly a maternal figure."

He tilted his head as though considering the matter thoughtfully. "The Navy took care of me for sixteen years of my life. Orphans can't be too picky about who takes them in."

Her smile faded.

"Still . . . why did you choose the financial sector when you became a civilian?" she asked.

He shrugged. "I'm good with numbers. I remember my

mom—my real mom—used to say my dad was, too, even though he only finished the seventh grade. When I was in the second grade, I asked my real dad who the founding fathers were, and he said, "I'm not sure about the other guys, but Lincoln headed 'em up." He met her gaze and smiled. "But numbers—that was different. He could just glance at a page-long column of three- or four-digit numbers and tell you if the bottom line was incorrect. I'm not quite as impressive as my dad, but I got the freak gene."

"He was a savant," Sophie murmured.

Thomas nodded.

"Thomas?" He met her stare. "Is that why you're so convinced that the FBI was wrong about their allegations about your client? Mannero?"

"I don't make mistakes when it comes to the books, Sophie. If the IRS gave the FBI a tip that Mannero was using crooked accounting, they were looking at different books than I saw."

Sophie nodded thoughtfully.

"Now I have a question for you," he said as he picked up another piece of toast.

She raised her eyebrows and took a sip of coffee.

"Your psychologist friend? Lancaster? Is that all he is to you? A friend?"

The abrupt change in his tone and topic made her blink. "Yes. He's happily married. I'm friends with his wife, Sheila, as well."

Thomas nodded. His earlier broad smile and light manner might have been a figment of her imagination. "And is he a good doctor? In your opinion?"

Sophie opened her mouth to say she knew why he was asking; she knew his brother had been Andy's patient. But she recalled what he'd said about not wanting to talk about Rick at the moment and swallowed her words.

"He's an excellent psychologist," she sufficed to say.

He nodded again, his gaze intent on her face.

"I wonder . . ." He began thoughtfully.

"What?"

"Maybe you were born with this proclivity for taking in strays, like I was born with the freak math gene."

She froze in the action of lifting a crescent of orange to her mouth and met his stare. She'd heard the mocking tone, the slight self-disparagement.

"Everybody gets a little lost sometimes, Thomas."

She couldn't quite read the message in his shadowed eyes, but he no longer looked amused.

"You should take care, Sophie. You're more like your friend Dr. Lancaster than you may think. A kind heart can be taken advantage of," he said quietly.

She took a bite out of the orange and chewed. "Have you ever noticed that you have a habit of warning me to stay away from you?"

He grunted softly and glanced out at the lake.

"So how's your newest patient doing?" he asked after a moment.

She exhaled slowly, recognizing she'd been rebuffed with the change of topic. "Guy is fine. He won't let me anywhere near that injured paw, of course, but hopefully if I can keep him fed, it'll heal on its own."

They spent the large portion of the remainder of the morning on the dock, leisurely eating the breakfast Sophie had supplied, swimming when they got too warm, and talking about what Sophie would term more "safe" topics—the sports they enjoyed, favorite restaurants in the city, their careers.

They lolled in the sun, and Sophie was glad to see that Thomas drifted off for a few minutes. She'd guessed he hadn't slept much last night. When he awoke, he mumbled something about dreaming he was a fish cooking in a frying pan. Sophie suggested a swim.

Later, she told him a story while they both treaded water about how she'd dared to ask a boy up to the lake house when she was eleven years old.

"I think he and his parents thought it was a bit strange, actually, for a girl my age to ask a boy to spend a weekend with her," Sophie explained with a grin. "But all my girlfriends were busy, and I hated to come to the lake house without a companion. So I convinced Eric Summers to come here, right?"

Thomas nodded, listening.

"And I was mortified when we were swimming together and a fish bit me in the butt. *Hard*, too," she added through Thomas's unabashed male laughter. "I mean enough to break the skin, make me scream like a banshee, and rush up onto the dock bringing half the lake water with me, grabbing my butt like I thought my hand was the only thing holding it onto my body. Eric Summers never did come back with me to Lake Haven after that. Apparently I'd confirmed all his suspicions about going away for the weekend with an eleven-year-old girl. I hope I didn't scar him for life in regard to romantic getaways."

Thomas was still laughing when he swam closer. Their water-lubricated skin slid sensually next to one another's and their treading legs tangled. He planted a quick, wet kiss on her mouth—grin to grin—and remained close, so that their lips caressed when he murmured, "If I had been that little boy, I'd have told you the fish around here have very good taste."

Sophie's eyes went wide when he slid his large hand beneath the panties of her bikini and gave a buttock a firm squeeze. His expression was distilled mischief, but Sophie recognized the appreciative male gleam in his eyes as well.

"I don't know how I kept myself away from you for two years," he said.

Sophie almost forgot to tread water she was so surprised by his sudden admission.

"I . . . I wish you hadn't," Sophie replied. "I'm still not sure why you made a point of it."

"Instinct, maybe." His slow grin took her by surprise yet again. He kissed her, quick and potent. "Self-preservation?"

"Do you honestly think I would cause you some sort of harm?" Sophie asked bemusedly, highly distracted by his nearness, not to mention his sensual stroking of her bare ass.

His knowing, amused look confused her.

"What?" Sophie asked.

He shook his head slowly. Sophie got the impression he considered her an innocent for not understanding his hesitancy in approaching her.

"It's hard, breaking that barrier. I was interested. I was *really* interested, but . . ."

"What, Thomas?"

He shrugged sheepishly, and Sophie understood by his manner he didn't want to make a big deal out of what he was saying. He lowered his head until his lips were a fraction of an inch away from her own. Their treading limbs rubbed and caressed each other's in the slippery water.

"You're not like the other women I've dated. I wasn't sure if you'd like me," he said quietly.

Sophie blinked. Surely he couldn't be serious. But he'd sounded so warm . . . so genuine.

"I *like* you Thomas," she whispered.

His smile at such close range hit her brain like an electrical charge.

"Good," he murmured.

She glanced up and saw him studying her through long, spiked wet eyelashes. "So . . . do I have to get bitten by a fish or have my hand caught in a trap—" He emphasized his words by sliding his fingers suggestively down the crack of her ass. "—in order to finish what we started earlier, Sophie?"

"You might be able to talk me into it without acquiring any major injuries," she replied breathlessly. He pressed closer and she felt her belly brush against his taut abdomen and the delicious fullness of his cock beneath his swim trunks. She hated to be so single-minded, but she'd never seen a more beautifully shaped, succulent penis in her life. The heaviness of it when he grew erect excited her beyond measure.

"I should probably shower first. I've been bathing in sweat and lake water," he mumbled, his eyes fixed on her mouth as the dense column of his cock whisked lightly against her hip, teasing and thrilling her.

"We'll shower afterwards," Sophie said, repeating what he'd told her last night.

His eyes flashed as he met her gaze. He placed his hand at the back of her head and gave her a quick, blistering kiss that made her toes curl in the cool water. He spoke near her lips.

"You were lonely when you were young. Weren't you, Sophie?"

Sophie's mouth fell open in surprise. The man made a habit of turning topics on a dime. He'd just been laughing and teasing her. Where had this sudden intensity come from?

"I guess I was," she said shakily after a moment, recognizing fully for the first time that what she said was true. Coming to the lake house without a companion had been the height of misery for her because she felt like a tag-along, a third wheel to her parents' passionate involvement with each other. When her parents weren't totally into the presence of each other, they were mostly focused on themselves . . . on their careers.

Thomas nodded his head slowly as his hands coasted over her hips and ass in a light caress that made her shiver.

"Lonely adults are sad," he murmured. "But a lonely child . . . It's worse."

She met his stare and nodded, her throat suddenly too thick with emotion to speak. His smile was apologetic, as though he regretted his maudlin change of topic. He caught her hand and urged her toward the dock.

"Let's go inside." His hoarse whisper and hot eyes made her hasten. She swam rapidly as anticipation built in her. When they'd clambered up onto the dock, however, something drew her attention away from the sight of Thomas's tanned, muscular body streaming with water, the shape and size of his erection made obvious by clinging, wet fabric.

Thomas noticed her glance toward the house. His chin swung over his shoulder. Before she could call out a flustered greeting to their visitor, however, Thomas's expression became cold and hard. He turned his back to her, as if blocking the sight of her from the male walking down the yard.

"Stay here," he instructed firmly before he strode off the dock.

"Thomas?" she muttered in rising confusion when she took in his aggressive demeanor and clenched fists.

"What do you want?" Thomas shouted as he ate up the distance between himself and the approaching man on long legs.

Sophie saw the man stop in his tracks halfway down the yard as he watched Thomas rush him.

"Sophie?" the man called out.

"I asked you, what the hell do you *want*?"

Sophie ran up the dock when she heard the fury in Thomas's voice.

"Stop. Thomas, stop it!" *What was wrong with him?* Her heart swelled in her chest, making breathing difficult, as she watched Thomas practically plow down the alarmed and increasingly angry-looking visitor. He stopped when he was toe-to-toe, just short of pushing over the tall, wiry, gray-haired man wearing his typical khaki shorts and golf shirt.

"Thomas, stop! He's my *neighbor*, Sherman Dolan," Sophie yelled as she ran up on the pair.

Sherman's eyes rolled slightly in the sockets as if he started to glance over at Sophie but thought better of it and remained pinned to the threatening man in front of him.

"Are you all right, Sophie? I spoke to Daisy. She said she'd stopped by earlier and she was worried that something might be wrong over here. Who *is* this man?"

She'd never seen her jocular, easygoing neighbor look so anxious. Sherman's nose pinched tight and he glared with a mixture of outrage and fear up at a very formidable-looking Thomas. What was it that Thomas did in the military? Sophie tried to recall dazedly. He looked absolutely deadly in that moment.

"Thomas," she said softly. "*Please.*"

He blinked. She took a cautious inhale of relief when she saw the tension leave his coiled muscles and he took a step back.

"This is Thomas Nicasio, Sherman. He's my guest. I'm sorry about—"

"You should be careful about sneaking around a person's property like that," Thomas told Sherman bluntly.

"Thomas, he's my *neighbor*. He comes over here all the time," Sophie snapped. She was worried about his overreaction, his hypervigilance toward what he considered to be a threat, but that didn't give him an excuse to be rude.

When he glanced at her slantwise, she saw the wildness in his eyes, the look of a creature cornered. His pupils were constricted into pinpoints. He was panting again, shallow and fast, like he had been the evening she saw him on her dock. Her breath froze in her lungs as she recognized the acuteness of his anxiety, the evidence of a fight or flight response storming through his blood.

"Thomas—" she began, but he cut her off.

"Excuse me," he muttered thickly before he stalked off toward the house, his posture stiff.

Sophie found herself staring at a pale Sherman Dolan. His mouth gaped open in amazement at Thomas's bizarre behavior.

"Sophie? Should I call the police? Who *is* that man?" Sherman demanded.

CHAPTER **ELEVEN**

Sophie shook her head, feeling guilty upon hearing the tremor in Sherman's voice. It was strange, to see someone she knew so well suddenly seem so vulnerable. Sherman was a fit man in his early sixties, but he looked somehow shrunken at that moment, shaken. There was little doubt that coming into abrupt contact with the cyclone of emotion that spun at Thomas's core could subtract a few years from one's life. It had obviously frightened Sherman as much as it had her. Her eyes burned and she realized they were filled with tears. It had pained her to see that trapped look on Thomas's face.

"I'm so sorry, Sherm. I appreciate you coming to check on me. I'm perfectly safe. Thomas is a friend."

She understood Sherm's incredulous look.

"He's just experienced a terrible loss," Sophie explained rapidly. "You've heard of posttraumatic stress syndrome? That's . . . that's kind of what he's experiencing."

Even though her explanation sounded lame to her stunned ears, she realized what she said was true. Thomas was indeed behaving like someone with posttraumatic stress syndrome. She'd suspected it before, after talking to

Andy—and even after her brief conversation with Agent Fisk last night—but the more obvious symptom of amnesia had thrown her off course.

Sherman pointed up toward the house. "That man nearly attacked me."

"I know . . . I'm so sorry. Please try to understand. He's not himself. People with his condition can suddenly become hypervigilant about threat; they're always waiting for something dangerous to happen. Their body and mind are sort of in a constant overdrive." She glanced anxiously at the house. What was Thomas doing in there?

God, what had happened to Thomas that had made him into this coil of twisted, stretched nerves? Was it just Rick's and Abel's unexpected deaths plaguing Thomas's soul?

It had to be something more . . .

She thought of the way he'd so carefully locked the doors when they'd arrived last night, the bruise on his head and his abraded knuckles. A nameless, uneasy fear buzzed in her gut.

"I hope you can understand, Sherm. I should go check on him. I'm so sorry about this."

She left her neighbor standing in the yard. She'd go over to the Dolans' house and try to smooth things over later. Right now, Thomas was her primary concern.

She hurried into the side entrance of the house and rushed past her untouched painting on an easel into the hallway. The living room was dim, cool, and empty. She heard a noise behind her and spun around.

"Thomas. What . . . what are you doing?"

He never stopped walking as he exited the hallway wearing the trousers from his suit. He pulled the rumpled white dress shirt he'd worn last night across his tanned torso and began to button it briskly. Sophie flinched when she saw the blood at his collar.

"Thomas?" she queried again shrilly when he walked into the kitchen, still not meeting her gaze. His expression looked rigid, like it'd been carved from stone.

"I'm going."

Sophie's eyes widened in disbelief when, without another word, he began to walk toward the back door. She ran. She barely had time to pass him and block the screen door.

"No," she countered bluntly.

Irritation flickered across his rocklike countenance.

"Step aside, Sophie."

"No. You said you'd stay for a few days. It's not time for you to go yet."

His mouth shaped into an angry slant. "What the hell is up with you?"

"What's up with *me*?"

"Yeah," he accused aggressively. "Why do you want me here so much? I almost flattened your neighbor out there in the yard. What, you like getting it good and hard from a crazy guy? Are you really willing to put up with someone who could be dangerous, that into the thrill of going down on a bomb, Sophie?"

Silence fell like a thick, toxic fog, only the sound of Thomas's rapid, irregular breathing breaking it.

Sophie shook with rising anxiety and anger. His nostrils flared as he stared down at her. She could see his pulse throbbing rapidly in the opening of his collar.

"Why are you doing this, Sophie?" he repeated in a rasp.

"I have my reasons. And *don't* talk to me like that. *Ever*," she bit out in a low voice.

The seconds dragged by in the charged silence. He abruptly clamped his eyes shut.

"What if I hurt you?" he asked through a tight jaw, his eyes still closed.

"I wouldn't let you stay here if I thought you'd hurt me."

When he opened them after a taut few seconds, he slowly . . . carefully . . . spread his hand along her collarbone, his long fingers touching her neck. He leaned down until their ragged breathing mingled. Sophie thought her heart had leapt straight into her throat, just beneath Thomas's palm.

"You shine like an angel in my eyes, Sophie, but everything feels so dark right now," he said through a throat that sounded as if it were surrounded by squeezing fingers. She saw his face flinch briefly in a concentrated agony of pain, but then it vanished.

"I'm sorry," he said starkly.

He dropped his hand and backed away from her. He stared blankly at her kitchen and shook his head once, as if to clear it. "Something's wrong," he mumbled.

"*Tell me* what, Thomas. What's wrong?" If only he could *say* it, she thought desperately.

His brows knitted together, as though he searched for the answer to her question but came up short.

"I feel like . . . the ground has dropped out from under me." He threw her a furtive glance before he looked away, but he couldn't hide the shadows in his eyes. "I never would have suspected it; that Rick's death would do this to me."

"Are you sure it's just Rick's and Abel's deaths that have you so upset? What about what's happening with your father?" Sophie asked cautiously.

His expression became shuttered. "That will pass. It has to." He sighed heavily. The heavy atmosphere of the room seemed to recede as the tension slowly eased out of his muscles.

"That reminds me," he mumbled, "I need to call my father about the warehouse explosion. The Feds have probably already contacted him about it."

"Thomas?"

"Yeah?"

"Do you believe you're . . . safe?"

His jaw swung around. "That *I'm* safe?"

She nodded her head.

"Why would you ask me that?"

"That . . . that way you responded to Sherman Dolan. It was like . . . like you thought someone was going to come here to . . . to hurt you," she finished shakily.

"Why would anyone want to hurt me?"

"I don't know, Thomas. I'm just going by your reaction."

He pressed his fingertips to his shut eyes. "Jesus. I don't know why I acted like that, Sophie." He dropped his hand and pinned her with his stare, looking a little desperate. "Why *did* I act like that?"

"You're ill," she whispered. "That's why you overreacted. You've experienced a great deal of stress in a short period of time. You're not yourself. Why don't you go take a shower and clean up. I'll make us some lunch."

He looked undecided. "That man . . . Dolan? Is he gone? I should apologize."

"He left. He's all right. If you like, we'll walk over to their place later, and you can apologize."

"Yeah. I should do that. I should definitely do that."

Not until he'd walked out of the kitchen did Sophie fully exhale. She stepped over to the counter and steadied herself while she gulped for air. His emotional state was so powerful that it affected everyone around him like a drastic drop in the barometric pressure and the threat of a storm rolling in, dark and fast.

Are you really willing to put up with someone who could be dangerous, that into the thrill of going down on a bomb, Sophie?

Was there any truth to his bitter accusation? Why was she insisting he stay, when he was so volatile and unpredictable? What the hell did she really know about Thomas Nicasio?

She stared down the hallway, suddenly realizing she was in the same position she'd taken after she'd left him in the bedroom when he'd first arrived. She took a long, restorative inhale and stepped away from the counter.

There was little doubt that sex with Thomas Nicasio was unlike any experience she'd ever had. It was quite possible he'd at least partially spoken the truth when he'd accused her, Sophie thought as she flashed back to what they'd done together behind the boathouse, how she'd gotten turned on to unprecedented levels just by letting him use her for his pleasure.

She'd trusted implicitly that he wouldn't hurt her, even in the midst of raw lust.

But sex wasn't what was primarily motivating her. Something else was guiding her, some deep instinct she'd learned to trust long ago.

CHAPTER **TWELVE**

Thomas toyed with his BlackBerry as he stood in the living room, staring out at the golden, rippling lake through the window. Sophie emerged from the hallway wearing a floral green and white haltered sundress that set off the peachy-gold tan she'd acquired this morning on the dock.

Earlier they'd eaten the salad she'd made them out on the front porch. Slowly, without him being entirely aware that it was happening to him, a measure of peace stole back over him as he looked at Sophie's luminous, calm face while they ate and talked of inconsequential things, the lake winking out of the corner of his eye. He still felt a sense of deep shame for the way he'd behaved earlier—couldn't begin to comprehend why he'd flown into a rage at the sight of a man penetrating the boundaries of Sophie's peaceful home—but Sophie's kindness went a long way in smoothing his frazzled emotional state.

He knew he was a jerk for taking advantage of her hospitality, not to mention her gorgeous body, but he couldn't seem to turn away from her. Something wouldn't let him. He didn't entirely trust his response to her, but he couldn't deny it. He didn't completely trust *her*, either, even though he wanted to. She was hiding something from him. Her behavior for the past several days made no sense whatsoever.

Or maybe he was just being paranoid? Wasn't it possible that she was having just as strong a reaction toward him as he was experiencing toward her?

Given how worked up he'd been lately, it wouldn't surprise him to be accused of paranoia.

"Did you get a hold of your father?" Sophie asked, breaking through his whirling thoughts. She stepped into the living room and nodded down at the phone he held in his hand.

"Damn battery is dead, and I don't have my car charger. Could I use your phone?"

"Of course."

"You don't have to get it now," he said quickly when she started toward the hallway.

A flash of guilt went through him when she turned around and he saw her earnest puzzlement. The truth was . . . a cancerous dread had been growing in him. He was avoiding talking to his family. It pained him to think of Joseph, Iris, and Kelly. The knowledge of their suffering was like a festering wound, something he needed to ignore for the moment in order to survive.

But he *couldn't* ignore it. The wound cut too deep. He knew he had no comfort to offer his family.

He was an empty shell.

He glanced down at Sophie's smooth cheeks, incandescent wavy gold hair, and full, parted lips. His body perked up in awareness, and he begrudgingly altered his opinion.

He still possessed the animalistic aspect of his manhood. Was that why he wanted to be around Sophie so much? She reminded him that he was alive, if only in the feral, primitive form of a rutting beast?

"What's wrong?" he asked, realizing she stared at him strangely.

"Thomas, you're sweating. Are you all right?"

"I'm fine," he muttered irritably as she reached out and

touched his brow. Her fingers felt cool . . . comforting. He hadn't even realized he'd started to sweat as he stood there with his phone in his hand. His fragmenting control over his body frustrated him. He tossed the BlackBerry onto the couch. Sophie's stroking fingers stilled on his jaw as his irritability bubbled to the surface. She started to drop her hand, but he caught it.

"Do you still want to walk over to the Dolans'?" she asked as he pressed her knuckles against his lips.

He noticed the uncertainty in her tone and felt like shit all over again.

"Yeah. I do," he said, forcing the civilized façade to the forefront. It wasn't a total lie. He *did* feel bad for the way he'd behaved earlier with Sherman Dolan, even if the part of him that wanted to drag Sophie off to bed like a caveman felt a hell of a lot stronger at the moment.

He inhaled, shoving his intrusive urges to the background and took Sophie's hand.

"Aren't you going to lock the door?" Thomas asked her sharply a moment later when she just pulled the door shut behind them.

Her smooth brow furrowed. "I never do."

Thomas scowled, his eyes scanning the driveway and surrounding foliage. "I'd appreciate it if you started."

For a second she hesitated, swaying in her sandals. "All right," she conceded finally, reaching for the door to go to retrieve her keys.

Sophie studied him surreptitiously from beneath her lashes as they approached the Dolans' white-sided Victorian house. She'd been alarmed at his appearance when she'd walked into the living room a few minutes ago. It reminded her of the evening she'd seen him on her dock. He looked like a man who had a fever raging in his body and mind.

Or a battle.

He seemed calmer now as they walked down the lake

road that was so little used it was more like a country path than a major thoroughfare. He was less agitated, but more thoughtful and withdrawn as well.

Was he dreading having to apologize for his earlier behavior to Sherm Dolan? His stoic profile told her little.

"Thomas?"

He glanced over at her.

"Sherman and Daisy grew up in Beverly, Illinois. They still have a lot of family there," Sophie said, knowing that Beverly and Morgan Park were next to one another, and that the histories of the neighborhoods were long intertwined. Knowing he had some common history with the Dolans might help to smooth over any awkwardness that had arisen from his earlier erratic behavior.

His mouth opened to respond but Daisy Dolan herself stepped out about fifty feet ahead of them through an opening in the hedge that lined the gravel driveway. Sophie smiled and waved and Daisy waved in return, her shoulder-length brown hair blowing in the breeze. As she walked forward to greet them, Sophie spotted a smudge of dirt on her neighbor's nose.

"Have you been in your garden?" Sophie asked with a smile as she bent to kiss Daisy's soft, pale cheek in greeting. Daisy spent a great deal of her time outdoors, flitting about in her garden or tending to her landscaped yard. How her skin remained so unaffected by the sun was a mystery to Sophie.

When she'd first met Sherman's wife, Sophie'd thought she'd be more aptly named Lily. When Daisy smiled, however, Sophie'd realized the name suited her very well.

"Yes, how did you know?" Daisy asked as she cast an uncertain glance at Thomas. The contrast in the two people she stood on the gravel drive with struck Sophie at that moment. Thomas was male vibrancy and power personified, while Daisy was thin, fragile, and delicate. Sophie knew that Daisy's heart wasn't strong. Her ill health was one of the reasons the Dolans had retired early and lived a stress-free, peaceful life at Haven Lake.

Sophie wiped the dirt from Daisy's nose and spoke lightly. "I know the signs, that's all."

"Is everything all right, Sophie? Sherman and I . . . We were worried . . ." Daisy trailed off as she glanced at a brooding Thomas warily.

"We wanted to come over and assure you that everything is okay. Daisy, meet Thomas Nicasio," Sophie murmured, her arm surrounding Daisy's thin shoulders.

Thomas nodded politely. "I'm sorry for causing you any worry and for overreacting with your husband. Is he around? I'd like to apologize in person."

Daisy's mouth dropped open at Thomas's deep voice and solemn manner. Her dove gray eyes—easily her most lovely feature—softened in her heart-shaped face, and Sophie knew Thomas had already won Daisy over. Sophie wondered if it was the shadow of genuine regret on Thomas's features or his sheer male potency that had swayed her. The latter must have affected her the other evening, as well, when Daisy had so trustingly given Thomas directions to her house.

"He's out on the dock fishing," Daisy told Thomas.

"That's a surprise," Sophie chuckled.

Thomas nodded, his green eyes meeting Sophie's briefly before he turned toward the lake.

Sophie went inside with Daisy to collect her mail, thankful that her neighbor didn't force her to elaborate on her earlier visit to Sophie's house.

"Is your Thomas going to be staying with you for a while?" Daisy asked when they eventually retired out onto the front porch and both sat on the large white swing. Sophie smiled at Daisy's turn of phrase. *Her* Thomas? Thomas didn't belong to anything much, at the moment, aside from his grief, she thought sadly.

She glanced out at the dock, where Thomas was now kneeling and nodding his head as Sherman gesticulated toward his fishing pole. Obviously it hadn't taken Thomas long to win over Sherman, as well. Sherman never could resist anyone who would converse with him on his two favorite topics: fishing and golf.

"I expect he'll stay for a few days at least," Sophie murmured as they began to sway gently on the porch swing.

"And am I right in calling him 'your Thomas'?"

Sophie blinked and turned to face Daisy, who grinned at her knowingly. Her return smile was a little wistful.

"For a few days, at least," Sophie repeated before her gaze returned to Thomas, who was now poking his hand in the depths of Sherman's tackle box while Sherman enthused, undoubtedly about some fish story.

When the two men came up on the front porch later, the first words out of Sherman's mouth were, "Thomas is going fishing with me tomorrow morning."

Sophie's eyebrows went up as she met Thomas's stare. His only concession to her amused glance was a sparkle in his green eyes and a slight quirk of his lips.

They ended up spending a relaxing hour with the Dolans, sitting on the front porch and sipping sweet tea while Thomas, Sherman, and Daisy reminisced about the Morgan Park/Beverly neighborhoods.

On the way home Thomas grasped her hand as they walked next to the gently swaying Queen Anne's lace and orange tiger lilies that lined the road. She met his eyes and they shared a smile.

"You didn't have to agree to go fishing with Sherm tomorrow morning. He gets up before dawn, you know. Just an apology would have been sufficient," Sophie said.

He shrugged. "I wanted to do it. He's a nice guy. Besides, I'm usually up early."

At least lately, anyway, Sophie thought to herself as she considered his insomnia.

"You remember a lot about Morgan Park," she prompted softly, referring to his and the Dolans' reminiscences about the close-knit, Southside Chicago bordering neighborhoods. Thomas had lived there until his parents' deaths, when he was ten years old.

"Some," Thomas murmured as he tracked a huge bumblebee with his eyes as it moved over some honeysuckle.

"And what about your parents?" His head swung around.

"Do you remember them very well?" Sophie asked hesitantly.

"Yeah. I remember them."

For a tense few seconds, Sophie thought he wasn't going to say anything else, but then he surprised her.

"My mom grew up in Morgan Park, the only daughter of an Irish bricklayer. She met my dad during the Southside Irish parade; he was a rowdy teenager, a first generation Italian who didn't know what to do when he stood in front of revolving doors for the first time. What he lacked in polish he made up for in street smarts. And in good looks, at least from my mother's perspective, I'd guess." He flashed her one of his rare grins and Sophie felt her heart leap in her chest.

"They used to listen to Elvis Presley. I remember my mom would tease my dad, saying that he looked like Elvis. I think there must have been some truth to it, too, because that's how I remember him—dark, wavy, slicked back hair, dark complexion, a serious expression that completely vanished when he grinned—it was like the sun coming out after a storm."

Sophie smiled.

"What?"

She shook her head. "If it weren't for the 'dark hair' that would be a pretty good description of you, Thomas."

He looked a little taken aback by her compliment, but then his grin widened. "Thanks."

A pang of something powerful went through her when she saw how genuinely pleased he was to be compared to his biological father. Perhaps no one had ever told him that he resembled James Nicasio?

"You're welcome. Do you have any pictures of your father?"

"I didn't when I was growing up, but after I left the Navy and came back to Chicago, Rick and I did a little investigative work and were able to unearth a picture of him from an old Teamsters photo." They paused on the narrow road while Thomas dug his wallet out of the cargo shorts he wore. Sophie couldn't help thinking that it was odd that the Carlisles hadn't supplied him with any photos of his parents; that he'd had to go searching for one as an adult.

He removed an aged newspaper clipping from his supple leather wallet and unfolded it, his long, blunt-tipped fingers moving with an agility and tenderness that belied their obvious strength.

Sophie took the piece of paper when he offered it and stared at a black-and-white photo of dozens of men. A man in the front row held a black-and-white sign that proclaimed them the Teamsters Local 126. When Thomas pointed, she drew the paper closer and examined the face of James Nicasio.

She smiled as she handed it back to him a moment later. "There's a very strong resemblance between the two of you. He's very handsome. So, he was a truck driver?"

Thomas nodded as he carefully—almost lovingly—refolded the paper. "He hauled steel and lumber."

"Did he work for your adoptive father?"

"Yeah."

"I was wondering about that. I was never really sure how you ended up with the Carlisles . . ." Sophie let her voice trail off, hoping he'd fill in the rest.

"Joseph took me in after my parents were killed. He's the kind of man who feels a lot of responsibility for the men who work for him and their families."

"But what about your parents' families? You mentioned that your mother grew up in Morgan Park?"

"Yeah, but my grandparents both died before I was eight. My mom was an only child."

"And your father's family?"

He shrugged. "He was an orphan. Like me. He ran away from the orphanage when he was thirteen, and he worked every day of his life after that."

He tipped his wallet to carefully reinsert the fragile newspaper clipping. A gold object slipped out of one of the leather folds.

"What's that?" Sophie asked, peering closer when Thomas caught it in his hand and opened his palm.

"It's a 'crab,' my Navy Explosive Ordnance Disposal badge," Thomas murmured. He ran a fingertip over the wreath and the star of the insignia before he reinserted it into the fold and put away his wallet.

"You mean like . . . dismantling bombs?"

"Yeah, in part. Only if we could do it securely. If we couldn't dismantle them, we'd detonate them safely. That was the fun part," he told her with a sideways amused glance.

"It must have been very dangerous work," Sophie said as they resumed walking. "Whatever made you decide to join a bomb squad?"

"I was a daredevil when I was a kid. Bit of an idiot, really." When he noticed her wry expression he smiled. "I liked the challenge. It's a difficult unit to get into. Besides . . . I wanted to play with all those cool disarming robots and high-tech toys."

"But to have to disarm a *bomb*," she said, the thought of it making her shiver.

"Disarming was only a small part of the job. We were usually searching and securing areas. It was a rarity to have to actually suit up and go down on a bomb."

She glanced over at him sharply. His smile faded, and she knew he'd also thought of what he'd said to her earlier while he was so agitated in the kitchen.

"I'm sorry I said that. I was upset," he said. "Foul things tend to come out of your mouth when you're riled up and have a history of working with a bunch of guys who don't even remember how to talk anything but dirty."

She nodded and they continued to walk in thoughtful silence.

"Sophie?" Thomas asked after a minute.

"Yes?"

"How did you know I grew up in Morgan Park?"

His abrupt question startled her. "I . . . what do you mean?"

He nodded his head in the direction of the Dolans' house. "Before we met up with Daisy back there, you mentioned that Daisy and Sherman had grown up in Beverly. You said it like you knew I'd grown up in Morgan Park; like you were trying to supply me with some common background to help ease things with the Dolans."

Her mouth hung open. "I . . . I must have heard it somewhere . . . back at the office."

"Who would be talking about where I grew up as a kid at the office? You and I didn't even know each other that well until recently."

Sophie met his sharp stare. For a moment, she wavered, wondering if she should tell him the truth about why she knew so much about his past. But something in his eyes—the hint of inner suffering and turmoil—made her retreat to a place of safety.

"Does it surprise you? You're very good-looking, Thomas. You're single. Lots of women in the building know who you are. People talk."

"You're saying some other woman told you about where I lived before I was ten years old?" he finally asked, his tone incredulous.

A bobwhite chirped its eternal question in the taut silence that followed.

"Actually, I think it was one of the doctors I work with who mentioned it. It was in the news back then, Thomas. People have long memories when it comes to something so tragic happening to a child."

She turned and started to walk again, fearful he would see her pulse thrumming rapidly in her throat.

CHAPTER **THIRTEEN**

Thankfully, Thomas didn't pursue the line of questioning in regard to how she knew intimate details of his life. They spoke of inconsequential things as Sophie took him on her favorite long walk through the woods and they examined the ripeness of the blackberries in a tangled thicket.

On the walk back to the house, Sophie saw from her side vision Thomas place his fingers on his right temple and shut his eyes briefly.

"Headache?" she asked.

"No. I'm fine," he replied gruffly, dropping his hand.

Sophie doubted that, but she was learning quickly enough that Thomas didn't want the spotlight of attention turned on him when it came to the topic of his health—physical or mental.

"I'm going to make a marinade for the chicken breasts I'm grilling tonight. Why don't you go down to the hammock and rest awhile. It's very relaxing in the shade," she said lightly. He didn't reply, so she wasn't sure if he thought she was patronizing him—treating him like a sick child—or not.

After returning to the house, she pulled out the ingredients she needed for the marinade and set them on the counter. While she was bending over to retrieve a container from a lower cabinet, Thomas came up behind her, his hard thighs brushing against her ass. When she straightened, his arms looped around her waist and he brought her against him. He leaned over her, his chin nuzzling her cheek. Something about Thomas's embraces overwhelmed her a little, Sophie realized dazedly. He was so tall, so male. She felt enveloped in his arms.

He placed his lips on her neck, making her shiver in pleasure.

She turned her head and they shared a slow, hot kiss. Sophie felt his cock stir against her bottom.

He lifted his head and examined her in the dim light.

"What?" she whispered, sensing his indecision.

"I want to make love to you again," he rasped.

"Oh," Sophie mumbled. She set the plastic container on the cabinet clumsily, all too willing to put aside her cooking preparations if it meant quenching the sudden flame in Thomas's dark green eyes as well as easing the growing ache between her thighs.

All that, just from one of his kisses.

Disappointment trickled into her awareness when he stepped away from her.

"But I have to admit, I'm a little tired. I didn't get much sleep last night," he added, his voice thick with regret.

"I understand. Take a nap. It'll do you good."

He hesitated, his gaze fixed on her mouth. "I don't get it."

"Get what?" Sophie asked, confused.

"Why I want you so much. Constantly. It's not normal."

Sophie laughed. "The way you put it, I don't know if I should be flattered or insulted."

She'd been trying to lighten the moment, but it didn't work. He just continued to study her soberly for a moment, as though he truly was trying to find the answer for the puzzle in her eyes . . . trying to discern her secrets. He finally shook his head slightly in frustration.

"Will you wake me up in a half hour or so?" he asked.

"Of course, if you like," Sophie assured him.

He seemed to waver on his feet a moment before he leaned down and treated her to another bone-liquefying kiss. Sophie just stared at his retreating back as he walked away a moment later, her brain temporarily wiped clean of everything but the taste of Thomas.

She watched him through the picture window in the living room as she prepared the marinade. He kicked out of his newly bought tennis shoes, peeled off his socks, and then straddled the hammock with long legs before lifting his feet and swaying for a moment. He leaned back and brought up his feet, settling into the mesh rope cradle.

Sophie smiled to herself. She knew perfectly well what it was like to be suspended between the thick canopy of the two supporting maple trees, the lulling effect of staring up at patches of blue sky and puffy clouds while the summer breeze rocked you gently.

Thomas would be fast asleep in minutes.

She let him rest for more than an hour. She would have let him sleep longer, but he already was having difficulty getting a full night's rest. He might suffer more acutely from his insomnia if he slept too long during the day. On the way back from setting out more food and some water for Guy she approached the hammock.

She studied his face for a moment before she caressed his cheek. The shade where he slept was relatively cool, but the day itself was warm. A light coat of perspiration dampened the hair at his temple. He didn't stir when she brushed his hair off his forehead, attempting to cool him. She could tell by the movement of his eyes beneath the closed lids that he was dreaming.

"Thomas," she called softly, beckoning him back to the realm of the waking world.

She squeaked in surprise when his hand jerked up, quick as a snake at the strike, gripping the forearm of her stroking hand in an ironlike hold. Her gaze shot to his face. His eyes were open, but she got the strange sensation that he wasn't seeing her at all.

"Thomas. It's just me," she assured, recognizing a nightmare in the depths of his eyes. His vicelike grip on her didn't lessen. "It's *Sophie*, Thomas. Everything's okay."

She twisted her forearm, willing him to release his tight hold. At first, he didn't relent. But then he glanced out at the golden lake and back to Sophie's face.

His hand dropped.

"Sorry," he mumbled gruffly. He wiped at a sheen of perspiration that had gathered on his upper lip. He grimaced and sat up partially in the hammock. Sophie watched as he flung his shirt off with a flex and ripple of ridged muscle.

"It's all right," she murmured, her attention captured by the compelling sight of his bronzed, bare torso. "It's a little warm. Do you want to go in to the air-conditioning?"

He lay back in the hammock and stared up at the trees. The color of his eyes reflected those of the scene above him, rays of sunlight spiking through dark forest green.

His choppy breathing slowly evened.

"No. It's better now," he said finally. Sophie wasn't sure if he referred to his fading nightmare or the fact that his body temperature was cooling in his half-naked state. He glanced over at her, his gaze flickering from her face down to her waist. He reached for her upper arms. "It'd be even better if you came here."

He guided her onto the hammock, her knees on either side of his hips. He smiled when he heard her soft laughter. Without saying another word, he drew her down to him, her breasts flush against his chest, and covered her mouth with his own.

Sophie moaned into his mouth when the impact of his taste and the pressure of his persuasive lips fully hit her consciousness. She tasted salt from his sweat and just the barest hint of the sugar from the sweet tea still lingering on his agile tongue. His singular flavor intermingled, the resulting taste so intoxicating that she found herself striking out for it again and again, seeking deeper in the depths of his mouth.

The kiss continued, as lazy, sultry, and sensual as the summer day. She felt the tension in his muscles, the evidence of an arousal that had flamed and then banked several times that day. But he seemed content for the moment in kissing her . . . in eating her mouth like it was the rarest, most succulent treat to be cherished. The only place he touched her was on her bare upper arms, where he lightly ran his fingertips over her skin and occasionally molded the muscles in his big hands.

Sophie found herself becoming hyperalert to those seemingly innocent caresses as Thomas continued to devour her mouth and his cock grew progressively stiffer until it felt like a thick, hot poker throbbing against her hip. Her flesh and blood turned to warm syrup under the influence of a kiss that went on and on, neither of them seemingly capable of getting enough of the other's taste and caressing lips. Something about the relative chasteness of his embrace and the graphic, illicit evidence of monumental arousal struck her as delicious for some reason—familiar and forbidden at once.

She groaned softly when he captured her tongue in his mouth and sucked gently, feeling the suction of his hot kiss all the way to the depths of her sex. Her clit twanged almost painfully.

She broke their kiss and pressed her forehead to his.

"Let's go inside," she murmured between pants.

"Why? It's nice here."

She swallowed the lump that had grown in her throat as she stared into his increasingly familiar face.

"Sit up a minute," he said.

Sophie did so, her movements causing the hammock to sway.

"Scoot back onto my thighs," he encouraged. Once she'd followed his instructions, she watched, frozen, as he rapidly unfastened his cargo shorts and pushed them down around his thighs. His white boxer briefs stretched tight over his enormous erection.

"Thomas—" She warned, glancing out at the lake. She could see the two houses across the water's expanse in the far distance. She doubted they could see any particulars, but there were also two speedboats within the area, although again, far enough away that the occupants wouldn't be able to observe anything crucial . . . unless they came closer, that is.

"Shhhh," he soothed. "No one will be able to see."

Her protest died on her tongue when he drew his underwear down over his cock where it'd been trapped along his left thigh. It flicked up at being liberated from the fabric as though it were a living creature. Sophie just stared, awestruck into silence when Thomas encircled the tumescent flesh with his hand, settling it on his belly, before he leaned back in the hammock again.

"Sophie?"

She realized she'd been gawking at him like she'd never seen his beautiful cock before—like she'd never seen a man *period*. Something about Thomas made everything about the experience somehow new . . . amazing, even, Sophie realized as she reached for the throbbing column that lay between them, the stark evidence of his male desire manifested into flesh. Perhaps it was the novel setting, the way dapples of golden sunlight filtering through the trees flickered across his cock like a magical dance.

Or maybe it was his expression when she glanced up and caught him watching her face while she stroked him.

"Come here, Sophie," he rasped.

Her tongue slicked her lower lip and she glanced out at the lake furtively before she shifted her hips, her opened vagina settling on the root of his cock.

"Don't worry about anyone seeing," Thomas murmured as he drew her down to him again with his hand on her shoulders. "Even if they did understand what was going on, they'd only be glimpsing something beautiful."

He seized her mouth with his own, his kiss scorching her when his former ones had stoked her fires so deliberately, so carefully. It felt like the equivalent of suddenly submerging her entire body in hot water, his embrace was so encompassing. She became mindless with sexual hunger, molding his upper lip between her own, gently biting his lower one, tangling her tongue with his. And all the while, the inevitable ache grew in her until it became a pain.

She flexed her hips, rubbing her cloth-covered sex over his rigid erection, stroking him like a feline in heat. Thomas groaned, deep and guttural, and nipped at her mouth.

"Reach into my back pocket."

She panted softly. Her body had transformed into a conduit of pure desire. Sexual electricity zinged through her flesh. She sat up dazedly, her eyes glued to Thomas's face as her hands moved behind his thighs, trying to locate his wallet.

"In the pocket of the right fold," he instructed when she found the supple brown leather holder and opened it with trembling fingers.

"Put it on," Thomas rasped a few seconds later when she withdrew a condom.

Sophie swallowed thickly and tore the package. Thomas encircled her wrist when she reached for his cock. She glanced up, her eyes going wide when she saw the feral gleam in his eyes.

"I want you to put it on. But I *don't* want it, too. I want to mark you, Sophie. I want my scent all over you. I want to fill you up with my come."

Liquid warmth bubbled from her slit as a myriad of illicit images and sensations sprung into her mind: Thomas's semen on her skin, on her lips . . . deep inside her womb. She thought of having him in her naked. She thought of telling him that she took birth control, but she didn't, of course; couldn't allow herself to be so foolish, so wild, so impulsive. But what he'd said perfectly paralleled her own desires. Without thinking, she ground her pussy against a hard thigh to ease the sharp pang of lust that went through her at the thought of having his steely flesh kiss her deepest reaches, of having his warm seed bathe her womb.

He noticed her arousal. His small smile was a caress of mutual understanding.

"Go on," he encouraged quietly as he released her wrist.

Her hands shook as she held his firm penis and carefully rolled the condom onto his length. His girth stretched the prophylactic tight. She already knew from experience with him that the rubber wouldn't reach all the way to the base of the staff. When she'd sheathed him, she fisted the cock head just below the rim and pumped him.

He hissed, taut and low, and reached for her hips.

"Come here," he demanded through a snarl.

His hands swept behind her back and he pushed her down to him. He leaned up to capture her mouth in a pillaging kiss. He wrapped his arms around her tightly and rocked her against his straining erection, making Sophie moan feverishly into his mouth. She flexed her hips, riding the ridge of his cock, bearing down until she got just the right pressure on her needy clit.

He broke their kiss abruptly and lowered his hands to her thighs, sliding his fingers beneath the fabric of her dress. She continued to grind her pussy against his cock, mindless with lust. He grabbed both her ass cheeks possessively before he transferred both hands to one skimpy side of her panties. Her eyelids snapped open when he tugged and she felt the rip of the fabric. She met his glittering gaze as he ripped the other side of her panties and grabbed the material from the back, yanking it away from her body.

Sophie's cheeks and her clit seemed to burn in unison.

He reached between their bodies for his cock. When Sophie realized she'd have to sit up to receive his length, her glance went skittishly back to the lake. But Thomas moved one hand to her upper back, keeping her body pressed down to his.

"Just lift your hips and I'll try to work it in," he muttered roughly.

CHAPTER **FOURTEEN**

He raised her hips and they shifted their bodies, both of them panting in tense anticipation. Sophie's scalding cheek fell to the cool mesh rope just above Thomas's head. She cried out in excitement at the sensation of him pushing his cock against her slit. When he'd fixed the steely head in her pussy, he lifted her dress to her waist and transferred his hands to her hips.

Sophie's face lowered down over his as he slowly impaled her. His mouth twisted, as though he were in pain, in an otherwise rigid face. Sophie shook as he carved his way into her flesh until he throbbed inside her . . . hot, vibrant, and volatile.

He shut his eyes suddenly as a shudder went through him. He spread his hands over her ass and began to slide her up and down his cock, several inches out, several inches in . . . just enough to make her gasp loudly and drop her forehead to his, overcome by naked need. His breath struck her opened lips in choppy puffs, their mouths less than a half inch apart. He leaned up as he continued to thrust his cock in and out of her pussy, not really kissing her, just rubbing their sensitive lips together until Sophie couldn't take the delicious pressure a second longer.

She delved her fingers into his hair and dragged his lower lip between her teeth. She dipped her hips again and again, frantically, increasing the depth and tempo of their fuck, crazed by the sensation of his cock filling her and firing her from the inside out. Her tongue sank into his mouth and she consumed him, flinging herself with abandon into the white-hot core of her desire.

She made a sound of protest into Thomas's mouth when he held her down in his lap a moment later. She struggled to resume her wild possession, wriggling her hips to get friction and seeking his lips hungrily when he twisted his chin slightly, breaking their kiss.

"Slow down, Sophie," he muttered gruffly. His cock lurched inside her when she continued to pluck at his lips, coaxing him back to her. She started and hopped back from him a few inches when he swatted her bottom hard enough to sting. Her eyes widened in amazement when the tingle faded to a delicious burn that transferred via some magical pathway to her clit.

His eyelids narrowed slightly as he studied her reaction. His hand gently rubbed the hot flesh where he'd spanked her. "I only had one more condom in my wallet," he told her in a tight, low voice. "I'm about to explode with all that writhing and hopping around you're doing. Could you please slow down? It feels too good. I want it to last longer than two minutes."

She inhaled shakily at the sight of his wry half-smile. She nodded.

"Thanks," he murmured, still stroking her ass. "Sit up for a second."

They both grimaced in pleasure when she slowly raised herself, altering the angle of his embedded cock in her body. For a few seconds, she remained with her hands on his chest, panting. She felt so filled with Thomas, so combustible.

"It's hot, isn't it?" Thomas asked quietly, his gaze flickering over her face and chest, which like his, were covered in a thin layer of perspiration. "Lower your dress. I want to see your breasts."

"Thomas," she hissed warningly, glancing out at the shimmering lake. He turned his head and squinted as he examined the shore through the mesh rope of the hammock. There wasn't a boat in sight, but that didn't mean there wouldn't be in ten seconds' time.

The hand that had spanked her ass, still lingered in a caress transferred to her hip. Sophie inhaled sharply when he reached with his thumb. She trembled as she stared down at him and he drew tiny little circles between the slippery folds of her labia, zeroing in on her clit. He watched her, his eyes narrow slits of glittering green beneath his heavy eyelids. When her mouth just hung open, not a sound issuing from her frozen vocal cords, he knew he'd found his target.

"Lower your dress, Sophie."

Her breath popped out of her lungs. Her hips made subtle little bucking motions against his finger, but he stilled her by holding her firmly down in his lap.

"Do as I say," he murmured, not unkindly.

Perhaps he saw the hesitancy in her eyes, because he added, "What would be so terrible about someone seeing from a distance while I was making love to you, Sophie? You're the last person on this planet who should be ashamed. You're beautiful. I'm not ashamed of how much I want you. Are you ashamed of wanting me?"

"*No*," she whispered honestly. Shame wasn't an unfamiliar emotion to Sophie, although she hadn't fully realized until that moment just how much it was part of the air she breathed, never noticing the toxicity of the emotion because she'd never experienced its absence. She felt shame for a body that sent all the wrong messages to other people, a shame that caused her to cloak not only her sexuality, but the vibrancy that accompanied her sexual nature.

But how could she possibly feel anything but pride that she was able to turn Thomas Nicasio's eyes into concentrated flames of desire?

He stilled his magical thumb as she reached for the tie of the halter at her neck. His nostrils flared when she lowered the fabric over her bare breasts. The warm, humid air tickled at her exposed nipples, making them itch to be touched. She murmured incoherently in longing when his cock surged deep inside her flesh, her cry increasing in volume when he resumed stimulating her clit with his thumb.

"That's better. Now touch them. Offer them to me like I taught you."

Her vagina tightened around him as lust stabbed through her. She cradled her breasts in her hands from below, moving her thumb and forefinger just below the nipples, pinching ever so slightly. She moaned when Thomas snarled and tightened his hold on her hips. He lifted her, moving her up just a fraction of an inch and back slightly, up, down, and back, rocking and rolling his cock in her pussy.

"*Thomas,*" she moaned, but he just continued to agitate her clit and fuck her ever so subtly while he stared at her breasts in her hands. The hammock did a jerky little dance in the air and Thomas continued to rock her on his cock until she clenched her teeth in swelling pleasure.

"Pinch your nipples, Sophie. *Do it,*" he commanded harshly when she just stared blankly as orgasm reared over her.

She pinched and rubbed her fingertips over her beaded nipples. Climax shot through her with lightning spikes of sensation. One hand dropped to Thomas's chest, bracing herself as pleasure shuddered through her flesh. She heard him curse, rough and low. He grabbed her buttocks in both hands and began to shift his hips up and down, thrusting into her pussy, causing the hammock to bob and rock in the air with his up-and-down movements. Coherent thought faded in her pleasure-infused brain as his mouth drew into a feral snarl and he fucked her with short, frantic strokes and she continued to come around his stabbing cock.

He lifted his head, his facial muscles tightening in an agony of pleasure or frustration; Sophie couldn't tell which.

"It's not enough. *God* . . . what I want to do to you," he muttered brokenly as he thrust into her madly. His need cut through her haze of orgasm and Sophie began to buck her hips, stroking him in return, giving him the hard friction difficult to find in the suspended hammock. Their pelvises slapped together in a rapid, wild tattoo as they bounced between the trees on the placid summer day. A profound sense of satisfaction tore through her when she felt his cock spasm inside her and his facial muscles tightened in a rictus of pleasure.

"Ah, God, *yeah*," he grated out between a tight jaw as he came. His eyelids clamped shut and with his hips still flexing powerfully, he leaned up and pushed her toward him, unerringly finding her nipple with his seeking lips. Sophie cried out in shock at the sensation of his hot mouth enclosing her and then this teeth nipping sensually over the hard crest. He suckled her as he came and continued to fuck her, the sensation sending her over the edge of climax once again.

After several moments of delicious orgasmic thrashing, Sophie felt all the trapped tension in Thomas's muscles slowly ease. He fell limply into the suspended hammock and Sophie sunk down on top of him. The hammock, which had been jerking and swinging during their lovemaking, eased into a gentle rocking movement, the sound of the ropes creaking loudly in protest against the bark of the trees becoming a lulling, low rhythmic squeak. Sophie panted onto Thomas's chest, feeling like she'd just completed the marathon of a lifetime.

When the hammock only swayed a few inches in each direction and their breathing had almost returned to normal, she turned her face and rubbed her opened lips against sweat-slicked skin, sliding softly against him, not thinking . . . just swimming through the heavy, sweet languor of the moment.

He palmed the back of her skull and held her against him while she mouthed his skin and his sweat melted on her tongue. She turned her head sluggishly, pressing her cheek next to Thomas's thrumming heart when she heard the sound of a motor boat grow louder. She watched through the mesh rope as the speedboat raced by, distantly wondering why she'd been so concerned about being seen. As if he'd read her mind, his fingers rubbed her scalp soothingly.

"I'm sorry," he murmured once the boat's motor had become a distant hum.

"I'm not," she whispered.

A couple of robins twittered in the lazy silence that followed. Thomas ran his fingers through her hair slowly, his caresses making her eyelids grow heavy. She sensed him stir in the hammock a moment later and glanced up, a question in her eyes.

"I wish I could make it last," he said.

"What?"

"How it feels. When I'm inside you."

Sophie's mouth dropped open. It was an incredibly sweet thing to say, but she sensed he hadn't meant it as flattery, or at least not entirely.

"What do you mean, Thomas?" she asked slowly.

He glanced out at the lake, the bright sunshine on the water causing a flame to flicker in his narrowed green eyes. "It wipes everything from my brain. You burn me clean, Sophie." He glanced into her face. Sophie wondered what her expression was when he smiled as if to reassure her.

Sex may burn you clean, but it's only for a little while, isn't that right, Thomas? Sophie thought sadly. He must have noticed her unrest because he murmured, "Shhhh," softly and placed his hand at the back of her head, urging her to return to his chest.

Sophie stared blindly at the sparkling lake, wondering how she was going to get him to speak of his pain when he was trying so desperately to deny its existence.

And worse . . . using her as a way to do it.

CHAPTER **FIFTEEN**

Thomas set the covered platter of marinated chicken next to the smoking barbecue grill and headed back into the house to ask Sophie for some tongs. He'd been a little amazed to see all of Sophie's preparations for their dinner, and he wanted to make sure his small part in making the meal matched up to Sophie's efforts.

The woman really didn't do anything halfway, he thought as he glanced at the vibrant colors of sunset she'd painted on the canvas on the screened-in side-porch. She disparaged her painting, but Thomas thought she possessed considerable natural talent. The cheddar potato casserole he'd watched her prepare with casual ease a few minutes ago had made his mouth water and it hadn't even baked yet. They'd taken a dip after working up a sweat in the hammock and Sophie had actually swum quite a distance with him, her stroke graceful and strong. Afterwards, she'd insisted upon looking behind the boathouse to see if her patient was lingering by the edge of the wood, but Guy was nowhere in sight.

No, there wasn't much Sophie couldn't do. She certainly had the ability to make him sweat. He wanted her almost every second he was with her. If he could bottle what she did to his libido he'd be the richest man on Earth. But he didn't just want her physically, Thomas realized as he walked down the dim hallway toward the kitchen. He longed for the sweet, clean scent of her skin, her touch, the sound of her low, soothing voice.

He heard her talking now, and it wasn't to him. He slowed his pace in the hallway. Her voice sounded quiet and muffled. She had her back to him as she stood in the kitchen, talking on the phone. Her voice, though soft, carried an edge of anxiety to it that made his spine tingle in warning. He halted in the dim hallway, still several feet from the entrance to the kitchen, straining to hear her.

"Yes . . . I understand. You're right. I hadn't been putting it into that context until this afternoon. The lapse in memory is just an extreme example of the symptom of numbing and avoidance of the trauma. It's part and parcel of the syndrome. You were right to question me about it yesterday in your office. What do you recommend?"

Was she talking about one of her patients? Thomas wondered with a growing sense of unease. Something about her tone made him think it was something weightier than a patient consultation.

"You and I both know that would be best, but it's not likely he'll be talked into that unless something breaks—" Her head dropped and she inhaled. "Unless some change occurs, I mean."

Thomas held his breath in his lungs until it burned as the person on the other end of the line with Sophie spoke. He eased closer to the end of the hallway and peered around the corner into the kitchen in time to see Sophie shake her head, her hair whisking across her shoulders.

"No. That's *not* going to happen. I'm not concerned about that." She listened intently to the other person's response. She shook her head again, but not as strenuously as last time. He strained to hear her voice when she spoke next; it was difficult to hear through his heartbeat pounding in his ears.

"No. I don't want you to worry about that, he's not dangerous. You've got to trust me. I can handle this. We'll talk tomorrow. Yes, I promise. I don't know how I ever got myself in this situation, but here I am." Her laugh sounded tired. "Of course it's not your fault . . . yes . . . I think what I'm doing might be telling, too. I'm not stopping now. I won't. I'll talk to you soon, okay?"

Thomas turned and headed back down the hallway stealthily when she pulled the phone away from her ear.

Once she'd gotten off the phone with Andy, Sophie cleaned the green beans at the sink, staring out the window, her mind churning.

The best thing would be for Nicasio to be evaluated and treated by a professional. There's no telling if a possible head injury is exacerbating a psychological trauma or not. But if you suspect he won't consent to medical treatment, try to get him to talk about what's happened to him recently, all the stressors he's experienced, in a roundabout manner. See if it dislodges anything.

She'd known Thomas was amnesic about certain events ever since last night when he'd behaved as though they'd just made love for the first time in her office. She just hadn't contextualized his localized amnesia as being a part of an acute stress response or PTSD until she'd seen the way he'd reacted toward Sherman Dolan this afternoon, when he'd looked *precisely* like someone suffering from the symptoms of an acute stress disorder.

What she still didn't know, precisely, was the *extent* of the trauma that he'd experienced in the past several days. She knew some of the internal demons he struggled against . . . but not all.

And Thomas couldn't tell her at the moment. His psyche was fighting like mad to make him *not* remember whatever had blasted into his consciousness like a lethal bullet, altering his entire world. She suspected he was doing everything in his power not to acknowledge that wound.

Her anxiety ratcheted up when she considered Andy's advice to subtly get him to talk about the trauma. The idea of temporarily increasing Thomas's discomfort and emotional pain was a little intimidating, mostly because she was afraid he would leave again.

The thought of confronting Thomas didn't make her nervous, however, despite Andy's warning that Thomas might be dangerous. No. She refused to believe that, Sophie told herself even as she once again recalled what Andy had said.

Sophie, listen to me. We're talking about a man who served in a crack military unit. Do you know how much psychological testing is required for a person to even qualify for the EOD? Those people stare right into the face of death again and again, and they can't fight it with fists and guns. They have to keep ultimate control while dismantling a bomb. Nicasio served and excelled in a unit like that, even becoming a decorated officer. If he could keep his head under those conditions, just consider what kind of stress he must be experiencing at the moment to make him respond in this way. Nicasio is no stranger to violent situations. I want you to remember that, Sophie. I don't know what he's reacting to, precisely. Maybe Rick's and his nephew's deaths were just the final straw that broke the camel's back after so many years of living under frequent threat of death. Either way, it's possible he's dangerous. Soldiers suffering from acute or posttraumatic stress disorders have been known to attack their spouses during flashbacks and nightmares. And that's not the only potential threat, Sophie. If it's true what you suspect about Nicasio—that something so painful happened that it made him amnesic for a short period of time— then he might resort to the defense mechanism of projection to deal with it. He might unconsciously start to blame the only other person in his vicinity. He might start to project his growing anguish and aggression onto you.

Sophie clamped her eyes shut tightly. It hurt her to think of Thomas suffering so acutely—like a wounded animal that felt pain, but had no understanding of why or how to make it stop.

But she didn't believe for a second that Thomas would ever harm her.

She started and choked on an inhale when a drawer suddenly opened behind her. She spun around and stared at Thomas, who stood in profile next to the opened drawer, a knife in his hand.

"Thomas? You startled me. What are you doing?"

He set the carving knife down and picked up a large silicone spatula and then tossed that aside, as well. "Sorry. I'm looking for some tongs for the chicken."

"Oh," she exhaled shakily and hurried across the kitchen. "In here," she said as she opened another drawer.

"Thanks," he murmured when she handed him the tongs. She noticed the way his dark brows pulled together slightly as he examined her before he turned and left the kitchen. Was he wondering about her edginess?

She shut her eyes again once he'd disappeared down the hallway, willing her heart to calm.

After she'd put the water on to boil for the green beans, Sophie walked out the side entrance of the house with a glass of wine in each hand. She'd already known Thomas was on the front porch, sitting on the old, cushioned gliding bench that faced the lake. She'd watched him from her cooking post in the kitchen as he'd settled there a minute ago.

They'd taken another swim after they'd made love in the hammock. Afterwards, they'd showered again. This time when Thomas had left the bathroom, he wore another pair of cargo shorts and a simple white T-shirt that highlighted his lean, muscular torso and deepening tan. Sophie noticed he hadn't shaved again, and a scruff darkened his jaw and upper lip. He looked so different than his polished city-self, but Sophie thought he had never looked more real, more savagely intense than he appeared here at Haven Lake. He may be a whirlwind of grief, but she'd never known a more vibrant man in her life.

He glanced up, seeming preoccupied, when she approached and handed him a glass of wine.

"Thanks," he said quietly as she sat next to him.

She inhaled the fragrance of soap and clean male skin, the scent causing an unstoppable cascade of awareness and arousal in her body. They watched the sun starting to make its descent over the lake and sipped their wine.

"Looks like we may get some more rain tonight," Thomas said, nodding toward the southwest where dark clouds hovered on the far horizon.

"I turned on the radio in the kitchen while I was cooking. We're actually going to get a lot of rain—the remnants of that tropical storm that hit the Gulf Coast so hard."

He met her eyes. "You were listening to the news?"

She nodded.

"Did you hear anything else?"

She studied him closely before she replied, but as usual, gleaned little from his stoic expression. "I was listening to a Chicago news station. They mentioned the destruction of the Mannero warehouse."

He shifted on the bench. "Was anyone hurt?"

"No," Sophie said.

"Did they mention anything else? Did they say what caused the fire?"

"No," Sophie replied honestly. "Thomas . . ."

"Yes?" he asked. She couldn't help but notice that his glance was wary.

"That explosion last night . . . do you think it was caused by a . . . by a bomb?"

He nodded.

"Then you believe the fire was intentionally set?"

Again, he nodded. "They didn't say anything on the news about the investigation against my father?" he asked.

"No . . . or if they did, not in the portion of the news I heard. They didn't mention anything about it. Why do you think someone torched the warehouse? Are you worried it will cast blame on your father?"

"Yeah," he stated bluntly. "Pretty damned convenient."

"So," Sophie began cautiously, "you think the explosion was meant to hide evidence?"

"Or cover up the fact that there *wasn't* any evidence to be found." His stare on her felt as incising as a surgical laser.

"What? You mean you think the *FBI* put a bomb in that warehouse?" she asked incredulously.

She saw his muscular throat tighten as he transferred his gaze to the lake. "You do realize the FBI was there last night?"

"I thought I heard someone shouting. I wondered . . ." Her voice trailed off as she considered. "Are you sure it was them, Thomas?"

"Yeah. I saw Fisk."

"I can't believe that," Sophie stated. "Surely the FBI isn't in the business of blowing up buildings. It doesn't make any sense. Given what you told me about those agents' visit, they had evidence from financial data that proved that Mannero was engaging in laundering money and connected him to the mob. The IRS had alerted them to that fact. Why would they want to destroy any further evidence of his possible illegal bookkeeping practices or potential money trails by destroying all the physical data at the warehouse?"

He glanced at her sharply. "I told you that you were too trusting. Do you really believe the FBI never does anything under the table? That every agent's a boy scout? Have you been reading the papers, Sophie? Watching the news? Top people on the state and federal level have been riding the FBI to shut down the Chicago Outfit, once and for all. Maybe the evidence the FBI got from the IRS was sufficient to arrest Douglas Mannero, but it sure as hell wasn't any connection between Mannero and my father. The feds were so desperate, they even stooped low enough to try and get *me* to make a connection. They don't have any rock solid evidence against my dad, but they're going to do whatever is necessary to make a bulletproof indictment—one with no holes in it. Do you think Fisk would hesitate about destroying evidence that would go against the case he's building against Joseph Carlisle? The agents who finally break the Chicago Outfit are going to be up for one hell of a promotion. Besides, that explosion makes it look like a criminal was covering his tracks . . . it casts public suspicion precisely where Fisk wants it: on my father."

Sophie just stared at him, unsure of what to say. Thomas must have sensed her doubt.

"It wouldn't have had to be the feds, you know," he said. "It could have been anyone who was trying to cast my father in a bad light."

"Thomas, *you* were almost killed in that explosion," Sophie reminded him softly.

His glance at her was a little impatient, as though she'd missed the point entirely. Perhaps she was missing the point, but that didn't change the fact that Thomas had been feet and seconds away from being blasted into oblivion.

A shiver went through her at the frightening thought. His eyes narrowed on her.

"Have you heard anything else about the investigation, Sophie? Talked to anyone about it?"

"No," Sophie replied. "We'll make sure and catch the news tonight, if you like."

Her rapid heartbeat eased in the silence that followed. Thomas resumed his stare at the golden lake. They began to slowly rock back and forth on the bench, the rhythmic squeak of the metal runners on the gliders creating a lulling sensation. The only other noise that reached their ears was the gentle breeze stirring the tops of the trees and the birds' occasional melodious communication with one another.

After several calming minutes, Sophie began to wonder how she'd gotten so unsettled in the face of Thomas' anxiety when their surroundings were the epitome of peace and beauty. She knew Andy's first concern was her safety, but she shouldn't have let him get to her with his dire warnings.

"Any places like this from your childhood?" Sophie asked him in a hushed tone.

For a stretched moment he didn't answer, and she wondered if he'd even heard her. Then he released a long breath.

"No. Not really, but it was beautiful where I grew up. We had a huge backyard. My mother—Iris Carlisle—belongs to the Lake Forest Gardening Club. When I first came to live with them, she'd scold Ricky and me for fooling around back there, hitting baseballs or practicing tackles or setting off one of Ricky's rockets." His mouth twitched slightly, but his eyes remained glued to the lake, lost in his memories. "So at first I thought that garden was just a huge pain in my ass, all that fussy stuff I had to be careful around, the fountains and sculpture and trellises . . . the thousands of flowers. Then, one day I was out there at twilight—must have been about twelve years old," he recalled gruffly. "And all of a sudden . . . Iris's garden was magic."

Tears burned her eyes, for some reason, but she couldn't look away from his stark profile. It didn't matter. His gaze remained fixed on the lake, as though it were a mirror to his past.

"Iris must have noticed me standing out there alone," he continued gruffly, "because she came out of the house. I pointed to this huge, purple flower and asked her what it was, and she told me it was a hydrangea. I kept asking about other flowers, even though I really didn't give a damn about flowers or their names. I just liked seeing her face when I asked her. I think that may have been when I really started to let her in. She wasn't my mother, but she was something different. Something special."

"You came to really love her, didn't you?"

His low grunt was an assent.

"It must have been so hard for you . . . to lose your parents so young . . . to suddenly be thrust into a whole new world." She took a sip of wine when she realized her heart had begun thumping against her breastbone, as though in a gentle reminder. "And was it so difficult for you . . . to accept your father as well?"

"Hmmm?" Thomas asked distractedly.

"Your father? Did you have as hard a time with him, as you did your mother?"

"No," Thomas replied with a shake of his head and a swift smile. "If you knew Joseph Carlisle, you'd understand."

"What do you mean?"

"Everyone who meets him likes him. The people who work for him would do anything for him."

"Really?"

Thomas nodded. "When I was a freshman in high school, a trucker that had worked for Carlisle Transportation for years was in an accident on the road. He was completely paralyzed from the waist down and lost a good portion of mobility in his upper body, as well. When the insurance company was dragging their feet in paying his disability claims, my dad supported him, his wife, and two daughters for almost a year out of his own pocket. My mother had the entire family over regularly. Rick and I are still friends with the daughters—Chelsea and Angie—and their husbands to this day. When Tim Mobly's disability finally did kick in, and my dad found out how small it was, he supplemented the family's income. That was twenty some odd years ago."

He paused, his gaze still on the sunlit water.

"My dad still does it today and probably will continue to, with some contingency in his will, until Tim Mobly and his wife pass away."

"That's amazing. Is he so loyal to everyone?"

He nodded. "To the people he cares about. To the people who work for him. A couple years back, when the gas prices were so high that a driver couldn't make a decent living even if he was on the road twenty hours out of a twenty-four-hour period, my father's was the only major trucking operation in the country to raise the mileage rates of the truckers in order to give them a fair chance. He raised them *considerably*, and took a huge hit in profit. My dad has one of the best employee retention rates of any company in the country. Even during that rough year, not one driver left him. Not one."

"With what happened to your biological father and mother, you must feel like you're in a similar situation to a lot of those people that Joseph Carlisle helped," Sophie said quietly. "You're just as loyal to him. Certainly . . ."

"What?" he asked sharply, turning toward her when she faded off. His longish bangs had fallen onto his forehead again, casting his eyes in shadow.

"Well, I was just going to say that James Nicasio would certainly have been grateful to him, if he knew from the afterlife what Joseph Carlisle had done . . . how he'd adopted his son . . . taken him into his home . . . raised him as his own. I . . . I believe that we take a piece of our loved ones with us when they pass, make them a part of us. Part of you must feel what your mother's and father's gratitude toward Joseph Carlisle would have been. Your admiration for your adopted father was earned, certainly, but knowing how your parents would have felt about his generosity must have had a big impact on you, as well . . ."

Sophie paused when she noticed his expression. She opened her mouth but he cut her off before she could speak.

"I better go check on the chicken." He stood and set the wineglass down on the table next to the bench. Sophie watched helplessly as he stalked around the bend on the wraparound porch.

They once again ate their meal at the small wooden table she kept on the porch. She tried to draw Thomas out in casual conversation, but although he responded politely, she sensed his distance and preoccupation. When they'd finished their meal, he insisted upon cleaning up the dishes, which she let him do while she made coffee and straightened up the counters. She was thinking of a way to address his reaction to what she'd said on the porch, but didn't really know how to frame an apology.

"Thanks for cooking. It tasted great," he said after he'd shut the dishwasher.

"You didn't eat much."

He shrugged. "My appetite isn't great; it's got nothing to do with your cooking. I think I'll go for a walk before sunset."

"Oh . . . okay," she said, trying to examine his face for signs of his mood without seeming like she was. "I'll see you in a bit, then."

He ran his hand over his lean, whiskered jaw, hesitating. He suddenly turned toward the door.

"Thomas?"

"Yeah?" he asked, looking over his shoulder.

"I'm sorry," she blurted out.

"For what?"

"For . . . for what's happening with your family. For

everything. You must have loved Rick and Abel very much. And your father . . ." Her voice wavered and cracked when she saw that while his eyes were moist, his gaze was wild and fierce.

Sophie instinctively took a step back.

His jaw stiffened at her reaction. He turned and walked out of the house.

He walked for miles on the mostly deserted country road that was just outside the turnoff to Sophie's and the Dolans' houses. Later, he couldn't have said exactly what the countryside looked like or where he'd been. He'd just walked and walked—at one point, running—until he finally noticed a few fat drops of cool rainwater splashing on his face. The splendor of sunset had been shut out by a dull, gray cloud cover. Only a muted dark purple glow lingered on the western horizon, a dull, bruised residue of the quickly fading, brilliant summer day.

He paused and wavered on his feet before he slowly turned back toward Sophie's. A vague realization of how far he'd gone struck him suddenly and his pace quickened. Sophie's house was in a very remote area. Why had he left her alone like that?

He began to run.

By the time he turned down Sophie's long gravel driveway, the blackness of night enveloped him. The air hung thick, still and humid. The rain had never done much more than spit irregularly for his entire run back, but as he stood there panting, it increased to an irregular sprinkle. He paused when he cleared the tree-lined path and just stared at Sophie's neat, white house for a full minute, his heart beating like a drum in his ears. The house seemed bizarrely both familiar to him and like a place he'd never seen except for in a hazy dream-memory.

He closed his eyes and then opened them again onto the picture-perfect house with the cheerful lights glowing through the windows.

What the hell was he doing here?

And what the hell was Sophie up to?

Why had she asked him to Haven Lake? Surely she could see he was a bundle of frayed nerves following Rick's and Abel's deaths?

A memory sliced through his mental haze—the vision of Sophie sitting in his lap while his cock was buried deep inside her flashed into his mind's eye in graphic detail, making him feel like he could reach out and touch the image: the soft, wavy hair tousled around her flushed face, her hands reaching behind her neck and untying her dress, the look in her eyes as she offered her breasts to him.

His cock stirred and stiffened.

He may not know what the hell he was doing with Sophie, but his almost rabid need for her couldn't be denied. He *wanted* to deny it, but it felt almost ridiculous to try, as stupid as the idea of willing his blood to stop surging wildly through his veins.

He jogged to the back door.

"*Sophie*?" he called out harshly for the third time several seconds later as he came out of the hallway back into the living room. The flicker of flames caught his eye through the large picture window that faced the lake. She must have started the lakeside bonfire before the sluggish rain began. He rushed down the hallway and swung open the screen door on the porch.

Dammit, why did she always leave this place wide open to all comers? She was too trusting, he thought in growing agitation.

He stalked through the grass and the pitch-black night, as silent as a hunter stalking prey. He couldn't explain why, precisely, his breath was coming in short, ragged pants and his cock was fully erect, his heartbeat throbbing dully along its turgid length.

When he was twenty feet away from the bonfire, which now hissed and sputtered from the sprinkling rain, he paused. The double-wide chaise lounge that had been pulled up to it was empty. A feeling of profound frustration and anxiety went through him. He scanned the area, but she was nowhere to be found within the globe of flickering light cast by the wildly dancing fire.

He opened his mouth to call out to her when he heard a sound like a stick popping beneath someone's foot and then a low, murmuring voice. His cock tingled in anticipation as he headed in the direction of the boathouse, his footsteps rapid and silent.

He paused when he rounded the back corner of the building. She carried a small handheld flashlight and knelt. He could see the dim outline of her behind the beam of light, which fell on the paw of the fox they'd seen earlier.

"It looks like it's healing okay, Guy. Shhh . . . I know. I won't touch the wound, I promise," she murmured soothingly when the animal whimpered and flinched away from her. She lifted the flashlight, tracking the animal and sighing softly when it retreated back to the woods. Thomas realized the fox had probably sensed his presence, even if Sophie hadn't.

"Sophie."

The hand that held the flashlight jerked.

"Thomas?" she gasped. The light wavered and fell on him where he stood several feet away. For several taut seconds, neither of them moved. Something dark and nameless rose in Thomas's chest and caused his cock to jerk in his boxer briefs, some primitive, biological mandate.

"That animal could hurt you," he breathed out, his emotional state making his voice low and harsh. He stepped closer to her. "How can you be so stupid?"

She made a sound of protest, like she'd started to rebut but suddenly checked herself. The light shifted, alerting him to the fact that she'd stood. He drew nearer. The air seemed to vibrate between them with electrical energy. The darkness in him, the bundle of twisted, taut emotion, felt like it'd burst out of his chest.

It had coalesced into a powerful, almost alarming need.

She made a little gasp of surprise when he swooped down and took her mouth in a voracious kiss. He swallowed her surprise and gave a groan of satisfaction when he felt her mouth soften and mold against his own. She pressed closer, participating in the kiss fervently, making the blood in his veins roar.

"Sophie?" he asked roughly next to her seeking lips a moment later.

"Yes?" she asked, her voice audibly trembling, making him wonder if she knew precisely what was happening between them.

"Better run."

"Thomas, I'm not going to—"

"*Run*, Sophie," he hissed.

The flashlight dropped to the grass. His erratic heartbeat made it almost impossible for him to hear her tennis shoes rustling in the damp lawn. But he made out the direction of her flight.

He lunged after her.

CHAPTER **SIXTEEN**

Sophie tore through the soft grass, the bonfire by the lake and the distant lights in the house her only guides in the pitch blackness. She had no idea why her heart bounded in her chest with so much excitement; no idea why she was running from Thomas when she wasn't afraid of him.

Not really.

But something elemental was making her run, causing her blood to race through her veins. Every nerve in her body was suddenly vibrating with energy, making her hyperaware of the velvety, thick cloak of darkness that surrounded her, of her straining muscles and drumming heart . . . of the mounting tension in her sex that was amplified by the friction of her pumping thighs.

In a fragmented manner she recalled the excitement of having a boy chase her on the playground for a kiss, an innocent reenactment of some atavistic instinct, some old trace of a primitive thrill.

But Thomas was no seven-year-old boy. And that kiss he'd just given her hadn't been a prelude to anything innocent. Warm liquid surged between her legs, dampening her sex.

She heard the sound of the fabric of his shorts swishing as he pumped his legs. He was just feet behind her.

Her eyes went wide and adrenaline poured into her veins, bursting into her muscles with a surge of electrifying chemical energy. She ran toward the house, some part of her brain associating it with normalcy and safety, but she could tell by the sound of his breathing that Thomas was closing in on her, her flight no match for his long, powerful legs. His low, harsh voice echoed in her brain.

Run, Sophie.

She nearly choked in rising anxiety. This was madness . . . pure lunacy. *Why* was she running from him? She considered spinning around and confronting him, but she wasn't ruled by logic at that moment.

She cried out sharply when she felt his hand on her elbow. He jerked her to a stop, cutting off the cry in her throat. She pulled at her arm like a wild creature caught in a trap, but he grasped her shoulders with both hands and spun her around.

He pulled her against him. She could feel how rigid his muscles were and the heat resonating even through his damp clothing. She felt his breath striking her face in warm, irregular jags.

He shook her lightly, causing their pelvises to thump together.

"Why did you ask me here? Why do you keep asking me all those questions about my father? What do you *know*? What are you trying to accomplish?"

She gasped at the impact of his staccato, harsh words striking her like gunfire.

"I don't know what you mean—"

"Good girls don't make good liars. Stop playing games, Sophie," he growled softly before he sank his tongue between her parted lips.

He ravaged her mouth; owned it. She not only allowed his possession, she gloried in it. Heat rolled through her body in an unstoppable torrent. Her awareness became a riot of broken thoughts and overwhelming sensation.

"Thomas," she moaned, half in desire and half in dazed confusion when he pulled her down into the cool, damp grass and rolled on top of her, his weight pinning her to the ground. His cock felt almost alarmingly engorged when he pressed it along her pussy and lower belly. She inhaled, her eyes going wide when her brain recognized on some instinctive level the scent of a male pitched into a feral frenzy to mate.

Her vagina contracted painfully, answering his silent summons. He reached between them and ripped roughly at the buttons of her shorts, shoving them and her panties down her thighs. The damp grass felt cool next to her heated skin. He ground his cock against her now exposed sex, grunting at the stimulation, before he lifted himself and clawed wildly at the fastenings of his own shorts. She panted as he lowered his clothing, anticipation building in her until it felt like the blood would burst through her veins.

She went entirely still beneath him, her breath catching on a jagged inhale when he grabbed her wrists and transferred them to one large hand. He pinned her arms to the ground above her head.

"I told you to make me go," he rasped.

"I don't want you to go. I want *you*, Thomas," she replied in a strangled whisper. Tears flowed down her face, their temperature hot compared to the cool drops of rain that mixed with them.

"Then you're going to have to take the consequences."

She gritted her teeth, moaning shakily between them when he thrust his cock into her slit. She was wet, aroused like a female in heat—the humid, thick air kissed her moist tissues—but Thomas was enormous with need, and her shorts and panties were gathered around her thighs, constricting their joining, making it impossible for her to open herself to him.

He grunted in profound frustration and whipped his hand down to her thighs, shifting his body and shoving her shorts and panties farther down her legs.

"Get out of them," he ordered starkly and she lifted her feet, allowing him to work the legs holes over her damp tennis shoes.

She moaned in rising lust when he was back over her a second later. He spread her thighs wide in the grass and pressed the steely head of his penis into her slit. He pushed her arms once again above her head, rearing over her, restraining her as he supported his upper body. Her cry mixed with his deep growl as he drove his cock's full length into her. Without pause, he began to thrust.

"God, *yes,*" she heard him mutter through a haze of rioting sensation.

He possessed her thoroughly in those moments, so that she was barely aware of the gentle rain falling on her bare legs and face or the prickly grass beneath her bare ass. Her muscles would be slightly sore the next day, but at that moment, she could only think about how inevitable it felt, how primitive and strong.

How honest.

She couldn't move much, pinned as she was to the ground, but she tilted her hips up eagerly to accept his powerful thrusts. A sharp cry popped out of her throat every time his flexing pelvis encountered her spread thighs. Distantly, Sophie realized the rain had increased to a steady patter. Their wet skin slapping together was what caused the loud smacking sound that intermixed with Thomas's harsh grunts and her own cries as sensation jolted through her.

His driving cock created a hot, delicious friction, an almost untenable pressure that made her frantic. Thomas seemed even more desperate to quench the wild hunger that possessed him, however. He abruptly released her restrained wrists and came up on his knees, cursing as he tried to position himself in the increasingly wet, slick grass. He spread his hands on the back of her bare thighs and pushed.

Sophie bit her lip, stifling her scream when he rolled her hips back and her knees came down near her ears. Thomas didn't bother to stifle his roar of pleasure as he rode her pussy fast and furious, like he thoroughly believed he could feel the breath of some dark demon prickling on his neck.

Like his only salvation lay at Sophie's farthest reach.

She couldn't have taken him like that for long, with her pussy spread wide and her legs pushed into the grass next to her ears and Thomas fucking her like his very life was at stake. But it didn't matter, because he was so pitched with need, so wild for release that it didn't last long.

She shut her eyes, her facial muscles pulled tight when she felt his cock lurch deep inside her, heard the almost amazed sound of his shout as he came. She knew she'd never forget the sound of his poignant, ecstatic moan as pleasure rattled and shook his body, driving his demons out of his mind.

The sensation of his cock twitching while he was sheathed in her body, of the warmth of his semen filling her, caused the unbearable pressure that'd grown in her muscles to break. Her pussy clamped around him as she joined him in an agony of bliss.

She welcomed his solid weight when he fell on top of her a moment later, gasping wildly for air. Her body felt over-stimulated, like she was a buzzing, vibrating, riot of nerves. She still hadn't begun to recover from the disorientation of their savage mating—and she knew Thomas hadn't either, given his ragged breathing and still stiff cock—when he suddenly lifted his head from the crevice of her neck and shoulder and withdrew from her body.

He made a hissing noise.

Sophie groaned. It felt as if a vital organ had been ripped out of her. His heavy, streaming cock fell against her external sex before he snatched it away, as though he thought it'd burned her.

"Thomas?" she whispered through numb lips.

But he didn't say anything, just rolled off her. Her legs lowered; her feet touched the wet grass. Raindrops fell on her bare legs, hips, and face. There was a rustling as Thomas adjusted his clothing and then he was kneeling over her. She murmured in surprise when he lifted her into his arms, and then stood.

"Put your arms around my neck," he ordered bleakly.

Neither of them spoke as he carried her through the slow, steady downpour to the side entrance of the house.

CHAPTER **SEVENTEEN**

Thomas was numb.

Every time he considered what had just happened out there in Sophie's dark yard, his consciousness seemed to fragment, to ricochet away from the disturbing image. The fact that the memory still had the power to arouse him made it even more shameful and confusing.

But he couldn't deny the truth for any more than a second, he realized as he carried Sophie into the bathroom attached to her bedroom. He really *had* just fallen on Sophie out there, held her down in the grass, and rutted on her like a mindless beast.

It hadn't been rape—she'd consented—but it had come closer to it than anything he'd ever done in his life. Never had he possessed a desire to take a woman so totally, to mark her . . . to fill her with his seed.

He'd never wanted to run so much in his life as he did at that moment. To escape that wild, blistering memory . . . to escape *period*.

But he couldn't, of course.

He couldn't leave Sophie. Not after what he'd just done.

He dropped a towel to the lid of the toilet seat and

lowered her to a sitting position. He mentally braced himself and turned on the light.

His mouth went dry at the image of her staring up at him with those huge, dark eyes set in a pale face. Her hair was wet. His gaze coasted down over her clinging gray T-shirt to her bare hips and legs. A few blades of grass stuck to one knee and dirt had smeared on her right thigh. White viscous fluid clung to dark blonde pubic hair.

When he realized he was staring, held captive by the power of the image . . . that his cock had just throbbed to life again, he looked away, forcing himself not to flinch. He stepped over to the bathtub and turned on the tap.

"Thomas . . . what are you doing?"

"I think you should take a bath."

"But . . . *Thomas*," she said when he picked up some bath salts at the corner of the tub and studied the jar before he opened the lid.

"Yeah?" he replied as he poured some of the light blue salts into the warm water filling the tub. Steam rose against his averted face.

"Will you please look at me?"

"Just a second," he muttered before he bent and swished his fingers in the water, testing its temperature. He turned and knelt, grabbing one of Sophie's wet canvas sneakers and untying it briskly.

"Thomas?" she repeated, sounding slightly exasperated. Her sneaker thumped onto the tile floor, only to be followed by its mate.

He glanced up at her before he stood and grabbed for the hem of her T-shirt.

"What?" he asked as he pulled the wet, soiled shirt over her head. Sophie sputtered into the fabric before she lifted her arms and he drew off the shirt. She grabbed at it when it crossed her hands and threw the shirt to the floor.

"Stop it! Thomas, what's *wrong* with you?"

He looked into her face incredulously.

"How can you ask me that?"

"I . . . I'm not sure . . ." She glanced around helplessly. "I'm on the pill. Is that why you're so anxious?"

Even though relief swept through him, so did another surge of regret. His fingertips grazed her damp cheek before he nodded toward the tub. "Why don't you get in the tub? I got you all dirty."

"I don't care about getting some dirt on me. You didn't hurt me. I enjoyed it as much as you did," she said in a rush. "And as far as not using a condom, I can assure you that I'm perfectly healthy and always have been. I just had my regular doctor's appointment two weeks ago—"

"You think that's what I'm thinking about?" he interrupted.

"I don't know what you're thinking about. I *usually* don't, you know? You're like some kind of . . . human jigsaw puzzle," she snapped. Something must have occurred to her because she started back suddenly. "Wait, you're not . . . are you trying to tell me you're not healthy?"

"Of course not. I practice safe sex. Religiously. *Always*."

The one exception being out there in the grass with you not five minutes ago, he thought.

"Oh . . . well . . . " Sophie glanced away in discomfort. He wondered if she was thinking the same thing he was. Why the hell had he made an exception for her?

Why the hell did he want to make that glorious mistake all over again, even knowing that she was lying to him . . . keeping secrets. His throat and chest tightened as he studied her profile, making it difficult to inhale for a second.

"Get in the bath, Sophie."

For several seconds she seemed undecided. But then she made to stand and he moved back, granting her space.

"Let me," he said gruffly when she reached for her only remaining clothing—her bra. He unfastened the hooks with a flick of his wrist and pulled the garment off her. Her breasts trembled slightly once they were liberated, the flesh looking firm and tender, the nipples delicate. His hand itched to touch her, but he remained at a distance.

"Go on," he said quietly.

When she stepped into the steaming water and lowered, he knelt next to the bathtub. Only about two inches of water had filled the tub so far, but the steamy mist made things warm and comfortable. Neither of them spoke as he wetted a clean washcloth. He sensed her watching him as he moved his hand over her knees and thighs, washing away the grass and dirt.

"I can bathe myself, Thomas," she said breathlessly when he gently bent one knee and washed the streak of dirt off the back of her thigh.

"I know that. I want to do it. I'm the one who got you dirty," he mumbled gruffly.

CHAPTER **EIGHTEEN**

Only the sound of the water trickling from her body back into the tub interrupted the silence that followed as he ran the warm washcloth over her shoulders and neck. Thomas was completely focused on his task: the gentle drag of the wet cloth across her smooth skin, the pulse that throbbed with increasing rapidity at her throat, the rise and fall of the round, pale globes of her breasts.

When he lifted the washcloth, a fat drop of water fell onto an erect nipple. His gaze remained fixed on the compelling sight as he draped the washcloth on the side of the tub and fumbled in the soap dish.

He dipped into the warm water, wetting the soap, before he lathered it between both hands.

She gave a furtive cry when he held both of her breasts in his shaping palms and lathered the nipples with gentle rubbing fingertips.

"Your breasts are almost indecently beautiful," he murmured distractedly as he coaxed the nipples into peaking higher for him.

Her hips shifted restlessly in the tub.

"Indecently?" she asked with a small smile.

He nodded.

"Are you flattering me, Thomas?"

He glanced up at her face, noting her wide eyes. "That would surprise you, wouldn't it?" he asked regretfully.

"No, it wouldn't," she corrected, her low voice tickling the back of his neck. A quiet, sensual spell seemed to have settled. He filled his hands with her firm, warm flesh, gliding his hands over the lather and soft skin, but his stare was locked with Sophie's. "I think it surprises you more that I have good expectations of you, doesn't it? That I could possibly be thinking that you're anything besides a confused, angry, grief-stricken man?"

"A grief-stricken animal, you mean?" he asked as he lowered his soapy hands over her rib cage and worshipped her unique shape and texture.

"No. I meant man," she whispered.

He didn't believe she could see much more than all the toxic emotional trash he'd been spilling all over her, but he didn't want to argue at the moment. Not when he'd fallen under the sensual spell Sophie always cast over him.

Neither of them spoke as he lathered his hands again and washed her stomach. Her belly and curving hips struck him as powerfully erotic for some reason, a soft harbor, a miracle of feminine curves and planes and tender patches of skin that made her catch her breath when he rubbed them with his fingers. He found those sweet spots everywhere on her body; the patch of skin a half inch above her pubic hair, for instance, or the spot on the inside of her right knee.

He pulled the plug on the tub after he'd finished washing her feet, letting the steamy water drain when he saw Sophie's cheeks had grown bright pink from the heat.

He moved back to the center of her body and once again dipped his hands beneath the surface of the water. A glance up at her face told him that her gaze was fixed on him as he lathered the soap and set it aside.

He'd saved her genitals for last. As he stared at the juncture of her thighs, he wondered why. Would he regret washing his semen off her body?

She moaned shakily when he opened his hand, fingers downward, and cradled her outer sex with a warm, soapy hand. After several delicious, taut moments, Thomas had his answer.

He'd wanted to see his come on her . . . wanted to smell it twining with Sophie's clean, floral scent.

He washed her anyway, subtly moving his hand, using the pads of his fingertips to discover and cleanse the delicate petals of her feminine flower. He heard her soft cries and moans as if from a distance. The feel of her sensitive flesh thrilling beneath his fingers left him spellbound.

His hand dropped lower between her thighs, his fingers gently seeking. She opened her legs wider, granting him permission and access. She whimpered when he ran the tip of his forefinger over her slit. It aroused him beyond measure, the feeling of the ample lubrication seeping from her pussy, the thick fluid feeling different than both the soap lather and the water.

He glanced up at her face, realizing for the first time that her pink cheeks and flushed breasts were the result of desire, not steamy water.

He held her gaze and inserted his middle finger into her snug slit, drawing a tiny circle in the narrow, silky confines, before he withdrew and repeated the process. She bent her knees and planted her feet, lifting her hips slightly, granting him free reign. His gaze fixed on her white front teeth biting at her lower lip as he gently attempted to rinse his ejaculate from her vagina.

Not that it would work, he thought with a grim sense of satisfaction. He'd exploded so deep in her, his semen would be in her for days to come.

When he realized the bestial direction of his thoughts, he glanced away from her face.

"Sore?" he asked gruffly as he watched himself fingering her.

"No. It feels so good," she said huskily as her hips made small gyrations against his finger.

"I'm trying to clean you," he said as he penetrated her

vagina again, but it was a lie, and he suspected she knew that, especially when he pressed the heel of his palm next to her tender cunt and began to stimulate her clit, as well.

He was becoming lost in another dense, thick haze of blinding need, the lure of the ecstatic void he'd found in the depths of Sophie's body beckoning him yet again.

The water level had fallen below her pussy now. He cupped his hand in the warm water and rinsed the soap from her pubic hair and labia. When he corkscrewed his finger in and out of her slit, he saw that his skin glistened with her abundant cream. He growled low in his throat at the sight. He opened his palm behind a smooth, warm thigh and tilted her hips back farther.

His focus on her was absolute as he pressed his fingertip to the delicate, tightly closed ring of her rectum.

She groaned shakily and he felt her thigh muscles stiffen in his grasping hand. Still, he continued to stare, held mesmerized by the vision of his finger sliding into Sophie's most private place. She felt smooth and tight . . . tight enough to squeeze his finger; hot enough to melt a stiff cock into limp, quivering, thoroughly sated flesh.

His mouth formed into a snarl at the heady thought. He used his hand to tilt her back more, until he held her with her knees bent, her legs suspended in the air. He pushed his forefinger into her clamping channel all the way to the knuckle, his way made easy by her slick juices on his skin. He paused to enjoy the heat that resonated into his flesh.

It was the second time this evening he'd held her like this, open and vulnerable, while he penetrated her body.

His gaze leapt to her face. She watched him with wide, glazed eyes.

"Are you all right?" he rasped.

She just nodded her head, apparently unable to speak.

He withdrew his finger and pushed it into her ass again.

"This is okay with you?" he asked as he slid his finger in to the hilt and began to draw tiny little circles over her clit with the pad of his thumb.

She gasped and nodded once again.

"Good," he murmured, watching her face for a reaction to his intimate caresses. He learned she liked it the best when he kept his finger deep in her ass and pushed on her clit subtly like a little button, vibrating his thumb tip over the well-lubricated, nerve-packed flesh. She gasped when he did that and the color rose in her cheeks.

"Do you want me to make you come like this?"

Her dark pink lips mouthed the word *yes*.

He moved his hand a bit more stringently and shook his head. "I wanted to make you clean, Sophie. I *wanted* to," he told her in a choked voice.

"I believe you, Thomas. But I like it when you make me feel dirty."

Her dark eyes rolled back in her head. He muttered a curse when he felt her body shudder. Maybe it was his imagination, but his finger seemed to burn inside her ass.

He wanted to nurse her through her orgasm, to feel every shiver of pleasure vibrate into his hand and then coax more from her body. But the red haze of lust had once again clouded his vision. He stood and placed one foot in the now-drained tub. He reached for her hands and pulled her to a standing position.

She just stared up at him, disoriented, still under the influence of her orgasm. He brushed her damp hair off her cheeks and kissed her parted lips softly.

"I don't know what's happening between us, Sophie," he muttered near her lips. "I would stop it if I could, but unless you tell me 'no,' I don't think I can stop myself."

She blinked and brought him into focus. "I don't want you to stop."

He just stared down at her for a few seconds, his brain buzzing and his cock humming like he'd been plugged into a low-grade electric jack. He finally stepped out of the tub and steadied her while she followed him. She said nothing, but he saw that her breath was still coming fast and choppy from her climax as he dried her off with a towel.

She put her hand in his when he extended it and he led her to the cool bedroom.

He hesitated when he got to the edge of her bed. A rage of lust roared through his veins at that moment, but he was hyperaware of Sophie, too, of everything he'd put her through tonight with his chaotic grief. He went still when she reached up and touched his jaw with warm fingertips.

"Do you want to tie me up, Thomas?"

His eyes went wide. What the *hell* had made her say that? How had she so perfectly guessed the truth?

"It's all right, if you do." Her whisper in the dim room made a ripple of excitement course down his spine, ending in a tingling sensation in his cock. He opened his mouth, but he couldn't seem to find the words. Her fingertips whisked over his opened lips.

"I'm not afraid," she said quietly. "I've never done it before, but I want to. With you."

"Never done *what*?" Thomas asked cautiously, wanting to make sure they were on the same page. Was she talking about being restrained, or—

"I've never had anal sex."

He swallowed with difficulty. Her eyes looked enormous and dark in the dim room, enigmatic and trusting at once.

"It won't be like . . . out in the yard," he said in a rush. "I promise. I don't know what came over me."

She nodded, her solemn stare humbling him.

He licked at his upper lip and tasted sweat. He glanced down, realizing she was damp and naked in the chilly air-conditioned room while he was fully dressed.

"I'm sorry," he mumbled. "Here. Get under the covers. Let's get you comfortable while I get a few things . . ."

His voice trailed off as he pulled back the comforter and sheet. Sophie slid beneath them and he covered her. He bent to kiss her—once in thanks for her generosity, once in rising need.

He walked over to her dresser and opened the top drawer. In the dim light he made out some neatly folded stockings. He lifted one and wrapped his hand in it, testing its strength, its flexibility.

The feeling of the soft, stretchy material aroused him for

some reason; probably because he knew the fabric had once swished between Sophie's silken thighs, existed within inches of her sweet, aromatic pussy.

He grabbed the stocking's mate and made his way over to the bags of items he'd collected when he drove into town. He already knew where the lubricant/scented massage oil was, noticed where the middle-aged cashier had bagged it while she gave him a speculative glance, which he ignored. At the time, he'd wondered at his nerve, buying lubricant given his new and strange relationship with Sophie.

But maybe it was the uniqueness of their relationship that had made him do it. Or maybe the animal in him just wouldn't be denied.

He thought once again of how he'd fucked Sophie out there in the yard.

Would he really be able to control himself? His level of arousal was different than his frenzied need to mate had been earlier, but Thomas couldn't say that it was milder in intensity, just more focused . . . more deliberate.

He moved aside a package of T-shirts and found the bottle. He felt Sophie's gaze on him as he placed the combination of lubricant and massage oil on the bedside table.

It was amazing, the stuff you could find at Wal-Mart.

He turned to her, the stockings lying in his hand.

"What's wrong?" she asked when he stared down at her in indecision.

"Are you sure you want to do this, Sophie?" he asked hoarsely.

She nodded.

"No. *Say* it," he demanded, needing to hear it in words.

He saw her throat convulse. "Yes, I want to, Thomas."

He exhaled slowly. "Okay. Well . . . usually it would require you helping me to get as stiff as a pike, because it works best that way," he told her, giving her an apologetic glance when he recognized his crudeness. When he saw her lips tilt in amusement, he continued, "But considering I've been stone-hard for a while now, I don't think we'll have any problems in that department. So how about if we just concentrate on you."

She bit at her lower lip. "Okay."

The small evidence of her anxiety made him forget his hesitancy about taking her in such a volatile act of sex when he himself was like a bomb that was about to go off. He promised himself then and there that if he did anything in the next few minutes that even hinted at harming Sophie, he'd leave.

And never come back.

That was dire enough of a consequence to ensure him that no matter what secrets Sophie might hold, she was completely safe with him.

"Reach up and grab the bedposts."

She did without pause, making his cock throb more insistently.

He leaned down and restrained her with the hose, his fingers going clumsy and stupid as lust pounded through his veins. After he'd affixed her wrists to the bedpost, he turned his attention to the end of the bed. He pulled back the bottom of the comforter and sheets and tied two stockings on the metal bed frame. She made a soft little sound in her throat when he spread her legs wide enough to reach the nylon restraints.

"Okay?" he whispered, as he held one of her elegant, arched feet in his palm. "I don't have to restrain your legs if you don't want me to. Just say the word."

"No, it's all right."

He shivered slightly at the sound of her low voice in the dim, silent room. He told himself to focus on his task instead of the arousing sight of Sophie, naked and tied spread-cagle on the bed, awaiting her pleasure.

When she was tied up, he straightened, one knee still on the bed.

"Nylons make a tight hold, Sophie. But . . ."

"What?" she asked shakily.

"You can pull loose of them. I tied you tight, but the loop will stretch. If you want it to."

"I understand, Thomas."

She'd sounded breathless, Thomas thought as he peeled the damp T-shirt he wore off his skin. He kicked off his tennis shoes and examined her as he unbuttoned his shorts. Was she aroused by the idea of being tied up, not only at his mercy, but at the mercy of the desire he planned to awaken in her body?

He hoped like hell she was aroused at being restrained, because it was driving him crazy with excitement. Too bad he didn't have access to any sex toys here at the cabin. It'd be nice to have a way to amplify her experience, he thought as he whipped off his socks.

Then again, making his lust even more powerful seemed not only unwise, but downright greedy. How could he become *more* aroused than he felt at that moment?

His gaze snagged on Sophie's when he leaned back up again. Without thinking about what he was doing, he shoved his hand into his boxer briefs and fisted his cock. It'd caused a wicked stab of lust to go through him to see her big, dark eyes watching him undress, to see the arousal and, yes, a touch of wariness in their depths.

"You say the word, Sophie—now or later . . . *anytime*—and I'll untie you," he rasped as he continued to stroke his cock.

"I know," she said shakily. Her gaze had transferred to his crotch, and she no longer looked wary; just excited. It sent a thrill through him, too, to know that she was aroused by the sight of him stroking himself. He lifted his penis out of his underwear and through his opened shorts. Her head lifted slightly off the pillow to get a better look when he began to run his hand up and down the sensitive shaft. Little pulses of pleasure leapt through him as he fisted the head and spread some pre-ejaculate on it until it glistened when he moved his hand to the turgid staff. Thomas knew it was his own hand jacking his cock but it was Sophie's big, wanting eyes that were giving him so much pleasure.

"I think I'd like to watch you bring yourself off," she whispered. Her voice had sounded a little awed, like she was surprised by the truth of what she'd said.

His cock leapt in his hand. He'd love to jack off for her, the vision of her tied to the bed naked and her eyes glued to his cock supplying ample fuel to complete the task with ease.

"I can tell you one thing," he said in all honesty as he continued to stroke himself. "The vision of how you look right this minute is going to be what pops into my mind whenever I do jack off from this day forward."

"Thomas," she whispered shakily when he reached for the comforter and sheet and pulled. The fabric slid sensually down her torso. He let go when it reached just below her bellybutton. As usual, the sight of the pale expanse of her stomach and her large, shapely breasts spiked his arousal.

"You have exceptionally beautiful breasts," he murmured as he stroked his raging erection. "I've never seen real ones that were so firm . . . so sweet."

She laughed softly. "How do you know they're real?"

He gave her a wry glance. "Give me some credit, Sophie."

"Oh, right. You're the breast expert," she said through a small smile. "Pardon me for even joking about your vast experience in such matters."

He smiled. "You're forgiven. I can tell by looking and touching that you've been thoroughly blessed by God, but even if I didn't know the truth already, I don't believe for a second you'd ever go for breast augmentation."

"How do you know that?"

"There's no way in hell you'd do something to draw additional attention to yourself. You always hide, Sophie."

Her smile faded slightly when their gazes met.

"It doesn't work," he told her gruffly. "I saw your beauty each and every time I caught sight of you." He twisted his fist over the sensitive patch of skin just beneath the crown of his cock. "I was blown away by it every damned time."

She didn't reply, just stared at him with her lips slightly parted and an amazed expression on her lovely face. He grimaced when he forced himself to let go of his cock.

"As much as your proposal appeals to me, I think I'll save this for my ravishment of you."

Her smile returned when he glanced down at his erection poking out between the fly of his shorts.

"You certainly make a formidable ravisher," she murmured.

He pumped his eyebrows. "You haven't seen anything yet."

Her soft laughter mesmerized him for a second or two. It stopped when he turned and headed out of the room.

"Thomas?"

"I'll be right back. I'm looking for something—"

She twisted her chin to see him when he walked back in the room a moment later.

"What are you doing?" she asked bemusedly as she stared at the dark red, silicone spatula he held in his hand.

"Improvising," he said before he set the spatula next to the bottle of lubricant on the bedside table. "Sophie?"

"Yes?" she asked, dragging her gaze off the spatula. The light spilling from the opened bathroom door was sufficient for him to see how flushed her cheeks looked.

"What we're going to do . . . it'd be best if you were as aroused as you can be. Do you happen to have a vibrator?"

Her lips fell open. Her blush deepened.

"Yes."

He smiled and pointed toward the bedside table drawer, his eyebrows cocked in a query. Her nod seemed hesitant.

"It's not a crime, Sophie," he murmured amusedly as he opened the drawer. "Believe it or not, I realize that women like to masturbate just as much as men." He paused when he saw the shape of what was obviously a dildo wrapped in a soft, dark blue cloth at the back of the drawer. He lifted the realistically shaped rubber phallus and whisked it out of the cloth bag.

His grin widened as he met Sophie's wide-eyed stare. "You like them big, huh, Sophie?"

She shut her eyes in embarrassment.

"It's not exactly the sort of thing I was asking about. Don't you have a nice little clit vibrator?" he asked, eyeing the monster cock he held standing up in his palm. The dildo was as large as his cock, and it certainly wouldn't help him prepare Sophie's ass for penetration.

"I don't have anything else," Sophie murmured, her eyes still closed. "It *is* a vibrator, though."

He glanced over at her, but she refused to meet his gaze. He reached inside the drawer for the vibrator controller and set both it and the rubber cock on the table.

She opened her eyes when he straddled her waist on the bed and leaned down to kiss a hot cheek.

"Don't be embarrassed," he whispered hoarsely as he peppered her cheeks and jaw with kisses. He hovered above her mouth and spoke quietly. "It's exciting to think of it—sweet, innocent Sophie Gable choosing one sex toy for her personal pleasure, and instead of getting a compact little clit vibrator, she gets herself a nice, big cock."

He kissed her mouth, sending his tongue between her lips to tease himself with her singular flavor. His cock throbbed on her warm, smooth belly. He didn't say it out loud, but it also gratified him that she'd purchased a cock that wasn't dissimilar in size and shape to his own penis, and she hadn't even known him then. He liked knowing that she had a preference for something he possessed. "Sweet Sophie," he murmured as he plucked at her lips. "You please me so much. How many more secrets do you carry behind those beautiful eyes?"

She said nothing when he lifted his head, but like him, she panted softly.

"I'm *so* going to enjoy using that cock on you," he said.

CHAPTER **NINETEEN**

Sophie's eyes went wide when she registered the gentle warning in Thomas's tone.

I'm so going to enjoy using that cock on you.

It *was* embarrassing revealing something as personal as her chosen method of masturbation to him—especially when the vibrating dildo was so large—but it was exciting, as well. What was he planning on doing to her while she was tied up to the bed, helpless and panting with desire?

Well, not helpless, precisely, Sophie reminded herself as she pulled slightly on the knots that bound her and felt the give to the material. She could escape if she wanted to, and Thomas had told her all she had to do was say the word, and he'd release her.

Not that she wanted him to stop, Sophie thought as she watched him sit up. He still straddled her naked body. His cock throbbed on her stomach, the cock head lying between her ribs. It excited her, as usual, the shape of him, the weight. She followed his movements as he leaned over to grab the little bottle, the vibrator, and the control mechanism. Desire twanged between her thighs as he turned on the vibrator and pushed a couple buttons, experimenting. She cried out softly in surprise when he placed the pulsating rubber cock tip next to the pulse on her neck.

"How's that setting?"

Sophie swallowed, feeling the weight of the dildo on her throat.

"It's . . . fine," she whispered.

He suddenly transferred the fat rubber cock tip to her lower lip. Sophie just stared up at him. She felt his cock lurch next to her abdomen.

"Your lips are very sensitive," he murmured. "Are you sure you like that setting?"

Sophie just nodded, speechless.

He removed the vibrator and set it on the bed. He picked up the little bottle. Perhaps he saw the question in her eyes when he poured several drops into his palm.

"It's a massage oil as well as a lubricant," he explained as he rubbed his right forefinger and the middle finger into the small amount he'd poured into his left palm. Sophie's breath froze in her lungs when he reached toward a heaving breast. Very slowly . . . very sensually, he rubbed his fingertips over the nipple.

She moaned and tried to shift her hips to get pressure on her pussy. She was trapped beneath Thomas's weight, however. He continued to rub the jasmine-scented oil all over the tip of her breast until the nipple was pointed and hard. Then he transferred his attentions to the other crest.

Sophie began to sweat when he picked up the dildo. He pressed the vibrating tip to a nipple.

"*Oh*," she cried out. The cock tip pulsed erotically next to her slippery nipple. The sensation sent a jolt of pleasure through her, but almost equally exciting was the image of Thomas holding the big cock on her breast and watching her face for a reaction.

"Feel good?" he asked, his voice like a low, rough purr.

Sophie wriggled beneath him, desperate to get friction on her spread pussy.

"Yes," she replied.

"Why are you twisting around so much, then? Try to relax, Sophie. Don't struggle against it."

She clamped her eyelids shut and willed herself to keep still as pleasure roared in her flesh.

"That's right. Just give into the feeling," she heard him say. She bit her lip when she felt him touch her other nipple with the palm of his hand, spreading the massage oil. Then his fingertips were stimulating that crest as well, plucking at the responsive tip, making her nipple distend and sending spikes of pleasure down to her pussy.

After torturing her nipples in this manner for several moments, the tension in her wet pussy mounted until it felt unbearable. The air-conditioned air seemed to have thickened around the juncture of her thighs. It felt as if it licked and teased her exposed tissues. It drove her mad.

She pulled on her wrist restraints in rising desperation, her back arching up off the bed. She gritted her teeth and tried to shift her hips. Thomas paused when he heard her moan of frustration.

"Shhhh," he soothed. He shifted his weight down her body. Sophie's groan only increased when she felt the thin stream of pre-cum he trailed along her skin as his cock slid down her abdomen.

"I'm sorry," Thomas said. "I'm not trying to taunt you, Sophie. I just want to make you feel good."

"It does feel good," she told him in a choked voice. "It feels *too* good."

She opened her eyelids in time to see his small smile. Her eyes remained glued to it as he lowered the dildo and pressed it to her ribs. She shivered at the sensual vibration.

"Look at your nipples."

Sophie glanced down. She'd never seen her nipples more dark or distended. She tried to shift her hips again, aroused by the vision of Thomas tickling her ribs with a big cock, but this time Thomas's weight held her firmly down onto the mattress.

"Thomas . . . *please*."

"I know what you want, Sophie. And I'm going to give it to you."

All of her muscles clenched tight again at the sensual threat she heard in his voice.

Her breath was coming fast and choppy by the time he rolled off her. He lay on his side and propped himself up on one elbow, his head at about her waist level. Sophie gasped when he transferred the cock tip of the vibrator to her inner thigh, just inches away from her spread pussy.

"Sophie?"

"Yes?" she asked, hyperaware of him moving the cock head around on her thigh, enlivening her flesh until Sophie felt like not just the patch of skin beneath the dildo, but her whole body vibrated with sexual energy. Her clit throbbed, needy for stimulation.

"Do you use this thing like this? Do you put it on your nipples? Or on your belly?"

She moaned when he moved the dildo a hair's-breadth closer to her pussy. She could tell by the way the cool air felt on her sensitive tissues that she was dripping wet.

"No . . . not really."

"How do you use it?" Thomas asked. He kept his face averted while he spoke. She sensed his eyes on the dildo pulsing between her spread thighs.

"I . . . I just . . ."

"Yes?" he prompted when she faded off as he moved the cock tip closer to her slit. When she didn't speak right away as lust pounded through her veins, he leaned over her pussy and shifted his hand.

"Oh, God," Sophie groaned when he pushed the head of the vibrating dildo into her slit.

"No lubrication required here," she heard him say under his breath. He sounded pleased. "Is this what you do, Sophie? Answer me, or I'll stop. Do you like to put it in your pussy? Tease yourself a little before you slide it all the way in you?"

"Yes," Sophie replied breathlessly as she shifted her hips against the dildo. She's always loved how similar it felt to a man's cock . . . not that she'd ever known a man's cock that compared to the sex toy until she'd met Thomas. Now she knew exactly how it differed from the real thing. It wasn't warm like Thomas; the protruding veins didn't throb with hot, surging blood; when Thomas had pressed it against her lips, the outer covering wasn't as soft as silk; it didn't smell like musk and semen and unbridled man.

She raised her hips as far off the bed as her restraints would allow and tried to get her slit down farther on the penetrating dildo.

Once again, Thomas made a hushing sound. She cried out in thwarted longing when he removed the cockhead from her vagina. He placed the heavy phallus on her labia. Sophie went entirely still in anticipation. The tiny vibrations resonated through the fleshy sex lips, humming her clit.

"Do you put this cock on your little clit, Sophie?"

"Yes," she whispered.

"Do you make yourself come that way?" he asked, his face still averted. She could feel his warm breath on her lower belly.

"Yes," she got out through a tight throat.

He shifted his hand and the cockhead burrowed between her labia. She cried out in triumph at the sensation of the vibrator directly on her clit. She'd felt it dozens of times before while masturbating, but it somehow felt more powerful at that moment, like a blast of concentrated pleasure. It must be Thomas's patient awakening of her flesh that caused it, or maybe it was just the fact that *he* held the vibrator and controlled her pleasure instead of herself.

Her cries became high-pitched and ragged as she neared climax. Her clit sizzled in pleasure. Every nerve in her body screamed for release; every muscle had grown tight as a drawn bowstring. She strained for orgasm. She could taste it, it hovered so close.

Suddenly he withdrew the vibrator. Sophie shouted when he inserted it into her slit.

"Take it, Sophie," he growled as he pushed. He leaned farther over her, watching as the big cock penetrated her pussy. "That's right, take it all."

CHAPTER **TWENTY**

Sophie whined and twisted in her restraints as he slid the dildo into her and it vibrated her all the way to her core. He finally stopped when the fat, rubber balls pressed to her cunt.

"Hold still," he ordered, his sharp demand cutting through her agonized pleasure. He began to plunge the dildo in and out of her slit. "Is this what you do with this cock, Sophie? Do you fuck yourself with it? Give it to yourself good and hard when you're all alone in this bed? *Sophie*?"

His voice penetrated her increasingly frantic excitement. "I . . . I . . ." but she couldn't finish a coherent sentence with Thomas plunging the big, throbbing dildo in and out of her.

"*Answer me.*"

His voice struck her like a lash.

"Yes," she squealed as her head thrashed on the pillow and orgasm loomed, promising release from this unbearable tension.

"*Good* girl," she heard him say through the roar of blood surging in her ears. He lowered his head and burrowed his tongue between her labia. He lashed at her burning clit while he continued to fuck her with the humming dildo.

Sophie felt as if he'd dropped a match on dynamite.

She screamed as orgasm blasted through her flesh.

The sensation of Thomas's whiskers brushing against her chin and lips filtered into a brain that felt as if it quivered in her skull from the impact of her orgasm.

"*Kiss me.*"

Sophie parted her lips to receive his pillaging tongue. Thankfully his attack, though potent, was short-lived because Sophie couldn't catch her breath. He fucked her mouth with his tongue and Sophie's awareness hazed with his singular flavor.

She whimpered into his mouth when her lungs burned for air.

"I'm sorry," he whispered gruffly as he released her from his kiss and bit at her lower lip while she gasped for breath. "I just . . . needed to surround myself in you."

"It's okay," she panted. "It felt so good. Thank you."

She saw his nostrils flare as he stared down at her.

"I'm gonna make you feel even better, Sophie. And I'm going to make you squirm a little, too . . . but I guarantee you it'll only make you burn brighter in the end."

She writhed slightly in her restraints as a shiver rippled down her spine.

Thomas had never experienced anything like it. He'd never comprehended the motives of a moth so perfectly. Kissing Sophie while she exploded in orgasm had been like leaping straight into the flames.

There was no turning back now; might as well savor the moments before he was completely incinerated by Sophie's fires.

He stood next to the bed, trying to ignore both the agony of parting himself from Sophie's naked, warm body and how heavy his erection felt when he stood and it fell, pulling on the fabric of his shorts. The stretchy material of his boxer briefs bunched near his balls, keeping his penis poking out from his body at a downward angle.

He instinctively stroked the length once, feeling Sophie's eyes on him. Jesus. As if he'd needed to warn her that he needed to be very hard for the deed.

She said nothing as he untied the restraints around her ankles, but he could hear her panting softly in the quiet room. He determinedly looked away from her face as he untied her wrists, worried he'd be tempted back to ravaging her sweet mouth if he did.

"Turn over on your belly, Sophie," he commanded gently, aware she was still dazed from her powerful climax. He guided her with his hands at her waist and hip as she flipped over on the bed. He made sure her head was turned comfortably, with her left cheek pressed into the pillow before he retied her wrists to the iron posts on the headboard.

His own breathing had roughened, just like Sophie's, by the time he trailed his fingers down the delicate line of her spine as she lay prone on the bed.

"Come up on your knees. That's right. Leave your breasts pressed to the bed." He gently kneaded a firm, round buttock before he swatted it.

She started at the cracking sound of flesh against flesh, and then suddenly went completely still.

"Have you ever had a man spank you before, Sophie?" he asked softly.

He strained to hear her soft reply.

"Just you."

He smiled slightly. He hadn't ever really *spanked* her, just swatted her ass in the heat of the moment.

That's not what he was planning to do now.

"Never were spanked as a child?" he asked.

"No."

"Good," he said as he rubbed her smooth bottom. "I'm not doing this to punish you, Sophie. I wouldn't want you to have any associations to that."

"*Why* are you going to, then?" she asked in a choked voice.

"Because it will turn me on a hell of a lot. And I have reason to suspect it'll do the same to you, Sophie. I'm not going to cause you pain. Just fire your nerves. Excite you a little while I ready you. Do you think it will?" he asked as he continued to rub her ass.

"Excite me?"

"Yes," he said as he moved to the head of the bed and smoothed her hair off her face so that he could gauge her expression. When he looked into her desire-glazed eyes and pink cheeks, he didn't really require an answer, but she gave it to him anyway.

"Yes. I think it will."

He smiled as he continued to stroke her hair in a soothing gesture. His other hand trailed along the side of her body, relishing in the softness of her skin. He coasted over a smooth hip and molded the bottom curve of a buttock in one palm.

Their gazes remained locked when he drew back his hand and landed a spank. She jumped slightly, her eyes widening.

"Okay?" he murmured as he caressed where he'd swatted. She nodded.

"You look surprised," he murmured as he spanked her in the same spot, trying to raise some blood into the flesh and fire her nerves. He massaged the warming buttock and tilted an eyebrow at her.

"I . . . didn't think it'd . . ."

"What?" he asked curiously as he smoothed a strand of wavy hair behind her ear. He paused when she didn't answer. "*What*, Sophie?"

"Excite me quite *that* much," she murmured.

He grinned and spanked her again, the sting of his palm and the taut whapping sound causing his cock to flick up an inch where it poked between the opening of his shorts. He thought Sophie must have noticed his reaction because her eyes fixed on his cock while he spanked her ass several more times. When he paused to rub the curving flesh of her buttocks to ease the sting he'd wrought, he let his fingers stray between her cheeks, lightly caressing her asshole. She bit her lower lip as he pressed a fingertip to her rectum and stimulated her by drawing tiny circles. The sound of her small whimper of arousal brought a snarl to his mouth.

He reached for the lubricant again.

"It's going to be difficult to get you ready," he admitted as he held one pink bottom cheek back while he poured several drops of lubricant directly on her rectum. She shivered in his hold. "Shhh," he murmured, holding her steady while he coated his finger in the silky liquid and then penetrated her ass. A growl vibrated his throat at the sensation. "I'd much prefer something sized between my finger and my cock," he said as he watched himself slide in and out of her ass. She clung even to that slender invader like a hot, sucking little mouth.

After a moment, she bobbed her ass slightly, meeting his down stroke, telling him without words she liked it. It felt decadent, but Thomas seriously had his doubts about whether he could make this work without any additional sex toys to prepare her. She'd never done this before. He burned to take her in this raw, primitive fashion, but he perhaps burned to make it good for Sophie even more.

Besides, he'd grown wary of the animal that grief had turned him into when it came to sex with her. Would he have reacted this way with any woman, given his tumultuous state?

He glanced into Sophie's face and admitted that he doubted it. What was happening between them was strange, but it was too good to be solely a product of just grief-inspired lust.

But what the hell did he really know, especially now, while his lust and need mounted to record-breaking levels?

He squeezed the ass cheek he held while he finger-fucked her. He spanked her several more times, enjoying the sensation of taut, hot skin beneath his striking palm and the sexy little sounds of arousal Sophie made in her throat. Liking her reaction so well, he withdrew his finger reluctantly from her snug ass and reached for the spatula he'd brought from the kitchen. He felt the tension rise in her when he smoothed the tiny paddle over a cheek.

"If I'm not mistaken, this is made of silicone," Thomas said as he traced the crack of Sophie's ass with the edge of the kitchen implement, admiring how the dark red spatula appeared next to her pink bottom.

"It is, I think," she said in a muffled voice. "I just bought it at that new cooking store that opened up near our offices. I haven't even had a chance to use it yet."

Thomas chuckled. "We'll break it in good for you, honey."

"Ooh," she cried out when he popped her ass with the spatula. Thomas paused. He could tell the spatula head was the perfect combination of tensile strength and flexibility for this particular task—the taut cracking sound of skin against silicone had been evidence of that—but he didn't want to hurt Sophie.

"Too much?" he murmured as he rubbed the buttock where he'd spanked her with the spatula.

"No . . . it . . . it's okay."

"You sure?" he asked, studying her profile.

"Yes," she said, her tone carrying an edge to it. Had it been caused by discomfort or arousal?

Thomas swung back the spatula and swatted her again. Her shaky moan gave him his answer. This was arousing her, all right, although there couldn't be any way it was turning her on more than it was turning him on.

He began moving the dark red paddle around, sensitizing every square inch of her beautiful ass. When he realized that she was arching her back and sending her ass up higher to greet his spanks he fisted his aching cock.

"Jesus," he groaned roughly. She was so damn sweet. "I don't think I can take much more of this, Sophie."

She turned her head on the pillow and watched him as he stroked his raging erection. "You don't have to, Thomas."

He clenched his teeth. "Actually, I do. You're nowhere near ready to get fucked in the ass," he stated bluntly. He forced himself to drop his erection. She was nowhere near being ready to be fucked in the ass by *that*.

By *him*.

He grimaced at the agony of the lack of stimulation on

his cock. Restraining Sophie, touching her, feeling her come, spanking her . . . all of it had combined to make him ready to explode at a few strokes.

Sophie lifted her head off the pillow, her eyes on him. "Try it."

"Try what?" he asked warily.

"Try and put it in my ass."

For what was probably only two cock-throbbing moments, but what felt like an eternity, he just stared at her.

"You don't understand, Sophie. It'll take a lot of patience and control on my part."

"You can do it, Thomas. I trust you."

He shut his eyes briefly, finding looking at her honest, lovely face a trial at that moment. He hated himself for it, but even as he tried to deny the allure of her, he was moving.

He shoved his underwear and shorts off his legs. The bedsprings creaked when he crawled onto the mattress. Sweat beaded on his abdomen as he looked at Sophie, naked and restrained before him, her ass blushing from his spankings.

Lust roared through his veins. He reached for the lubricant.

"I'm not going to fuck you," he rasped as he spread the lubricant all over his cock. He didn't know if he was making the vow to her or himself, but he suspected the latter. "I'll . . . I'll wait for another time, when I have something to prepare you better. I'm just going to . . . to . . ." He'd lost the ability to speak as blinding need tightened every muscle in his body. He lifted his cock and spread one of Sophie's ass cheeks. "Put the tip in you. I just want to feel your ass around my cock."

"I'll tell you if I want you to stop, Thomas. I want to try it."

He blinked some sweat out of his eyes as he pushed the tip of his well-lubricated cock to her asshole. Why had she sounded so certain? She didn't realize how dangerous he was, that he might lose control . . . detonate like a bomb? Her calm trust in him caused a taut friction in his stormy spirit.

Her body tightened, resisting him when he pushed his cock head against her rectum, willing her to open for him.

"You have to press against it, Sophie," he said tightly. "Awww—" He bit off his groan as she did what he requested and his cock head squeezed into her ass. For a few seconds, he just knelt there and panted, praying silently to reestablish a splintering control, the tip of his cock throbbing in Sophie's ass. It was a cruel challenge. All he could consider was the mindless nirvana that would come from plunging in and out of her hot little hole, fast and furious.

His balls pinched in agony, the semen in them feeling like it was boiling, like it was going to erupt into Sophie's ass whether he wanted it to or not.

And God, did he want it.

He flexed his hips, sinking into her a quarter of an inch farther. Hot spikes of pleasure rippled through his flesh.

"Sophie?" he asked roughly. She was so silent. He needed to hear her voice.

She turned her chin, trying to look back at him. Tendrils of blonde hair fell on her face, but beneath him he thought he caught a nuance of the tension in her muscles.

"Are you all right?"

The eye that was turned toward him was opened wide, but he didn't sense any discomfort in her expression.

"It . . . feels strange," she murmured.

He winced, both at her words and the pleasure of pushing his cock another half-inch into her. She moaned softly and he cursed. The sensation of her ass constricting the top of his cock in an elastic-tight, hot grip sent another convulsion through his flesh.

His control frayed the more he tried to grasp a hold of it. He wasn't going to last.

"I shouldn't have tried this without a dildo or a plug," he grated out as he reached around Sophie's hips. Burrowing between her labia was like dipping his finger into warmed honey. Her cries of excitement as he stimulated her clit told him she wasn't far from release. His control snapped at the evidence of her reciprocal desire. His cock twitched and swelled, demanding its due.

But he didn't move, even as his need made his blood scald his veins.

Even when she cried out and climaxed against his hand.

He grimaced and suppressed a howl a moment later as he came in Sophie's ass. The entire time both of them climaxed, he fought the urge to plunge deeper; the need feeling like a frantic creature trapped inside of him, demanding release. The struggle against his orgasm caused him to coast on a nearly unbearable razor's edge between pleasure and pain. He wanted to stroke himself at least, pump the frothing semen until his testicles were utterly spent, but he wanted to hear Sophie's sharp cries of ecstasy more.

Later, he wondered how he'd endured it.

He withdrew when they'd both quieted. He leaned over her, his still throbbing, overly sensitive cock pressing against her ass. Neither of them spoke as he worked to untie the knots that restrained her.

Thomas barely panted, his orgasm had been so locked down, so restrained.

Sophie turned into his arms when she was unbound. Her breath fell on his chest in soft, irregular bursts of air. His awareness focused on the sensation to the exclusion of all else; it hypnotized him. As she calmed, and her breathing smoothed, his body followed her rhythm. He felt the tension easing out of his muscles.

Maybe he didn't know Sophie Gable all that well. But he knew a treasure when he held it in his arms. He pressed his mouth to the top of her head and pulled her farther into his embrace.

"I've dreamed about you, Sophie."

She tensed in his arms. "What do you mean?"

"I've dreamed about you . . . about making love to you here. About tying you up, in this very bed."

"They weren't dreams, Thomas. You *have* made love to me here in this bed. You have tied me to it."

He chuckled softly and kissed the top of her head again. "That's not what I meant." He nuzzled her temple in the silence that followed. "Those dreams . . . it's like every time I make love to you, I'm trying to bring those dreams to life. Make them real somehow. Make sure *you're* real." He gave a bark of laughter. "I really am going nuts, aren't I?"

He started to get a little concerned when she didn't respond.

"Sophie?" He brushed a hand over her hip and then an ass cheek. "I didn't hurt you, did I?"

"Of course not," she murmured. "You held back. You didn't have to, Thomas."

He knew what she meant. But he *did* have to restrain himself. After what happened out there in the yard, it'd been an absolute necessity to prove that he could control himself, even in the midst of the most trying, arousing sexual situation he could imagine.

He felt as if he had to relearn his personal limits all over again. Because who knew, really, what this stranger who had overtaken his body was capable of, in the end?

CHAPTER **TWENTY-ONE**

Sophie murmured sleepily and craned up her lips when they were caressed and molded by a firm, masculine mouth.

"Thomas," she murmured without opening her eyes. His scent surrounded her; his taste soaked into her sleep-hazed awareness, making her crave more. Her kisses became hungrier as her hands found their way to his shoulders and she molded dense muscles in her palms. She was pleased that he shared in her need. His kisses altered from slow and warm to deep and hot.

He broke away several seconds later.

"If you keep kissing me like that, I'm going to insult Sherm twice in a twenty-four-hour period, this time by not showing up for fishing."

Sophie sighed in disappointment at the unwelcome intrusion of reality and opened her eyes. They'd turned out the light in the bathroom after they'd cleaned up last night following their lovemaking. The room was swathed in blackness.

"It's the middle of the night," she protested groggily.

"No. It's about fifteen minutes until dawn," he corrected before he dropped another kiss on her mouth. "I'm going to go shower." But he didn't move. Instead he gave her another long, sultry kiss that made Sophie feel like her body was going to melt right into the mattress.

"You really know how to kiss, Thomas Nicasio," she murmured when he lifted his head awhile later.

"Back at you," he said gruffly, and then after a pause, "I don't want to go."

"You better go," she said regretfully.

"Okay. But I don't want to."

She sensed his small smile rather than saw it. She laughed softly as he turned over and got out of bed. A sadness came over her at the absence of his solid male warmth, but so did a feeling of happiness, for some reason.

"I got the coffee ready for you last night. Just turn it on."

"Thanks," he replied in a sleep-roughened voice.

She heard him turn on the shower, but must have fallen asleep again, because she didn't recall him leaving.

When she awoke, she saw through the window that the cloud cover from last night hadn't dissipated. She hoped it hadn't rained on Thomas and Sherm while they fished, although Sherm would be totally enthusiastic if it did, Sophie thought with a smile as she got out of bed. He'd just say the rain would make the fish bite more.

She was still smiling a minute later when she stood at the kitchen sink sipping her coffee and staring out the back window onto the gray morning. Slowly, the weight of what was happening to Thomas—what was happening to her— settled on her spirit, dampening her mood. What right did she have to feel so warm, to be so cheerful when things were so volatile and uncertain?

What right did she have to be happy about falling in love with a man who was in the midst of a personal crisis, was quite possibly in grave danger, and *certainly* was emotionally unavailable?

She set down her coffee cup heavily on the counter, the realization of what she'd just admitted to herself striking her consciousness like a blow.

Was it even possible? To fall in love with someone in such

a short period of time? Not in Sophie's experience it wasn't. She'd considered herself to be in love a few other times in her life, but it had always come on more gradually than this. In fact, what she was experiencing with Thomas felt unlike anything she'd ever experienced before.

Was it just an infatuation? The result of an unprecedented sexual attraction?

She thought of what she'd said to Andy yesterday when they were speaking on the phone.

You must be having strong feelings, Sophie. It's not exactly your typical MO with a guy. I can't help but think it's telling that you're going out on a limb like this for Nicasio. Be careful, okay?

Sophie swallowed and stepped away from the counter. Andy was right. It wasn't her typical MO. Sophie was usually cautious with men, especially at the start of a relationship. She'd been accused of being standoffish often enough that it'd become something she'd come to dread . . . the inevitability of it happening again.

She thought of herself last night, of how she'd responded to Thomas's volatile, dominant lovemaking. Might as well admit it. She'd been the direct opposite of standoffish. She'd given herself to him without reservation, even in these bizarre circumstances, where caution *surely* should prevail.

Even in the midst of his crisis, Thomas had ended up showing more restraint than her. It pained her a little, to recall how he'd leashed himself there at the end, how she'd heard both pain and intense pleasure in his climactic groans. She sensed that he sought her out to somehow ease the impact of his trauma . . . to escape it. Recently, she'd experienced a simultaneous desire to do precisely that.

They'd become partners in that unspoken goal.

But Sophie knew his crisis would come to an end. Whatever he'd pushed out of his memory, it would eventually return. Andy was right. The unit that Thomas had belonged to in the Navy required an enormous psychological tolerance for stress. Whatever had happened to Thomas in the past several days—what short period of time was hiding in the darkness of his consciousness—would eventually return, and likely very soon. Localized amnesias from acute traumas typically didn't last long.

It was one thing to be able to withstand the stress of war and imminent death. But Sophie knew personal loss, family grief—and betrayal?—was a different matter entirely.

Sophie couldn't precisely see what had caused Thomas's anguish, but she could see the murky outlines of it through the lens of how he was reacting. He had withstood sixteen years of stressful duty in the military, and not only endured it, but excelled, becoming a high-ranking officer and commanding his own unit. He'd survived three tours of duty in the Middle East. But despite all those years of constant, almost daily stress, events that had transpired in the past few days that related to his family had turned him into a bundle of tightly wound nerves and precipitated an anxiety response in him that he'd never begun to manifest as the leader of a bomb squad.

Sophie didn't *need* to know the precise details of what had happened. To see Thomas's response was sufficient for her to know whatever he'd seen in the past week, whatever he'd experienced . . . whatever he'd learned, had slashed and torn at his very soul.

It might have just been the unexpected deaths of Rick and Abel that had caused his traumatic reaction. But knowing what she knew through Andy's consultations about the Carlisle family and her cryptic, yet telling conversation with Agent Fisk, Sophie doubted it.

I feel like the ground has dropped out from under me.

Her face tightened with emotion when she recalled Thomas's anguish as they'd stood in the kitchen yesterday. In a psychological sense, he'd spoken a literal truth. Thomas Nicasio's entire world, his foundation, had crumbled and disintegrated beneath his feet.

She walked over to the window that looked out onto the lake. It seemed smooth and gray today, like an opaque mirror. She saw a fishing boat puttering into a cove at the far side of the lake, recognizing Thomas and Sherm by the dark red color of the craft and Sherm's bright orange fishing cap. Her gaze lingered on the other figure sitting at the back of the boat before it disappeared behind the trees that lined the cove.

He was safe, for the moment. She exhaled slowly, not realizing until that very moment she'd been anxious about his safety while he was absent.

She didn't know what she should do. All wisdom had abandoned her. It must have, to be falling for a man who could probably never return her feelings, given what he was experiencing.

She could only take each hour as it came.

She sighed and turned away from the window. They needed groceries and other supplies. She'd feed Guy the hamburger that still remained and try to check on his paw. Then she'd drive into Effingham and do a little shopping while Thomas was out fishing with Sherm.

It seemed like as good a plan as any, under these precarious circumstances.

And then later, when Thomas came home . . . she'd seduce him. Sophie felt a little guilty about being so premeditative. But the fact of the matter was, Thomas's strong desire for her was being fueled by his grief and trauma. Sophie had understood that from the beginning. The knowledge hurt, but Sophie didn't hold it against Thomas.

How could she?

After last night, she also knew one other crucial bit of information. He wasn't just using their sexual attraction to keep the memories at bay. Part of Thomas *wanted* to remember what had happened that first night when they'd made love, even if another part of him grasped for the darkness of forgetfulness. And whether she liked it or not, the electrical attraction he felt toward her had somehow become twined with his localized amnesia.

Previously, she'd conceptualized his hypersexuality as a means of escape from his trauma. Now, she'd grown to suspect that he was grasping for something as well when he made love to her so ravenously. He tried desperately to recall, even as another voice in him demanded he forget.

She needed to reach him. And if she could do that by drawing him closer to her using the only language his anguished body and mind would allow at the moment— volatile sex—then Sophie could accept that challenge.

It was a dangerous dance she was engaging in with Thomas. They moved right on the precipice of disaster. The realization that she was falling in love made her gambit even riskier.

She could only hope the situation didn't explode in her face at the smallest misstep.

An hour and a half later she went into her bathroom and closed and locked the door. She set the sack she'd just brought in from the car and the bottle of lubricant they'd used last night on the counter and glanced at herself in the mirror. The faint hint of a blush still lingered on her cheeks. Thank goodness Thomas hadn't arrived back at the cottage yet, or he might have noticed it.

It hadn't been anywhere near as mortifying and anxiety-provoking as she'd thought it would be to enter the adult sex store that wasn't far off the interstate near Effingham. She'd imagined sex-starved truckers, indecent proposals, and possibly illegal prostitution rings awaited inside the small shop. Instead, she'd found an empty parking lot and a bored middle-aged woman manning the cash register.

Thankfully, reality had paled compared to her fantasies.

The sex-shop sales clerk had asked Sophie if she needed any help finding anything, but her weary tone and the way she barely pulled her eyes away from the television perched behind the counter made it easy for Sophie to say *no*. She'd proceeded to walk up and down the aisles, her curiosity slowly starting to overshadow her worries about being harassed by sex-crazed truck drivers.

She withdrew the item she'd bought at the store and opened the box. Inside was a butt plug. Sophie had hesitated about which size to buy. It would be easier to insert one of the smaller ones, but wouldn't that make things more difficult in the end? She'd finally purchased a medium-sized one, thinking it would be better to get over any discomfort alone instead of having it interfere when she made love to Thomas.

She withdrew the black silicone plug and ran her fingertip over the fat head that would keep it in place once it was inserted. It looked like it might hurt considerably, so it surprised her that a flash of heat went through her pussy. She'd been too determined about her mission to seduce Thomas— to draw him closer, to break down some of his defenses—not to mention too embarrassed by her foray inside the adult store, to be aroused before.

But now, here in the privacy of her bathroom, excitement intertwined with her anxiety.

She wasn't sure precisely how to proceed in her little experiment, but the physician in her told her that the most important thing would be to relax. She stripped out of her floral print skirt, T-shirt, bra, sandals, and underwear and turned on the shower. After her flesh had grown warm from the jets of water, she picked up the soap and lathered her hands, the motions calling to mind vividly the image of Thomas swirling the soap in his large, masculine hands last night.

Without ever intending to do so, Sophie began to trace the trail on her flesh that Thomas had made in this same bathroom hours ago. She closed her eyes while her hands slicked over her belly and hips, then cradled the weight of her breasts. She thought of Thomas's gruff yet gentle command, *Offer them to me, Sophie.*

Her fingers rubbed and pinched at her nipples as she stood in the shower and imagined doing just that: offering her flesh to Thomas, making his eyes go dark with need . . . giving herself freely for his consumption. Her pelvis arched up against the pressure of the jetting water, eager for the stimulation on her cunt.

A moment later she turned her hips out of the water spray. Her hand moved in her soap-lathered pussy, stroking her burning clit. She used her other hand to penetrate her rectum, using the soap to ease her passage. Her fingers circled more frantically on her clit as her excitement mounted. She moaned; her eyes opened dazedly at the sound. She'd been so engrossed in her memories and fantasies, she hadn't even been aware of making a choice to masturbate.

She rinsed quickly and opened the shower curtain. The steam in the small room had grown so thick she didn't even catch a chill when she stepped out of the tub. She dried off and stood before the sink, naked.

She carefully washed the butt plug and coated it liberally with lubricant.

Her face looked wary in the mirror when she bent slightly over the sink and parted her bottom cheeks. She winced when she experimentally tried to slip the thick head into her rectum.

It wasn't going to work, she thought in rising frustration. Thomas had been right to doubt the possibility of the maneuver.

But she had taken his cock head into her ass last night; surely she could manage this.

She pressed her ass determinedly against the silicone plug. Pain shot through her body. She removed the plug from between her ass cheeks, but she didn't give up.

She applied the lubricant to herself and finger-fucked her ass for several seconds. Slowly, heat began to spread in her sex until she found it necessary to slip a finger between her labia and stimulate herself.

She had been a virgin to anal play until last night, and had been surprised by how much it had aroused her. Thomas may have thought she was being kind by asking him to put his cock in her, but she hadn't been. As she'd lain there restrained to the bed with her ass in the air, all she'd been able to think about was Thomas's beautiful cock, of him filling her in such a private place . . . of him taking so much pleasure in what she offered him freely.

It'd pained her, a little, when he'd refused her.

But if she could ready herself for him, maybe he wouldn't feel the need to restrain . . .

This time when she picked up the plug, she reached between her legs instead of around her hips. Thanks to the new angle and her increasing arousal, she was able to work the slippery plug into her body with only minimal discomfort.

When the silicone plug was lodged snugly in her ass, Sophie placed her hands on the vanity and panted, examining her reflection in the mirror. Her cheeks and lips were stained dark pink and her eyes were shiny with arousal. Her nipples stood at full-alert status.

She looked every inch a sex-primed woman: flushed, warm, and wet. For a few seconds, she just stared, so unaccustomed was she to seeing her sexuality fully exposed.

Thomas had given her this gift, she realized with dawning amazement. He'd introduced her to the creature who had always resided behind her conservative blouses and low-heeled pumps.

He'd taught her to like this earthy, sexy woman.

Her soft, soughing breath was the only sound in the silent room. She felt full and incendiary, but the inserted plug also created a pressure on her sex, making her pussy tingle with excitement.

What if Thomas didn't come home for hours? What if Sherm and Daisy asked him to stay for lunch?

Sophie's worries about having to wear the plug around for an undetermined period of time were shattered instantly when she heard the back door open.

"Sophie?" she heard Thomas call down the hallway.

Sophie froze, still bent over the sink. Her ass clenched around the invading plug and arousal stabbed at her clit.

"I . . . I'm in the bathroom, Thomas. I'll be out in a minute."

She leaned up and washed her hands, using cold water to try to dampen the heat that plagued her body. She applied some scented lotion and deodorant before she redressed carefully.

She hesitated before she opened the bathroom door.

It was useless; she couldn't prevail. She wasn't as strong as Thomas. She reached for the bottom of her skirt and lifted it.

She bit her lip to prevent a cry when she made herself come with her hand a few moments later, the plug in her ass and her desperate plan to seduce Thomas adding a hot spike of excitement to her orgasm.

CHAPTER **TWENTY-TWO**

Thomas knelt on the carpet in Sophie's living room, flipping through the old record albums stored in a crate. Sophie's parents might have been too self-involved to cherish their only daughter, but he had to admit, they had excellent taste in music. He smiled and withdrew one album. He'd just figured out how to operate the record player when he saw Sophie walk into the room from the corner of his eye. The vision of her snagged his gaze and held as firmly as one of Sherm's handmade lures in a fish's mouth.

"Wow," he said.

The becoming color in her cheeks deepened.

"Wow . . . what?" she asked, just as the opening notes of Elvis singing "Can't Help Falling in Love" resounded from the speakers.

"You're not wearing a bra." He glanced up from the riveting site of Sophie's full breasts pressing against the thin fabric of a light pink T-shirt. He realized he'd sounded stupid, but in fact, he was just dumbfounded by her beauty. "You *never* go around braless."

He experienced a moment of regret at his bluntness when

she glanced away in embarrassment. "I . . . I hurried out of the shower when I heard you."

"I'm not complaining. Trust me, I'm not complaining. Hey . . . look at this," he said, holding up the record album in his hand in an attempt to ease her bout of self-consciousness. That such a gorgeous woman would ever feel uneasy about her body was shocking to him, but he'd come to accept that in Sophie's case, it was a plain fact. She'd been born with the genes of a Hollywood film goddess, but no one was more interested in denying that obvious truth than Sophie herself.

He hated that her self-consciousness bordered on shame at times, but he cherished that character trait as well, because it helped him to know Sophie better. To understand her. He doubted she'd ever get to the point where she strutted around in low-cut dresses and spiked heels, but he was more than thrilled to see she'd dared to greet him with only a scrap of material cradling her breasts.

Besides, Sophie braless, flushed and warm from a shower, was sexier than stilettos and half-bared breasts any day.

"This is an original recording," he continued, awe tingeing his tone as he held up the album.

He stared, transfixed by her small smile.

"My parents have quite a collection. I keep telling them I'll send it to them—it must be worth thousands—but they're apparently happy with their CDs and iPods."

"Their loss is my gain," he said gruffly. Even though he was trying to make up for his earlier bluntness, he found that he couldn't stand it another second. He needed to have Sophie in his arms. He set down the record album and beckoned to her.

"Come on. Dance with me."

Her smile broadened as she walked toward him. He didn't know why, but the image of her coming to him on that gray, rainy day—her face luminous, her hand outstretched, her hips swaying subtly, a secret in those dark eyes that always drew him in like a moth to flame—something told him that vision of Sophie would stay with him for a long, long time.

He reached out his hand and she took it.

"That's better," he murmured as he enfolded her in his arms and breathed in her scent. He pressed his lips to her neck as they moved to the music. "God, you smell good." He smiled when he felt her shiver.

"Did you catch any fish?" she asked.

He glanced up distractedly. "Fish?"

"Yeah . . . you know . . . what you were trying to catch on the end of that pole out there in the lake? No fish stories, huh?" Sophie laughed softly when he didn't answer because he was dropping kisses on her cheek, jaw, and the corner of her lips.

"I've got better things to do than tell stories," he mumbled before he dipped his tongue in the center of the beguiling target of her lips. She responded to him with equal hunger, coming up on her tiptoes to meet him, pressing her breasts against him, her stiff nipples poking between his ribs, tangling her tongue with his and applying a slight suction. His body buzzed in pleasant anticipation.

Touching Sophie, surrounding himself in her taste, always kept the dark shadows at bay. Had he really only been away from her for four hours? It felt like days.

The beast in him had fully wakened a moment later. "You taste like sex, Sophie Gable."

"Do I?" she whispered next to his lips.

"You know you do," Thomas said as they slowly turned on the carpet and Elvis crooned to them. *Wise men say only fools rush in, indeed,* he thought with a mental roll of his eyes as he considered the lyrics to the song. Unfortunately, foolishness had never before felt remotely this potent.

"Why do you keep looking at me like that?" he asked after a moment of enjoying the ensnarement of Sophie's liquid dark eyes. Sometimes, it felt like he was falling into them.

"I'm planning on seducing you," she said.

His lips and his cock twitched in unison. "*Nice.* But since when does that require planning?"

She gave him an arch look. He chuckled and kissed the end of her nose.

"So, how are you planning to do it?" he asked in a conspiratorial whisper near her ear.

"I don't know," she replied. She shifted her head back from his seeking lips and studied him soberly. "I was just going to wing it—"

Wing away, he thought dazedly when she placed her hand at the back of his head, pushed him down for a kiss that blew him away. It managed to strike him as sweet and voracious, innocent and skilled all at once.

His entire world collapsed to the feeling of Sophie's soft, vibrant body in his arms, the seductive movement of her lips and tongue, her delicious, pervading flavor, the prized scent rising off her skin that always perfumed the air after—

He sealed their kiss. She gave him a startled look when he abruptly started to lift her skirt.

"What are you doing?" she murmured at the same moment that he dipped two fingers beneath the tiny panties she wore. He grunted in arousal.

"You're all creamed up, Sophie," he rasped as he slid his finger into the juicy crevice between her labia. She inhaled sharply when he flicked at her clit. He smiled down at her. Just like it had last night, when he'd pulled out that big cock she kept in her bedside table, the contrast in Sophie's fresh, girl-next-door appearance and the evidence of her deep sensuality aroused him monumentally. His eyes widened as he continued to stroke her and he realized just how wet she was.

"This isn't just from getting turned on. You just came, didn't you?" he asked quietly.

"Thomas. Don't." She grabbed his hand and pushed him away, giving him a reprimanding look. "I'm supposed to be seducing you."

His smile widened. God, she was amazing. He reached for her hand when she used it to smooth her skirt back over her hips and thighs.

She gasped in disbelief when he lifted it to his mouth and slid her forefinger into his mouth.

"Never mind. I have my answer," he said, his voice sounding garbled while he laved her skin with his tongue.

He closed his mouth around her. Her taste inundated his brain and had far-reaching effects on his body. He took one last gentle suck on her finger before he released it, only to capture the second one greedily with his lips. He kissed her knuckles after he'd found every last remnant of her sweet essence.

"What got you so turned on, Sophie?"

It wasn't entirely fair that he'd asked her a question because he wouldn't allow her to respond. He was too busy devouring her. He couldn't keep his mouth off hers. Something about tasting her juices on her own fingers had made him go a little nuts.

A lot nuts.

He pressed her to him tightly while his hands explored every straight line and curve on her body and his tongue searched avidly for more of her secrets in the depths of her mouth.

He grunted in dissatisfaction when she backed out of his arms.

"Thomas, no . . . wait."

He paused and took stock of himself as he stared at her and panted lightly.

"Sorry," he said after a moment. "I really do turn into an animal around you, don't I?"

A tendril of light gold hair fell onto her cheek as she shook her head decisively. "No. It's not that. I like the way you make love to me. I . . . I love it." He sensed both her softness and her strength when she met his gaze. "But you always bowl me over. I want to be the one to make love to you."

His heartbeat throbbed in his ears in the seconds that followed. "Just tell me one thing."

Her elegantly arched brows rose.

"Is that what you were thinking about when you were touching yourself in that bathroom?"

"Yes. In part." The color in her cheeks became even more vivid, but she held his stare and her voice sounded smooth and even.

He threw up his hands. "Then I'm all yours. Do whatever

you want to me. If it got you that turned on, I'm all for it. The way I've been behaving lately, it wouldn't surprise me if you wanted to be the one to take charge. Probably safer all around," he added under his breath.

She stepped toward him. "No. That's not what I meant. I'm not worried about *safety*. I was just thinking I'd like to be able to . . . to touch you without interference."

"Really?"

She shook her head in mild exasperation. "Why would that surprise you?"

He shrugged. "So . . . what do you want me to do?"

She licked her lower lip. Thomas suspected she did it out of anxiety, but his whole body tightened anyway. Why did he think everything she did was sex distilled?

"Why don't you start out by taking off your clothes. And . . . you can lay on the couch, if you like."

Thomas stripped with rapid efficiency while the notes to "Puppet on a String" resounded from the speakers and Sophie watched him with dark eyes that shone like moonlight on two deep pools.

CHAPTER **TWENTY-THREE**

The plug seemed to throb in her ass as she watched Thomas remove his shirt with a compelling flex of defined muscle. It surprised her how much the sensation aroused her. Apparently there were sympathetic nerves between her ass and pussy that had never been fully awakened before, because her clit tingled with excitement. It'd felt delicious when Thomas had stroked it just now.

She inhaled slowly when Thomas dropped his boxer briefs and his long, firm erection sprang free. The buzz of her clit amplified to a burn.

The silicone plug felt slightly uncomfortable lodged in her body, but the pressure it caused was undeniably arousing. She was surprised to learn the far-flung effects of the plug. The bottoms of her feet felt hot and her breasts were heavy and achy, as if they possessed a mind of their own and were demanding to be touched and fondled. Even the nerves in her mouth seemed to tingle, making her lips feel warm, swollen, and overly sensitive.

Thomas flung off the last of his clothing and sprawled back on the couch, pulling a pillow beneath his head, and Sophie had to admit . . . maybe it wasn't just the ass plug that was making her entire body hum with sexual awareness. He lay there—a long stretch of defined muscle and male tumescence—and smiled at her.

"Okay. I'm ready to play doctor."

Sophie snorted with laughter. He joined in her mirth as she walked toward him. It felt so good—so *right* to laugh with Thomas. His humor had been cloaked by the shadow of his grief. She realized that Thomas Nicasio was meant to laugh. The fact that she'd rarely seen him do it in their short acquaintance caused sadness to stab through her arousal.

"What?" he asked, still grinning broadly. He must have seen her falter in her mirth.

"Nothing. I just . . . hold on. I'm going to get something."

His eyebrows shot up on his forehead when she returned a few seconds later carrying the bottle of lubricant.

"You said last night it was a massage oil as well," Sophie murmured as she knelt beside the couch.

She glanced up at him from beneath lowered brows as she poured some of the light, silky liquid into her palm. She rubbed her hands together, smearing the oil. Sophie couldn't help but notice that his cock lurched up from where it rested on his belly when she touched him. He said nothing when she began to smooth her hands and curious fingertips over his skin, lightly massaging dense pectoral and shoulder muscles. She watched the progress of her exploration of his body, but she sensed his stare on her face, and knew that he watched her with as much focus as she studied him.

It felt like a decadent treat, to be able to stroke and caress such a beautiful man without constraint. She discovered a ticklish strip of skin along his right rib. She glanced up when he started and they shared a smile.

"Would you put your arms above your head, please?" she murmured.

He did so slowly, holding her stare.

"You can't expect me just to lay here for much longer," he said while she applied more massage oil to her hands and they made a squishy sound as she rubbed them together. The inserted plug in addition to the opportunity to touch

Thomas unhindered was making things between her thighs exceptionally wet.

"I *do* expect it," she assured him.

She felt the tremor in his flesh when she swept her hands down the fascinating diagonal slants at the sides of his torso that ran from just below his armpit to his waist. It did something to her . . . to feel such a strong man tremble with excitement from her touch, to hold his heart between her hands.

Her gaze flickered down to his erection, which looked firm and delicious. A drop of clear pre-ejaculate beaded at the slit. It shifted on his belly, as though her glance had been a physical caress.

"Touch me, Sophie," he murmured.

She leaned down and inserted a tiny, erect, dark brown nipple between her lips. He groaned roughly and cradled her head in his palm, pressing her to him as she studied the tiny bumps on his nipple with her tongue.

When she lifted her head a moment later, Thomas didn't appear to like her absence.

"Come back," he demanded, reaching for her.

Sophie laughed softly. "I will. Put your hands back above your head first."

He did so, albeit with a scowl.

She felt the tension rise in his muscles as she continued to explore his body with curious fingertips. She molded his strong, hard thigh muscles in her hands while her gaze remained fixed on his full testicles and swollen cock. Everything between her legs, from her clit to her pussy, from her perineum to her ass sizzled with sexual energy.

He grabbed her wrist when she slid her hand partially beneath him and palmed a tight buttock. His other hand captured her free hand. Their gazes held as he placed her palm on his teeming cock. He folded his hand above hers and guided her motions, lifting the heavy column of flesh off his abdomen.

For several taut, delicious moments, they stared at one another as he moved her lubricated hand up and down the length of his cock. Sophie felt the air burn in her lungs. He looked magnificent at that moment, his muscles tight with arousal and gleaming from the oil, his dark green eyes pinning her with a fierce, feral stare.

"I'm not very good at giving up control," he rasped.

"I didn't want you to give up control. This isn't about that," she whispered. She clamped her thighs together tight, trying to alleviate a pinch of arousal, when he began to move her hand more rapidly over his cock.

"What is it about then?"

"I wanted to show you that I trust that you won't lose control." She placed another lubricated hand beneath the one that already fisted his penis and moved it in unison with the other, jacking him more thoroughly. He hissed in pleasure. "I want you to believe it; I want *you* to trust in yourself again. You're grief-stricken, Thomas. Not dangerous."

A muscle flinched in his cheek. "How can you be so sure?"

"Because. I am," she stated, knowing what she said wasn't logical, but that it made perfect sense to her, nonetheless. She released his cock. "I'm going to undress," she explained when he kept her hand clutched in his, unwilling for her to stop touching him.

He let go of her reluctantly.

She stood and grabbed the hem of her T-shirt, glancing out the large window that looked out on the yard and lake, assuring herself there were no unexpected spectators. She felt slightly feverish, she realized, as she shrugged out of the shirt and let it drop to the carpet. Her skin was overly sensitive and prickly.

Things felt positively molten between her thighs.

She panted lightly as she pushed the print skirt off her hips and stood before Thomas wearing only a skimpy pair of pink silk panties. His nostrils flared as he examined her and his gaze predictably stuck on her breasts. Sophie had a long history of becoming annoyed when men stared at her chest instead of her face, but Thomas's gaze was different.

It made her feel beautiful.

And because he'd given her that, she returned the gift by

cradling her breasts in her hands and making him an offering of her aching nipples.

He growled low in his throat and lowered his arms, extending them toward her.

"Come here." This time, his low command wasn't something she was even faintly interested in disobeying.

She winced as she straddled his lap and the pressure of the butt plug amplified. Thomas didn't seem to notice, though. He was too busy staring at her breasts and leaning up from his pillow.

She cried out shakily when he surrounded a nipple with his hot mouth. Her cheeks felt so hot. Her clit and the soles of her feet burned in sympathy with her nipple. She laced her fingers through his thick hair and held him to her, her facial muscles clenching tight when the need inside of her grew so sharp, it verged on pain.

He drew on her demandingly, amplifying the growing pressure swelling in her body. She shifted her hips and captured his penis between her thighs. She ground her pussy down on the stiff pillar.

"*Use your teeth,*" she begged.

She felt his teeth on the tender flesh. She cried out as her body shook in orgasm.

A moment later, she opened her eyelids, only to see Thomas leaning back on the pillow. He looked a little incredulous.

And a lot aroused.

"What's got you so primed, Sophie?"

She licked her upper lip and pressed down on his solid chest with her hands, steadying herself as she stood next to the couch. She kept her eyes averted as she pulled her panties down her legs.

She turned her back to him.

Even as aroused as she was, it still was one of the hardest things she'd ever done to expose herself to him in these circumstances. She peered over her shoulder when he didn't respond immediately. As she would have guessed, his gaze was glued to the base of the black plug that was wedged between her ass cheeks.

If he'd appeared a little incredulous before by the evidence of her wild arousal, he looked downright stunned now.

"Where did you get that?" he asked as he slowly sat up from his reclining position.

"I bought it this morning," Sophie whispered. She turned, feeling both vulnerable and aroused at the impact of his scorching stare. Her ass throbbed around the plug and her clit answered with a pinch of pleasure. She was really going to have to check out her medical books on the nervous system to discover why ass stimulation could have such amazing effects on the body—

"Why?" Thomas asked sharply. He stood slowly, his long, unfolding body, stiff, glistening cock and feral expression seeming a bit intimidating. He stepped toward her. "Why the hell did you do that, Sophie?" He came closer, so that their bodies were just inches apart; the moist tip of his cock head almost kissed her bare hip.

"Sophie?"

She jerked her gaze off his erection.

"*Why?*"

She swallowed convulsively. Was it her imagination, or was he asking why she'd uncharacteristically walked into an adult sex shop and bought a butt plug or why she was doing this with him . . . sheltering him, having wild sex with him . . . falling in love?

She held his stare and took a steadying breath. "I did it because I wanted to."

He leaned down over her until Sophie drowned in the depths of green eyes flecked with fire. She felt emotion swell in her chest, like subterranean water finding an outlet and surging wildly to the surface.

"You wanted to *what*?"

"I wanted you to trust yourself again." When his stare just continued to bore through her, she added in a whisper, "I wanted to give myself to you, Thomas."

"*Sophie,*" he hissed. He shut his eyelids for a moment,

his facial muscles going rigid. She felt his cock flick up against her hip, dabbing her skin with warm moisture. His eyes opened, but he avoided her gaze as he turned and grabbed the bottle of lubricant. He reached for her hand blindly and led her toward the hallway and her bedroom.

Sophie had to hurry to keep up with his long-legged stride. A mixture of anxious anticipation and wild arousal caused her blood to pump wildly in her veins and her ass to pulse around the inserted plug, creating a low level, pleasurable burn all along her cunt.

She was breathless by the time he pulled her into the bedroom.

"Get on the bed on your hands and knees," he rasped. She crawled onto the mattress. "No. Move a little farther up on the bed."

His rigid expression and taut orders didn't offend her. She sensed the edge of his excitement like a sharp file scraping gently across her sensitive skin. When she settled in position, he flipped open her bedside table and took out the vibrator and control box. She watched him, as she panted in excitement, while he lubed up his straining erection, his actions rapid and perfunctory . . . like he meant business.

She moaned softly, her arousal mounting exponentially at the sight of him readying himself. He crawled behind her on the bed, bringing the vibrator and control panel with him.

"Put the vibrator on your clit while I try to get inside you. It'll help," he added gruffly when she turned to look at him. His gaze snagged on hers.

"Are you sure you want to do this?"

"Oh, yeah," she replied with emphasis.

He tried to smile, but his muscles appeared to be too tight to cooperate.

"Just tell me to stop at any time if you get too uncomfortable. Okay?"

She nodded as he flipped the *on* button for the vibrator. A tremor went through her when she used one hand to hold the rubber cock head to her overly sensitive clit. When she moaned loudly at the sensation, Thomas leaned over her, his slick, stiff cock brushing an ass cheek, and turned down the power a notch. He kissed the side of her heaving ribs with a hot mouth before he knelt behind her again.

"Jesus, you're beautiful," she heard him mutter under his breath from behind her. "You're gonna kill me, Sophie."

She cried out shakily when he turned the base of the plug, withdrew it ever so slightly and pushed it back into her.

"Hurt?" he muttered tightly.

"No," she gasped. Pain hadn't been what made her cry out.

She felt him move behind her, positioning himself. He spread his hand over her left hip and gently pried back her ass cheek. Sophie whimpered when he removed the plug.

He cursed under his breath. Her vocal cords seemed to vibrate in tandem with the sex toy when he arrowed the first several inches of his cock into her ass.

"*Ahhhhh*," she moaned. She felt every muscle—including the one that encircled Thomas's cock—clamp tight.

"I'm stopping," he grated out behind her. "Are you okay?"

Her head had fallen forward and her hair hung around her face. The minimal discomfort she had experienced at his penetration faded. Her entire awareness had zeroed down to the sensation of him inside her ass. She pressed the vibrator tighter to her clit and a ripple of excitement traveled all the way up her tailbone to her neck. She responded to Thomas's inquiry with one word.

"More."

He grabbed both of her ass cheeks and sunk into her another few inches. He hissed in pleasure.

"Christ, you're so hot. And so fucking tight."

Sophie pressed back with a hand on the mattress and mewled in pleasure as she slid his well-lubricated cock deeper. He grunted and spanked a buttock in gentle reprimand.

"*Don't,* Sophie," he bit out. "If you had any idea what I wanted to do to you right now, you wouldn't tease."

Sophie felt so full, so excited that she found she couldn't respond. But she hadn't been teasing. She had a good feeling she knew exactly what Thomas wanted to do, because she wanted it, too.

It felt incredible. He seemed to throb directly into her flesh, feeling closer than she'd ever harbored a man in her body, more immediate . . . more incendiary.

She held her breath in cresting excitement as the vibrator tickled her clit and Thomas began to pump gently, edging his cock farther and farther into her.

"That's right. Try to relax," he murmured behind her as he fucked her ass carefully with the upper half of his cock, pressing slightly deeper into her with each stroke. Sophie uncrossed her eyes.

Had he really just said that? *Try to relax*?

She showed him just how unlikely that was when her entire body seemed to seize in orgasm.

When the crashing waves of pleasure had receded and she came back to herself, the sound of her own soughing breath resounding loudly in her ears, Sophie realized that she'd dropped the vibrator to the mattress and Thomas's hair-sprinkled thighs pressed directly against the lower curve of her buttocks. His balls nestled between her spread ass cheeks and the length of his cock throbbed deep inside her.

"I can't take it anymore, Sophie."

The palpable tension in his body and the strangled sound of his voice made her heart squeeze tight in her chest.

"Then don't, Tom."

He made a choked sound.

"Brace yourself."

Sophie's eyes went wide at the tautly uttered words. Her mouth hung open but her breath froze in her lungs when he withdrew his cock and plunged back into her again. He held her ass in his big hands and began fucking her with long, thorough strokes. His low, feral grunts of satisfaction and the staccato rhythm of his pelvis smacking against her buttocks filled her ears like a drumbeat of desire.

Gone was his restraint. He had endured while she found pleasure, but now he seemed intent on taking his due.

Sophie gloried in the storm of sensation and emotion that crashed all around her.

His thrusts grew more rapid and forceful, making her groan roughly.

"I told you to stay away from me."

He firmed his hold on her ass and bent one long leg, resting his foot on the mattress, using the extra leverage to take her harder.

"I . . . don't . . . want . . . you . . . *away*," Sophie muttered between clenched teeth, every word popping out of her mouth at the same moment he smacked against her ass and filled her to capacity with his straining desire.

"Aww, Jesus . . . *Sophie*."

She used all of her strength to brace herself, barely keeping herself from pitching over, when he plunged into her and held her to him with a desperate grasp. Her eyes went wide when she felt his cock swell. His howl of release stood in direct opposition to last night, when he'd restrained himself so carefully.

Sophie gasped raggedly while he came, her face tight with emotion. His cock was so swollen, so primed that it caused her some mild discomfort when he held her ass and thrust tightly, emptying himself into her. But it gave her more satisfaction than she'd ever experienced, knowing that he'd trusted himself once again to let go.

Knowing that she'd pleased him.

Feeling Thomas throbbing in climax in such an intimate place aroused her all over again. She remained still when he eventually withdrew and leaned over her, breathing heavily. But when he caught his breath and fell to the bed, pulling her down next to him and turning to face her, Sophie pressed her hand between her thighs and winced.

"I'm sorry," Thomas muttered. He stretched out next to her on the bed and pressed his face to her neck. Sophie whimpered when his hand moved between her thighs, and he worked his magic. It took her all of thirty seconds before she shuddered once again in orgasm. He pressed kisses to her neck and shoulder while she came.

When she'd quieted, he settled his mouth on hers.

"Sophie," he whispered against her lips a moment later as their stares held.

She inhaled slowly, praying she wasn't imagining the myriad of messages she read in his eyes.

"My whole life," he said quietly, "I never had anything that was just mine."

Her eyes burned. For some reason, she knew exactly what he meant. In a way, they were both orphans: both belonging, and yet knowing deep down that they *didn't* belong, recognizing on some level they were extras to a family unit that had been intact and self-sufficient without their presence.

She furrowed her fingers through the thick hair at his nape while her other hand cupped his jaw. She could feel his heart still beating erratically where his chest pressed against her ribs.

She wanted to tell him that she understood . . . that her heart had never been truly owned any more than she'd ever owned another's, but her throat was suddenly constricted with emotion.

"Shhh," he soothed softly before he pressed his fingertips and then his mouth against hers in order to still her trembling lips.

CHAPTER **TWENTY-FOUR**

Let's go take a shower," Thomas murmured after she'd cried silently in his arms for a minute or two and then quieted. She was glad he didn't ask her for the reason for her tears. Or at least she was grateful until she realized maybe he didn't want to hear her answer.

They showered together, talking only minimally, letting their caressing fingertips speak for them. Thomas gently washed the remnants of their lovemaking off her body. She turned away as he attempted to clean her cheeks, but he held her chin with his hand and continued, refusing to be rebuffed, and using a damp washcloth to wipe away the tracks of her tears.

She felt like an idiot when more fell to take their place—why was her chest so full of emotion?—but he didn't seem to mind, silently washing the fresh tears away with the washcloth and finally drinking them with his wet, warm lips.

They got back into bed after their shower and held each other while raindrops pattered on the windowpanes. Slowly, cautiously, she let it happen—allowed the spell of her growing love to settle and encompass her just as surely as Thomas's embrace.

They didn't sleep, but continued to commune with touches and softly murmured conversations.

After a while, however, her stomach felt hollow with hunger and Thomas began to move restlessly. Sophie sensed that he was too active of a man to spend long awake in a bed . . . if he wasn't making love, anyway. He seemed increasingly eager to do just that. His lazy kisses on her breasts were becoming hungrier by the second. It amazed her that she found his fascination with her breasts endearing—and arousing—instead of annoying, and she was increasingly focused on the trail of his talented mouth. Before he could reach a peaking nipple though, her stomach growled loudly.

He raised his head, looking adorable and sexy with his hair tousled on his forehead and an incredulous expression on his face.

"I never ate breakfast," she laughed.

He hugged her tightly, rolling her across his body until she was at the edge of the bed near the door. "Go on," he growled, swatting her ass playfully, the resulting crack making her jump out of bed. "Better get you fed before I make another meal out of you."

Thomas said that Daisy had made them a large breakfast in celebration of the six fish Sherm and he had brought back, so Sophie ate her meal of toast and fruit alone. Thomas sat with her at the breakfast bar, turned in the swivel stool so that he could see the steady rain falling onto the gray lake. He sipped his coffee, his mood becoming more and more somber with each passing second.

A sense of helplessness pressed down on her when she once again recognized that he was emotionally withdrawing. She wondered if her earlier bout of crying following their lovemaking had ruined her chances of trying to have an honest conversation with him . . . of trying to reach him. He'd been so intent on trying to soothe her unrest that she hadn't taken a chance—not just with seducing him, but with encouraging him to talk to her, by telling him the truth—like she'd promised herself she would.

"Thomas," she began impulsively, "there's something I wanted to—"

But he had begun talking at the same moment she did.

"You seem like you're in good shape. Do you want to go running with me?"

Her mouth hung open. She glanced out the picture window.

"It's raining outside."

He stood.

"Not hard. And I feel . . . restless."

Sophie studied his face, seeing the tension that had crept back into his muscles and pinched at his features. How could she deal with his inner demons, invisible as they were to not just her, but him as well?

Well, at least he asked you to go with him this time, instead of taking off all worked up like he did last night, Sophie thought, trying to staunch her disappointment.

She gave him a small smile and nodded. "Sure. Just let me change."

They returned forty-five minutes later, both of them soaked through with rain and a healthy salting of sweat. Thomas hadn't said much during their run, once again seeming preoccupied. When they returned, Sophie said she wanted to open the boathouse door for Guy. She didn't like to think of the little fox out there in the woods, drenched and injured. She'd told Thomas to go into the house without her, but he'd silently accompanied her to the boathouse and helped her arrange a little den of old blankets for the fox.

They entered on the side porch afterwards so they could remove their wet tennis shoes and socks on the tile floor before entering the house. Sophie's gaze was snagged by the image of Thomas whipping his T-shirt over his head and the flex and ripple of gleaming, supple muscle. It was on the edge of her tongue to suggest they shower again together— maybe this time she wouldn't melt into a puddle of tears— but she stopped herself when he turned his back to her and headed toward the house.

"I smell like the inside of a marching boot," he muttered. "I'll shower in the extra bedroom."

And Sophie was left standing alone on the screen porch, holding her soggy tennis shoe and knowing her attempt at cracking the barrier of his defenses had utterly failed.

Seduction hadn't worked, she thought grimly as she peeled off a wet footie. She might have broken down the walls *she'd* erected against honesty and intimacy, but apparently Thomas's remained intact.

She was going to have to take a risk. She was going to have to do it—just tell him.

It was time to go, Thomas thought as he stared out the picture window morosely later that afternoon. He needed to get back to his work . . . back to his life. It was *past* time. It'd never been time to *begin* with, he thought with rising exasperation.

He'd tell Sophie as soon as she finished her shower. What he'd said earlier about not being able to walk away from her was true, but he could see her in the city . . . it wasn't like they lived on opposite sides of the country.

A voice inside him kept shouting out that he should leave her for now, though.

His life was too up in the air at the moment. He was too much of a downer . . . a heavy burden on what should have been a relaxing vacation for her.

She walked into the living room a few minutes later wearing a pair of faded jeans, a long-sleeved, ivory button-down shirt that ghosted her full breasts and not a trace of makeup, her bare feet padding silently on the carpet.

The voice demanding that he flee faded to background noise. Sophie had a way of taking center stage in his awareness.

Even though she looked all soft and touchable after her shower, there was a determined cast to her features.

"Thomas, we have to talk."

"You want me to go, don't you?" he asked grimly. He may have just been contemplating leaving, but the idea of Sophie not wanting him there anymore felt like a kick to the gut with a steel-toed boot.

"No. That's not it. No, of course not." She opened her mouth, as if she wanted to say more, but she stopped herself. She walked toward him, glancing distractedly out at the lake and the heavy downpour. "Jeez, it's getting worse, isn't it?"

"What do you want to talk to me about?"

"Sit down," she said, nodding at the couch in front of the picture window.

She didn't speak once they'd sat, but just looked down at her hands folded on her thighs. A strange expression overcame her face. She shifted her right hip up and reached between the sofa cushion, extracting his BlackBerry. He barely acknowledged it when she handed it to him.

"Sophie, what's wrong?"

"It's not that anything is *wrong*, necessarily—maybe you'll think differently—but . . . well, there's something I've been meaning to tell you, Thomas. Something about your brother."

"What about him?"

"You know how I'm friends with Andy Lancaster? Well, sometimes Andy would consult with me about his cases. He wouldn't give me any names," she added quickly, her big eyes glued to his face. "But . . . well, I was there in the offices. You remember? . . . We used to see each other . . . on . . . on the nights when . . ."

"When my brother Rick was there for his sessions," Thomas finished woodenly when she faded off.

She nodded.

He studied her narrowly. "Isn't that sort of unethical for Dr. Lancaster? To blab about his patients to someone else?"

"No . . . it's really not, Thomas," she exclaimed in a rush. "I used to work as a clinical social worker years ago. There's no other psychologists in our practice, so I was the only one with any degree of expertise that Andy could talk to. It's common for psychologists to consult—to try to get distance on their cases, to gain some objectivity. And like I said, Andy never says names. He maintains confidentiality. I just sort of . . . put two and two together on my own."

He felt as if ice water rushed down his spine and was slowly seeping to his extremities. "You *know*? You know about what Rick's source told him? About his investigations into the mob?"

He didn't even realize he was standing until Sophie stood, too. Gone was the vibrant, apricot tint of her skin. Her face looked washed out of color. Her throat convulsed, as though she were having trouble swallowing. His heartbeat began to pound out a warning in his ears when he read the compassion and anxiety in her dark eyes.

"Rick's source lied, Sophie. He *lied*."

"How . . . *how* do you know?" she asked shakily.

"Because it's *ludicrous*, that's how I know," he bellowed. "Do you think I wouldn't know if the man I'd lived with for eight years of my life, the man who I've called *Father* for twenty-six years, was a fucking *sociopath*?" He started to walk away from her, but then jerked around, making her start back. "Is that why you keep asking me about my dad? Because you suspect he's guilty? What the hell did Rick tell Lancaster? It's not like *Rick* believed the crap his source was feeding him!" He grabbed her shoulders. "Did he, Sophie? Are you trying to tell me Rick told his psychologist that he actually *believed* that his own father was a criminal?"

"*No*. Andy told me that he was confused and upset by the information his source gave him about your father's long-term involvement in illegal activities."

"*Alleged* involvement. Rick was a highly respected investigative reporter for the *Chicago Tribune*, as you probably already know—since you probably know every other damn thing about my life," Thomas added bitterly. "Rick used a pseudonym for his articles and books. He believed that the two-bit criminal he'd cultivated as a source—a weasel by the name of Bernard Cokey—didn't know Rick's real name. But the son of a bitch obviously *did* know he was feeding his lies to the son of Joseph Carlisle. He probably planned on extorting money from Rick for not going to some other journalist or cop with the information. He just never got the chance to do it before Rick was killed."

He felt like throwing something when he saw the expression in her eyes.

"Why are you looking at me like that?" he seethed in a low voice.

"Thomas . . . you're sure? You're *sure* that Bernard Cokey is a liar?"

His brows furrowed in puzzlement. "You said that Rick didn't believe the crap Cokey fed him. Why are you even asking me? I've told you my opinion."

She licked her lower lip nervously. "Well . . . according to Andy, Rick said that he *did* trust Cokey. Everything else he'd told him about Outfit operations checked out. He couldn't understand why he'd fingered Joseph Carlisle—"

"The rat-bastard did it because he knew Rick's real name and planned on squeezing him for money," Thomas boomed. When he saw Sophie flinch, he released her as if her shoulders had burned him.

"I'm going for a drive."

"Thomas . . . wait . . . The weather is awful. You're upset."

But he didn't pause as he stormed toward the back door. He felt violated . . . like Sophie was some kind of freaking psychic who had pried into his brain against his will. All this time, she'd known about the fiery splinter in his spirit, the volatile lie that Rick had revealed to him less than two weeks before he'd died.

He slammed the door shut behind him, ignoring Sophie's pleas for him to stop and stepped out into the heavy downpour.

He couldn't *believe* Sophie had known about Bernard Cokey and his defamations the whole time. The whole fucking time . . . ever since the first moment he'd touched her, she'd known about the shocking, bitter lies that had plagued not just Rick in the last days of his life, but Thomas as well.

A wave of vertigo and nausea struck him a few seconds later as he sat in the driver's seat and turned on the ignition.

He'd been wondering about Sophie's motivations for the past few days. It'd been damn strange, the way she'd shown up at the Mannero warehouse just minutes before it exploded. And hadn't he been suspicious of her as he sat in this very seat and drove behind her on the interstate on the way to the lake house? Hadn't he become suspicious of why she'd insisted that he—a new lover, but still . . . a near stranger—come with her to the intimate surroundings of her vacation house on Haven Lake? But then he'd spent time with her . . . become overwhelmed by his consuming desire and her soft, soothing touches.

An image sliced through his spinning, chaotic thoughts, jarring him—the memory of Agent Fisk standing in his office and studying Thomas with his penetrating stare.

Our informant isn't a criminal, Mr. Nicasio. Not in the slightest.

Jesus.

Sophie was an upstanding citizen, and she'd known all the murky, explosive details of Rick's investigations. What if she'd gone to the authorities after Rick was killed and told them what she knew? He thought of how she'd been there along with the FBI at the warehouse parking lot before it exploded.

What if she was still collaborating with the authorities, even now?

The curtain over the back door fluttered and he saw her pale face glance out at him. His gut lurched.

He didn't believe Sophie was capable of such cold-heartedness . . . capable of manipulation and betrayal.

He *couldn't* believe that.

But given all available evidence, how could he *not*?

He saw the back door opening and tossed the BlackBerry he still clutched in his hand into the passenger seat. He shoved the car into reverse and stomped on the accelerator. His gaze was on the rearview window as he hurtled down the long, gravel path, but his focus was on the corner of his vision, where he saw Sophie rushing out the back door.

For a split second, his attention broke. He stared at Sophie's anxious face, the sound of the gravel spitting as he nearly went off the road snapping him out of his trance.

CHAPTER **TWENTY-FIVE**

Hours later, Sophie picked up her cell phone for the tenth time, cursed under her breath, and tossed it back down on the kitchen counter.

Who was she going to call?

She didn't know Thomas's cell phone number, not that it would matter if she did. His battery was dead, and she doubted he'd answer her call even if she could get through to him.

She'd gotten into her car and followed on Thomas's heels as soon as he'd shot like a disoriented bat out of hell down her driveway, nearly careening into the ditch that lined the path before he'd neatly corrected and resumed his escape. She hadn't caught a glimpse of his car anywhere—not on any of the increasingly wet and flooding surrounding country roads, not at the gas stations or Wal-Mart in town, not in Sherm and Daisy's driveway, not at the fish and tackle shop at the north end of the lake.

She stared out the kitchen window. The rain continued, relentless and steady. Through the thick mist, she made out that the ditches at the side of her driveway were flooded with several feet of water.

She thought of the pain on Thomas's face when she'd told

him she knew about what Rick's investigations had uncovered. The betrayal.

She picked up her cell phone again. *The police*. That's who she should call. She'd just tell them that Thomas had left here in a highly agitated state, and that she was worried about his safety.

But she received an incoming call after dialing two numbers.

"Hello?" Sophie answered.

"Sophie? It's Sherm."

"I know," Sophie replied, slightly impatient. Sherm and Daisy didn't use cell phones and never seemed to understand that Sophie could see who was calling on her screen.

"Are you doing all right over there? Had any flooding?"

"I'm fine, Sherm. The sump pump is working overtime, but I haven't had any problems so far. What about you and Daisy?" she asked dutifully, even though she was biting at the bit to call the police now that she'd made the decision. Thomas was out driving around in these conditions.

"Daisy and the house are fine—had some flooding in the basement—but nothing major. I hit some pretty serious flooding on Route 2, and your friend Thomas pulled me out of a ditch."

Sophie straightened and held the phone tighter to her ear when Sherm continued.

"Ran into a little lake covering the road . . . made it through without stalling out—knew enough to keep my foot on the accelerator—but there was a damn landslide of mud after the water. Slicker than an oil spill. I went into a ditch. Thomas found me on his way back from Effingham. He dug me out, but I had to leave my car. We took a roundabout way to get back to the house."

"Are both of you all right?" she asked rapidly. Her mind buzzed with questions, perhaps the most glaring one concerned Sherm's rambling reference to Thomas *returning* from Effingham. Had he been on his way back to her house when he encountered Sherm and pulled him out of a ditch?

Or had Sherm been confused by his accident, and assumed that Thomas was coming when he'd really been leaving?

"We're both fine. Just made it back. We look like we've been wrestling with pigs in the mud, but we're healthy. Damn weathermen never gave us any indication the rain would be this bad. Country roads are flooded out from here to Charleston and—"

"Sherm, where is Thomas?" Sophie interrupted.

"Oh, he's here. Right here with Daisy and me at the house."

Sophie shut her eyes and inhaled slowly. Thank goodness he hadn't left after dropping Sherm off at his house. "May I speak with him, please?"

"He's in the shower. Both of us were covered in mud . . . well, I still am, come to think of it."

"All right. I'm on my way to your place," Sophie said.

"No . . . *no,* girl, you stay put. The lake road is flooded out in parts as well. I don't know what the stretch is like between our house and yours, but I do know that our drive back in Thomas's car was a chancy thing. You can tell that boy served in the military; never flinched flying through patches of three-foot-deep water and kept that car solid on the road the whole way. I couldn't have done it, that's for sure, and I'd cringe thinking of you trying. Daisy'll never let up about the fact that I drove into town under these conditions, but I needed some tying silk for a hackle fish fly—"

"But Thomas can't stay there with you. I'm sure the road will be okay—"

But this time Sophie was interrupted by the sound of a deep, authoritative rumble in the background.

"Is that Thomas?" Sophie demanded.

"It is. And he agrees with me. He says for you to stay right where you are. It's dangerous out there. I could feel undercurrents tugging on Thomas's car when we went through some of those floodwaters. It was a miracle we didn't lose contact with the road. As soon as the rain lets up, the flooding will go down, and then we'll see about things."

"Sherm, put Thomas on the phone," she begged. She needed to know if he was still upset.

"Well, it looks like he headed back to the bathroom, Sophie. I'll have him give you a call as soon as he's finished cleaning up, how'd that be?"

"Make sure that you tell him to call me, Sherm."

"I've made a note of it. Don't you worry now. Give us a call if anything should happen over there."

Sophie hung up the phone a few seconds later, feeling helpless and frustrated as she stared at the heavy downpour outside her window.

Obviously, Thomas had provided her with her answer as to whether or not he was still angry at her for knowing his secrets.

Sophie hated the rain. She'd never despised a force of nature so much as that steady, relentless downpour. It was only eight o'clock in the evening, but the sky was so overcast that it was pitch black outside.

She switched on the light in the kitchen, the cheery glow seeming unusually bright compared to the impenetrable darkness outside the windows. In the background, she heard the sump pump churning endlessly and wondered when the machine would finally give out from overuse.

At this rate, Thomas might have to spend the night at the Dolans'. The thought of him being a quarter mile away and not being able to see him, to try to explain things to him further, was driving her crazy. She felt like a caged animal.

The damn rain was her prison bars.

She put some hot water in the pot for tea and flipped on the burner, all the while listening to the weather report on the radio she kept on the kitchen counter. She scowled at the announcement that I-57 had been closed due to flooding. Multiple rural roads had been barricaded for hours, but the closing of a major interstate suggested that conditions were worsening, not improving.

Thomas hadn't called, despite Sherm's assurance that he'd

ask him to do so once he was finished cleaning up. She was worried he'd take off come morning, and the gap that had opened between them when she told him what she'd known would slowly widen until it was an impassable crevice.

She poured some hot water into a mug with a tea bag and stared out the wet window into the impenetrable darkness. She'd called Andy earlier and told him what had happened. He'd been concerned for Thomas's safety in his emotional turmoil, but he'd tried to assure her she hadn't done anything wrong.

"Maybe it's best that he's not there with you, Sophie. He needs time to pull himself together . . . regroup. He has to work this out—"

"At his own pace. I know, Andy," Sophie had finished for him. But she couldn't help but thinking then, just as she thought it now, that Thomas's "pace" for recovery might not be fast enough for an encroaching threat.

She saw the great, round bloom of fire in her mind's eye and imagined the *boom* of the warehouse explosion. She shivered and stepped away from the sink.

For a few seconds, she considered trying to call the Dolan house again. But Sherm had assured her he would tell Thomas to call her. If he had done so, it must mean Thomas wasn't willing to talk to her at the moment.

Sophie took her tea and curled up at the end of the sofa with a knitted afghan drawn over her legs. She flipped on the television to the all-news network.

Her anxiety only amplified when the anchorman reported that the FBI and the U.S. Attorney's office were preparing to announce a formal indictment on a host of federal charges against Joseph Carlisle within the next few days.

A loud cracking noise made her startle, causing a few drops of tea to splatter on the afghan. She hopped up off the couch and peered out the picture window—the noise had issued from the direction of the lake. She jumped when she heard it again, a sound like wood knocking against wood forcefully. What was it? Something hitting her dock?

She considered going out to check, but thought better of

it. There was nothing she could do about it in the pitch blackness and heavy downpour.

Again, she heard the loud cracking noise and shivered. She'd never felt isolated here at the lake house, but she felt very alone at the moment, like she existed on an island with an ocean surrounding her on all sides. She hurried into the kitchen and locked the back door, then traversed the long, dark hallway to secure the door that led to the screened-in porch. Since she never used the front door, it was already locked up tight.

When she returned to the kitchen, she picked up her cell phone to call the Dolans' house, but their residential phone line was dead.

CHAPTER **TWENTY-SIX**

Sophie started into wakefulness and glanced around the living room cautiously, using only her eyes instead of moving her head. She'd fallen asleep with the television on. It cast the room in dim, flickering light, but the kitchen was swathed in dark shadow.

She held her breath in her lungs, listening.

The sound of the churning sump pump and the patter of rain on the roof told her the rain hadn't abated. But the rain or the sump pump hadn't been what had awakened her . . .

Her eyes went wide and a scream tickled her throat when a shadow separated from the thick blackness and the form of a tall man began to move toward her.

"Shhhh, it's just me."

She realized she'd sat up and was tensed to spring up off the couch.

"Thomas?" she gasped.

"Yeah."

He stepped into the living room and she saw that he was completely naked except for a pair of white boxer briefs.

"I was . . . am . . . soaking wet. I stripped in the kitchen."

Sophie just gaped at him, knocked off balance by his sudden appearance.

"How did you get in the house?"

"Picked the lock," he replied levelly. Perhaps he noticed her stunned expression as she stared up at him. "It wasn't that hard. I used the deadbolt to lock it once I got inside."

"Oh" was all she could think of to say for a moment. "How . . . how did you get here? You didn't drive, did you? The rain hasn't stopped—"

"I walked. Well, swam during one part. There's nearly four feet of standing water in one dip in the road."

She stood. "Thomas, that was dangerous. Some of those currents can be strong, especially if the lake is meeting the floodwaters." She noticed how erect his small, brown nipples were. "You must be freezing. Do you want something hot to drink? Or a shower to warm up?"

"No."

His hair hung wet on his brow. Even though he'd removed his clothing, his naked skin gleamed with moisture. She tried to study his face, but his expression was unreadable in the dim, flickering light. It suddenly struck her with force that he was there in the house with her. She'd been hoping to speak with him—to see him—for hours, and now he'd suddenly appeared.

"Thomas, I'm so sorry. I wanted to tell you about Rick and Andy all along, but—"

"So why didn't you?" he interrupted.

"I . . . I was worried about how you would take it," she replied honestly. "I feel guilty about knowing such private things about you and your family, but the circumstances were so strange. When we became involved, they became even stranger."

Sophie felt the weight of his stare as he studied her for several taut seconds.

"Have you told anyone what you knew about Rick? About Bernard Cokey?"

She shook her head. "No, of course not. Andy and I have discussed it, but—"

"*No one* else?"

"No."

"You didn't go to the police with the information? The Feds?"

"No, Thomas."

"And your friend? Andy Lancaster? Is he trying to convince you my father is guilty?"

"*No,* absolutely not. Do you believe me?" she asked breathlessly.

"I don't know what to believe anymore," he admitted, his chin lifted, his stance wary. "Agent Fisk told me that they had a star informant, someone of spotless character who was feeding them information about my father."

Her heart seemed to thud and then stop for a suspended second in her rib cage.

"It wasn't me, Thomas. Is that what you're thinking? That *I* gave inside information on Joseph Carlisle?"

He didn't reply.

"It wasn't *me*," she repeated in a whisper.

"Bernard Cokey is dead."

The sound of rain pattering on the roof turned into a dull roar in her ears.

"I couldn't sleep over at the Dolans' so I turned on the television. Cokey and his wife were shot, execution-style, in a roadside inn in Wisconsin earlier this evening."

"Oh my God," she whispered through numb lips. She longed to turn on a lamp so that she could make out his expression through the dark, flickering shadows. Rick's source—the man who had once been a small-time crook within the mob—was dead. Perhaps the only people alive who knew about Cokey's and Rick Carlisle's connection were Thomas and Andy.

And herself.

Thomas just stood there, existing on a knife's edge of indecision. He believed her; he thought she was lying.

Something told him to get away from Sophie as fast as he could.

He wanted her more than he'd ever wanted anything in his life.

The friction arising from the battle waging inside his spirit felt unbearable.

"Thomas?"

Her soft query brought him back to himself. She sat at the edge of the couch, her body tensed as if she was about to rise. He realized it was his presence that kept her motionless, her uncertainty about his intentions standing there in her living room almost naked in the middle of the night. His glance lowered over her, taking in her bare, pale limbs. She wore a nightgown—nothing fancy.

It looked sexy as hell on Sophie.

He inhaled slowly, his nostrils pinching tight, as he stared at the way her breasts shaped the soft fabric of the gown. Suddenly, unbidden and unwelcome, the potently erotic memories of making love to her that morning stormed through his brain. His cock lurched in his damp boxers.

Her dark eyes lowered and lingered on his crotch.

She'd noticed. Good, he thought grimly. What she'd said earlier today had made him vulnerable. Exposed. Angry. He didn't feel so worried about protecting Sophie from his volatility at the moment. She'd asked him here. She knew the consequences.

"Why did you come back?" she whispered.

"One guess."

Her elegant throat convulsed. She remained perched there at the edge of the couch, looking as if she was considering fleeing. But there wasn't a chance he was letting Sophie Gable go anywhere at the moment.

"Take off your gown," he demanded hoarsely.

"Thomas . . . you're angry at me. I don't think—"

His gaze flew to her face. "Take it off, Sophie."

She hesitated for a split second before she whisked the filmy garment over her head. Underneath, she wore a pair of those modest, white cotton panties that drove him crazy with lust. He stared at her breasts. His cock strained against his boxer briefs as if it were iron and Sophie a powerful magnet.

He stepped toward her.

"Stand up," he ordered quietly.

"Maybe we should talk first—"

"I don't want to *talk*. Stand up," he repeated.

She did so slowly as he approached her. He could see their reflections cast in the picture window behind her. He towered over her.

He reached out and cradled her breasts. Blood rushed into his cock. So soft . . . like new flower petals. So responsive, he added to himself as he flicked his thumbs over the rosy tips and she tightened for him. He became completely absorbed in his task as he fondled her, shaping her fulsome flesh to his palms, rubbing and tweaking her nipples until they grew incredibly hard and distended. The storm that held them captive, the inexplicable terror that crouched just outside of his vision, all of that receded.

He lifted her breasts with his hands and let them drop. A pang of lust shot through his cock when he saw them fall back into place with an erotic jiggle.

"I've never seen breasts this large and yet so firm," he muttered, completely enraptured.

"Thomas," she whispered shakily. He looked up at her face. Her glance seemed to entreat him, but he didn't want to consider Sophie's pleas at the moment.

Not unless she begged him to make her come.

"I know what I want right now, Sophie, and it's not a heart-to-heart talk. If you don't want to play, just say no, but don't try and make me feel guilty because I want to fuck you blind."

He didn't feel guilty when he saw her lower lip tremble . . . Didn't feel much of anything, really, except the potent blast of lust rushing through his veins. He molded her firm breasts to his palm and massaged her while he held her stare.

"What's it going to be, Sophie?"

"If it's . . ." She swallowed. "If that's what you want," she finished throatily.

He stared at her magnificent breasts in his hands. "Oh, it's what I want, all right. Lay down on your back on the couch." He didn't like letting go of her soft, warm flesh, but he did when she moved to do what he'd demanded.

He hurried out of the living room and returned a few seconds later carrying the little bottle of lubricant. There wasn't much left. They'd made quite a dent in their supply over the past few days.

Sophie lay there, still wearing her girl-next-door panties, watching him with those big, dark eyes that were going to be the death of him. He jerked down his boxer briefs and matter-of-factly lubed up his swollen cock.

Her eyes widened.

"Don't worry. I'm not going to fuck your ass again. Not at the moment," he rasped. He dropped his heavy erection. "Move farther down on the couch."

He waited while she scooted away from the pillows and armrest. He straddled her chest with one leg, pressing his knee into the couch next to her ribs. His other leg wouldn't fit on the narrow couch. He bent his leg and kept his foot on the floor, leaning over Sophie and placing both his hands on the armrest.

"Squeeze them together. I want to fuck those beautiful breasts."

He groaned in pleasure a moment later as his cock burrowed between silky, firm flesh. He thrust his hips, drowning in the delicious sensation. It was selfish of him to stimulate himself in this way, and he knew it. He *knew* it. Christ, he couldn't even see Sophie's expression, positioned as he was.

That was when he realized the last thing he wanted to see at that moment was Sophie's breathtaking face or to stare at his own reflection in her haunted eyes.

He just wanted to lose himself in the bounty of Sophie's sweet body.

He watched his cock sliding like an oiled piston between the fulsome globes, aroused beyond measure by the sight of her holding her full breasts in her small hands, making a pagan offering of her flesh for his greedy cock.

Selfish. That's what he was when it came to Sophie. And he couldn't seem to stop his endless greed.

Her nipples rose from the mounds like hard little darts, tempting him, making him starved for the feeling of them sliding against his tongue. But he couldn't bring himself to stop fucking Sophie's breasts. He was like an addict when it came to her.

She moaned when he became more forceful in his thrusts, popping the lower curves of her breasts with his pelvis and aching balls. The sight of her flesh bobbing up with every lusty stroke drove him crazy.

"Touch your nipples," he growled. He watched with a feral focus as her forefingers and thumbs slid over the erect crests. "That's right. Pinch them."

He groaned gutturally and grimaced in mounting pleasure as his balls smacked against her breasts rhythmically.

Pleasure swamped his brain for the next several moments, washing away everything in its wake.

Her eyelids blinked open when he jerked his cock out of the sweet crevice of her breasts. He stood and swung his leg to the floor. She seemed dazed when he grabbed her hands and pulled her up next to him, but he was glad to see that her cheeks were stained pink with arousal. He was so turned on, so primed to detonate, that he couldn't speak. He merely turned her until she faced the picture window and urged her to bend over, still holding one of her wrists.

She leaned over. He grabbed her other wrist and bound her hands at her lower back with one hand, using his grip on her to keep her steady. He arrowed his cock to her slit.

"Spread your legs, Sophie. Let me in," he insisted in a tight, low voice.

He hissed as she complied and his cock sunk into her slowly.

"Jesus," he mumbled tensely. She was molten. He felt like he was sinking into bliss. He had to press firmly to gain ground she was so tight, but it was a hot, sweet struggle. His cock carved through her snug, juicy channel like a hot knife through melting butter.

She whimpered once he pressed his balls to her moist tissues. The sound may have come from discomfort or it may have come from arousal. Thomas couldn't tell which. He didn't care.

He was stone drunk on greedy lust. He shook with a need to leap into the forgetful fires of hedonistic pleasure.

He held her hip firmly and began to fuck her, fast and furious from the get-go. This wasn't about wooing Sophie; it was about his desperation. His need. There wasn't room for anything else. She mewled in surprised arousal as he plunged into her from tip to balls, driving into her firm, yet giving body like he thought salvation lay at her depths.

It was too much. Emotion and wild pleasure swamped him from every direction, making him sweat . . . making him dizzy.

"God, I want to fill you up with my come."

She said his name on a moan, and he realized he'd spoken his thought out loud. It was true. Why the hell did the mere thought of Sophie drenched with his semen turn him into a rabid animal?

He snarled as he lifted one foot onto the couch, his thigh forcing Sophie downward slightly until her forehead hit the cushion of the couch. He thrust with even greater force, watching with fixed intensity as his cock pounded into her with all the relentless power of a charging piston.

Nirvana winked at him out of the corner of his eye.

"Sophie. *Sophie*," he hissed from a clenched jaw. He released her hip and furrowed his fingers through the soft hair at her nape. He grasped a handful of it, jerking her head back slightly as a hurtling wave of climax seized his entire body.

Sure enough, he went temporarily blind as a jolt of pleasure consumed him.

Sophie cried out at the sensation of him swelling inside her and pressing tight, her eyes going wide at the erotic feeling of his cock jerking as he exploded inside her. He continued to fuck her as he came, releasing her hair, but using his grip

on her bound wrists to push her pussy back and forth on his
throbbing penis.

His volatile possession continued. She felt his cock lurch
inside her and realized with a sense of wonder that he was
still ejaculating.

After a moment, he let go of her wrists and reached for her
shoulders, pulling her up against him. He pressed his mouth
to the crown of her head and gave a low, plaintive moan.

Her heart squeezed tight in recognition of the sound of
a wounded creature.

She studied the erotic tableau of their reflection in the
picture window. He leaned down over her from his great
height, his neck bent, his large hands on her shoulders looking dark next to her skin.

She reached around and encircled his hips with her arms,
palming the rock-hard muscles of his buttocks. Her vagina
clamped tight around his cock, securing him in her embrace.

He raised his head slowly. Sophie couldn't make out his
eyes in the reflection, but she sensed his gaze on her.

He suddenly withdrew and turned her in his arms. He
lifted her. Neither of them spoke as he carried her down the
dark hallway to the bedroom, his hand at the back of her
head pressing her cheek to his chest. Sophie couldn't find
words to speak. But as Thomas had said earlier, conversation
wasn't his focus at the moment.

He pushed her tighter against his body when they reached
her bedside so that he could use one hand to whip back the
covers. He laid her on the cool sheets and settled on the
mattress next to her. She put her arms around his shoulders
and stroked his dense back muscles while his hand caressed
her waist, belly, and hips, and finally settled between her
thighs. She whimpered in pleasure as he skillfully amplified
the friction that had grown in her flesh during his volatile
possession.

When she climaxed a moment later against his hand, he
covered her mouth with his, eating her cries of pleasure.
After she'd quieted, he transferred his lips to her cheeks,

where he wetted them with her tears. Her hand found his
cock and she stroked him while he kissed her, feeling the
fever amplify in his flesh yet again.

"What's happening to me?" he whispered roughly next
to her lips after she'd opened her thighs and guided him
back inside her.

"I don't know for sure," she replied in a hushed voice.
She moaned shakily when he began to roll his hips, fucking
her with slow, firm, delicious strokes. She cradled the base
of his skull and leaned up to press her mouth to his. "But I
wish you would trust me," she gasped as he subtly rotated
his pelvis against her clit, "because I think I'm falling in
love with you."

He went still for a moment before he seized her mouth
in a branding kiss and resumed making love to her, this time
more heatedly.

CHAPTER **TWENTY-SEVEN**

The next morning she awoke to the ceaseless drone of falling rain. She was beginning to wonder if it would ever stop. She glanced at Thomas, her gaze sticking on the sight of his usually tension-filled face relaxed for once in sleep. He didn't stir when she got out of bed and tucked the blanket securely around him. She shrugged into a thick robe—the house felt chilly and damp—and wandered out into the kitchen to start the coffee.

Peering out the kitchen window into the gloom, she was heartened to see that the water in the ditches next to her driveway had receded. Even though it still rained, it came down lighter than last night, and must have been doing so for a while. She thought of the Dolans and was about to try their downed phone line again when Thomas came up behind her.

"Good morning," she whispered when he wrapped her in his arms and pressed his mouth to the juncture at her neck and shoulder. She laughed softly when he didn't answer, but turned her around and lifted her. She encircled his waist with her legs as he carried her back to bed.

He made love to her with a fierce focus. Just before he'd

nearly driven her over the edge into ecstasy, he bit at her lower lip as it shaped a plea.

"Tell me, Sophie."

And she did: She told him she loved him.

God help her.

Afterward, he held her in his arms and they stared out the wet window onto the sodden day. Dread settled on her chest.

"You're in danger, Thomas," she whispered. "The people who knew about your brother's and Bernard Cokey's conversations are dying."

He paused in stroking her upper arm. "Cokey had a long history as a criminal, Sophie. Word must have leaked out about him sharing secrets with Rick. Obviously Cokey was fearful for his life."

"How do you know—"

"I doubt he and his wife make a point of vacationing in roadside dives. They were on the run."

"But doesn't that mean—"

The next thing she knew, Thomas had pushed her onto her back and leaned down over her.

"I think it means my brother and my nephew might have been murdered."

A chill convulsed her as she stared up at his face.

"Rick told me about Cokey's background," Thomas said, his mouth grimacing as though he spoke of these matters reluctantly. "There's little doubt Cokey knew inside information about the Outfit. He gave Rick loads of information— dozens more names—than just the lie he told about my dad. But even if it were true that the mob was targeting people who knew about Cokey feeding information to my brother, it's a far leap to try to implicate my father."

"Thomas," she spoke softly. "Whoever this witness is that the FBI has, whoever this impeccable witness is, he must have had good reason for going to the FBI. Maybe they aren't the traitor that you're imagining—"

She paused when she noticed how his eyes gleamed at her between narrowed eyelids.

"Let's not go there, Sophie," he rasped. "Please," he added, seeming to recognize his harshness too late.

"Okay," she whispered.

He inhaled slowly before he rolled over on the bed and stood. He went to the window and stared out at the gray lake for a moment. Sophie could almost feel his mind churning. His muscles looked rigid and tight, as though they strained against the weight of his anxiety. She suddenly understood perfectly his overwhelming need to make love. It was only during the brief period of time afterwards that she'd felt his muscles relax.

"But maybe you're right. We should leave here," he said.

She came up on her elbows. "Does anyone know you're here, Thomas?"

"The Dolans. And your friend Lancaster."

"I doubt they pose a threat. And no one would associate us being together, would they? We were only together for the first time last week, and surely no one saw us that might plan to harm you. But you just mentioned Andy and the Dolans . . . I thought you'd called your family—"

"I never got around to it," he said, his face still turned toward the window. "My cell phone is useless without a battery."

She hesitated, wary of his volatile mood.

"Thomas . . . I told you that you could use my phone to contact them. Why haven't you?"

He didn't turn toward her, but she saw how he went utterly still.

"Thomas?" she whispered.

"I don't want to speak with them," he said after a moment.

"Why not?"

When he turned his chin toward the bed, his eyes looked flat and lifeless.

"I just don't. Is the lake house property under your name, Sophie?"

She inhaled shakily, aware that a crucial moment had come and gone, but unsure as to whether she was relieved or regretful of its passing.

"No. As a matter of fact, it's still listed under my father's name—my father's stage name. I don't think we're in any danger while we're here. But, Thomas . . . if what you said about Bernard Cokey is true, we need to contact the FBI."

"I'm not telling the Feds what that little weasel Cokey said about my father," he said in a hollow voice.

Sophie rose from the bed and hastily grabbed her robe, flinging it over her shoulders and tying the sash.

"But if what you're saying is true, then *you're* in danger, Thomas. What about those agents you mentioned? Maybe we should try to call—"

She paused when he turned fully toward her, a nude, beautiful male animal poised to pounce. But Sophie didn't retreat. Instead, she stepped toward him slowly, wishing like hell she knew what he was thinking behind those shuttered eyes. If she'd tried to guess his thoughts at the moment, however, it turned out she would have been dead wrong.

"Do you *really* think it's possible?" he asked.

"For your father to be the head of a crime syndicate?"

"No," he replied, his nostrils flaring, "for someone to fall for someone else so fast?"

Her lower lip dropped in surprise. Had he been referring to her telling him that she loved him? Or had he been referring to himself?

She stepped close and cupped his jaw in her palm.

"All I can do is go by personal experience," she said softly.

He turned his chin and rubbed his whiskers against her skin, making her shiver.

"I wish I could trust my personal experience at the moment," he said in such a low rumble that she drew closer to him in order to hear him. He gave her a brooding glance before he dropped his forehead to hers. "All I know is that I've never wanted another woman the way I want you. I can't seem to make it stop."

"Stop trying then," she whispered against his lips. "Please. I'm not your enemy, Thomas."

He abruptly opened her robe and pressed her naked body to his. He wrapped his arms around her, shielding her in his encompassing embrace. Sophie held him tightly, giving him her warmth when he shivered in the chilly room.

CHAPTER **TWENTY-EIGHT**

Sophie tried the Dolans' phone again after they ate lunch, expressing her frustration to Thomas over the fact that their phone line was still dead.

"I hadn't realized," Thomas said after he closed the dishwasher. "Their electricity never went out, so we didn't notice. The phone lines are separate from the electric though. It'd be easy for a tree or a branch to fall on the lines in this weather."

According to the news, the incessant rain was nearing an end, but severe damage had been done throughout central Illinois and Indiana. Roads were flooded, and several major interstates were closed as crews worked overtime to clear the huge amount of debris that clogged the drainage routes, exacerbating the flooding. Sophie was relieved that Haven Lake, although bloated with water, was being well controlled by the dam and drainage into the spillway, and then the Little Wabash River.

They watched the weather channel together, Thomas lying on his back on the couch and Sophie curled up on her side next to him, her knees bent on his thighs and her head on his chest. He seemed to crave her nearness. He couldn't stop touching her.

Sophie didn't mind, because she felt the exact same way about him.

Still, the thought that his singular attraction toward her was made exponentially more potent by his emotional turmoil hovered in the back of her mind like a dark cloud. Anguish and anxiety as acute as Thomas's couldn't last indefinitely.

His need for her, his desperate craving, would diminish once his memories returned and he began to deal with his grief. The constant pressure, the internal emotional friction that he alleviated—at least in part—through making love to her with such focus and intensity would inevitably come to an end.

Later that afternoon, Thomas volunteered to venture out into the soggy yard to bring Guy some food and milk. Sophie was in the kitchen preparing a chicken casserole for their dinner later when her cell phone rang. Her brows furrowed quizzically when she saw the Chicago area code, but didn't recognize the number.

"Hello?"

"Sophie?"

She set down the wooden spoon she was holding. "Sherm? Is everything okay?" she asked, alarmed by the edge of panic in her neighbor's voice.

"It's Daisy," he gasped. "She insisted on going down into the basement to check on the flooding, and on the way back up the stairs, she got winded. She started having chest pains, and our damn phone line is dead. I didn't have any idea until I tried to call you."

Sophie's brow wrinkled in puzzlement. *How was Sherm calling her if the lines were dead?* she thought fleetingly, but then her mind raced to the far more critical matter of Daisy.

"Is Daisy conscious? Have you had to do CPR?"

"No, she's awake and lying on the sofa. We're both scared to death."

"Has she taken her nitroglycerin?"

"Yes."

"Okay, listen to me, Sherm. I want you to hang up and call nine-one-one."

"But the roads—"

"The roads are improving. It may take some doing, but they'll be able to get an ambulance to your house. And in the meantime, I'm on my way this very second. Just try to keep Daisy comfortable, okay? Everything is going to be fine, Sherm," she ended with firm assurance, attempting to steady him.

Sophie shoved her cell phone into a sealable plastic bag and rifled quickly through her spare bathroom cabinet, stashing a small bottle of aspirin in her jean pockets—just in case Daisy was running low on her nitroglycerin tablets. She hurried into an old rubber pair of boots that used to belong to her mother that were shoved into the back of a closet. Thomas was returning from the boathouse when she ran around the corner of the house, her feet sinking into the muddy ground. Miraculously, the rain had slowed to a steady drizzle.

Thomas pulled up short some thirty feet away when he saw her.

"It's Daisy's heart. Sherm just called. I need to get over there right away," she shouted through the rain and mist.

"Okay. Let's go," Thomas called out tersely as he jogged toward her.

Sophie noticed when Thomas left the nurse's station and came to join them in the waiting room. He gave her a small smile of reassurance and she smiled back, thankful for his presence in these difficult circumstances.

"The nurse says the bed next to Daisy's is free, Sherm. It's yours for the night, if you want to stay," Thomas said.

"Thank you for arranging that, Thomas," Sherm murmured. He looked pale and shaken. Sophie patted his hand where it rested on the armrest of his chair. Both Daisy and he had known about the weakness of Daisy's heart, but it was the first time Daisy had ever actually had an emergency situation because of it. Sherm's safe little world had been punctured, and Sophie knew the Dolans had some difficult choices to make. She adored having them as neighbors on Haven Lake, but as a physician, she knew it was advisable for them to move somewhere where emergency service was always easily accessible.

"Dr. Hanlon says Daisy is going to be fine, Sherm. It was a relatively minor heart attack. You decide if you want to stay here or if you want Thomas and me to drop you off at home. Either way, I want you to try to get some sleep. You're exhausted."

"I'll stay here with Daisy," Sherm said. "I can't thank you two enough for all you've done." He glanced up at Thomas. "And *you* . . . that's twice you put your neck on the line for me in twenty-four hours."

Thomas shrugged. "I didn't do much of anything but take a dip a time or two," he said wryly, glancing down at his damp clothing. He and Sophie had had to wade through several feet of standing water to get to the Dolans' house that afternoon.

"Well, I surely do appreciate all you did," Sherm said in a reedy voice. He grabbed Sophie's hand and squeezed it.

"It was nothing, Sherm. That's what neighbors are for. And friends," she added.

"It made all the difference in the world having you there while we waited for the ambulance, Sophie. You calmed Daisy, and you calmed me just with your presence, and Lord knows that's what we most needed at the moment. Now you two go home, and get yourselves warm and dry. You've been here for hours, soaked through the whole time. Michelle will be coming as soon as I-57 opens, along with Tad, so don't you two worry about us anymore," Sherm said, referring to his daughter and son-in-law, who still lived in Beverly, on the Southside of Chicago.

Despite Sherm's protests to the contrary, Sophie insisted she'd be back the next morning with some clothing and other supplies.

The flooding had receded minimally on the country roads on the way back to her house, but Sophie was infinitely glad it was Thomas driving through the water and not her. He never flinched and never hesitated as he plowed into the miniature ponds, seeming to have an instinctive understanding of what his car could withstand. When they reached the standing water between the Dolans' house and Sophie's, however, Thomas came to a stop thirty feet away. Sophie glanced at him, and he just shook his head. The water was still too high for them to drive through.

So he parked his car in the Dolans' driveway and he and Sophie resignedly waded through the deep water once again.

Sophie was showing signs of exhaustion by the time they stripped out of their wet clothing on the side porch. Thomas immediately guided her into the bathroom for a hot shower, ignoring her protests that she wanted to finish her interrupted preparations for the chicken casserole.

When she came into the cheerily lit kitchen a half hour later, Thomas was reading the instructions on the back of a frozen pizza box. He'd already showered, she realized as she stared, a little dumbfounded by the sight of him leaning against her counter wearing a pair of low-riding jeans and an unbuttoned cotton shirt with the sleeves rolled back to his elbows. His hair hung damp on his forehead, creating a parenthesis around his eyes.

"What about my chicken casserole?" she asked lamely, her gaze glued to the appealing sight of his forearm dusted in brown hair. Several veins popped from the surface, highlighting his strength. He lowered the pizza box and Sophie found herself staring at his tanned, ridged abdomen instead.

"I'm cooking," he said resolutely. "And since I can't cook, we're having pizza. You just sit right up there at the counter, and I'll pour you a glass of wine, and you can watch the chef at work."

Sophie laughed and sunk onto one of the counter stools. She'd rather have eaten chicken casserole, but it was too much of a temptation to resist watching a beautiful man cook for her.

Thomas made a salad to go with the frozen pizza. The meal tasted wonderful, maybe because she wasn't used to having someone else prepare a meal for her, or maybe because she was starved.

Or maybe because she was submersed in the first, heady rushes of falling in love.

After they'd cleaned up the dishes, they watched television while lying on the couch, embracing each other as they had that afternoon. It occurred to her, as it had done countless times since Thomas had come to her lake house, that she needed to confront him, encourage him to talk about what was troubling him . . . haunting him.

But she recalled only too well what had occurred when she'd forced him to talk about Rick and Bernard Cokey last time. He'd left. He'd returned, but maybe next time, he wouldn't.

Thomas wasn't the only one who seemed to want to take shelter. It was becoming increasingly easy for Sophie, as well, to try to ignore the harsh realities of the world outside Haven Lake . . . to find sanctuary in Thomas's arms.

She fell asleep during the last part of a suspense movie, the sensation of Thomas caressing her scalp and running his fingers through her hair lulling her.

She awoke later to find herself in Thomas's arms as he carried her down the darkened hallway to her bedroom.

"I didn't understand the plot of that movie in the slightest," she said. She barely made out his small grin in the shadows.

"That's because you kept falling asleep."

"Umm, that could be it," she murmured as she nuzzled his chest with her mouth.

Sophie didn't say anything when Thomas set her on the edge of the bed and began to undress her. In fact, they only spoke with their bodies for the following moments as they made love, and Sophie was stunned anew by the intense, blazing quality of Thomas's desire.

Afterwards, they held each other, Sophie becoming hypnotized by the sensation of Thomas's warm breath falling on a patch of her left breast.

A thought penetrated her languor. She opened her leaden eyelids.

"I kept forgetting to ask Sherman how he called me today with the phone lines down," she said groggily.

But Thomas didn't respond, and Sophie realized as he continued to breathe evenly that he'd fallen fast asleep. She rubbed her cheek against his chest, inhaled his scent deeply, and quickly followed him.

CHAPTER **TWENTY-NINE**

The morning dawned crystalline and golden, making a mockery of all the gloom that had dared to come before its splendor. Sophie walked into the still boggy yard after getting dressed, squinting in the bright summer sunshine as though she'd been secluded in a dark den for weeks. She paused in the front yard and called out in amazement.

Thomas didn't turn at her shout; he was busy at the moment.

Sophie watched as he overturned the submerged canoe next to her dock with a flex of powerful, gleaming shoulder, back, and arm muscles.

"I heard it hitting the dock the night before last," she said as she walked onto the dock. She recalled how eerie the cracking sound had been when she'd been in the house all alone while the rain fell ceaselessly around her. "It looks like it's in perfect condition."

"It is," Thomas said from where he stood in four feet of water next to the dock. He found a frayed nylon rope on the bow of the fiberglass craft and clambered up onto the dock. Sophie noticed he was wearing his newly purchased swim trunks and once again admired the way he filled them out.

"With all the drains being opened to the spillway to keep

the water level from getting too high in the lake, there would have been some strong currents. The canoe must have broken free and gotten snagged. I saw the underside of it beneath your dock when I came back from my swim. We'll figure out who owns it, but in the meantime—" He flashed her a grin. "We're going to borrow it. It'll help keep us dry."

"What do you mean?" Sophie murmured, her gaze glued to his mouth. He was an extremely handsome man, but Thomas became nothing less than riveting when he smiled. The radiant sunshine following days of oppressive gloom didn't even compare.

"I saw some old paddles in your boathouse when I was checking on Guy this morning. He's doing fine, by the way. That paw is on the mend. I'm thinking your patient is getting used to all the food and hospitality, though. He's going to take up permanent residence in your boathouse, the little freeloader."

He chuckled when he saw her mock scowl at his disparagement of Guy. He finished deftly tying a knot in the rope and stood. "Anyway, you said we should take Sherm and Daisy some supplies this morning, so we'll take the canoe in the lake versus wading through floodwater."

"Brilliant." Her eyebrows went up when he put out his arms for a hug. He was teasing, since he was soaking wet, but Sophie went anyway. He laughed, low and soft, when she pressed tight to him, soaking her jean shorts and T-shirt. She wrapped her forearms around his neck. His skin felt smooth and sun-warmed.

"I'm getting used to you being wet all the time," she said as she urged him down for a kiss.

His hand moved between their bodies and settled between her thighs, cradling her sex possessively.

"I'm getting addicted to the same thing about you," he murmured gruffly next to her lips before he seized her mouth in a toe-curling kiss.

Later that morning, they paddled the canoe over to Sherm and Daisy's dock and made their way up to the house. Thomas walked down the road to check on the status of the flooding while Sophie gathered some clothing and personal items.

A night's rest appeared to have done Sherman and Daisy a world of good, Sophie decided a half hour later when they walked into the hospital room. Daisy was sitting up in bed and she and Sherm were working on a crossword puzzle together, bickering good-naturedly about answers.

They only stayed long enough to drop off the supplies and exchange news. The doctor had given a good report to Daisy after she'd made her morning rounds. Thomas assured the couple that their daughter and her husband should have no trouble making it to Haven Lake, as the water had receded to safe levels on the roads between the hospital and the Dolans' lake house. When a nurse came in to alert Daisy that she'd be going for some testing, Thomas and Sophie said their good-byes.

Sherm turned his good ear toward the hallway. He'd been waiting for Daisy to return from her testing, steadily working his way through the crossword puzzle they'd started together. He'd just heard a man's voice coming from the direction of the nursing station saying Thomas Nicasio's name.

Sherm set down the crossword puzzle book and stood. The gruff baritone hadn't really sounded like his son-in-law's voice, but who else would be asking for Thomas Nicasio? Sherm had told Michelle and Tad about Sophie's and Nicasio's invaluable assistance over the past few days.

When he walked out of the hospital room and down the hallway the short distance to the nursing station, however, he knew immediately that the large man with the jet-black hair and thick stubble on his jaw was most definitely not his son-in-law. The man turned toward him when he called out.

"Are you looking for Thomas Nicasio?"

Sherm realized the man was wearing dark glasses. Well, the sun was exceptionally bright today, after all, following all that God-forsaken rain.

"I am. I'm an old friend. I thought I saw him here earlier, but he didn't hear me when I called out . . ."

"You did see him. You just missed him. He and Sophie were just here . . . oh, twenty minutes ago?" Sherm said as he checked his watch. "You say you're an old friend of Thomas's?"

"Yes, from the Navy," the man said, smiling as if in reminiscence.

Sherm noticed the flashing Rolex watch and the suppleness of the man's thigh-length leather coat. It was a tad strange to wear a coat on a summer day—even a lightweight one like the man wore—but Sherm supposed the air-conditioning in the hospital could get chilly. Thomas's old friend must have done well for himself since leaving the military. He practically exuded power and money. The guy had fifteen, maybe twenty years on Thomas, but like Thomas, he appeared to take excellent care of himself. His shoulders and chest were thick with muscle, and there wasn't a sign of a paunch on his belly. Well, the military taught a man the value of keeping fit, Sherm thought with a trace of good-natured envy.

"Does Nicasio live around this area? I'm visiting an aunt here in the hospital, but I'd love to be able to catch up." The man's voice had a slight nasal quality to it, and Sherm noticed his nose was swollen, like he'd been hit.

"Oh, no, no. He's just staying with Sophie."

"Sophie?" the man asked with a wide smile. "Don't tell me Nicasio finally tied the knot. He was the youngest officer of us all, but we all said he'd be the last to dangle on the noose."

Sherm laughed. "No, they aren't married, but Nicasio would be lucky to get Sophie. She's a gem, that girl. Daisy and I look forward to every summer when she comes to Haven Lake."

"Haven Lake? Is that far from here?"

"Barely ten miles. You could make it there and back while your aunt took a nap. Do you want directions?"

"That'd be very kind of you."

"No problem," Sherm assured, glad to do something

pleasant for Thomas when he'd done so much for Daisy and him recently. The man didn't write down the directions, but Sherm got the impression he wouldn't forget as he listened soberly and nodded.

When Sherm finished, a thought struck him and he tapped his forehead in irritation at himself. "Forget my own head if it wasn't attached. Bit out of it, I guess—worried about Daisy," Sherm mumbled under his breath as he dug in his pant pocket and withdrew the BlackBerry. "Would you return Thomas's phone to him when you see him? I forgot to give it to him; even been using it to talk to my daughter and tell her about her mother and all. Damndest thing. If it weren't for this phone, my wife might be a lot worse off. You know all that flooding we've had?"

Thomas's friend nodded once, eyeing the BlackBerry.

"Well our phone lines went down. It about gave *me* a heart attack when my wife started having chest pains yesterday, and I was surrounded by floodwaters with no working phone. But Thomas had left this on the counter," Sherm explained, holding up the BlackBerry. "But *it* didn't work either."

Sherm saw a gray eyebrow arch up behind the man's sunglasses. Strange . . . when his hair was so pitch black.

"No battery in it. But the thing of it was . . . " Sherm continued, warming up to the topic. He'd been too preoccupied with Daisy to have told anyone yet, and it *really* was a good story. " . . . I'd been with Thomas in his car that evening—he pulled me out of a ditch, bless the boy. He'd been using a flashlight, and when he put it back in the glove box, I saw the phone battery inside of it."

"Nicasio had taken the battery out of his phone?"

Sherm nodded and threw up his hands in a "hell if I know why" gesture.

The man's grin widened as he backed away. "Knowing Nicasio, he was probably trying to avoid some clinging woman."

Sherm laughed amiably and waved when the man turned away.

CHAPTER **THIRTY**

Thomas walked through the dim hallway, knowing Sophie was in the kitchen because he could hear the faucet running. The woman was probably making them a gourmet lunch, he thought with a mixture of amazement and amusement. He couldn't convince her to stay on the dock with him in the sunshine and make out until they both got so hot they'd have to rush up to the bedroom to cool off. She'd just laughed and slapped away the hand that had been caressing her breast beneath her bikini top.

"I'm hungry," she'd protested.

"You're always hungry," he'd mumbled as he ran his lips over the delicious upper swell of her right breast.

"Well you're always horny, so that makes us even," she'd replied briskly.

The smile that had curved his mouth at the memory faded when he saw Sophie standing stock-still at the sink and staring out the window.

"Sophie?"

She jumped and turned around, sloshing soapy water out of the overfilling pan she'd been washing.

"Thomas. You scared me."

He grinned bemusedly. "What were you staring at?"

"Nothing," she said quickly when he crossed the kitchen to glance curiously out the window. "I mean . . . there was a deer out there. At the edge of the woods on the right-hand side of the driveway."

"Well, it's gone now." He turned toward her. "What are you making for lunch?"

Thomas thought the odd moment had passed when Sophie answered lightly, but he began to wonder when she seemed distracted as they ate the delicious lunch she'd made of a walnut and pear salad and hot rolls.

"I think I'll go and stretch my legs," she said from behind him as he knelt in front of a cabinet, putting away a pan in a lower cupboard.

"The paths in the woods will be a muddy mess," Thomas commented as he lifted several pans and slid the larger one beneath them.

"I know. I'll be careful," she said, giving him a bright smile when he glanced over his shoulder.

He watched her from his kneeling position in front of the cabinet as she went out the back door, his brow furrowed in puzzlement.

When she reached the end of her driveway, Sophie paused on the lake road and glanced anxiously from right to left. Sophie's house lay at the end of an extension of the lake road. The blacktopped road ceased in a crudely shaped, forest-lined cul de sac. She glanced warily back toward her house. The thick foliage on either side of the road obscured the view.

She walked over to the man who had just stepped out of the woods lining the dead-end road.

"What are you doing here?" she asked Fisk in a pressured whisper. She'd been shocked into immobility when she'd seen the young agent signaling to her from her driveway earlier, his motions conveying both a beckoning gesture and a plea for secrecy. Gone was Fisk's dark, sober suit. Instead, he wore a pair of jeans, a green T-shirt, and very muddy hiking boots.

"Is Nicasio in the house?" he asked in a low voice.

Sophie studied him searchingly, finding that she trusted his face this time as much as she had on their previous meeting.

"How did you find me?" she asked, ignoring his question.

"I was eventually able to trace you to your parents. It wasn't that hard after that, to locate any property listed under your father's stage name in the near vicinity. I checked airline passenger lists, so I knew you and Nicasio hadn't flown anywhere. I figured you had to be within driving distance. I would have found you sooner if the damn interstate hadn't been shut down. I need to talk to Nicasio. It's extremely important."

"You can't," she said so starkly that he gave her an astonished look.

"I need him, Dr. Gable. And he needs me. He needs protection. Have you heard what happened to Bernard Cokey?"

"I know. I know. But you don't understand—" Sophie broke off, glancing around the vicinity nervously.

"I think I understand more than you might think. Is Nicasio still . . . out of it?"

She shook her head in rising agitation.

"He's experiencing a trauma reaction," she said, the truth spilling out of her in a pressured rush. It wasn't as if Fisk hadn't already suspected the truth, after all. He'd known something was amiss with Thomas after that meeting in his office last week. "I don't know if it was caused by a concussion or from a psychological trauma, or both, but he doesn't remember a short period of his life."

She gave Fisk a pleading look.

"Forcing a person to confront memories before they're sufficiently ready to face them can cause even more damage. You have to trust me on this, Agent Fisk. His memories will come back, probably anytime now, any day . . . any hour.

Cases like these are more common than people might think. Someone is in a car accident, and thinks they can't recall the incident because they bumped their head, but the memory returns after they're able to psychologically deal with the memory, or someone sees a random violent act and becomes amnesic for the actual event. Thomas's trauma must have been a doozy, though," she hissed, "because he's suffering a localized amnesia for about an eighteen-hour period, as best as I can figure."

Agent Fisk just stared at her for a moment.

"Jesus, *amnesia*?" he blurted out. "I thought he wasn't talking openly to me in front of Larue because I'd warned him about possible security breaches in the Bureau. I knew he seemed agitated and out of it, but I didn't expect this."

"His agitation and localized amnesia are both symptoms of PTSD. I spoke with a psychologist friend about it. In some cases of severe traumatic stress, the person blocks out the central trauma entirely."

Something shifted in Fisk's expression. "Holy . . . He doesn't remember talking to me at all, does he?"

Sophie's heartbeat began to throb loudly in her ears.

"He remembers talking to you and that other agent in his office," she said slowly, her voice sounding raspy and thin with the background cacophony of the crickets and tree frogs chirping in the nearby woods. "He's amnesic for the period before that, I think. Eighteen hours or so . . . maybe less—"

"How do you know, Dr. Gable? How do you know he lost his memory? He can't *tell* you, can he?" Fisk interrupted.

She met his stare levelly. She thought of that passionate, life-altering night they'd made love and the fact that Thomas seemed completely unaware it'd ever happened.

"I just know," she said firmly, holding Fisk's stare.

She paused when she saw the agent briefly close his eyes at hearing the conviction in her tone.

"Last Thursday afternoon? Did this missing eighteen hours happen last Thursday?" Fisk asked her more insistently when she didn't immediately answer.

"Yes."

"He doesn't remember what he told me last Thursday? *Any* of it?"

She hesitated. "I don't think so. Although lately . . . I've wondered if things are slowly starting to come back to him . . . Shadows of the truth, if not the thing itself. He's not defending his father as stringently as he used to. And I see the doubt in his eyes at times."

"*Defending* him? Joseph Carlisle?"

"When he first came here, he wouldn't hear a word against Carlisle," she murmured. She straightened and met Fisk's stare. "Agent Fisk . . . that star witness that you have that gave you inside information on Joseph Carlisle?"

"Yeah?"

"It's Thomas, isn't it?"

Fisk hesitated for a split second before he nodded once.

He placed his hand on her shoulder comfortingly when a spasm of emotion shook her.

"Was what he told me trustworthy, given his condition?" Fisk asked, obviously alarmed at the thought.

Sophie inhaled shakily, bringing herself under control. She'd suspected the truth. But she now knew firsthand suspicion and the truth were two entirely different things.

She glanced grimly back at the driveway.

"You can trust whatever Thomas revealed to you. He told you nothing but the absolute truth," Sophie said.

"How do you know?"

"Because only the truth could have had this much of an explosive impact on him," she whispered.

The first thing Sophie did when she returned to the house was turn up the air-conditioning. All the extra moisture and the hot sun were making for humidity you could slice, it was so thick.

Or perhaps she was just sweating following her conversation with Agent Fisk. Fisk had promised not to confront

Thomas for now, saying he would stay in the background and watch over the house.

"You're going to have to try to get through to him," Fisk's voice resounded through her brain. "If anyone can break things to him gently, it's probably you. His testimony is crucial to stopping a cancerous, powerful organization, not to mention putting away a very bad man."

"His father," Sophie had whispered, her tone thick with dread.

Fisk's mouth had tightened. "Thomas Nicasio may be in denial at the moment, but I can assure you, Dr. Gable, that inside, where it counts, he despises the sound of Joseph Carlisle's name."

"What do you mean?" she asked sharply.

Fisk had frowned as if unsure whether he should say more, but something had decided him. "We've had some leaks at the FBI in regard to our investigations into the Outfit; enough breaches in security that my superior has funneled a lot of high-level information exclusively to me. Last Thursday afternoon, when Nicasio called headquarters from a pay phone, saying he needed to talk to the person responsible for the investigation, my boss had the call sent to me.

"We've been building a fairly convincing case against Joseph Carlisle and several of his top lieutenants, mostly based on illegal accounting practices, tax fraud, and gambling. Frankly, we wanted more, though. With the right lawyers and legal abracadabra, Carlisle might have gotten off with a slap on the wrist. Best case scenario was that we put away Carlisle, the Outfit would put another guy in his place, and the mob would continue on its merry way. But what Nicasio told me during that phone call convinced me without a doubt that we could put Joseph Carlisle behind bars for good and slice out the legs of the Chicago mob on a permanent basis as well. Nicasio was obviously pressured and agitated, but he was also entirely convincing."

Sophie's anxiety had ratcheted up a few notches when the agent paused.

"What is it?" Sophie had prompted uneasily.

"One of the things he told me," Fisk had continued in a hushed voice, "was that Thomas had discovered that afternoon that Joseph Carlisle—his adoptive father—had ordered the execution of James Nicasio when Thomas was just a kid. Apparently, James had noticed some irregularity in his trucking invoices. Carlisle Transportation was racking up the miles on James Nicasio's runs, beefing up the charges on certain customers' deliveries. It's just one of the ways that Carlisle launders money. Those customers were in on a scheme to hide profits from illegal operations. I guess James Nicasio poked around after that, and noticed similar altered bookkeeping on some of his buddies' invoices, so he knew it wasn't just isolated to his truck. The books were being cooked on a company-wide level. Nicasio confronted Carlisle. He refused to back down when Carlisle ordered him to keep silent about it.

"When Thomas called me last Thursday," Fisk continued, "he said he was in possession of a recording made by his brother, Rick Carlisle, of Bernard Cokey describing how he'd overheard Carlisle give orders to a hood named Newt Garnier to execute James Nicasio. Apparently when the hit happened, Marion Nicasio threw herself in front of her husband when Garnier broke into the house that night. So Garnier shot her as well."

As she stood in her living room, Sophie re-experienced the flash of horror that had jolted through her when Fisk had said those words just minutes ago. The effect on Thomas when he had made the same discovery was infinitely more damaging. The man he'd considered his father had murdered his real parents, and then taken Thomas into his home.

Could there be any worse knowledge than learning you'd not only lived with the devil for most of your childhood, but called him *Father*? Carlisle had robbed Thomas of his parents, his brother, and his nephew. But Sophie suspected she knew what had been the very first blow, what had psychologically sent Thomas into a posttraumatic tailspin following all his recent horrific losses.

That sick fuck had made Thomas love him.

She thought of how wounded he'd been that night she'd found him standing on her dock. That wound still existed, despite Thomas's frantic attempts at ignoring it.

Sophie rushed over to the picture window, searching the dock and lake desperately.

"Thomas?" she called out shrilly when she saw no sign of him.

She started to race down the hallway, thinking she must have missed him in the yard, when she saw him walking toward her.

"What . . . what are you doing?" she asked in confusion when she noticed that he wore the pants to his suit and the same bloody dress shirt he'd worn when he came to Haven Lake with her so many nights ago. She stepped back when she took in the expression on his face and the hard, dangerous glitter in his green eyes.

"Are you finished having your talk with Agent Fisk?"

Air popped out of her lungs as though she'd been punched. It had been the last thing she'd expected him to say.

"I . . . I—"

"Come on, Sophie," he prodded. His quiet voice struck her as being bizarrely at odds with his damp brow and tense posture. "If you're going to make a habit of lying, you'll have to get better at thinking on your feet."

"I don't know what you mean. I haven't been lying."

"You've been *conspiring*," he spat, the biting force of his accusation startling her more than his volume. "You've been talking to that man—" He waved wildly toward the driveway. "—behind my back. That's why you asked me here, isn't it?" he demanded as he came toward her slowly. Sophie shook her head as she stepped away from him. "You wanted me to open up to you. Maybe give you some incriminating evidence about my father that would bolster the FBI's investigation?"

"No. No, Thomas. That's not true," she murmured. Her hip hit the kitchen counter, halting her. Thomas kept coming, his presence as dark and intimidating as it might be to stand in the path of an oncoming cyclone. Sweat beaded on his brow and glazed his face.

"I wondered why you insisted on me being here," he said in a hollow voice. "I even suspected you of talking to the Feds about what you'd learned from Dr. Lancaster. Still . . ." His slashing smile struck Sophie as alarming. "You can be very convincing, Sophie. I have to give credit where it's due. Those big eyes and soft touches. You're one hell of an actress." He shook his head, his fixed smile remaining eerily intact. His bark of laughter made her jump like gunfire had gone off.

"I even believed it when you told me you were falling in love with me. I even believed *that*."

"You should have believed it. It's the truth," she whispered through numb lips. He stepped toward her, until his thighs and pelvis made contact with her body. She felt the heat pouring off him. Her gaze up at him entreated him . . . begged him to remember.

She went very still when he leaned down over her and placed his large, opened hand on her collarbone, thumb and forefinger pressing to her neck.

"It's a lie," he hissed softly. "*Everything* is a fucking lie."

"No. Not everything." Her lips moved to say more, but the wildness in his eyes, the reality of his lancing pain, froze her vocal cords.

"You're the FBI's informant," he grated out.

"*No, Tom. It wasn't me.*"

She saw a convulsion of emotion go through his face, but then it was gone. Tears dripped into her open mouth as she watched helplessly as he stormed out the back door.

CHAPTER **THIRTY-ONE**

He saw the world in blurry two-dimensions, as though he were a trapped goldfish swimming around frantically in a bowl of glass. Brilliant color blinded him from all directions as his car hurtled down the country road. Sweat poured off his brow. His demons rose, one by one: They were his own memories, thoughts . . . emotions.

He fought them like a person fights rising nausea, but they encroached on him anyway, hitting him in a series of disorienting flashes.

Agent Fisk's hand on Sophie's shoulder, their heads bent together as they spoke intimately.

Flash.

Sophie staring up at him, pleading with him with those soft, dark eyes that cut down to the very core of him. "No, Tom. It wasn't *me*."

Tom. She'd called him Tom. *Why had she called him the name he'd gone by as a boy?*

Flash.

Joseph Carlisle staring at him coldly from behind his huge walnut desk.

Pity. You ended up being just like your father, in the end.
It happened in two quick blinks of an eye.

He started to rise on a small hill in the road and a midnight blue Buick was suddenly topping it, headed straight at him. Thomas jerked the wheel and struck loose gravel, careening over the rise in the road at a skid. He braked, lurching to a halt, just barely stopping himself from going into the ditch.

He could no longer see the Buick because of the bump in the road, but suddenly he could divide his life into before the moment he'd seen that speeding vehicle and everything that came after.

He shut his eyes and shook as memories slammed into his consciousness with the force of a locomotive.

The interior of Joseph Carlisle's office was cool and dim. His father hadn't been going into his office at the trucking company since Rick and Abel had died. Thomas sunk into one of the leather chairs in front of his father's desk and briefly shut his eyes. They burned. He had slept maybe three or four hours in days. Ever since the funeral.

Ever since he'd finally done what Rick had asked and listened to the recording Rick had given him just days before he died.

He opened his eyes, and noticed Joseph had taken note of his haggard appearance, unshaven jaw, worn jeans, and an old T-shirt from his Navy EOD days.

Mighty are those that flirt with fate.

Mighty? Perhaps. Or maybe he'd just been lost. He'd been fearless as a kid, accepting almost any dare, because he figured deep down, he didn't deserve the stability of a family. Now that he was beginning to experience the shakiness of what he'd assumed was a stable world, the idea of going down on a bomb seemed downright tame.

"You look like shit . . . and like you've been getting about as much sleep as your mother," Joseph said as he sunk down into the chair behind his desk. The chair was a large, winged-back number. Joseph used to overfill it, not only with his large, once powerful body, but with his charisma. Presently, it looked like the chair had grown.

Or Joseph Carlisle had shrunk.

"You should contact your doctor and ask for sleeping pills," his adoptive father continued in a toneless voice. When he clutched his side and winced, a large figure stepped into Thomas's peripheral vision. He scowled as he watched Newt Garnier—Joseph's longtime right-hand man—open up a drawer and take out a bottle of antacid.

"You're the one who needs to see a doctor," Thomas said. His irritation mounted when his father accepted the tablets from Garnier, washing them down with a swig of coffee.

"It's just my damn acid reflux."

"How do you know? Who diagnosed you? Has Garnier gone and got his medical degree in the past few months?" Thomas snapped. He ignored Garnier's malevolent glare. He and Thomas had never gotten along. Thomas figured Garnier was jealous of anyone who shared a special relationship with Joseph Carlisle. He knew his mother and Garnier had never been on the best footing either, but his father refused to hear a word against the man.

"Don't let your mother hear you saying stuff like that," Joseph said wryly. "The last thing she needs at this moment is something else to worry about."

Thomas went still, only his gaze moving over Joseph. Had what he said been a subtle threat? Had Joseph noticed the way Thomas had scrutinized him from across the crowded rooms at the wake and the funeral, as though he were trying to bring the sight of his adoptive father into focus? It disoriented him, this necessity for suspicion, this compulsion to try to consider the man he'd known and loved for most of his life in a different light.

When Garnier slammed the drawer shut and Joseph grimaced as he took another swig of his coffee, Thomas inhaled slowly, attempting to smooth over his confusion and a rising anger that he wasn't quite sure how the hell to contain. He'd been having more and more trouble controlling his temper since Rick had died. Now that he'd listened to the tape, he found himself increasingly at the mercy of his fury.

His adoptive father looked old. The thought drained the rage and helplessness out of him. He sagged into the leather chair, suddenly feeling too weary to complete the task that had brought him to his father's house in Lake Forest today.

But he *would* finish it. Too many questions were buzzing around his head. He needed answers.

He'd continue for Rick.

"I'd like to speak with you alone," Thomas muttered.

Garnier opened his mouth as though to protest—the man was becoming increasingly proprietary over Joseph in the past several months—but Joseph waved his hand dismissively.

"I'll be right outside if you need me," Garnier rasped.

"We won't."

Garnier swung around his square jaw at Thomas's pointed comment. Thomas held his stare until the big man stepped out of his vision.

"That guy's an asshole," Thomas said under his breath.

"He says the same about you," Joseph Carlisle replied without rancor. "Maybe that's why I like both of you."

Thomas distractedly picked up the trophy sitting on his father's desk.

"I can't believe you still have this thing," he mumbled as he flipped the cheap trophy in one hand so that he could read the inscribed plate. FIRST PLACE, DIVISION IA, THE LAKE FOREST PANTHERS, 1985.

"The day you hit that winning homerun was one of the best days of my life," Joseph said.

Thomas glanced up. "You've gotta be kidding."

"I'm serious."

Thomas shook his head, his brow wrinkled perplexedly. "It had to be one of the worst days of Ricky's," he mumbled, recalling how Rick had completely fallen apart in the outfield during the Little League championship game.

"The kid was a mess when it came to sports."

"Yeah. He was," Thomas said quietly. "And was brilliant at a lot of things that really counted."

He set the trophy on his father's desk carelessly. *Stupid, useless fucking thing.* Maybe it was the jolt of anger that went through him that gave him the will to proceed, despite Joseph's vulnerable state and the subtle allusions to his mother's condition, as well.

"You should have cut Rick more slack."

"We all should have done a lot of things," Joseph countered, his brusque tone belying his wasted appearance. "It's easy to second-guess our actions when someone close to us passes."

"Second-guessing yourself is a waste of time, right?" Thomas mused. "'Regrets will only weigh you down?' 'You've gotta move on, never look back,'" he quoted a few of Joseph's parental mantras.

Joseph shrugged. "Some of the best advice I ever gave my boys."

Thomas just shook his head grimly.

"What's wrong with you?" Joseph demanded.

Well, here it was. Best to just get it over with.

"Rick had been investigating the Chicago Outfit just before he died," Thomas began. "He planned to write a book on the topic."

Joseph's face looked gray in the dim light . . . waxy, like he wore a mask. "And you're bringing this up . . . Why? Because you know these FBI sons of bitches are nosing around, asking me stupid questions about my trucking company, about gambling operations and illegal bookkeeping . . . insinuating *I'm* a criminal. Those assholes are turning your mother into a walking zombie—"

"I'm just stating a fact," Thomas interrupted, although he tried to keep his voice even. "And Mom's in the state she's in because her son and grandson are dead."

"You think I don't know that?" Joseph fired at him.

"I'm trying to talk to you about Rick's investigations."

"What has that got to do with me?"

Thomas met his father's stare. His fierce eyes used to

have the ability to make him quake in his Nikes, not that he'd let Joseph ever know that. At the moment, Joseph's blue eyes looked watery and . . . washed out. Still, Thomas sensed the fight and toughness of an old bulldog in him.

"It's got everything to do with you," Thomas replied. "Rick found an informant, a man who had done small deals with the Outfit since he was practically a kid, who was willing to talk to Rick about what he knew—to detail operations. To name names."

The silence that followed felt so thick that Thomas swore it pressed like a weight on his chest. He studied the face of the man that he'd known and trusted since he was a ten-year-old boy.

"I guess you already know who Rick's informant fingered as the head man of the Outfit," Thomas said.

Joseph's indifferent shrug jarred through his consciousness.

"Me, right?"

Thomas nodded, his entire awareness . . . his entire world narrowing down into a surreally sharp focus on the man who sat behind the desk.

"Are you telling me that Ricky believed that liar?" Joseph barked.

"He didn't, at first. I told him that this man—his source—must have known Rick's real name. He must have been trying to con Rick, implicate you as a criminal so that he could later blackmail Rick for money."

Joseph made a "well there you have it" gesture with his hand. Thomas just continued to pin him with his stare, however, and Joseph added bitterly, "Let me guess. My loving eldest son decided in the end that his ol' dad was guilty. What . . . was he going to devote a whole chapter to me in his book? 'My Dad, the Crime Boss?'"

"I don't know, Joseph." The old man's chin shot up at Thomas's usage of his given name. "Is that what you were worried would happen?"

An unhealthy-looking pink flush stained his father's gray cheeks. Thomas realized with a distant sense of amazement that now that he'd crossed the line, he was starting to see his adoptive father in a shockingly clear focus. The vision was slowly, inexorably turning his world upside-down.

"Rick gave me a tape of his interviews with his informant several days before he died. I refused to listen to it," Thomas rasped.

"You always were loyal. More like my own flesh and blood than my own son." Joseph's voice sounded proud and sure, but Thomas saw how his hands shook.

"Rick was ten times the man I am. *Ten times*," Thomas enunciated slowly.

"He was weak and ungrateful—"

"He was *your son*."

Joseph didn't flinch when Thomas stood abruptly and reached for the wooden box sitting on his father's desk. Ricky and he had known what was inside that box since Thomas was fifteen years old. The two of them had been bored one Saturday afternoon and Rick had dared his brother to smoke one of their father's strong, pungent cigars. They'd snuck into Joseph's office—forbidden territory.

That was when they'd found the gun.

Thomas removed the Glock automatic, quickly checked to see that it was loaded and then slammed it down on the desk between them. His breathing came raggedly now.

"But after Rick and Abel were incinerated in that *boat accident*, I decided . . . why not? Give the tape a listen. It's what Rick wanted, wasn't it? Do you know what that man told Rick on those tapes, Joseph?"

Joseph's nostrils flared but he didn't reply.

"He told Rick that you had given the order for dozens of murders over the years. *You*," Thomas repeated, half in fury and half in incredulity. "The same man who coached our Little League team, who invited half the city to our house on Christmas Eve, and made the biggest donations to the children's hospital every year. *You*."

Thomas leaned down over the desk until his face was less than two feet away from Joseph's and spoke in a low, gravelly voice.

"The informant told Rick that two of the people you had murdered were my parents because my father had noticed some inconsistencies in your books, Joseph. What do you say to that?"

For a stretched moment in which Thomas thought his fury was going to erupt through the top of his head, Joseph said nothing. Finally Joseph nodded at the Glock that lay between them.

"If you believe that I had James Nicasio killed, what are you just standing there for? Why don't you shoot me, Thomas? Why don't you shoot your old man?" he asked roughly.

"Maybe I just wanted to see if you'd pick up that gun and kill *me* in cold blood just like you did your son and grandson," Thomas hissed. "But no . . . that's not your style is it, *Dad*? You wouldn't just blast a son's brain out in your own house, would you? No, it's much more your style to have one of your hoods cut my brake lines, or maybe arrange for another explosion? A gas leak, maybe. Yeah, that sounds more up your alley, doesn't it?"

Joseph's taut leer struck him as obscene.

"At least I taught you something after all these years. But not enough, apparently," he said, shaking his head. "I should have known, in the end, that blood was thicker than water. You're just like him. You're just like your father. He was so indignant at the idea of someone making a little extra money on the side. 'Not on *my* truck; not on *my* runs.' That's what James Nicasio said when he came to me with his great discoveries about the jacked up invoices all those years ago. As if that stupid dago even owned that truck; as if *he* had the right to say what would happen in my company. You're just like *both* of them—your nosy father and your self-righteous, holier-than-thou brother." He shoved the gun toward Thomas. "*Go on*. Prove me wrong. Neither of *them* would have had the guts to pick up that gun and shoot me."

Fury blinded him. Thomas wasn't aware of having picked up the weapon, but he suddenly trained it on Joseph's face. Hatred raced through his veins like a poison, the strength of it amplified exponentially by the presence of a lifetime of love and respect.

"You're admitting it? You had them killed? My parents . . . Ricky?"

Joseph gave him a disdainful glance. "I won't deny it. I might have done so for a son, but I see I don't have one anymore."

His finger twitched on the trigger, but something stilled it. He lowered the weapon.

"You're right," he rasped. "I *am* like my father. I'm not such an animal that I'd shoot a pitiful, helpless old man."

Joseph rose from his desk, incensed.

"You worthless piece of shit," he raged, spittle shooting from his mouth. "I should have left you to the orphanage. I should have left you on the streets with the trash, where you belonged."

"I should have been so fucking lucky!" Thomas roared. "Instead I was lured into the house of a monster . . . played at his feet, ate his cursed food."

Asked for his love . . . been so proud when I mistakenly believed it was given . . .

The truth burned.

He was barely aware of the door opening behind him. His words were flying out of his throat now like boiling drops of acid, scalding him to his very core. "You asshole . . . you *devil*—" He struggled when Garnier put him in a restraining hold, locking his arms down next to his body, but his baleful stare remained locked with the man who had transformed into a monster before his very eyes. "I'm going to send you away forever, do you hear me? I'm going to see you roast. You're *finished*."

In a fit of wild rage he dropped the Glock and broke free of Garnier's restraint. Spinning, he clocked Garnier on his square jaw, the solid punch splitting the skin on his knuckle. He followed with a left to Garnier's solar plexus that made the big, gray-haired man double over and gasp for air.

Thomas snarled and put all of his pent-up rage into a vicious kick to Garnier's face.

"You're going down with him, asshole," Thomas seethed. "You worked for him back then. Did he send *you* to my parents' house that night? Were you the *big man* who murdered two helpless people in their bed while their kid slept in the other room?" Garnier started to stand—blood gushed out of his nose and ran down into his gaping mouth.

Thomas sank another punch to his gut. Garnier gasped and then howled with fury.

"Thomas? Joseph? What in the—*Oh my God.*"

Iris Carlisle stood in the doorway to the den wearing a green robe, her usually meticulously coiffed brown hair mussed and slightly greasy, the skin of her face looking like pale parchment paper stretched thin over the delicate bones. Her familiar light green eyes pinned Thomas with a bewildered, anxious stare.

"Mom . . . I'm sorry," Thomas whispered gruffly.

Garnier took a measure of revenge while Thomas was distracted by the sight of Iris. Light flashed in front of his eyes and then air rushed by his ears.

He hit the floor before pain shot through his head like a jolt of electricity.

He must have passed out for a moment; he couldn't be sure. Garnier had nailed him on the temple. The next thing he heard through the dense haze of pain and confusion that encompassed him like a thick cloud was his mother's frantic, fearful voice, and then Joseph's roar, cutting through everything else.

"Leave him alone, you moron; that's my wife standing there. Just get him out of here!"

Thomas realized that Garnier had hauled him into a sitting position, and that one of his fists was cocked, ready to strike Thomas again. Garnier growled at Joseph's order, but he did his boss's bidding. Instead of hammering Thomas again, he jerked him up off the floor. Thomas staggered when Garnier shoved him toward the door.

His memory of leaving the house was spotty. He vaguely recalled his mother's frightened face, her calling out to him, and Garnier's snide insults and threats as he shoved Thomas out of the house he'd grown up in.

It'd been a living nightmare . . . Worse, an acid trip choreographed by the devil.

Thomas couldn't even recall most of his drive from the Carlisle's home back to the city. Garnier—and likely Joseph—had probably hoped he'd crash, he was so out of it. By the time he'd pulled over at a gas station just before the junction of the Kennedy and Edens expressways, however, Thomas was thinking more clearly. He wasn't himself; not by any means. He was an automaton, moving and thinking, but not feeling. In the past few days, feeling had grown dangerous.

In the past hour and a half, feeling had become agony.

He'd walked into the gas station, bought a bottle of water and some Tylenol, and asked for quarters with his change.

Then he'd used the pay phone in the parking lot to contact the FBI. He'd had a long conversation with an agent named Fisk. He'd told Agent Fisk that he was in possession of a tape that incriminated his adoptive father, Joseph Carlisle, in multiple crimes, including the murder of his real parents, James and Marion Nicasio. At the conclusion of their talk, Fisk had told him about some leaks at the Bureau and warned Thomas not to speak with any other agent about the information. Thomas had agreed for no other reason than through the haze of his shock he'd made an assessment of Fisk, and decided he seemed all right.

Thomas'd explained that he'd turn over the evidence to Fisk within a few days. He'd hung up to the sound of Fisk asking him repeatedly where he planned on going following their conversation.

"You're in danger, Nicasio!" Thomas had heard the agent shout right before he'd replaced the receiver in the cradle and walked away from the pay phone.

He'd lingered at the gas station, ensuring himself that he wasn't being followed. Joseph and Garnier must have been nearly as discombobulated by his unexpected visit as Thomas had been. They'd regroup, though. Eventually.

When he was convinced that he hadn't been followed, Thomas got into his car and removed the battery from his cell phone.

He drove, longing for distance from a terror that Joseph Carlisle had just confirmed as a reality—desperate for something to hold onto while his life careened wildly off balance.

He thought he'd been driving aimlessly, but now, as he sat at the side of that country road, the roar of the blue Buick's engine still humming in his ears, Thomas knew he'd traveled with a single-minded focus. He'd seen a luminous face in his mind's eye, said her name silently like a mantra that might save him.

Dr. Gable.

Sophie. Sophie.

And somewhere in the monotonous process of driving down a strip of interstate for miles and miles, a fever of forgetfulness had settled upon him. The toxic memories became distant. They faded.

Then they were gone.

Until two seconds ago, when that blue Buick topped that rise, and Thomas had a flashing image of Newt Garnier's rocklike profile, his gaze trained with focused intensity on the road that led straight to Sophie.

He shoved the ignition into reverse, but someone slapping their palm against the window stopped him from stomping on the gas.

What he saw outside the window caused a sensation as though all the blood in his head had rushed to his legs.

He lowered the window.

"You left Sophie alone?" he bellowed.

You're the one who left Sophie alone, you asshole, he admonished himself.

"I'm here to protect you, not Dr. Gable," Agent Fisk said, clearly set off balance by Thomas's greeting.

"Fuck."

He started to back up, but Fisk held onto the window frame and staggered after him.

"She's there all alone," Thomas shouted. "I just saw Newt

Garnier pass in a car. *Just now.* He'll kill her without thinking twice."

He thought Fisk might have let go of his car willingly then, but Thomas was too agitated to even notice. The vision of Sophie looking up at him with those dark eyes . . . eyes that were pleading with him to remember.

It was the wrongness of accusing her, of forsaking Sophie that had caused all the memories to explode to the surface. How could he want to block out that night in his father's office if it meant erasing a single second with Sophie?

Which is exactly what he'd done.

He saw her standing there in her kitchen, her breasts looking so soft and firm beneath the thin bikini top, her dark eyes full of compassion and concern as she handed him a glass of lemonade. He remembered holding her in the guest bedroom, her scent filling his nose, soothing him and arousing him to a fever pitch at once.

Sleep with me, Sophie. I need your cleanness so much right now.

She'd rebuffed him then, but later, when he'd awakened after hours of healing, dreamless sleep, he'd staggered down the hallway to her bedroom, Sophie's presence calling out to him like siren song.

He'd opened the door and murmured her name. A lamp from the living room cast enough light down the hallway for him to see her curled on her side at the edge of the bed. Her eyes shone in the dim light. She didn't look surprised or startled at his intrusion into her private sanctuary.

"Do you feel better?" she'd asked quietly.

He'd just nodded, unable to remove his gaze from her face. *How the hell had he ever succeeded in staying away from her before?*

"Let me feel your forehead," she'd whispered.

He'd gone to her and knelt next to the bed, a supplicant before her beauty. Her hand had felt cool on his skin. Her scent enveloped him: sex and flowers and clean cotton.

When their gazes had met, she'd put her hands on his shoulders and silently urged him toward her.

And now, as he hurtled down the road toward her lake house in rising panic, he recalled how later they held each other fast as their tears mingled on their cheeks and his cock grew soft in the snug, warm sanctuary of Sophie's body.

It's going to be all right, Tom. I promise you. Someday, it's all going to be okay again.

He'd made love to her again and again on that night, and she'd given herself repeatedly, let him restrain her, let him find solace from his anguish in her sweet, soft flesh. Those hadn't been wet dreams he'd been having about Sophie; they'd been reality.

He'd never spoken to her of what had happened to him; his mind had blocked it from him even as he sought her out like a wounded animal. But somehow, she'd sensed the parameters of his fury, his loss . . . his grief.

Somehow, Sophie had known.

"It's going to be all right, Tom. I promise you. Someday, it's all going to be okay again," she'd whispered.

Oh God.

God, please let that be true. Not for him, who had ripped into her peaceful world like a torrential storm.

For Sophie.

CHAPTER **THIRTY-TWO**

Sophie had resisted an urge to go after Thomas in her car. It would be a useless exercise. It's not as if she could somehow overtake him on the road.

She couldn't force him to trust her . . . couldn't make him come back to her.

Would he be all right? Surely not. He wasn't safe. Her only comfort was that Agent Fisk was there, guarding him. Fisk would have tailed Thomas. The FBI agent would protect him—maybe even help him come to terms with his poisonous memories—better than Sophie could.

She wandered out to the boathouse. Perhaps Guy sensed her helplessness and misery, because he didn't start and go wary when she entered. The fox had been snuggled into a nest of blankets near his feeding dishes. When she sank down onto the dusty concrete floor of the dim boathouse and began to cry, the fox stood and began to inch toward her slowly.

The little animal finally stopped, his nose just inches from her knee. Laughter mixed with her sorrow when Guy lowered his head, allowing her to pet his neck and rub just behind his ears.

He backed away after several seconds, but Sophie had never appreciated a gesture of sympathy more.

It gave her the strength to stand and brush off her dusty shorts.

"It's going to be okay," she murmured to Guy, attempting to brace herself. "It's not over yet."

A shadow moved across the sunlight shining through the opened door. She saw Guy flinch. Sophie started to turn.

Someone—someone large—came up behind her and pinned her right arm against her ribs and pushed her body weight back against his solid length, setting her off balance. The hard, ungiving bone of a forearm pressed against her trachea.

"It might be over sooner than you think," a man rasped near her ear.

Thomas peered through the dusty window of the boathouse, struggling to see inside the shadowed interior. He saw a movement—Sophie's pale T-shirt as she jerked in Newt Garnier's hold. The dark outline of Garnier's gun showed up starkly against Sophie's belly. The sight sent a jolt of electricity through him. But what he heard made it worse. Garnier spoke in a low, rough voice while Sophie made choking sounds as she struggled.

He knew Garnier would just as soon strangle her than leave the evidence of a bullet behind.

Spots began to appear before her eyes. The intruder was cutting off her oxygen supply with his strangling hold. Just when she thought she would lose consciousness, however, he lessened the hold slightly, restoring a minimal amount of air to her burning lungs.

He began to question her again.

"Where's Nicasio?" Sophie felt him press the hard barrel of a gun between her ribs. "Better tell me, Blondie, or I'll shoot you point-blank in the gut. Very painful way to die, and it takes forever. You'd die out here all alone—"

A loud thwacking sound exploded into her ears. The hold on her trachea lessened, but then she was being pulled backward by a heavy weight. She twisted to get out of the man's hold, throwing her elbow into his ribs. He cursed viciously. Just as she was lunging for freedom, he grabbed at her hair and pulled her back once again.

Sophie found herself staring at Thomas's rigid face. Her heart leapt in her chest at the unexpected, welcome sight of him. Dread settled when she recalled the man's gun. Thomas held one of the paddles from the canoe in both hands, his biceps flexing tightly beneath the arms of his T-shirt. He looked furious, but focused; his glare not on Sophie but on the man who held her and pressed the barrel of his gun to Sophie's temple.

"You shoulda hit me harder, Nicasio," the man behind her taunted. Her positioning was different than before, and she had a little more room to maneuver. She glanced up to see the face of the man who held her and saw the profile of a man in his fifties with steel-gray hair, a rough-hewn face, and a swollen nose. From her angle, she could see that blood trickled out of his right ear, a result of what had sounded like a vicious blow of the paddle against the intruder's head.

Sophie also noticed that despite the man's bravado, his speech was slurred. The blow to his head was having an effect, even if the man didn't realize it. He blinked several times, as though trying to clear his vision.

"Most men's heads aren't quite so thick, Garnier," Thomas muttered. His eyelids were narrowed so that Sophie could see nothing but two crescents of gleaming dark green. His focus on Garnier seemed absolute. "Let go of her. She's got nothing to do with this."

Sophie gritted her teeth in pain when the man shoved the barrel of the gun farther into her skull.

"Who says she's got nuthin' to do with this? She was here, wasn't she? She got in my way. Just like your ma did all those years ago, huh Nicasio? I didn't go there for her. Joseph just wanted James Nicasio dead. But seein' as how she was stupid enough to throw herself in front of Nicasio, it was no sweat off my back to do her like I did your dad. Now . . . drop dat paddle, or I'll do the same to this little girl—"

Several things happened at once. Garnier tried to shake Sophie in front of him for emphasis, but he stumbled slightly on his feet in doing so. Sophie seized the moment and put all of her energy into another backward jab with her elbow. She heard an animal growl from below and Garnier squalled.

Apparently, Guy had chosen the precise same moment to attack and bit Garnier's leg.

"Don't move, Garnier!" Fisk barked. The agent swung into the doorway, his weapon drawn and aimed near Sophie's head.

The various attacks on Garnier caused him to lower his weapon from Sophie's temple. The second he did, Thomas didn't swing the paddle, he jabbed the handle straight into Garnier's face, one hand guiding the weapon, the other providing the forceful forward shove from the end of the paddle.

Thomas never flinched. In that fleeting second, Sophie glimpsed the incredibly tight focus, the sheer fearlessness of a man who had faced off with a live bomb time and again.

She heard a sickening crunch of wood against bone and suddenly the tight trap of Garnier's steely arms went slack. She spun away in time to see Garnier sinking to the floor in slow motion, a surprised look on his face. When his knees hit the floor, he slumped over into complete unconsciousness. Thomas had lanced the handle of the paddle into Garnier's right eye socket.

One thing was for sure: Garnier would never use the eye—or what was left of it—again.

The paddle fell to the concrete floor with a clack. Thomas came up behind her. He encircled her in his arms, hugging her to him, before he let go and turned her to face him.

"I'm okay," Sophie said when she glanced up and saw

the palpable anxiety on his features as his gaze ran over her, searching for wounds.

His nostrils flared when she spoke. The expression she saw in his eyes made her touch his jaw, and then wrap her arms around his shoulders.

"I'm okay, Thomas. I'm okay," she repeated.

His arms came around her and her feet came off the floor when he lifted her. He held her to him so tightly it squeezed the air out of her lungs for a few seconds.

"Sophie," he spoke roughly near her ear. "Sophie . . . I'm so sorry—I . . . I didn't remember."

A spasm of emotion tightened her face when she heard how his deep voice cracked.

"It's okay. Everything is going to be all right. Are you hurt?" she asked in a rush after he'd set her back on the floor and she'd caught her breath.

He lifted his head and shook it. She saw his muscular neck convulse as he swallowed.

"You shouldn't have done that, Nicasio."

Sophie pushed her way out of Thomas's arms—although he seemed hesitant to let her go—and stared at Fisk. The agent knelt next to the fallen giant, his fingers on Garnier's neck.

"Is he dead?" Thomas asked woodenly.

"No. I'm surprised after that shot you gave him with that paddle. In fact, I'm shocked the damn thing isn't still in the guy's skull," Fisk finished wryly under his breath before he stood and removed some handcuffs from the back pocket of the jeans he wore.

"He killed my parents," Thomas said, his lip curling in hatred as he pinned the unconscious Garnier with his stare. "He killed them under Joseph Carlisle's order."

"Yeah, I heard that part. And even though you should have let me handle things with Garnier—" The agent rolled his eyes at his unintentional double entendre. "I not only need to thank you for saving Dr. Gable, but garnering us that confession," Fisk admitted with a small smile. He extricated his cell phone and began to dial emergency services.

Sophie turned her attention to Thomas. He must have noticed the way she was staring at him. His arms were still slightly outstretched from when he'd been holding her a second earlier. His glance at her was regretful.

"I remember, Sophie. I remember all of it."

He lowered his eyes and his arms at once, but Sophie flew over to him, flinging her arms around his shoulders. When he realized she wasn't rebuffing him for his earlier behavior, he hugged her to him just as forcefully. He lowered his head and she pressed her face to the side of his neck.

"I'm so sorry, Thomas. I'm so sorry," she murmured, hating the idea of him experiencing so much anguish.

"No," he said gruffly. "I'm the one who's sorry. I'm the one."

She heard a plaintive whine and looked down to see Guy looking up at them with black, anxious eyes.

"Look at that," Thomas murmured. "A three-and-a-half-legged hero."

"Four-legged. He's pretty much healed. Thank you for helping me, Guy," Sophie whispered to the little fox. Guy whimpered and sat on his haunches, looking completely comfortable for the first time since Sophie had begun taking care of him.

Thomas's arms tightened around her. Sophie just stood there in the dim boathouse, telling herself to focus on the feeling of holding a vibrant, whole Thomas in her arms. She tried like hell not to consider what came next . . . now that he no longer needed her to help him forget all of his pain.

CHAPTER **THIRTY-THREE**

Sophie sat in front of her laptop computer and scowled at the screen. It was a hopeless cause. She might as well face it. She would not be turning in her journal articles on the holistic treatment of Type II diabetes.

Not this year, she wouldn't.

She glanced over at Collin Fisk, who sprawled on her couch and was reading *The New England Journal of Medicine* as though he actually found it interesting. Sophie had gotten to know the young agent very well over the last three weeks—ever since Newt Garnier had attacked her at her lake house; ever since Joseph Carlisle had been arrested on multiple criminal accounts, including conspiracy to commit murder.

Thomas had returned to Chicago with several federal agents who had been charged with protecting him. The FBI had offered to put him in a witness protection program until he was able to testify against Joseph Carlisle, but Thomas had refused.

It had been driving Sophie mad to think of Thomas up there in Chicago without her, giving testimony against a man he'd once loved and respected. She was worried sick that despite FBI protection, the mob would find a way to silence the man who had the power to kill the many-tentacled criminal organization once and for all.

Thomas had insisted that Sophie stay away from him, however, at least until he'd been able to give his testimony and the dangerous players, like Joseph Carlisle, were rendered powerless. He'd also insisted on one other thing before he'd left Haven Lake. Thomas would not accept another bodyguard for Sophie other than Collin Fisk.

That'd all been weeks ago now. So much had happened in the interim. Newt Garnier had agreed to come clean on other members of the criminal organization in exchange for a lighter sentence.

Four days ago, Joseph Carlisle had died of a massive heart attack while under police custody at the Dirksen Federal Building.

Sophie felt as if she'd been dying a slow death of her own being cooped up there in the lake house and watching the heart-wrenching footage of the Carlisle funeral . . . of Thomas holding up his very frail-looking mother, Iris, as she collapsed on the way to the burial of her husband.

God, she couldn't imagine what Thomas was enduring. She hurt so much for him.

"You said you wanted to stop biting your nails," Collin said as he flipped one of the pages of the journal and continued to read without looking up.

Sophie grimaced at her fingertips.

"Now isn't the time to give up bad habits," she mumbled. She set aside her computer and stood. "What's taking them so long?"

"It does take *time* to drive from Chicago to here, Sophie."

"I know, but they're past due," she said, checking her watch.

She nervously went to the window over the sink and checked the driveway. It'd been three long weeks since she'd seen Thomas in person. When he'd said good-bye to her, the two agents who had arrived from Chicago to guard him were standing annoyingly close. They hadn't gone much farther away when Thomas had barked that they needed a little privacy.

He'd called her on the phone several times, but once again, she got the impression he was either distracted by the stress of giving evidence at FBI headquarters or by tending to his mother, who was not doing well at all since her husband had been charged with so many crimes and taken into custody.

At other times, she got the impression that Thomas wasn't alone when he called. She imagined from the terse, slightly irritated quality of his tone that his bodyguards were standing nearby.

At least Sophie *hoped* those were the reasons that Thomas had been so unrevealing in their brief interactions. It might also be that he felt guilty for the way he'd behaved with her during his emotional crisis. Now that he was starting to accept the brutal facts of his life—that the man he'd loved and called "Father" had, in fact, been the man who had murdered his own parents—perhaps he was embarrassed by his acute need for Sophie during his trauma.

She knew from experience that it wasn't uncommon for people to feel ashamed of their vulnerability during an acute stress response. Thomas was even more used to dealing with his stress in a private manner than most. He'd been accepted, trained, and then had excelled in a military unit that required a high degree of tolerance to stress and danger. He'd been used to overcoming his personal demons in a private manner.

How did he really feel about the fact that his mind had shut out a part of his life that had caused him so much pain? Would he forever associate his short-lived vulnerability with Sophie? Had he called to tell her that he wanted to meet with her this evening because he wanted to apologize once again . . . and then proceed to exit her life once and for all?

The anxious ruminations caused a surge of nausea in her gut. When she heard the gravel snapping beneath the wheels of an arriving vehicle, Sophie couldn't be sure if she was experiencing intense anticipation or dread.

She flew to the back door, but then stopped several feet

away, not wanting to seem too wildly eager. She veered over toward the window, instead. She saw that it was Thomas's car, and that Thomas himself drove with two agents in the passenger seats.

As soon as the dark green sedan came to a halt, the driver's-side door flew open and Thomas sprung out of the driver's seat. He left the door hanging open, just like he had on that first night he'd come to her. His brown hair was slightly mussed and hung on his brow in the fashion to which she'd grown accustomed while he was with her at Haven Lake. He must have come from some kind of meeting, however, because he wore a pair of dark gray dress pants that fell elegantly on his tall, powerful frame and a striped dress shirt with the sleeves rolled back and the collar open.

When she saw how he walked purposefully toward the house with that familiar long-legged stride, Sophie forgot her self-consciousness and barreled out the back door.

He stopped abruptly at her appearance, his leather dress shoes causing the gravel to pop and scatter beneath them. Their gazes met across the fifteen feet that separated them. Sophie stood frozen, one hand on the screen door. He seemed just as disarmed by the sight of her.

"Why don't you try hugging him?" Collin asked wryly from behind her.

Sophie glanced back, a smile pulling at her lips. She saw that Thomas didn't seem as amused as he took in Agent Fisk standing behind her. Her foot hit the sidewalk when Fisk gave her a soft shove from behind.

Thomas came toward her as she approached him. She studied him but she couldn't decipher his expression.

Then he wrapped her in his arms and the familiar feeling of being encompassed by Thomas Nicasio—of coming home—overwhelmed her. She wasn't sure how long they remained like that—just hugging, pressing their bodies close, so that Sophie could feel his strong, steady heartbeat pounding next to her own.

Eventually, she turned her face into him, covertly wiping her tears on his shirtfront.

"You've lost weight," she said shakily into his chest.

"I haven't had the benefit of your good cooking," he replied in a low voice near her ear.

Sophie leaned back and felt herself sinking into the depths of Thomas's fiery green eyes. Someone cleared his throat from behind them.

"Agents Hargrove and Ellis and I will occupy ourselves out here for a while," Fisk said levelly. He stepped out of the screen door and waved Thomas and Sophie inside the house. Sophie smiled gratefully at Fisk and grabbed Thomas's hand.

"Wait," Thomas said gruffly from behind her when they neared Fisk. He addressed the young agent. "I told you that I had something for you, many weeks ago. I want to give it to you now."

Fisk's brows rose in interest. "The tape of Bernard Cokey?"

Thomas nodded.

"We have enough evidence to put away the major players for good, thanks to you," Fisk told Nicasio. "But if that tape exists, it'd be the icing on the cake."

"It exists. It's what my brother and nephew died for," Thomas said soberly. Much to Sophie's surprise, he tightened his hold on her hand and led her into the kitchen. He stopped once Fisk had followed them into the house and the screen door had closed behind him.

"Where's your briefcase, Sophie?" Thomas asked.

"My . . . what?"

"Your briefcase," Thomas repeated. "The one with all your journal articles inside it?"

"It's right there, next to the chair," Sophie said bemusedly, pointing to the supple brown leather bag that was nearly as stuffed as it had been that evening a month ago, when Thomas had helped her to retrieve her spilled papers.

Thomas released her hand and picked up the briefcase. He deposited it on the kitchen counter. Agent Fisk and she watched as Thomas searched amongst the pouches, finally extricating a journal—*The Lancet*. Sophie's mouth opened in wonder when he opened the magazine, tapped it on the counter, and a tiny cassette fell out.

He picked it up and handed it to Agent Fisk, who looked nearly as surprised as Sophie.

"It . . . it's been there? All along?" Sophie asked Thomas.

Thomas nodded. His gaze flickered over Agent Fisk before it settled on Sophie. He must have read the stunned question in her eyes, because he shrugged.

"I guess part of me trusted you with the truth all along, Sophie."

Sophie broke out of the trance of Thomas's eyes when Agent Fisk spoke.

"This is great, Thomas. Thanks. Like I said before, icing on the cake. I'll take good care of it."

Sophie continued to stare at Thomas as Fisk left, shutting the back door behind him.

She and Thomas stood alone for the first time in weeks. It seemed like an eternity.

"I was really out of it after Rick and Abel's funeral," he said gruffly. "I didn't know what to think about what I'd heard on that tape . . . about Cokey's allegation that Joseph Carlisle had given the order for my father to be executed." He hesitated for a moment, seeming unsure of his words. "I know I told you on that night we met in your office lobby— the night you were leaving for Haven Lake—that I was looking for Andy Lancaster, but I was lying."

Her eyebrows rose on her head in puzzlement. She took a step toward him.

"I was looking for you, Sophie."

His deep, husky voice seemed to linger in the air around her after he'd spoken. She couldn't help but think of that first night he'd come to Haven Lake, when he'd been so disoriented and traumatized . . . how he'd told her the same thing.

I came looking for you, Sophie.

"The amount of stress you were under was extraordinary, Thomas. I'm not blaming you for putting the tape in my briefcase. I just . . . I just don't understand why you did it."

"I don't know," he said, and she knew the incredulous

query hadn't faded from her expression. He sighed and threw up his hands in a helpless gesture.

"It's okay, Thomas," she whispered when she saw his bewilderment.

His gaze sharpened on her. "What's okay?"

She swallowed thickly and tried to infuse her voice with a measure of firmness she was far from feeling.

"It's okay. I'm . . . I'm glad I was here for you, when you needed it. I'm so thankful that you're on the mend. Andy told me that you'd been seeing a friend of his, Dr. Cassetti?"

"Yeah," he replied gruffly. "He's a good guy."

Sophie smiled tremulously. "I want you to know that I don't regret it. Not any of it."

His expression turned wary. "What do you mean by that —that you don't regret it?" he asked slowly.

"I know that what happened between us was a . . . a sort of side effect of your trauma. You needed an outlet for all the volatile emotions you were experiencing, emotions you couldn't put a name to. You found an outlet for your anguish by . . . by—"

"Fucking you like an animal, again and again?" he supplied quietly when she floundered.

She flushed with heat at his graphic language. His eyes looked hot as he studied her, but Sophie still couldn't entirely comprehend where he was coming from.

Or what he was feeling.

"Sophie?"

"Yes?" she whispered when he stepped close. Close enough for the fabric of his dress shirt to just touch the fabric over her breasts. Close enough for her to sense the coiled strength of his muscles and the hardness at his groin.

"If your theory about why I wanted you so much before were true, then it wouldn't make much sense for me to want you even more right this minute, would it?"

She stared up at him, her breath stuck in her lungs. She shook her head.

He joined her, shaking his head as well.

"Because I do. I want you even more than before. I'm going to take you back to your bedroom in a second and show you firsthand just how much. So the thing of it is," he muttered, his rough tone highly at odds with the deliberate gentleness with which he caressed her jaw and cheek, "there must have been some other reason that even when I was losing it, I trusted you with that tape; why later, I trusted you with *all of me* while I was falling apart. There must be some other reason that I sought you out, some other cause for why I can't get enough of you or why I've gone nearly as nuts for the past three weeks, being away from you," he murmured through lips that tilted with amusement.

Sophie blinked the tears out of her eyes, determined that he not see her vulnerable. "You were in the midst of a trauma reaction, Thomas. Don't feel like you have to say these things."

He paused in caressing her. His mouth settled into a grim line.

"I don't feel like I *have* to say anything." He suddenly pulled her tightly against him, making her hyperaware of his hard, masculine length. "Don't even try to do it, Sophie."

"What?" she asked, confused by his hard tone.

"I have all of my memories back. I remember everything. Well, almost all of it."

"What's that supposed to mea—"

"I remember you specifically telling me that you were falling for me. Are you going to deny it?" he interrupted, green eyes flashing. Sophie cried out in surprise when he suddenly lifted her into his arms.

"What do you think you're doing?" she asked him as he headed down the hallway.

"I'll make you tell me again. I have my methods," he said determinedly.

She laughed even though tears wet her cheek—tears of joy, at knowing he didn't regret seeking her out in the midst of his anguish and pain.

"As if I could ever deny a force of nature like you," she said against his neck.

He paused next to her bed and urged her head back so that he could look into her eyes. When she saw his expression, her smile faded.

"What, Tom?"

"I remembered all the crap about Joseph Carlisle—all the shit that had become my life for one reason. Do you know what it was?" he murmured.

"Why?" she mouthed, overcome by emotion.

"Because I couldn't sacrifice you to the darkness that was taking over my mind. You were this one exquisite, shining, beautiful thing set amongst all those awful realities. I couldn't have gone on forgetting you, forgetting the first night I ever touched you . . . forgetting the first night I felt you shake in my arms . . ."

"Thomas," she whispered. She pressed a finger to his lower lip, and then kissed his mouth softly.

"Why didn't you remind me of that night, Sophie?"

She shook her head. "I couldn't. I was afraid if I pushed you it would dislodge other memories of what had happened in that same time period. It had become all tied together in your unconsciousness. I didn't want to worsen your condition."

"How did you know, though? What made you realize that I didn't remember being here with you, on that first night?"

She traced one of his eyebrows and cast herself back into her own memories.

"I knew when we made love in my office. Afterwards . . ." She swallowed thickly. "You apologized for making love to me so forcefully for the first time."

She met his gaze. He winced.

"Jesus, Sophie. I'm so sorry. When I look back on it, it seems so strange. I remember what it was like *not* remembering, but it's like I was someone else. No . . . more like the pieces of my life were removed and replaced, but out of sequence. I remember almost everything now . . . although I can't really recall how I got back to Chicago after coming here on that first night, or what I was thinking in returning to work as though nothing had ever happened."

"I didn't understand what was happening to you at first,

either," Sophie admitted. "I thought you were just amnesic—possibly because of your head injury, possibly because of grief . . . maybe both. It wasn't until I'd been with you for a while and spoken with Andy that I realized your amnesia for that period of time was just one of the many symptoms that come from a trauma reaction. You returned to work that next morning as if nothing had ever happened because part of you *wanted* that, needed it . . . to forget what had happened when you confronted your father, to erase the horror of what he'd done to you."

"Another part of me wanted to remember that period of time," he said gruffly. "I wanted to remember you."

"I know," she replied. "I could see it in your eyes at times when we made love. I knew the memories would come back when you were ready. All I could do was wait . . . and pray for you."

He dried a tear on her cheek with a blunt-tipped fingertip. "You called me Tom on that night."

"You told me to," she whispered.

"It was what my parents and friends called me, when I was young," he said huskily. "I became Thomas with the Carlisles. For some reason, I wanted to hear my old name—my real name—on your lips on that night."

He lay her down on the bed and sank down over her. She closed her eyes briefly, cherishing the sensation of his long, hard body pressing her down into the mattress.

"I want to hear it again. I want to hear you scream it, Sophie."

He leaned down and seized her mouth in an explosive kiss, making speech, let alone a feeble thought, an utter impossibility.

EPILOGUE

FIVE WEEKS LATER

Thomas didn't have anything against Andy Lancaster and his wife, Sheila, per se. He'd just never wished two people would vanish so much as he did this easygoing, amiable couple.

He watched Sophie climb up on the ladder attached to the dock with a narrow-lidded gaze, took in every nuance of her shifting body weight, the slight sway of her breasts in the bikini top, the erotic manner in which rivulets of water ran across her golden, apricot-hued skin.

It was the first weekend in September, and it was a hot one. Just days ago, the FBI had finally, *finally* said that Thomas no longer required constant surveillance for his safety. Thomas had insisted he didn't need a bodyguard practically since day one. He had become even more vociferous about it since Joseph Carlisle had passed away and Newt Garnier had provided testimony that led to the arrests of every high-ranking lieutenant in the Outfit that the FBI had ever hoped to put behind bars.

He'd finally gotten rid of the omnipresent bodyguards only to have Sophie announce that Andy Lancaster and his wife would be coming for a weekend visit at Haven Lake.

Andy stopped in mid-sentence when Thomas abruptly lurched up from his reclining position on the dock. He had no idea what Lancaster had even been saying.

Thomas would apologize to Andy later.

"Sophie? Can I talk to you for a minute? Up at the house?" he clarified when Sophie just stared at him blankly for a second, a towel pressed to her cheek.

"Oh, sure," she replied levelly enough, although Thomas saw the reprimand in her laughing eyes.

He pulled her up the porch stairs behind him and into their bedroom. He snapped the door shut and locked it before he turned to her with a grim expression on his face.

"I should turn you over my knee, do you know that?"

Her eyebrows arched in amusement. "For what?"

"For running around in that bikini and driving me nuts." He grimaced when he cupped his aching balls and then his erection. "Don't tell me you didn't notice this. What are you, some kind of a sadist?"

Sophie just smiled, all sweetness and sex. She was going to fucking kill him, he swore it.

Daily.

"Take off that top," he snarled as he shoved down his trunks and stepped out of them.

His cock bobbed in the air when she did so. Her nipples were still tight and beaded from her swim. He growled and reached for her bikini bottoms when she ran her fingertips over them.

A few seconds later—Thomas was in no mood for seductions—he had her on her back on the mattress, his cock skewering her.

"Aw, God, yes," he muttered gratefully through clenched teeth at the divine sensation of Sophie's pussy sucking and squeezing at him. He began to pump. He glanced up and noticed Sophie's smile as he slammed into the heaven of her.

"How can you grin like that at a time like this?" he asked.

"I remember a time when I was worried that your need for me might diminish once you started to feel better," she murmured.

He pushed his cock all the way into her and rotated his hips slightly, grinding down on her clit. When she shut her eyes and her lips formed a little "O" of pleasure, he knew he was stimulating her sweet spot.

"You feel that? I feel fucking great at the moment. Does that feel like my need for you is diminishing?"

He made sure he gave her a climax before he raced for the finish line, fucking her with rapid, short strokes that had the bed rattling against the wall and both of them gasping wildly for air.

Later, after they'd both quieted, he heard Sophie call out to him softly. He lifted his head from her breast and met her stare.

"There's . . . something I've been meaning to ask you. If you don't want to tell me, you don't have to. But I know that in your therapy, you've been trying to put all your memories of what happened back then into sequence and perspective . . ."

"It's okay, Sophie. Go ahead and ask," he said, sensing her uncertainty.

"I was wondering . . . about your cell phone? I noticed it, you know. That first night that you came here, when you were so disoriented? I noticed that you'd removed your battery. It didn't occur to me until later that you'd likely done it so that your phone couldn't send out a signal."

He just stared at her for a moment before he exhaled and shook his head. "You don't miss much, do you?"

She just looked up at him silently . . . searchingly.

"Are you wondering if I purposefully made it so that I couldn't call anyone, because I was worried about Joseph Carlisle tracing me?"

She just nodded her head.

"Not consciously, no," he said as he once again reviewed the jumbled sequence of events. "That period of time was black for me in those days when I first came here with you after the warehouse explosion. I wouldn't even let myself consider the missing time." He shrugged. "It seems strange, but it's true. Dr. Cassetti says the human mind can do amazing things in order to protect itself. But I've been talking things over in therapy, and Cassetti pointed out that I had a clear, returned memory of wanting to make sure at that gas station, after calling Fisk, that I wasn't being followed or traced."

He glanced at Sophie. "So even though I wasn't consciously making sure I didn't provide an opportunity for a trace—"

"Some part of you knew to protect yourself," she finished for him.

He caressed her jaw. "Some part of me wouldn't have led those jackals to you." He smiled grimly. "It's like Dr. Cassetti said, I was traumatized, not stupid."

She put her hand on his jaw in a mirroring gesture. "I'm so glad to hear you say that," she whispered.

He leaned down and kissed her when he saw the expression on her face.

"'Course, my unconscious mind's plan didn't work too well," he muttered darkly.

"Sherm would die if he knew that he'd inadvertently led Newt Garnier here by using your phone. I'm so glad you agree that we shouldn't tell him," Sophie said.

He agreed one hundred percent, so he didn't respond. He shifted his hips, stimulating his sated cock in her tight sheath. She must have sensed his slight puzzlement.

"What?" she whispered through a smile as she pushed his bangs off his forehead and, as usual, they fell forward once again.

"You know . . ." he murmured thoughtfully, "I could never figure it out, why I wanted to fill you up with my come all the time. It's kind of strange, huh?"

"Is it?" Sophie asked. They both blinked when they heard a distant splash from the direction of the lake and then Sheila's laughter.

"For me it is. You know what I think?"

"I think you're wishing Andy and Sheila would go," she replied, giving him an amused, quelling glance. "But, Tom, we can't say anything, and you know it. And next weekend, remember that we invited Iris and Kelly to come and visit. A weekend here at Haven Lake will do them a world of good. I'm so glad you're maintaining your relationship with your mother, despite it all. So please don't pull anything like dragging me off to bed in the middle of lunch while she's here—"

"I think I've been trying—against all the odds," Thomas continued as though she'd never spoken, "to put a baby in you."

She blinked at his matter-of-fact admission.

He grinned broadly.

He supposed he could understand Sophie's surprise. He'd been thinking about it a lot lately—he'd even been talking about it with Dr. Cassetti—while this was all news to her.

It'd been hell, dealing with all the loss. All the betrayal. But Sophie had entered his life, and she shone like a beacon in all the darkness.

Her fingers froze in his hair. He grimaced in pleasure when he felt her vagina tighten around him.

"I'm completely serious," he said, when she glanced up at him searchingly, her eyes like dark, deep pools. He felt himself sinking into them. He loved Sophie's smile, and he adored the end of her nose, and he worshipped her breasts . . . but her eyes were sacred to him. "It goes beyond wanting to mark you. I honestly . . ."

"What?" she asked when he shook his head and grinned even wider.

"I've never even begun to feel this way about another woman," he confessed quietly.

After a moment, her fingers began running through his hair again.

"If you're really serious about that baby thing, you'll have to marry me, Tom," she murmured in such a flippant manner that he knew she wasn't sure if she should take him seriously or not.

He caught her chin and tilted it up, urging her to meet his gaze. Her body went entirely still. He leaned down.

"Name the day, Sophie," he said gruffly near her parted lips. "Name the day."

Keep reading for a special preview of Beth Kery's

PARADISE RULES

Available now from Heat Books.

Lana Rodriguez's eyelids narrowed suspiciously as she watched the buxom blonde in the minuscule bikini follow their surf instructor to a back room. She thought she recognized the expression of sly excitement on the young woman's face. Undoubtedly a man with their instructor's looks—the annoyingly potent, flashing grin and abundant, gleaming muscles—had female tourists throwing themselves at him with the consistency of a perfect Oahu day. Irritation bubbled up to the surface, an irritation that went far beyond her presence in Waikiki and taking a stupid surfing lesson.

Lana slammed the skin suit back into place, causing a brisk clang of the hanger against the metal rack. Her personal assistant and longtime friend's face fell at the evidence of her pique.

"Jeez, you weren't kidding when you said you hated Waikiki, were you?" Melanie pulled her skin suit's top down over her bathing suit. "You really *didn't* have to come, Lana. And you certainly didn't have to agree to take these surf lessons with me. I've taken vacations by myself before, you know."

Regret immediately lanced through Lana's flash of temper. Melanie was in the midst of a soul-scarring divorce that had already gone on for two years more than it should have. Sure, Melanie might have gone on a few vacations by herself before she married that sleazeball David Mason. Still, there was no way in hell Lana was going to allow her friend to be alone when she was still raw and hurting from her soon-to-be ex-husband's latest underhanded courtroom maneuver to get full custody of their four-year-old daughter, Shawna.

She gave Melanie an apologetic grin. "Sorry. Didn't mean to go diva on you."

Melanie laughed. "Girl, if you ever showed a *hint* of the diva gene, I'd have abandoned you years ago."

"Your shirt is too loose, hon." Lana chose a shirt that read *Jason Koa Surf Schools, Waikiki* over the left breast and handed it to Melanie before she picked one for herself. The tight long-sleeved shirt would partially protect them from the shearing Waikiki surf and the friction burn of surfboard against bare skin . . . as well as ensure that a woman's bikini top would stay in place.

Melanie shrugged out of the top and took the one that Lana handed her. "Why *do* you hate Waikiki so much?"

"Too touristy."

Melanie eyed her. "You seem really tense. And on the plane—jeez, Lana, I thought a few times you were going to have a panic attack like you used to have before you went onstage, back when you were still a kid."

Lana waved her hand impatiently. "Flying to Hawaii is worse than flying to Europe. I should have asked my doctor for something to help me sleep."

For the whole damn trip, she added to herself.

"Are you afraid people will recognize you? You could be anybody under that hat and ginormous pair of sunglasses." Melanie's blue eyes dropped doubtfully over her friend's figure. "'Course . . . there's not much I can do about disguising your body when you're wearing a bikini. The boring, baggy clothes I usually buy for you just won't work in Waikiki. Even the homeless people wear swimsuits."

Lana was only half listening. Her gaze had wandered back to the corridor where their surfer-dude instructor had disappeared with the blonde on his tail.

"I'm not worried about being recognized. People don't care about the blues in Waikiki," she said grimly.

"There are blues and jazz lovers everywhere, Lana, and you know it."

Lana scowled. She hadn't actually been referring to a genre of music. "Waikiki is all surface and no substance—a flashy whore decked out in skimpy designer clothes, a perfect tan highlighting a perfect boob job . . . It's so fake."

So vicious. So primed to use the poor and underprivileged to serve the tourist industry's endless greed, she thought privately.

Melanie's eyebrows rose. Lana realized she'd allowed her bitterness to show and immediately made her face settle into impassivity.

"Well, it's certainly a happening spot," Melanie said. "I needed someplace with this kind of energy and excitement after what David has pulled over the past month. A secluded tropical island just wouldn't have done the trick." Melanie stretched the dark blue fabric over her generous breasts. "I need the distraction of a party atmosphere. And these native guys are phenomenal. Don't tell me you didn't notice how gorgeous our surf instructor is. He's a walking god. He could be the inspiration for a tropical drink—Hawaiian Wet Dream."

"He's awfully tall to be a Hawaiian."

Melanie paused in the action of readjusting her bikini top. "You don't think he's Hawaiian?"

Lana shrugged negligently. "Sure, he might have been born here and have some roots. I just meant there are few pure Hawaiians left. He's part Anglo. And he's got some Filipino influence, I'd guess, in addition to Hawaiian."

"Well, the combination is one hundred percent phenomenal." Melanie's blue eyes sparkled mischievously. "I'd *love* to have him help me forget about David on this vacation."

Lana smirked.

"Don't give me that look, Lana. Not *you*—of all people. No one knows better than me how single-minded you are when it comes to men. Surely you wouldn't deny me the pleasure of a few rounds of sex with a gorgeous stranger when you're such an expert on the activity."

Lana shrugged and leaned down to put on a pair of surf shoes. "You're right. I'm here to see that you have a good time, after all, and I'm going to make sure it happens. No better way to celebrate saying sayonara to that louse husband of yours than steaming up the sheets on your vacation. Hell, I'm only too happy to do the same." She nodded toward the back room. "Just don't count on doing it with our hunky surf instructor, though. It seems he's otherwise occupied."

Melanie checked her waterproof watch. "Jeez, he's already twenty minutes late. If he doesn't hurry, we're going to be rushing to make the luau I scheduled."

Lana clamped her back teeth together. "You have yet to learn about *Hawaiian time*, hon," she muttered with a scowl.

Melanie laughed. "Care to explain how you're such an expert on *Hawaiian time*? I've worked for you since you were a nineteen-year-old kid recording your first album. That was ten years ago, and I've never heard you mention Hawaii *once* in that time period. Did you spend time here before you came to the states from Mexico?"

"You know, this loser is really starting to bug the shit out of me," Lana said, choosing to ignore Melanie's questions. She dropped her beach bag on the floor and stalked toward the dim corridor at the back of the facility. "He's a little old to be playing irresponsible surfer dude, don't you think? I've got half a mind to report him to his boss."

"Lana, maybe you should just hang loose . . ."

But Lana ignored her friend. The familiar Hawaiian phrase made her clench her teeth even tighter.

She turned into a large room that contained several surfboards on tables in the process of being repaired or waxed. Her eyes immediately found the figures of the tall man and the curvy woman, despite the dim light. He leaned back casually, one foot propped against the wall, his hands tucked behind a pair of tight buns that Lana hadn't failed to notice as he strutted around, giving instructions about preparing for the lesson earlier. He looked down at the blonde, a half-amused, half-irritated expression on his shadowed face. His profile was as arresting as the rest of the package. That straight, bold nose had immediately pointed out his Caucasian heritage to her, along with his height.

"Excuse me. My friend and I have a schedule we'd like to keep. You would think you did, as well, considering the fact that between the two of us, we're shelling out four hundred dollars an hour for your services."

The woman started and gasped in surprise. Her hand jerked, and she hopped back with a guilty glance at Lana.

Lana was glad that she wore the dark glasses so neither of them saw how wide her eyes went. He had the nerve to not even hurry as he lowered the pant leg of his board shorts, covering a long, shapely, semi-erect cock. Even with his shorts lowered she could still perfectly make out the outline of it next to his thigh.

It was far from being the first cock she'd ever seen, and it wouldn't be the last. But that quick glance informed Lana it was the most beautiful. A flash of pure, primal heat surged through her along with a lightning bolt of irritation.

She was comforted by the fact that she knew her face gave nothing away.

"Four hundred dollars an hour should help you get over your discomfort. If you start doing your job now, I'll agree not to tell your boss about your negligence, Mr. . . . ?

He didn't move from his lazy pose against the wall. She couldn't really make out his eyes in the dim room but sensed his stare boring into her. She'd noticed earlier that his eyes were a singular color—dark gray with flecks of green and amber.

"Koa. Jason Koa. And I'll be happy to reimburse you for the half hour of your lesson and still give you the full two hours."

"Good," she replied briskly, unmoved by the fact that he was apparently the owner of the two-bit surfing school. She started down the corridor, only to notice that he hadn't moved. "Well? Aren't you coming?"

"That gives me another eight minutes. I'll be with you in a moment, undoubtedly more comfortable and better prepared for teaching what I don't doubt will be a challenging lesson."

Lana stiffened when he reached for the giggling blonde. She thought of where she'd like to tell Jason Koa to stuff his insolent attitude and gorgeous smug face, but then she thought of Melanie. She imagined her friend's look of disappointment if Lana marched out there and self-righteously informed her that they were leaving.

She doubted her sunglasses disguised the glare of pure loathing she threw him before she turned away.

He set down the board in the grassy area near the beach. "Okay. Which one of you ladies is up first?"

Jason was glad when the blonde with the round face and nice smile stepped forward. He'd have to work with her man-eater friend at some point, but he was still steamed by her insulting display of arrogance back at his shop. He wasn't sure why her bitchiness had gotten to him so much, but it had. He'd been so preoccupied by her frigid superiority that he hadn't been able to concentrate when pretty little Katie eagerly resumed her hand job.

Not that he'd really been interested to begin with. Katie had taken a lesson from him three days ago. He'd taken her up on her blatant offer of her body that night, but he'd quickly become annoyed by her pursuit of him. Her California-girl good looks, large breasts, and curvy hips and ass went a long way to making him forget his rule not to get involved with customers. He'd been irritated when she followed him into the back room today and thrown herself at him. His cock had responded to her eager hands but not with much enthusiasm.

Still, if she'd kept it up, he would have grudgingly let her finish him off. He was just a guy, after all.

But then the man-eater interrupted and ruined a little

afternoon delight. He'd pushed Katie's industrious hand away after the woman left and made small talk with her about her job as a financial analyst. Apparently Katie had a hell of a head on her shoulders. That was the vacation mentality for you. Jason seriously doubted Katie was in the habit of throwing herself at males in the everyday business world, but give her the tropical breezes and the sensual rhythms of the island, and she was suddenly shameless.

He'd made his customers wait the full eight minutes, which caused him to feel a little guilty, he realized, as he positioned the blonde named Melanie belly-down on the board. Melanie was obviously nice and excited about her lesson. It had been rude of him to make her wait longer just because she had shit taste in friends.

Five minutes later, after he was satisfied that Melanie had the basics of paddling, kneeling, positioning herself in a standing position in the center of the board, and falling in the safest way, he suggested that she go and pick out a board from the beginner rack he kept on the beach.

He gave Melanie's silent friend a bland look. "You're up."

"I don't need instruction on the basics."

"Is that right?" he asked mockingly.

He glanced down over her. He had to admit she had the body of an athlete. It wouldn't surprise him if she knew exactly what she was doing. He'd immediately taken note of the casual manner in which she took off her sundress earlier in his shop. She was as used to baring her body as the female swimmers he knew—as most native Hawaiians, for that matter.

He hated to admit it, but she had excellent reason to be comfortable stripping down in public. She had a jaw-dropping body—strong and supple, but soft and feminine, too. And even though she wasn't tanned, her smooth skin held a golden hue that promised to soak up the sun thirstily. If she stayed on the island for two weeks, she'd probably be ready to contend in a Miss Hawaiian Tropic contest.

"I'll be the one to decide whether or not you need instruction. Get up on the board, and show me the basics."

Her muscles stiffened. For a second, he thought she'd refuse, which would be fine by him. He'd be more than happy to leave her on the beach.

She surprised him by stepping up on the board, however. He stopped her with a hand on her elbow when she started to go lie down on her belly.

"Take off the hat and glasses."

She started. Despite her frigid nature, her skin felt warm and satiny beneath his appreciative fingers.

"Why? What difference does it make?"

"I like to be able to look into the eyes of my students. Got a problem with that?"

He felt her stare on him from behind the dark glasses.

"Look, Waikiki isn't Waimea in March—or even Sandy for that matter," he said, referring to a few Oahu advanced surfer beaches. "But it ain't the wave pool at the water park, either, lady. Those waves can pound the hell out of you. If you don't do what I say, it can be dangerous. Call me an ass, but I tend to like to know what I'm dealing with before I take responsibility for you out there. If I can't look into your eyes, it makes it a little difficult for me to know what you're made of. Play by my rules, or don't play at all."

He realized he'd tightened his grip on her firm biceps. Without speaking she removed the straw hat and tossed it on the grass. Brown hair with golden highlights spilled around her shoulders. The glasses landed on top of the hat. Exotically tilted hazel eyes studied him coldly through thick, long lashes.

He knew those eyes. He knew that face. So did half the population.

He dropped his hand.

Okay, so half the population wouldn't recognize her. She wasn't pop-star famous by any means, but she did have a loyal following, not to mention the fact that her work commanded the respect of blues and jazz aficionados across the globe.

"Show me what you got," he said grimly. He watched her as she gracefully came up into a surfing stance.

"I told you," she said coldly over her left shoulder.

Jason spread his hand on the back of her thigh. "You know the actions, but you need to loosen up. You're too tight. Relax." He almost broke out in a huge smile when he slapped her thigh lightly. Her eyes widened in disbelief.

"Get your hand off me."

"Give me a break, lady," he muttered as he slid his hand down to her ankle, urging her to widen her stance an inch or two. "You saw me touching your friend as well. You need to relax more than just your body. Your attitude could use a Hawaiian adjustment as well."

"Think I should just *hang loose*, dude?"

He paused with his hand on her firm calf and glanced up at her. Her face was livid with fury.

"You know, I don't think I've ever seen you wear that particular expression on the front cover of a magazine. I guess that's for the best, considering the publisher wants people to *buy* their magazine, not be repulsed by it."

She clamped her jaw shut. He watched in fascination as her face smoothed into a beautiful mask of impassivity. He stroked her satiny skin ever so lightly, preferring her fury for some reason. Must be turning into a masochist in his old age. When she tensed even further, he knew she'd noticed his subtle groping. Out of the corner of his eye he saw Melanie approaching with a short board under her arm.

"Lana." Her name lingered on his tongue. "That wouldn't be short for *'Ailana* now, would it?"

This was interesting, Jason thought when he saw her cheek muscle twitch. He rose slowly until he looked down at her, holding her gaze all the while.

"It means 'loving' in Hawaiian. Of course without the *okina*, the word *ailana* refers to raw, fuck-me-till-I'm-blind sexual intercourse," he said softly, referring to the punctuation mark before the name. He saw the fury return to her expression and smiled insolently. "Ah—I see you already knew that, 'Ailana."

"There isn't a damn thing you can teach me that I don't already know and wish I didn't, Mr. Koa."

He leaned closer, catching her fresh, floral fragrance combined with healthy, sweet sweat. *Onaona*, he thought, instinctively using his admittedly primitive knowledge of the Hawaiian language to describe her scent. She even *smelled* like the islands.

"I beg to differ."

He saw her nostrils flare. His eyes fastened on her lush mouth.

"Is this board okay, Jason?" Melanie called out. He stepped back, glad for the interruption. He was only too happy to consider something else beside the fact that his cock had just stiffened to a lead pipe as he verbally sparred with a prima donna who clearly had some *serious* issues.

Not his problem.

So what if her personality was a far stretch from what he'd thought it would be given her low, sultry singing voice. Her voice, face, and body had thrilled many a male before him. He didn't need to be a fan of the entertainment industry to know that most famous people were whacked. Why should it surprise him that Lana Rodriguez was no different?

Still, Jason acknowledged he was disappointed. Her voice and bluesy arrangements brought out the pensive, moody side of him—the side he rarely showed others, certainly not in his role as an athlete or as an extroverted businessman in the Hawaiian tourist industry. In truth, he'd always been a little haunted by her songs.

He suppressed a frown when he fully registered his thoughts and gave an easy grin instead.

"Yeah, that's perfect, Melanie. Why don't you go and pick a board, Lana, and we'll catch a wave."

"Bitchin'," he heard Lana mutter scathingly under her breath before she walked away.

All it takes is one moment for your life to change—
One night of desire to make you feel alive…

FROM *NEW YORK TIMES* BESTSELLING AUTHOR
BETH KERY
writing as
BETHANY KANE

Addicted to You

A One Night of Passion Novel

Irish film director Rill Pierce fled to the tiny backwoods town of Vulture's Canyon seeking sanctuary and solitude after a devastating tragedy. Once, his raw sex appeal and sultry Irish accent made women across the globe swoon. Now, he's barely recognizable…

But Katie Hughes, his best friend's sister, is not the type of woman to give up on a man like Rill. She blazes into Vulture's Canyon, determined to save him from himself. Instead, she finds herself unleashing years of pent-up passion. In a storm of hunger and need, Katie and Rill forget themselves and the world. But will Rill's insatiable attraction to Katie heal his pain—or will it just feed the darkness within him?

"Really packs an emotional punch."
—*Smexy Books*

"Explosive and intense."
—Lisa Marie Rice

bethkery.com
facebook.com/beth.kery
facebook.com/LoveAlwaysBooks
penguin.com

M1345T0713

BETH KERY

Captured By You

Aussie playboy, world traveler, and landscape photographer Chance Hathoway recognizes a miracle of nature when he sees it. He comes upon her unaware, swimming in the nude. Camera in hand, his instinct is to capture her ripe, naked abandon. But he longs to possess more than just her image . . .

When Sherona Legion suddenly discovers that she's being watched at her most vulnerable she's surprised at her reaction. It's not embarrassment or anger. It's pure, unabashed arousal. She likes it—enough that she's willing to take an unprecedented risk with the sexy photographer.

Thrilled at having the exhibitionist in her awakened, Sherona agrees to Chance's offer to pose for a series of nude photographs—stimulating tableaus of bondage. It leads Chance and Sherona to intimate and unparalleled experimentation. But how much is Sherona really ready to give to a complete stranger? And how much more can Chance take?